Under the Mountain

By the same author

The Glass House

Under the Mountain

SOPHIE COOKE

HUTCHINSON
LONDON

Published by Hutchinson 2008

2 4 6 8 10 9 7 5 3 1

First published in Great Britain in 2008 by
Hutchinson
Random House, 20 Vauxhall Bridge Road,
London SW1V 2SA

www.rbooks.co.uk

Addresses for companies within The Random House Group Limited can be found at:
www.randomhouse.co.uk/offices.htm

The Random House Group Limited Reg. No. 954009

A CIP catalogue record for this book
is available from the British Library

ISBN 9780091799441

The Random House Group Limited supports The Forest Stewardship
Council (FSC), the leading international forest certification organisation. All our
titles that are printed on Greenpeace approved FSC certified paper carry the FSC logo.
Our paper procurement policy can be found at www.rbooks.co.uk/environment

Mixed Sources
Product group from well-managed
forests and other controlled sources
www.fsc.org Cert no. TT-COC-2139
© 1996 Forest Stewardship Council
FSC

Typeset in Adobe Garamond by Palimpsest Book Production Limited,
Grangemouth, Stirlingshire

Printed and bound in Great Britain by
CPI Mackays, Chatham ME5 8TD

for Malcolm

who was there at the beginning
and differently at the end
which can be a beginning again.

Chapter One

Catherine picked a flake of sandstone from her thigh, flicked it sideways and shifted her buttocks on the step above the pavement. Her short skirt stayed stuck against the undersides of her thighs for a moment or two before falling down again, blue roses on viscose.

Thick cloud banks had rolled in from the west at six, sealing in the heat from the June noonday sun; in its windless state the tail-end of the day seemed to be coiling back on itself, a collapsing lung. As the hours pushed further into evening, so the evening pushed further into the city's stone, its porous bones, pressing out the humid afternoon that had soaked there with all its odours, its sweat and cola, to mix here on its skin now with the looser dust of lateness falling, the cooler time as should be. Streaks of the gone day were replaying, spooling past the proper hour of their dying, into the hours for dining, the eights and even nines now as Catherine sat waiting on the step of a once-fine house in the New Town, waiting for Rosa in the warm dusk, and rearranged her legs, and ran her hand across the step, the flaking sandstone that was gradually turning into beach again.

She leaned forwards, an elbow on her knee, cupping her jaw in the heel of her propped-up palm, its soft joint with

1

her crease-lined wrist. Head turned sideways, hair knotting in the forking of fingers; gazing through the railings to next door's street stair that also clung above the plunging of a basement. The stone had worn down there, just as here, at the edges of its steps, but someone had replaced it. New stone blocks shone pale and sharp-edged right where the lips of the steps must once have crumbled most.

A man walked up over the steps next door. There, she saw his brown brogues, and the hem of his hemp summer trousers. When she could hear that he was busy at the intercom, then she turned to look at the rest of him, the back of him, his white crumpled shirt, the way he curled and uncurled the fingers of his left hand into and out from his palm, while he spoke his name, waiting. His neck inclined forward, so that his lean sunburnt cheek fell into darkness. The slow drone of the buzzer admitting him. She turned back to the street and heard the door heave closed behind him, its final crash cutting short the starting sound of his feet on the stone stair.

She turned her attention to the windows of the new apartment block on the other side of the road, which was merely a resculpting of the Standard Life building, that brave office brick that had smashed its way into the Georgian street in the nineteen seventies. So sure of itself back then, but today's developers had wisely rubbed their fingers over the edges of its bluntness, swapped its concrete skin for stone, fitted natty balconies and a set of *brises-soleil* whose rows of lowered lashes cast shadows on the stairway glass and wall. There were security gates and secluded penthouse decks. The whole effect was one both of greater sophistication and of modesty, a slick elusiveness built in. Like a grown woman, the redesigned building attracted attention in order to deflect it. It was hard, very hard, to imagine the plain administrators who had toiled there once in nylon shirts, with filing cabinets and typewriters beneath fluorescent strip-lights.

Catherine Farrants was looking across at those apartments now, sitting with her hands clamped over the brim of the topmost step that she sat upon, tight in, either side of her body. She watched as Venetian blinds descended in a room on the second floor, the serried slats clattering soundlessly down the spotless floor-to-ceiling glass.

The figure beyond was pulling at the cord, and letting go. Walking away, smoothing her Von Furstenberg dress. It took Catherine a full few seconds to work out what was wrong with the scene: that, having closed the blind, the woman ought to have been invisible. Instead, she was quite clearly lifting a glass of wine from an island unit in her open-plan living space. She was turning, speaking and making a motion with her hand. There was someone else in the room. A man, sliding in from the right, cutting across to the sofa end with a bottle of beer in hand. They think the blinds are closed, realised Catherine. The woman has pulled the cord the wrong way, and she doesn't know that the world can see in, because from her side, she can't see out.

Catherine turned her head and looked the other way down the street, towards the peeling mosque and the distant dome of the bus depot.

It will be better if you tell her, Bernadette had said this morning, a calm hand resting on the carnage in the foreign magazine. The faces of the dead had smiled out from cropped holiday snaps, fluttering in the breeze at the far left edge of the page, as if they might still be alive.

And Catherine hadn't thought about that business, or Sam, not in years, but sitting on the step here, it was all coming back. Maybe it was because she had been thinking of Humberto and Rosa, of how she was going to tell Rosa that he was one of them. Or why she must – when really, so easily, the facts in the newspaper could have been a matter of no personal importance. And of course the three of them had been quite entwined back then, Humberto, Rosa and Sam, in that particular year when everyone was young and she especially. Maybe it was the summer heat, maybe it was the waiting, maybe it was the blood in the newspaper, or the thoughts of nylon shirts, a different time, maybe it was the thing she ought to tell although she didn't want to, maybe it was all these things, but when the woman pulled her blinds the wrong way, there was no stopping Catherine's recall. Her memory was tumbling backwards, snagging once as passing petrol fumes unfurled and hooked her nostrils.

Chapter Two

It was a beautiful house, Catherine had noticed, when she'd last returned there – what, fourteen years ago, fifteen, must have been – passing with a brief boyfriend in a student car, her wrist in leather bracelets pointing ahead, her younger, louder voice saying, That's where I used to live, less from nostalgia than pride, owing to the size of it. On the road to Oban, a pile of girlish sweeties and the hash tin balanced on her thighs. And he of course had pulled into the drive, the gravel that was empty, and he had snooped around; she'd been stuck with this. With how rudely impressed he'd been. By its age, as much as scale – he kept remarking on how old it was, and how amazing, that her family had always lived here. It's only Victorian, she said. They were textile barons, she said, not the real thing, you know.

Lucky to be any kind, he had called, treading away from her across the lawn, but she wasn't really listening. She was looking up at the house, its blond sandstone blocks, the tower that soared square above the porch. The high windows under great gables in which the upstairs quarters lay – the corridors and cupboards, the billiard room, the pipistrelles, the smell of unslept beds, though surely that was different now – she was walking over the gravel, in spite of the sound it made, to the furthest edge of the drive, the lavender spikes, and new plants that she did not recognise, where now she stood gazing down the long frontage of the house. The dining room, thrust out upon this corner like a mullioned rosette, where for one summer she had slept; and then the fenestrated sweep of the drawing room still serene behind its balustraded terrace, its windows catching the April light, reflecting darkly the treetops across the river and the distant mountain beyond. The kitchen, half-sunken, beneath the library, down there on the end where it belonged. Past it, among far-off shrubs, still stood the gate in the wall to the Farishes' garden next door.

On the architect's original plans the dining room and the library had been labelled the other way around, but old William Farrants did not want his reading to be disturbed by comings and goings of carriages and motor cars on the gravel, and also reasoned – kindly, considerately – that swapping the two would make it less far for the maid to carry the sandwiches that he always liked to take when reading even gentle works. He didn't notice that the servants then had to carry great tureens and stacks of plates all the way down the hall to the new dining room for breakfast, lunch and dinner, because this was not something that he personally asked them to do. Perhaps it didn't matter anyway, given that he was paying them, but details like this became stories that Catherine liked to tell.

Her great-grandfather seemed to her to have been a blithely ignorant creature, although perhaps he was only ignorant of the future, and besides, she herself, standing there aged twenty in the spring of nineteen ninety-two, could not have foreseen a future where people once more vied to serve the very rich; to source, concierge and manage; to massage and advise. She thought her generation of anti-fashion and irony, its proud snubbing of materialism, was here to stay; had no idea back then that culture is only the face society puts on things and changes with the tautness of the purse-skin.

Catherine had stood fidgeting with her lapiz earring. The ancient sinews of wisteria still twisted above the terrace, though the laburnum was gone; and now Kyle was clambering over the balustrade: she watched him shade his eyes as he peered in close to the drawing room glass. They've got a fucking zebra skin rug, he called.

She had scuffed her trainer in the gravel, ignoring him. She was looking at the house, and feeling that it must be much more than six years since she had lived here. She was wishing that they hadn't stopped, were somewhere on the road ahead instead, slowing through Killin; but now that they had stopped here, she couldn't help but gaze on the collected turrets and soft grey-lichened sills through Kyle's eyes, and see that it was all hugely handsome. This appreciation of the house's aesthetic value upset her greatly. She thought she would have loved Falls anyway, but its beauty meant that anyone else would, too. The beauty of it denied the uniqueness of her affection. Its architectural perfection prevented intimacy, for there was nothing in it to forgive.

She strode back towards the car, past the old dining room, whose walls, she saw, glancing sideways, were now lined with books after all. Hunkering down in the passenger seat, Catherine had begun to skin up, and by the time her boyfriend returned, was a third of the way down the reefer.

So these were the things she had thought of when she visited the house last. Its great beauty, which irritated her and pushed her away. How she would never proudly point it out again to friends. How much less she liked her boyfriend for being so easily won by it. How her period was three days late, but then again, often had been. How strangely her best friend Parker had been behaving lately.

She did not think of Sam at all, although perhaps, somewhere in the shady allotments of her mind, swayed some remembrance of Lori's fate. Because she frowned, and poked a fingertip into her belly-button as she inhaled, and was doubly, triply, glad when they pulled out of the gateway and were gone.

Why did you move? asked her boyfriend.

We couldn't afford to keep it, answered Catherine, which was the truth. The roof was about to fall in, she said, tapping the ash out of the open window. Do you want a Refresher? she asked him.

Chapter Three

Slowly Catherine in two thousand and eight was blinking her eyes as a blue car passed her on the street. She remembered her last visit in the sound of an engine as it slowed, changing gears; the scent of petrol fumes and dirty candy on the air.

The old summer at Falls, drawing her towards it, pulled her swiftly through its in-between time. Her last sighting of the place passed in the lowering and the raising of her eyelids: a whole landscape, torn past the window of a speeding train. When her lashes lifted again, she was entirely gone. She was looking at a chunk of city street – blank farmland built over with terraced townhouses, ripped down and replaced with offices, remoulded into flats – and she was flying backwards, down, into a time when everything had seemed to be a field, a building site. Back before recent remodellings, the pasting on of an air of ease, of varied pleasures, the layered dissemblings. Back before the coolly pragmatic righteous anger of the preceding demolition, its sensible right-angled second beginning. She was looking at a chunk of city street, but it wasn't now, at all, and she was elsewhere.

Chapter Four

It wasn't a bad illness, not one big one, but a pile-up of quotidian childish sickenings, each ramming into the bumper of the one in front: whooping cough, chickenpox, measles straight and German, that knocked her all summer long, nine years old on a scrolled couch in the erstwhile dining room of Falls House.

Catherine lay in sweats or shivers, or the tiredness between, on a white towelling sheet, stretched over protective woollen underblankets, stretched over the tattered grey damask daybed. Her mother had fitted it with several over-layers, too: a thin cotton sheet, a yellow cellular cot blanket, another in white, and a stained once-blue quilt. It won't matter if you're sick on it, her older sister had observed, in a kindly tone, on the inauguration of the sick-room.

I won't be sick, Catherine told her, from under a wrinkled brow. I don't feel sick at all.

You might be, Bernie persisted, and brought a sick bowl. Just in case, she said, encouragingly.

The purpose of the several layers was ostensibly to keep Catherine at a comfortable temperature, easily controlled by peeling off or pulling on according to the fluctuations of her skin, the breeze from the window. In reality, the most useful function of the elaborate bedding options was in giving Catherine something to do; in allowing her to believe that once she had folded back the second cot blanket, then she would be quite at ease, or once she had got the quilt so that it was not pressing down on her feet in that irritating way. Having performed these alterations, she could lie back and gauge whether or not the new configuration of blankets was in fact an improvement on the last. And if it wasn't, she could rearrange it. That was the thing: to be the one who arranged one's own discomfort, that was the comforting thing.

Through May and June she lay inside the room, cupped southerly to the great house's breast. She would be better, she kept telling herself, by the time that Sam and Rosa came. She imagined herself racing ahead of Sam through various parts of the garden, running in a particularly splendid way so that her adored older cousin would again look at her, out of breath, bent over with his hands on his knees, smile up through sweated forelock and say, You're a great runner, Catherine.

Catherine wasn't better at all by the time that Sam and Rosa came – and Aunt Ellie, she came too, of course, although Catherine always forgot to count her because everything always happened just as it would have done if she hadn't been there. They said hello, put their heads round the door, but she hardly even saw them, her fever was so high.

She watched them all outside, in the garden, and they seemed like shapes instead of sister, father, mother, cousins (aunt). She was so emptied of herself by the illness that it had become impossible to imagine other people. The most she could manage was to see them. Their voices, likewise emptied of sense, fell on her ears in sounds that water or birds might make as well, mingled with the distant roar of the river in the gorge, the clattering of petals in the vase upon the floor. Now and then shrieked the fighter jets that sometimes practised overhead, but not today, today they had been quiet, or rather, screaming somewhere else.

Catherine curled and stretched across the mattress, her whole body shrinking into a ball and re-expanding before shrinking back, and rolling, like the whole of her were one tormented stomach muscle, but, as she had so sagely predicted, the sickness never came. She kicked the whole lot of her bedding to the floor – whether in crossness or offering – and fitfully shivered now that she was so exposed.

Eventually she twisted upwards, slung her legs out and pressed the bare soles of her feet down against the smooth sun-warmed parquet floor, tried to stand. She managed this, and was standing now, close to the kicked-off sheet. All she had to do was stoop and collect its edge. But the brooches of her kneecaps had her pinned now, the needles of their fastenings lanced her stringy shinbones all hot and snapping, and she knew, she just knew, that if she took one more step, if she stooped, if she moved at all, then her knees would scatter past her ankles and end up on the floor. And then what would hold her legs up? If she moved, if she moved one inch from here, she would quite definitely fall apart.

Something like Mummy was in here, talking now, lifting her up and putting her back, and asking if she would like the sheet, and how about the yellow blanket, should we have that halfway and then folded back? All Catherine had to do was nod, and be tucked in, and have her dirty water glass taken away sideways. Everything was sideways when you were ill. And lie there now in the silence, and rest

12

under the coolness of the sheet, with the breeze from the window lapping at her cheeks.

She could hear them picnicking outside.

Mine and Rosa's names is foreign, Bernie was saying. So's Mummy's. Natasha is a Russian name. But Sam isn't foreign.

Catherine closed her eyes. It was too much effort to comprehend the sense of what Bernadette was saying, but she recognised the sound of Sam's name as something comforting. She pulled the sheet up over her face so that its cotton completely shaded her, and laboriously breathed her way towards sleep.

Chapter Five

'Nor is daddy,' said Bernadette. '*George*,' she gravely intoned, looking at a bowl of broad beans before turning to her mother. 'Why do only females have foreign names?'

'I don't know. Perhaps they're booty,' said Natasha Farrants. 'Ladies get tossed between ships, while men must fly the flags on the masts. Pass me the mayonnaise, please.'

'Skull and crossbones?' Bernie enquired.

'That's a different sort of man.'

Rosa looked up from her orange Tupperware plate piled with salad. 'Are you a feminist, Aunt Tash?'

'Women's Lib? Lord no. I'm far too busy.'

'What's women's lip?' asked Bernadette, but Rosa was already asking,

'What about Boadicea?'

'I imagine she was too busy for it too,' said Natasha.

'What's women's lip? What's Boda's ear?'

'Boadicea was a warrior queen,' said Rosa. 'She led a tribe against the Roman army.'

'Britons' Lib, really,' said Natasha.

'That's the way you get things, though, isn't it?' Rosa persisted. 'By fighting for something else. Uncle George says that process is the most important thing. He says the trick is to slip the ends into the means, and that's the way to get things done.'

Still half a child inside, thought Natasha. Her niece might be sixteen, but she was still enough of a child to enter into everything entirely, to treat every notion as if it might very well be real. A child's respect for internal logic over external proofs, because not yet thinking everything had been seen, she would listen to all tales from the still-broad *terra incognita*, countenance all possible creatures and towns, customs and sounds. And not having been there yet herself, could test these only by the sense they made. Rosa would agree to believe anything as long as it made sense inside.

'Yes, well,' said Natasha. It was a long time since she had wondered about the actual meaning of her husband's ideas. These days, she merely cared about the outside shape of them within their shared life. Repercussions, reverb, concerned her more than tunes. When George had stumbled down from his library the other evening and grabbed her in the kitchen, with his scraps of paper and his Ancient Hebrew script, she had only been glad to feel his hand around her wrist.

'Look,' he had said, beginning to draw symbols on the page. 'The Ancient Hebrew letter A, *Al*. It's a pictograph for an ox's head. Associated meanings – leadership, strength, yoke, pillar. B,' he had breathed, quickly scratching a shape like a squared spiral. '*Beyt*. A pictograph for the layout of their tents. Associated meanings – home, family, inside. The *letters* have meanings. Isn't it amazing?' Natasha had only been aware that he had taken his hand away from her and was entirely absorbed now in the piece of paper, leaning his arm upon the table where she had been about to roll pastry. He was not even glancing round. He seemed to simply assume she was still there and it did not occur to Natasha, who never took anything for granted herself, that this might be an act of trust rather than indifference.

'You put them together to create the meaning of the word. *Ab* – the strength of the home – meaning father. But still also meaning the tentpole itself.' He had laughed. 'Both, do you see, a literal meaning and a conceptual meaning too, each word a joining-point between two worlds.'

Natasha had looked at him, and the way he had co-opted the tabletop, and the way he still had not turned around to see whether she was there and whether she cared or not about the joining-points on his piece of paper when the joining-points that mattered to her, the joining-points of his hands and eyes, had been taken away from her, when the strength of her home was preventing her from flouring the Formica and rolling out the pastry that waited in the bowl.

'Was Boda's Ear a princess before she was a queen?' Bernie asked, sitting with her head wedged in the crook of her mother's shoulder.

'I don't think they really had princesses then,' said Natasha. 'I imagine she was just somebody who wasn't the queen yet.'

'Do you think Lady Di rides a motorbike? I'm going to write and ask her.'

'I think feminism's great,' said Sam, who Natasha had not even realised was paying them any attention, sat apart and staring down the short lawn to the tall fence, the rabbit wire, and through it to the rapids of the fast-flowing river. His knees drawn up, and that dark brown hound of his resting its nose on his foot. The dog Julab closed its eyes as she looked at it. It was as if it had felt Natasha's gaze and spurned her: utterly loyal and obedient to Sam, utterly disregarding everyone else. Which was the way things should be, thought Natasha, between dogs and their masters, but still, she found it a little unnerving here in the grounds of her own house. It seemed offensive to George, somehow. Everyone ought to cede to their hostess, on the tacit understanding that she ceded to the host behind closed doors: this was how things were gently done. How could she deliver her guests' respect up to her husband, if they did not first deliver it to her? But really – it was only her nephew's dog. It was only a dog lying in the sunshine with its eyes closed, resting at its master's feet. And Sam was only eighteen: still a child also, really. It was summer, wasn't it, and the sky was very bright.

The outside walls of the house loomed peacefully sun-baked, as strong and firm as ever behind the nearby flowerbeds, and she decided not to think of the way that when the rain came she had to run to and fro in the hall indoors with buckets and pots to catch the drips beneath the leaking skylight; decided to ignore the fact that it would again be autumn soon, and that the leaking would be worse, as it was every year, a little bit worse than the last. Not to think of the way that the wine set aside by previous gener-ations was slowly shrinking lower against the cellar walls.

She looked at the red poppies that bloomed in a hot scatter against the puffs of pale blue catmint, and the bril-liant creamy lilies with their long throats and kissed-out lips, the stately suck-and-spit of their faultless trumpets. Beneath them, soft rabbits' ears of stachys overlapped the border, tumbled luxuriantly on the edges of the lawn. A dandelion clock drifted slowly past. Everything was so ripely coloured and so perfectly clear in the garden around her, and her daughter was so warm and heavy and real against her body, and the house was standing so solidly and close, that she felt foolish for thinking that her husband in any way really required her shoring up of him. In a world such as this, he surely could not subside or crumble. Not that Natasha feared a breakdown: George wasn't the type to shatter so much as somehow slide and recombine. He did it with words all the time: slid sideways; appeared in one corner and then suddenly was in the other, opposite the place you'd thought. Used his words like mirrors so much that perhaps it was not surprising she sometimes found it hard to trust his flesh. Sometimes, when she was with him, she had the feeling that she was in a dream. There was that same unsureness as to what might happen next. With George you often felt that he might, at any moment, turn into a cat. Which was just a madness on her part, not his, but all the same explained the way she turned her back on his eyes sometimes and busied herself with inconsequential clothes pegs.

She was reaching a hand up to her throat now, fingering her necklace, a wreath of fine gold threads that George had bought her when Bernadette was born – not yet Bernadette then, but a small pink crumpled shock that slept. The necklace had seemed like a promise of good things to come: a miraculous abundance to match her own bodily gift, the great achievement of her womb in creating something where nothing had been. She wasn't to know that George had sold the remaining first editions from the library – *Treasure Island*, Hume's *Enquiries*, and all the Walter Scotts – in order to pay for it. She had enjoyed supposing, rather, that good fortune was befalling New Albion Press. Bernadette had been a honeymoon baby, born before the year of their March wedding was even out; Natasha did not, at that time, entirely understand the way the coins were stacked. It had not, for a long time, occurred to her that George's material confidence could be grounded on nothing of real substance but merely expectation, old security, a sense of due.

She wrinkled her nose as a fleeting memory buzzed against her bones: Ruaridh's face, flushed, having drunk too much wine as usual. Staggering in the kitchen, with an unpleasant laugh. 'George, you bloody ponce. All your fucking fanciness. You can't smell the shit for the flowers that grow in it.'

18

Had Ellie been there too? Natasha didn't think so, although it was always hard to recall because in truth Natasha had scarcely been aware of Ellie as a separate entity until after Ruaridh's death. If she had been there, then she would have faded away to the drawing room at the first sign of the disturbance, because that was what Ellie always did, and afterwards would smile brightly with nervous eyelashes and draw your attention to something small and silly – a bird flying past the window, some embroidered motto on your own cushion.

Natasha brushed her fingers briskly across the skin of her forearm, as if she were being bothered by an insect. That was how it felt. The irritating memory, its legs and wings: the ugliness of her brother's face – whom she greatly wished to remember only in the finest of lights, now that he was gone – and the perpetual irritatingness of Ellie, to whom she wanted to be kind; and then the interruption of her thoughts by the whole thing, the rudeness of it, the *bothering*. Inside it, the sharper sting of the preceding scene, which she had no desire to suffer again, again. If only memory were a bee, and not a wasp. She dusted her arm quite hard and blinked.

Carefully, Natasha noticed another dandelion clock blowing gently past her. Went back to holding her necklace, pressing the precious bundle of tarnished threads between her fingers. She must get the clasp mended, she reminded herself. Lately it had been feeling as if it were about to break – too loose, where it joined. It was pulling out of the hasp. She would take it to the jewellers in Stirling next month. The Gills would have left by then; there would be enough slack in her budget to pay a small bill, if she spread it over two weeks and postponed her next tub of Atrixo handcream. Which was her only remaining cosmetic indulgence, but really, oatmeal worked almost as well, didn't it, to condition the skin.

Where had Ellie got to? Natasha was determined not to be irritated by her at all this afternoon. She wanted to start being kind right away.

'Of course women are equal to men,' said Sam.

And what were you supposed to make of that, Natasha wondered. And why, she wordlessly frowned, was her sister-in-law taking so long.

'Look at mother,' he said.

She was already turning her neck, looking for his mother quite literally, when he said this, so that she seemed a little absurd and had to stop and pretend to be admiring the far azalea instead, beyond the drained pond. But where was she? She'd only gone to fetch an egg slicer.

'Yes,' said Rosa. 'I think Mum's done a very good job of bringing us up since Dad died.'

What a strange pale shade of tangerine that azalea blossom was. How strange it was that once the pond had had water in it. It had been drained when the children were born, for safety's sake, and now they were older, everyone had got used to using its nice stone bottom and sheltered walls for barbecues, so that somehow there never seemed much point in refilling it; yet bulrushes still grew around its edge. Natasha knew it had had water in it once, but she couldn't begin to picture it. How strange that although she could remember the fact of it, she couldn't imagine it at all.

How strange it was that Ruaridh should have gone and left so many strange things behind him. Things in her own garden that could take her by surprise. And the strange sudden fragility of her past, a childhood or a rearing, a bringing up, as Rosa had phrased it just then, that had seemed so solid when her brother had been here to have witnessed it with her and turned out surer.

The surest of them both, broken and gone. No sliding in Ruaridh: he had never been one for tricks and transmutations. He was all or nothing. Shattered and gone. Leaving

20

the changedness of her same garden. Leaving her own brittle arches of built-up basis, unbuttressed. The childish assumptions on which she had stacked herself seemed small and random now – not certain at all. An adult moss of pragmatism and age might still helpfully cloud the bricks, make them seem a unity and not a cobbled chance, but she had seen her brother's grander structure crumble. He had gone, leaving her past, alone, to sustain itself or fall.

Leaving also these two strange children of his. And the thread between her fingers.

'Mummy,' said Bernie. 'You're hurting me.'

Her daughter's hair.

Ellie was walking towards them on the path that ran along the front of the house, lugging a picnic flask, smiling in that funny brave apologetic way she always had.

'I found some peaches,' she gasped, planting the flask beside the rug. 'I've made some iced tea.'

Natasha's sister-in-law always paused at the end of her sentences, like a pony, wanting to be coached over the next jump. She was smoothing her long dress down around her thighs, folding it in like a tulip and sinking to the ground. Breathing out with a small sigh that asked to be happy, as if to say, where are the words that I'm waiting for. Where is my hay.

Despite her best intentions, Natasha could not oblige. She was too maddened by Ellie's unauthorised commandeering of the peaches: as if, in finding them in Natasha's kitchen, she had somehow procured them all by herself. She had no idea, really none, of what it was to worry about where one's money was coming from.

George, of course, carried on as he had always done. Everything had turned out all right for such a long time that he thought his wife's concern absurd, and faintly offensive, and would get cross and say that it was like

21

worrying whether or not the oaks would have acorns next autumn.

He seemed to have forgotten that his grandfather's grandfather was a navvy, born on a scrubbed kitchen table in a dank little two-room but-and-ben not twenty miles from here; seemed so sure that the intervening period of prosperity had safeguarded the family from a return to that state of affairs for ever that in fact he never gave it a moment's thought. It seemed inconceivable to George that he should ever have to give it all back.

And yet Natasha's housekeeping money shrank smaller and smaller every quarter, calculations in the back of her diary tighter and tighter. Inflation bloomed around them but sales of dictionaries and poetry remained the same, all those printed words upon the pages quite stubborn in their fastness – quite useless, she sometimes felt, in their inability to provoke the passions that printed numbers on free-floating bits of patterned bank paper could. Not her business, of course, in every sense, and George would not really speak about it; only handed her the same amount of cash every month as if that were enough in spite of the state of things, in spite of the real prices on the stickers. She was growing vegetables at the end of the lawn and pretending that pointed cabbages were a new hobby of hers. The children did not have ice creams in the town, because she bought them at the cash and carry and kept them in the freezer at home; their clothes were genteel hand-me-downs from friends. Her own were home-made, or quietly bought from the Oxfam shop in safely distant Stirling, because it would have been peculiar to have worn Nuala's old skirt, in a way that was not strange when it came to children. With children, you could pretend that the clothes were just equipment, no different from borrowing a highchair or a trigonometry set. It didn't wash for grown-ups.

Natasha did not grudge the secret poverties. She loved the

house too much, loved waking with the sun washing through the muslin inner curtains after George had drawn the faded teal velvet ones and gone to make his coffee. She loved the vastness of these rooms in which he had grown up, liked the idea of her children taking it for granted, the sound of them riding their bicycles down the hall. She liked the servants' bells that ran to the kitchen from every room, stoutly labelled, that were silent now though the wires still worked, if you didn't mind ringing to serve yourselves.

And she was glad, amongst other things, that the house had last been redecorated in nineteen fifty-three when George's father's publishing business, brave and newborn then, had won the contract to supply fresh Atlases to every school in Britain. It could have been the plastic orange sixties, she liked to remind herself, or we could all still be languishing in dark tobacco-stained eighteen ninety-five. George's uncles, to whom the unwanted textile business had woven its silvery way, had given his mother a good deal on the furnishing fabrics that were so frayed around the edges now. Battered damask roses bloomed above cold radiators, which required so much oil to run that it was better just to use the log fireplaces, which was fine, because a fire was always nice, wasn't it, Natasha thought. Paisley silk cushions had quietened to torn lilac from once-glorious purple, but Natasha was glad of this also, because judging from the brightness of the old colour where it had hung on in the tight corners of the seams, she thought it must originally have been a bit *de trop*.

Kirsty thought that she should paint the kitchen canary yellow, to jazz it up a bit. I like it like this, Natasha had said, not wanting to think about the colours she might paint the walls if there were the money for it.

She liked the house. She liked it just the way it was, all of it, and she insisted on this.

*   *   *

23

But those peaches! They had cost her one pound thirty, had studded her careful basket at the expense of aubergines, a pomegranate, other exotica. Her one calculated treasure from the greengrocers. People like Ellie would never understand the continual exclusions of frugality's choosings, the way that each choice meant choosing what not to have. That a peach wasn't just a peach, but stood too as no-black-grapes, no-orange-juice, margarine-instead-of-butter.

And Ellie came to stay here for week upon week with these children of Ruaridh's, Sam, and Rosa, whom, in fact, Natasha rather liked, but that wasn't the point in this instance. The point was, Natasha was finding it extremely difficult to feed them all, given Ellie's haphazard notions of household contribution, and now Ellie had taken the peaches, and she felt quite physically angry.

It wasn't so much that Ellie assumed that, living in a house this size, and married to a Farrants, her sister-in-law must have money to spare. It was more that she never thought about money at all. It was there when she needed it, and nothing more. She had that curiously unmaterialistic air that only the very rich or the saintly can. When she bought gifts for her host and hostess, it was not because she thought they might need them but rather because she enjoyed giving the things. So Natasha had received a basket of excruciatingly expensive Provençal lavender bath products and a bottle of twelve-year-old malt whisky, but still almost wept when she tried to stretch her money across the three extra mouths, irritated all the more because she knew that Ellie was not ungenerous, and knew too that she could nevertheless never ask for cash. On the one occasion where Ellie had donated some food – a squash, bought for amusement rather than nutritional purposes: isn't it a funny-looking thing? I couldn't resist it, I hope you don't mind; planting it on the kitchen table like a clever child with a home-made bomb – Natasha had been so absurdly grateful that she had thought Ellie surely must notice, might repeat the experiment.

Ellie was regarding her with perplexed patience now, brow furrowed in the midday sun.

'Did you use all of them?' Natasha asked, rousing herself at last, couching her ill-mannered words in casual tones, as if she were only asking for the recipe. Ellie tucked a lank strand of fine hair behind her ear. 'No. Two. Three. No, two.' Imagine, wondered Natasha in silence, imagine not even knowing how many peaches you'd used. And also relenting now, envisioning the five surviving peaches, still there, after all, in her fruit bowl, that could be stretched with junket and still do for seven.

It was lucky that Catherine was ill. Humberto took her place at the table half the time, but he brought things to it too: blueberries, trout, a rabbit for a stew; and helped her in the garden.

His tent beyond the Himalayan pine flickered in the sunlight, a splash of orange peel in the grass, bright nylon.

George had not been sure, until he'd gone to meet him: this Spaniard in the garden who had asked to stay. Natasha had let him set up camp there while she waited for her husband to come home from work, and broke news of the request; and really it was fine, and George had seemed surprised by how fine it was, when he saw the neatness of the hiking boots set at the opening of the tent like well-behaved front paws; the cleanness of the scrubbed steel cooking pots, burnished like the insides of seashells by sand. Humberto's politeness, and shaven skin – for some reason, said George afterwards, he had been sure that he would wear a beard. The way that Humberto had beaten all the pegs down close to the ground, and stood, smiling but not smiling too hard. It was always nicer to give things to a chap who did not try and force your hand. Yes, fine, George had said to her, returning. Nice set up he's got there. Wouldn't mind a simple fir-girt frithsoken for myself. He's not to come in the house, though, Natasha. Other than to scumber, I suppose.

What?

To disencumber. His bowels.

Sometimes Natasha wondered why George insisted on using words that made him hard to understand. Because that was the point, wasn't it, of speaking? To make yourself understood? It wasn't that he suavely hedged or dissembled, like some people did, for politeness' sake – sometimes she wished he would – no, he seemed always to be perfectly honest, but honest in some strange code that required time and questions to break. It was as if he knew he could say whatever he liked, because there was a delay built in to the explosion of its meaning. He would give the words over to people and then sit back, let them open the sentences out by themselves, without getting his own hands either kissed or dirty at all. He was always gone by the time you answered the door; his eyes had already moved on, disappeared around the corner.

Dappled light flickered again brightly on the orange nylon. Yes, Humberto was fine, thought Natasha. A lot of the time you didn't even know he was there. Sometimes he would walk up behind you on the gravel and you would completely fail to hear his sandals, or rather, the sound he made was such that he could just as easily have been the river water splitting on the rocks, or the breeze in the stiff ruff of the hedge, or beech nuts, pine cones, rolling over dry roots. He could have been wind-fallen detritus scattering in the wake of cars upon the road. Those were the sounds that surrounded him, and his feet on the gravel would sound no different. It was admirable, wasn't it, to have such a skill for camouflage, assimilation. Admirable and only a little unnerving. He seemed to have attuned himself quite perfectly to the landscape – had taken the physical country, and not its inhabitants, as his yardstick – so the thing was, that he at once seemed alien to Natasha and yet on intimate terms with the ground beneath her feet. He seemed to be part of it, in a way that could sometimes accuse her. Knowing it better than she did, and wasn't there also something quite improper about that? It was like watching a stranger tuck your mother's hair behind her ear and tell you she was beautiful. So Natasha was being kind to Humberto in preferring to think of his affinity with the woods and hills as resulting from some set of practical scouting skills rather than from a peculiar inherent disposition. 'Where's Humberto today?' she asked. Expecting Sam to answer, because Sam always knew where Humberto was, and exactly what he had done the day before, and the fact that Zaragoza was named by the Romans for Caesar Augustus. But Sam was staring sulkily out to the river, and shrugged, and said, 'Ask Rosa.'

And Rosa was picking at her lettuce leaves, and stopping, and stretching for a tomato quarter, dipping it in salad cream, and not answering.

'Have you seen Humberto?' asked Natasha. Watching her niece eat the piece of tomato. Rosa was swallowing, looking steadily sideways at the pale yellow spikes of the mulleins. Natasha glanced too, at their grey foliate velour smudged up against the sandstone of the balustrade, and looked back at her niece, and saw the tautness in her cheeks. The sun was showering down from somewhere high behind Rosa's head. She continued to gaze steadily over there to the left of Natasha's shoulder. 'He said he wanted to be on his own today,' she announced.

'Don't dip your tomato in the jar,' said her mother. 'Put some salad cream on the side of your plate.'

Which was not at all the point, thought Natasha, seeing Rosa's over-composure.

'I don't want any more,' said Rosa.

'I hope you two haven't been pestering him,' Ellie looked from one teenager to the other, but they were each as inscrutable as the house windows, black against the sunlit noon. She sighed. 'It was very nice of him to take you shooting, Sam.'

'He didn't take me shooting. I took him, and I let him use my gun. Which was nice of *me*.' Sam turned and looked at his mother in a callow way that hadn't yet learned to curdle insolence from bravery.

'Mummy,' said Bernie, twisting her neck upwards in the crook of Natasha's shoulder. 'Is it Sam's gun, or is it still Uncle Ruaridh's?'

Sam rose to his feet, picking up his plate. 'It's mine,' he said, loping off towards the path that ran around the side of the house, with Julab trotting at his heels.

Natasha sat staring at the patch of space that Sam was passing through. Sun flashed brightly from white china in his hand. Her thoughts were drifting on the back of a third dandelion clock as it crossed him, and then the world seemed to hang there as if that fluffing seedhead clock had been frozen in a glass ball, a paperweight that pinned the day still.

Sam was sulking, of course, thought Natasha, but he had been right in his assertion that he had led the shooting trip and not Humberto. Ellie might like to arrange everyone younger than herself according to seniority, but when it came to Sam and guns, age was immaterial. He had a unity with the machine that went beyond mere manual experience. His mind must surely have operated in the same way as his rifle – via aims and mechanisms and well-greased unhesitating barrels – for his use of it to be so seamless, and perhaps this alarmed Natasha a little. When Sam held the gun, it was no longer a gun, but an extension of him. The confidence of it disturbed her, but then, perhaps it was only the physical confidence of all male youth.

28

And he was not a bloodthirsty boy, Natasha told herself. He never seemed excited by blood or death or violence. But then, it never upset him either. It failed to disturb him in any way at all. He simply had a single-mindedness that applied itself to ending rabbits as steadily as it once had to building radios. A devotion to accuracy and logical sequence, a calmness with which he maximised the number of birds falling from the sky until his bag was on the brink of obscene, George told her, home from the Rednock shoot last October break.

She was replaying their conversation in her head now and, although she could not reproduce it perfectly, she knew George's way of speaking and the gist of the thing that he'd been saying, so the memory, if not exactly true, was at least a fair impression. Natasha sat staring at the halted garden, seeing George, who was pulling off his britches and sitting on the bed in his long-johns as the taps ran in their pale pink-carpeted bathroom next door. She was now standing by the open bathroom door, keeping an eye on the water level, and then looking back at him, there on the quilt. She was thinking that there was something very appealing about George, something that elicited more in her than merely to-be-expected conjugal affection. He always seemed to be looking for something and wondering if you could help him, and silently he always seemed to be laughing darkly at the futility of his fumblings, and was he also sad, she wondered? – but did not ask him, because few men seemed so happy as George, which would have made it absurd, wouldn't it, to ask him.

George is sitting on the bed in his long-johns and she is standing beside the open door to the bathroom, its sounds of hot running water and pink steam. 'I had to ask him to leave some for the others,' George is saying. 'I don't think he understood me at all. Smiled, of course, and took a rest, but I don't think he understood at all.' He is doing something small with his hands – there must be a fastening, a button perhaps. 'There is a balance between games and gravity, and he's got it the wrong way round,' she hears George say. 'He plays the game as if it were deadly serious, and then he treats death as if it were only something in a game. Fails to comprehend that the point of a shoot is to kill things – really kill them – within the context of a waltz among friends. Isn't it, darling? Gravity in levity? Death in leisure? Blood, falling, shot hot stillness – distributed, yes. Death known for what it is, taken seriously, and respected, but placed purposely, pleasingly, in a pattern where it is meant to be. Death in a dance, or some such thing.' Perhaps she is nodding, or smiling at him; she must be, because he is looking at her now, and when he continues, he is suddenly almost jocular in tone. 'Off goes your nephew, marching through the ballroom by himself, killing things off as if he were only picking fluff from his jacket buttons – and not in time to the music at all – and then he stands at the far wall all bemused, wondering why the others take so long. Amiable boy, but somebody should have taught him about death and games. I really don't think he understands.'

With a start, Natasha realised that Sam was standing in front of her. Hadn't he gone to the kitchen? She'd seen him, with a white shine of china plate in his hand. I'm not eating off a plastic plate, she recalled him saying in the kitchen before lunch, in that ironical tone he had lately adopted of deadpan affrontedness. Yes, it was a china plate he'd been carrying, that she'd been looking at five minutes ago, the spark of it in the sunshine by the mulleins as she thought of George's story of him, of the Rednock shoot. He must have gone inside and laid it in the kitchen while her thoughts had hung on the same spot, and he must have walked back through them without her noticing, and now here he was.

'Shall I carry the other things in?' he was asking.

She smiled guiltily. Oh, he was a nice lad, she thought,

no matter if Ruaridh hadn't taught him the things George thought important. 'No,' she said. 'It's fine, Sam. Thank you, though.'

'I've just sliced you an egg,' said his mother peevishly.

Sam darted a smiling glance at Aunt Tash. Conspiratorial: my mother thinks I'm still a child; let's pretend, because we both love her. Natasha smiled back, but stopped smiling when he turned away to take the proffered egg, sandwiched in a chunk of soft white bread.

Sam was standing, eating, while the four of them sat on the ground: she and Bernie on the garish red Royal Stuart tartan rug, Ellie lodged on it too, the other side of the mainly empty tubs, the broad beans – somebody should finish them – and the salad cream. Rosa over there, who was far too pretty for her own good, sitting purposely on the grass and not the rug, but so close to it that her bare knees brushed its tasselled fringing.

Ellie screwed up her face, Thermos cup in hand. 'Do you know,' she said, 'I think it's better without the peaches.'

And Sam's legs were very hairy, Natasha noticed. Like a man's.

'Would somebody like to have these broad beans?' she asked. But it seemed that nobody did, so she took the tub into her lap with the arm that was not wrapped around Bernie, and picked at them herself.

Chapter Six

Bernie spent the afternoon upriver with Sam. If you went to the end of the garden, past Humberto's encampment, through the pines, you could clamber down the riverbank and get around the end of the boundary fence, climb up the other side and carry on, under the overhanging branches of the ash trees, hop from rock to rock where the earth gaped out beneath tangled brambles. Undergrowth sealed off the wild woods, and sealed off the river from anyone who didn't take its own route.

Grey stone rose from the river in great long elbows and shins over which the water spilled, in stepped falls, but Bernie and Sam hugged the edge as they climbed, clamping their hands on the black wet mounds of moss. Now and again Sam stopped to haul the coil of rope tighter over his shoulder.

Beyond the falls always seemed a very secret place. Partly it was its inaccessibility, but also it was the slowness of the water that flowed here – so different from the rapids downstream – that meant you could hear every sound, every lazy whistle in the leaves, every flipping scale of trout in the umbrous pools. The quietness hung sweet and heavy.

Bernie stood at the river's edge, halfway between the dozy

heat of bracken and plantains, and the coolness rising from the water that circled as if it could hardly even be bothered to flow downstream. Rings of pinprick bubbles formed and fell on its dark amber depths. She had taken off her wet plimsolls and the flat rock that she stood on was baked and lovely under the soles of her feet. Half in the light, shadows from the branches striped the backs of her legs, likening the stripes of her green and white towelling shorts. She could feel the bars of sun warmth on her skin, and the gaps between. Like a tiger, she thought; this must be how it *feels* to be stripy. Look at me, she called to her cousin. I'm like a tiger.

Sam nodded. She couldn't see what he thought of her tiger-ishness, because he was wearing black Raybans, but she suspected, from the way that his head was craned backwards, the way that the plane of his face was slanted up towards the canopy of leaves, that he wasn't actually paying her much attention.

She wasn't really sure that she wanted to make a death slide any more. It would be quite fun enough just to balance here, on the rock, like she always did; and maybe go for a swim, like she always did; and take pebbles to make drowned mosaics for minnows to swim over, like she always did; and twist plantains into plaits while she dried out, like she always did. That was what she would have done if Catherine had been here, and not tucked up in the sick-room at home. These were the things that she and Catherine always did, and talked quietly in the gaps between.

Her sister's long absence had changed things. Catherine's habitual activities had been displaced by rest and nothingness, but Bernie's share had to be replaced by something else, because she was not ill. So sometimes she sat on Rosa's bed, reading her music magazines, and quietly applying apricot nail lacquer, but she always felt a bit restless in there, stifled by pretending to be interested in things she didn't much care about. She dropped in on Catherine, but the sick bowl was always empty and even when Catherine was awake she didn't seem really to be there, so Bernie could neither nurse her nor talk to her in any satisfactory way. Sometimes she helped her mother in the kitchen, but that wasn't quite right either, because her mother kept giving her the same jobs she'd always given her, even though Bernie was undoubtedly taller than last year as she stood there, podding the exact same beans. She liked visiting Humberto in the garden; she liked the way he called her *princesita* and the way that he listened while she told him made-up stories that she pretended were real, but now Rosa was there all the time and he called Rosa *preciosa* and talked to her in a different kind of voice. And Rosa's voice changed too, when she was sitting near him. And then Rosa would send her away from them, to go and find things that were stupid and difficult, like a four-leafed clover or an oak apple or a toad, as if it were a fun game, but it wasn't. She knew they just wanted to be alone. And that only left Sam, who was a boy, and so in a fit of bravery, in a crazed bid to cleave to this last potential ally, Bernie had suggested that they do the most boyish thing she could imagine and rig a death slide across the river.

Now they were here, she was feeling some trepidation. Not about riding on the actual slide, because she hadn't thought that far ahead, but about putting it here. About hanging a great big rope, there in the sky, between the tres-passers' trees that belonged to her and Catherine but not, surely, to something that you left after you'd gone away. It didn't seem right. You couldn't be a tiger and leave a death slide behind you. You would have to be a human, now, for ever.

Slowly Bernie lifted her right leg behind her, bending it

34

at the knee, caught her ankle in her hand behind her back, and stretched her left arm forward. Her palm was holding itself up in a stop sign to the opposite bank. But really she was just trying to hold her balance.

Chapter Seven

'Sam's awfully good with the girls,' said Natasha, stacking dry dishes from the draining rack. On the worktop, and then heaving them up to the open cupboard. The beaky milk jug on the cupboard's upper shelf looked down imperviously on her efforts. Natasha was still bothered by thinking ill of Sam earlier. She hadn't actually thought much ill of him at all, of course. She hadn't allowed herself to, but it had been there, the pull of it, the attractiveness of those thoughts. Because she had been cross with his mother about the peaches, of course; it wasn't Sam at all. And then she had been wrong about thinking he had gone off in a sulk, when really he had only been clearing away his plate and coming back to help. Ruaridh's boy. Who nevertheless was not Ruaridh, and did not look like Ruaridh, not in the slightest; perhaps that was the source of her rancour.

'I think he's quite happy that Bernie asked him,' said Ellie, wiping down the kitchen table far too gently, as if she were dusting mahogany and not pale blue chipped Formica. 'He feels he's too old for that sort of thing but he still rather likes it. It's probably fun for him to be able to build a death slide and pretend it's just for her.'

Natasha paused in her plate-lifting. 'Well,' she insisted. 'It's nice of him, all the same.'

36

Gingerly Ellie's wrist flicked the cloth about the corner. As she scooped up the rag and carried it to the sink she was careful to keep an eye on it, there in her hands, in case it tried anything unusual. 'Oh,' she said, distractedly. 'He wouldn't do it if he didn't want to.'

Natasha shoved the pile of plates into the cupboard, hard. She frowned to herself, to her sore arms and the milk jug, cross. When she turned round, she was smiling in a very determined way. Yanking out a chair and sitting down. Thinking of how much nicer she was when Nuala Farish was here instead of Ellie. That was who she really was, wasn't it? That calm and even-tempered woman, who laughed with Nuala? Why couldn't she be like that all the time?

'It's lovely and cool in here,' approved Ellie, sitting down too.

'Chilly in winter,' said Natasha, because of course the kitchen quarters ceded sunshine to the reception rooms. This section had been built with its walls part-submerged in earth, designed to keep the food cool in the larders, rather than to keep scullery maids comfortable in January. William Farrants' architect could never have imagined that the lady of the house would spend so much time in here, or that the cook and the maids would all vanish back to the town, operate tills and go home to double glazing and their own sofas. Otherwise he might have arranged the windows differently: those high jail-like lozenges of daylight at the level of the path outside, through which you could see nothing at all, unless one of the girls had taken it upon themselves to run outside and press their nose against the glass. They were still at an age where it was funny to see each other's faces so high up on the wall, and liked to hang upside down out of their beds to see what it would be like if the world were the other way up.

'But yes,' said Natasha, 'it is lovely on a day like this. I like it in here,' she said. 'Kirsty thinks it's poky, not being able to see out, but do you know, I don't think I mind that either. I think I rather like it. So does Nuala, actually.' She removed her hair clasp; caught her hair up freshly behind her head in one hand. 'We agree.' Fastened the clasp again. 'It's quite monastic, isn't it. Quite relaxing, in a way, not having to worry about what's going on outside.'

'Out of sight, out of mind,' said Ellie.

Which annoyed Natasha all over again, because she couldn't help thinking of Rosa and Humberto, and how inappropriate it was for Ellie of all people to presume to use such a smug and hackneyed remark in summing up, inaccurately, her sentiments. The sentiments of her, Natasha, who kept all things in mind at all times, when Ellie couldn't see what was right in front of her, not even when she was staring at it under her own nose with her eyes wide open. Natasha brought her arms back down crossly.

But Ellie was not, in fact, casting any aspersions on her sister-in-law. She simply couldn't think what to say in response to Natasha's bizarre comment about the monasticism of the kitchen. The idea of nuns and monks appalled Ellie to her core. She was intensely disturbed by the suggestion that this room whose temperate comfort she had been praising might have anything to do with silence and fasting and queer deprivations. So she said the first thing that came to hand, to prevent the silence from swelling into anything like a cowl. And now she was brushing her hand over a small patch of tabletop, and wondering out loud if she should put the kettle on.

Natasha watched her uncouple the flex. Ellie was a slim woman, with slim hair, which lay down flat against her head, and slim movements that seemed more like embroiderings in space. It was always a surprise that those funny small flittings of her fingers could actually achieve things. When Ellie handed her a mug full of tea, it was as if ornamental grasses pink-seeded in a breeze had somehow knitted a scarf. Everyone was absurdly impressed when Ellie managed to do things properly, and yet, she managed to do things properly quite often. Perhaps it was her own air of surprise that led them. The way her eyebrows were tentatively raised as she slid the mug across the table, the way the outcomes of her actions always seemed so novel and potentially pleasing to her, but only potentially. Always she was also half-sorry for the things she would undoubtedly have got wrong.

The competent mug sparked a fresh pang of guilt in Natasha. 'I can't tell you how grateful Catherine was to have Pello back,' she said, raising her forehead earnestly. 'You know, she still talks about that. You'd think Sam had crossed hell and high water to save him. Well, I suppose he did, didn't he? The high water part at any rate. Poor little Pello.'

'Oh yes, the bedraggled bear.'

'It was awfully good of him. God knows what histrionics we would have had if Pello had been carried off to sea.'

Ellie smiled.

At least she wasn't unpicking it this time, thought Natasha. And sat back quietly now, pleased to have had atoning praise of her nephew accepted. Sam's bravery was a thing that no one could question: his body was fearless to a point that sometimes verged on foolhardiness.

Everything fine now, Natasha drank her tea too quickly and scalded the roof of her mouth. 'Bugger,' she said, wincing, and put her mug back down.

Chapter Eight

Catherine lay on the daybed, in the same place she had lain for days on end. She knew the window panelling too well; the brass hoops on the sash windows; the flutter of the curtain cord against wood; the pitting of the pale gold sandstone outside the glass, the flake of it that hadn't quite come loose in the second block up from the bottom of the sill. The arrangement of criss-cross old bricks that paved the path that ran around the house, arranged in this small section here outside her window, level with the gleaming floor inside. The groove between the two, into which the sash window boomed down when it closed. Don't worry, Bernie had told her, I'm quite sure the frogs and mice shan't come in. If they do, you can call me.

But so far they hadn't.

The grass outside lay level for a short distance before it fell away sloping to the old pond that had never had any water in that Catherine knew. And on beyond that shimmered the tall mesh fence, and beyond that, she knew, was the brief cliff dropping down to the river. You could see it from the island.

Catherine lay with tetchy brow and weariness, watching the comings and goings in the garden outside. From her vantage point she could see straight down to the river and also most of the lawn as it ran eastwards downstream, because of the way that the giant dining room windows were angled around this corner, and the other, like animal eyes, like the way an animal keeps its eyes on the sides of its head instead of fixed to the front. If she lifted the blinds on the other ones, she'd be able to see all the way westwards too, across the gravel driveway to the pine grove, but the sun shone in too hotly over there and so she had been planted on this side instead. You can see more from here, anyway, her mother had said, which had given Catherine the vague idea that watching from the window was in fact a task she had been given, a proper part of getting better.

It was harder to see the things that were straight in front, having the windows on the side corners, of course, but overall you could definitely see more. Than if they were just at the front like a blinkered horse.

She had seen the others laying out the lunch things on the grass in front of the drawing room, just there, sideways from her. Then she must have fallen asleep; she remembered hearing something nice, and then when she woke it was horrible and quiet. That thick quietness that you knew wasn't going to lift, the kind you only found in places from which the people had gone.

So everyone must have gone out. Everyone except one, because always one person stayed behind with her, but she never knew which of them the person would be. And also the person wasn't going to make a noise all by themselves, were they, not a human kind anyway, because there was no one for them to call to. There would just be rustling, or mainly nothing. Sometimes she tried to guess which of them it was, but really she never knew until they came to poke a face round the edge of her door and ask if she was all right, and take away her dirty water glass sideways.

Catherine would nod, at Mummy or Bernie, Aunt Ellie or Rosa or Sam. And while she was nodding, what she wanted to say was: *I didn't know who you were.* It made her want to cry, but lots of things made you want to cry when you were ill.

Lately the Spanish man, whom she didn't know at all and was a bit afraid of, had been doing it too. Almost she preferred to see his face around the doorframe. If you weren't going to know who was in the house with you, at least it made more *sense* if they were a stranger. The horrid thing was having people you knew so well be strangers and leave you stuck here with all the things you thought you knew taken away and waiting, and waiting.

Footsteps sounded in the hall, and paused outside the door.

Maybe it was Sam. That would be good.

Maybe it wasn't.

She waited, but the footsteps carried on away towards the kitchen without announcing whose they were and Catherine lay feeling staggered and cheated again and wondered if she would feel better if she turned her pillow over to the cool side. She leaned her head against Pello. And stared through the glass at the outrageously green lawn, and the brightness of the sunshine that fell there; the giant red poppies that splattered brightly in beds of blue catmint, and the blackness of the shadows that managed to hide; but mainly the light, mainly she stared at the sunshine that fell on the grass outside like it was pulling each blade out from the ground.

When the footsteps came back, Catherine made sure to lie very still and not be in the least bit interested in whose they might be, smoothed her curiosity as thin and flat as the cotton sheet that covered her chest, and lay with her head turned sideways, away from the door, not moving an

42

inch. Not thinking, at all, about anything other than the flick of the curtain cord against the panelling, the way it drew and then kissed its own shadow line, over and over again.

Patience is not a virtue but a skill. Catherine learned it all summer long.

'Are you all right?'

Rosa. It was Rosa's voice, there at the opened door. Catherine nodded, still watching the curtain cord.

'I made you toast and honey.'

Catherine turned her head from the daybed then, and looked at her cousin, almost beside her now. The sound of her sandals on the floor, stopping. 'You're very pretty,' said Catherine. 'I wish I had curly hair.'

Rosa laughed. 'Thank you,' she said, standing there in her tight dark denim shorts that clung all the way down to her brown knees, her loose blue Indian blouse that floated out when she stooped and put the plate down, the shine of the wet honey in the dull room. 'The aunts have gone shopping,' Rosa said.

'We've got no money,' observed Catherine, but Rosa thought she was referring to the two of them there in the room.

'Oh, I do,' she said. 'It's hard to spend your allowance in the holidays, isn't it.'

'I don't have an allowance,' said Catherine.

'Well, you will when you're older.'

'Does Sam have an allowance?'

'Yes.'

'Remember when he saved Pello?'

'Yes.'

'Where's Bernie?'

'With Sam. They're building a death slide across the river.'

'Where?'

43

'I don't know. Past the falls.'

'Oh.' Catherine fiddled with the edge of her sheet. 'Why were you and Sam fighting yesterday?'

'When?'

'In the evening. When the others were on the island.'

'Did you think you heard us fighting? We weren't fighting. I'm going to be in the garden, gorgeous. Call if you need anything.'

Catherine watched as Rosa's blouse caught the breeze out there in the garden, and her brown hair billowing sideways. She was sashaying slowly down the slope, and Humberto was standing at the bottom, with his hands on his hips, watching her.

It seemed as if she might slip over when she got to the bottom, because Humberto put out a hand to steady her.

They climbed down into the drained pond. Catherine could still see the tops of their heads for a while, and then not. She waited for barbecue smoke but there wasn't any.

Chapter Nine

Natasha laid the palm of her hand down softly on the top of a pile of pale angora sweaters. How absurdly pillowy they were! Like her daughters' cheeks, but these you could take home and keep soft in a drawer for ever. Swiftly she considered the probability of their pilling and bobbling after washing. Really, it was better just to touch them brand new in a shop. There had been a time she would have found the sweaters exquisite, and straightforwardly adored them, and thought about them afterwards, and wanted one quite desperately, but after years of practice she was able to touch them and only think them amusing and pleasant for a moment or two. Besides, none of those pale colours suited her.

Natasha found fault with things not out of any natural pessimism or ill-will, but to draw the sting from her un-requited love for them. Sweaters only returned affection if you had the money to pay for them: otherwise they stayed there on the shelves, quite impervious to your longing. It was best to find reasons not to want them.

Natasha was thirty-four, and years of practice were showing, hardening slowly from defence against a kind of love into the beginnings of a cynical approach to things beyond expensive knitwear, to the trappings of the very day. Things that were free – the fluffing seed that bowled along the roadside, the sweet-tasting rain that fell – she had begun accidentally to shutter herself against also, so that they brushed against her only in irony, as rude weeds and chill discomfort, where once she had loved them openly, unconditionally.

Anything that she had loved, now she saw faults in. The things she had never much cared for were the things that others thought she liked best. Anything insipid and unlikely to inspire her heart, seemed good. She could like cheap Battenberg precisely because she had always preferred rich fruitcake. She could like poplin shirts because they were not silk. She allowed herself to like the things she knew she would never want too badly. The things that were safe.

Anyway, things aren't important, she often said. People are.

Which was why it was especially hard for her to suspect that she might harbour uncharitable thoughts towards her nephew; to know that she certainly thought unkind things about Ellie.

And now Ellie was emerging from the fitting rooms in a sweep of tweed, a swirling coat with princess collar and bell-shaped sleeves, her fine limp hair scooped up into a flat cap. 'What do you think?' she was asking, half laughing.

'Oh, the coat's lovely,' said Natasha. Thinking, the sleeves would fall in your food when you were eating. Although, you would probably take the coat off for eating. But what about picnics? If you were picnicking, you often kept your coat on. And then the sleeves would fall in your food, trail in the mayonnaise, which would be a shame.

'What is it? You don't like something. Is it too tight across the shoulders?'

'No, no,' Natasha exclaimed. But she was pleased that Ellie knew the coat had not attained her unqualified approval. She was now quite happy to draw attention to

46

all its other merits: the covered buttons; the dashing sky blue silk lining, which looked so spry against the beige check; the fine bracelet cuffs inside those perilous sleeves, how neat, how sweet.

Always Natasha was making amends.

And Ruaridh would have adored her in that silly hat.

'Do buy it,' she said. 'I think you should.' And watched as Ellie left the coat and hat behind the till in order that her arms could be free to rake prettily through the rails on another trawl around the store.

In case she'd missed something.

Standing by the pickles and preserves, Natasha saw from the corner of her eye that Ellie had lifted up one of those angora sweaters from the pile, there in the carpeted section of the shop. She couldn't help turning round to properly look. And it was astonishing, it really was, the way that her sister-in-law hardly thought twice about it; simply ran her hand over the pale green silken rabbit hair; glanced cursorily at the other colours – paused for a second, but no, this was the colour she wanted – and carried it off on her arm.

Natasha would have chosen the pale blue. If she'd been Ellie. She stared at the jar of green tomato chutney that she was pretending to consider buying. Ninety pence for a jar of chutney! No wonder they called Royce's the Harrods of the North. She took the jar to the till and paid and was glad.

Natasha was standing by the doors to the car park, reading the ingredients on the label of her jar with unwarranted interest. Her heart was beating hard. Ellie smiled at her uncertainly, in her usual way, as she approached with her bags.

Getting into the car, Eleanor took all of the bags into the driver's seat with her, was half-submerged with them all on her lap. Which wasn't the cleverest way of doing it, thought Natasha, who was belted into Ellie's passenger seat – Natasha always wore her coat belt – and who was now being handed the plastic cushions of booty as if she were an attendant maid. It would have been easier, thought Natasha, to put the bags in the boot.

'The top one's for you,' said Ellie; and with her hands free, turned the key. Natasha opened the bag as they pulled out of the car park and onto the open road. She looked at the pale green angora sweater nestling in tissue paper inside.

'Do you like it?' Ellie asked.

Natasha looked at it. 'Yes,' she said. 'It's very soft.' She closed the bag again, and looked at the brilliant hedgerows flying by her, the road stretching out in front. 'You're too kind,' said Natasha. 'You shouldn't have.' Her voice was rather quiet; its defeated note made Ellie glance sideways as she drove, but Natasha's head was turned away now and she was wearing her hair loose, which hid the side of her face. She would have had to be looking straight at you.

They drove past the strawberry farm, its rows and rows of precious neatness, and pickers in between, rolled out in giant squares across the open hillside. 'I love it,' Natasha suddenly declared. She had turned her face back towards Ellie and was quite normal and herself again. 'I really do,' she beamed. 'I really do.'

Look at them all, bent double, and she was in here with a lovely angora sweater, guiltily liking Ellie, which was better than not liking her because it meant she only had to contend with guilt for her past sentiments rather than the current ones also.

She wished she hadn't bought the chutney.

Chapter Ten

One leg braced against a lower branch, high in the ash tree, balanced, Sam tightened his rope around its trunk. Breathing out between his teeth as he tugged the knot fast. It was easy for him but he liked it all the same; he liked being up here where you had to be on purpose. Nobody was accidentally up a tree. You could only be up here because you'd chosen to be, and everyone else would know it when they looked up at you from down below. And when you were alone, still the world knew it; the birds and leaves knew to reckon with you. Here was somebody who did what he chose, and starlings could not choose to come and sit on his sofa; leaves could not choose to fall upon his dinner plate.

He liked being out here with the starlings and the leaves. He liked it that he was stronger than these things, always. You could be at peace with things like that.

The leaves, tattooed with layers of the leaves above, hung over him and all around him, shelling the sunlight so that he worked in a built-up shade. Somewhere beneath him he could hear Bernie dabbling in the water, the plish of a finger or toe. He was fond of his cousins, of their prim sweetness; they were like a pair of elderly ladies in little ungrown leotard bodies. He liked their frankness, and he liked their frank admiration of him. 'Are you still being a tiger?' he called, not looking down.

But there was no reply. 'Bernie?' he called. And sat with his head held very still, for a moment, listening. Swiftly he finished off and scrambled down the tree, branch to branch, dropped into the plantains. It took him a second to catch his balance, to look around, down here on the ground.

Bernie was standing right there, the other side of the tree trunk, a few feet away on the riverbank, looking straight at him. He frowned. 'Why didn't you answer?' he asked, striding back toward the coil of rope. It lay in the long grass and the plantains, connected by a tentacle through the branches to the tree above. He was stripping off his T-shirt. He was stooping, hoisting the coil, slinging his arm through it, lassoing his shoulder. Tramping towards the water's edge. He looked around again before entering the water, at Bernie standing there watching him. 'I thought something had happened to you,' he told her. He couldn't understand why she was just standing there, looking at him in that funny way. 'Why didn't you answer?' he asked again.

'I didn't hear you,' said Bernie, bravely looking at him still, but the rest of her face, all of her except her eyes, falling away from his gaze.

'Don't be a liar,' said Sam.

'I'm not lying!'

And she wasn't, in a way, as she watched him wading through the water, and swimming now, with his tennis shoes strung by the laces around his neck; surely they would drag him down, Bernie thought, and he'd drown, she half-fretted, half-wished, but he didn't.

She wasn't lying about the way that she was feeling, in the moment that she cried out, *I'm not lying*. She was standing on the rock feeling more honest and raw than she'd ever done. She'd been lying a few moments earlier,

50

when she'd said that she hadn't heard him; of course she had been fibbing then, but she'd just thought that it would be nice for him to wonder about her. And he had: she had made him wonder, she had brought him down from the tree: she, Bernie, had done this. And then standing there, feeling very much herself, feeling towards all the things that this Bernie might do, how unbearable it was for him to accuse her *then* of lying.

She watched him haul himself out on the opposite bank.

Julab was panting and pacing beside her, ducking his head towards the river's edge and sniffing at it, retreating. She would have liked it if Sam's dog had stayed with her, but it didn't, it plunged in now and ploughed off in pursuit of its master, head held barely up above the water, eyes nervous and hard.

Bernie sat down on the rock and dangled her bare legs in the slow amber flow. She was refusing to look at Sam, and staring instead sideways towards the big ash tree nearby; the rope hanging down, twitching now: he must be pulling at it from the other side. She wished they hadn't come here and done this. It would have been better if she'd kept this place for herself and Catherine. With a rope tied across, it would never again feel like they could trespass here as tigers.

Sam glanced up from his tethering, at Bernie over there sulking, staring pointedly sideways. Her cheeks were full and rigid, like she was holding something in. God knew what had got into her. She was swishing her legs in that same overly intentional way that Rosa often used; except Bernie was only ten.

He'd wanted to come here with her because of her straightforward pleasantness, and now here she was behaving like his sister. She must have been spending too much time with her. Everyone seemed to be spending too much time with Rosa lately.

Humberto was an idiot anyway, Bleeding Spic

And it was only that he'd been worried about her, about Rosa, that was why he'd warned her, standing there yesterday in the hall with the bottle of HP sauce in her hand, in front of the kitchen door, her cocksure curls that didn't really know. Her brittle laugh in return as she dodged sideways, her silly hurry, *puellae festinant ad silvam*. He thought of them then, in his Latin book, the only girls there were at school: crude line drawings in short but shapeless togas. He had thought of them as his sister laughed, there in front of him, so close that he had been able to grab her arm. Before her billowing shapeless blouse receded down the hall. Had girls always hastened toward their doom in this slippery eyes-averted way?

Come on, he'd called, turning and following her towards the evening light that filtered through from the porch. You know he's only interested in you because of what's between your legs, Rosa. He wouldn't give a shit about you if you were a boy.

Fuck off! she'd hissed, and turned to face him before she stepped out; all her prettiness a heaving glare. I'm not a boy, am I? You're pathetic. You're just jealous.

As if.

And he'd stood there in the porch, watching her on her way across the footbridge to the island, still carrying the bottle she'd been about to put away. He couldn't very well go there now, with her and everyone else. Now he wouldn't see the kingfisher that they had all run to look at, that Humberto, of course, had spotted. And he would have liked to, and the thought of not seeing it pricked at his eyes. He ambled down to the drained pond and picked up the last frazzling burger from the barbecue grill, blackened on bricks, its comforting heat.

It was a sheltered spot.

There were kingfishers in books. There were books in Uncle George's library.

It wasn't quite the same, of course, because having seen a kingfisher in a book you could not say to people, I saw a kingfisher today. You had to see a real one, to be able to say that.

But still.

Sam climbed down from the oak that grew on this side of the river. Collected his thoughts as he stood in the grass. The grass would make a perfect landing patch for the girls, who would be too scared to jump off into the river. He could stand here and fetch Bernie down; Catherine too when she was better. He could reach up and catch them as they flew in, little bats, homing. He wouldn't let them bang into the tree and hurt themselves. He liked to look after Bernadette and Catherine.

Bernie seemed to have stopped sulking now, he was pleased to see, and had gone back to balancing on the rock with her ankle in her hand, like she always did. He smiled. He liked her unselfconsciousness, the way she was looking upriver, forehead blank, lips parted, concentrating only on not falling over. It didn't occur to him that her unselfconscious air was entirely intentional, and done for him.

Bernadette was learning cleverness and the art of peripheral vision, grimly aware of him there where she was not looking. A girl looks at what she wants; a woman does not. Bernadette was still a girl, but she was finding that there were many womanly things she could do, including acting like a girl. Looking upriver as if that was where the things she wanted lay, so that the boy on the other bank would think her charming.

The funny thing was, she wasn't even sure if she liked Sam, and certainly not the way that Catherine did. But

53

now Catherine was ill in bed, and doing nothing, Bernie felt some responsibility for living her sister's life on her behalf until she was better, keeping it going in a way she would have wished so she could hand it back when Catherine finally rose from the daybed and say, Here, I kept it warm for you.

Already she felt guilty for bringing Sam to their place, for stringing up a death slide across it. The least she could do was make Sam fall in love with Catherine now that they were here. So she balanced in a comely innocent fashion, knowing he was watching, being Bernie-and-Catherine. It just so happened that Catherine wasn't here, but that didn't mean that Sam couldn't see her in Bernie, did it? She would make him fall in love with the pair of them, of which Catherine was definitely a part. It made her feel very noble and clever.

Bernadette was nonchalant as Sam crossed the river once more towards her. He was climbing the ash tree above her, to try out the rope slide first, to make sure it was safe, he said.

She watched as he took off whooping, the length of his legs bunching up from their backward take-off into a kick that hurtled ahead of him as he flew by, out into broad sunshine, and suddenly dropped, arms and legs wide as if he'd hit a window, falling free, plummeting into the water. Bernadette smiled uncertainly as he emerged, and felt very strange about the fact that she was here alone with him, because really they were very different.

'I'll catch you on the other bank,' said Sam, dripping wet, standing under her where she perched in the ash tree, pulley in hand. Her knee was quivering a little where she had braced her leg against a lower branch. The swooping descent of the rope looked very long and deep from here; and here

54

was very high, from here; the river all of a sudden a strange and frightening thing. 'Wait till I'm at the other end,' he said. 'And push off with your legs from the branch when you jump, otherwise you might get stuck halfway. You need to give yourself a good push-off.'

'Okay,' answered Bernie, trying to sound casual. She was doing this for Catherine, she reminded herself. She was showing Sam how brave she and Catherine were.

Look at him down there, wading into the river, with his dark hair all wet and plastered round his head, like on a Roman bust, or an otter. She'd seen the busts in books at school; she'd seen the otters on the riverbank at home. A Roman otter, she thought, watching him. Why did Catherine like him so much? Bernie found herself a little frightened of him, and felt it was very good of her to be here doing this for her sister.

She looked at him standing there on the opposite bank. 'Okay,' he called. 'Let's have you, Bernie.' Beckoning with a broad sweep of his arm.

Bernie took a deep breath and pushed as hard as she could, with her feet, off from the dear grey trunk, where really, really, she would have liked to stay. Screwed her eyes up not quite closed as she flew through the gap in the foliage, the leaves that brushed her cheek so that she nearly screamed; the sunlit blaze of the open air, mid-air. The whooshing coolness of making your own wind by swooping fast enough, confusing the air around you so it made way as if you were a bird, but you weren't, you were just holding on.

Sam the other side, waiting to catch her.

Her bravery.

She swallowed up the air and sun, and let go. A lurching flash, a dark gasp, and total cold wet blackness. Her eyes wide underwater, still going down, how far down? And when would the river return her? She hadn't even touched the bottom.

Fingers splayed, legs pedalled and stopped, suspended in the river pool. Hanging deeper than she'd ever gone, here where she and Catherine told of giant pike. Here in the darkness. Hair spooling up above her head, streaming scalp bubbles tickling as they left her. Her hair began to fall and wrap against her neck, and she breathed out in the deliciousness of the silence. The crude sound of her outward gurgle startled her, made her small body push and straighten.

She'd bloody done it, though, for a moment, even as her arms panicked and propelled her back.

Rising now, slowly it seemed, to the surface. Pushing through the crust of sunlight on the water. Grabbing at the air, and then smiling and frowning and splashing out towards the opposite shore, wet plimsolls dragging at her ankles. She'd done *something*, for a moment, although she wasn't yet sure what.

'I told you I'd catch you!' Sam was shouting, furious. 'You shouldn't have done that. What if you'd jumped too late and hit the rocks?'

Bernie couldn't understand why he was so cross. 'You did it,' she said.

'I'm older than you,' he said. 'I'm responsible for you.'

He looped the pulley up in a high branch of the ash tree where Bernie couldn't reach it, and stormed off back towards the house by himself.

Bernie sat on the rock, plaiting plantain stems.

Chapter Eleven

Catherine, ignorant of her sister's travails on her behalf, lay exactly where she had lain yesterday, and the day before, and the week before that, watching the sway of the poppies whose petals were quartering now and flipping on tiny blackened hinges from seedpods that fattened and hardened and rattled: *our turn next* they said. She saw Julab first, and brightened a little, partly because she was fond of the dog, partly because it always meant that Sam must be close by. And sure enough, here her cousin came, striding across the lawn towards the other end of the house and the kitchen door. He was wearing cut-off army surplus trousers, which were wet and mud-smeared, and a blue T-shirt, which was crumpled and dry. His hair was plastered round his head. I expect his shoes are muddy, thought Catherine; that will be why he is going to the kitchen door. Maybe he is going to put on dry sandals, I imagine that is why he has come back to the house. I imagine he has jumped off their death slide into the river; that will be why he is wet. And watched as he disappeared from view, like she knew he would, and was not disappointed by this because she had got very good at patience, and the art of patience is the art of not wanting things. She was good at letting things wash past the window frame when they chose, and letting them go.

She was doubly pleased, then, when ten minutes later Sam pushed open the dining room door. 'Hello trooper,' he said.

Catherine grinned. She was feeling a little better since waking from her nap, had eaten the toast and drunk the water that Rosa had brought.

'What can I get you?' he asked.

'Nothing,' said Catherine. 'I'm fine.'

'How's your skin? Do you want me to rub some cream in?'

Really the spots weren't that itchy any more. 'Yes please,' said Catherine.

She lay on her front and pulled up her nightie, with the bed sheet tucked over her bottom, so that Sam could dab calamine ointment on the fading red bumps that punctured her body from her shoulder blades down to her waist. His fingers were very light, she thought, like he was hardly touching her at all. Still, it was nice. She knew it would have to stop soon, once he had dabbed the last spot, and she had learned not to be upset by this, but she had also learned how to make the most of things while they were with her. She knew how to drink in every drop of a moment, wring its guts so she could savour it later, in the long waiting times. The closeness of the cotton pillowslip pressed against her mouth, even with her face turned sideways, and the upholstery of the daybed pressing into her ribs, so that her breathing was shallower than usual; the flick-flack of the window cord, that was so regular, more familiar to her than her own heartbeat, marking the bit-by-bit disappearing of the time but also holding it, in a pleasant way, holding the dusty floor and the scent of dry grass, the sunshine warmth somewhere outdoors, between each knock it made. Holding it all in between the beats, the long drawn-out moment of those hands upon her skin.

Years later, after Larry had died, Catherine would lie face down in the double bed they had shared, with a metronome on the bedside table. She would set it ticking to exactly this beat.

'All done,' said Sam.

'I've got some on my legs.'

'But you can reach those yourself, can't you?'

Catherine hesitated. 'Yes,' she confessed. 'If I stretch.'

'Stretchiest girl I know,' said Sam. 'You could show those Romanians something.'

'Which ones?'

'The gymnasts. The girls who do backflips on the beam.'

'Do you mean Romans?'

'No. Togas would get in the way, wouldn't they?'

'The Greeks did gymnastics naked.'

Sam looked at her and laughed. 'Yes,' he said, 'they did.'

Catherine thought this was the happiest she'd ever been in her life.

Funny little thing, thought Sam. So matter-of-fact about everything. He hoped she stayed like that always, with that innocent frankness of hers, and did not go like Bernie, and sulk, and jump off rope slides when she wasn't supposed to.

'Will you play hangman with me?' asked Catherine.

'Are you well enough?'

'For a bit. Feeling a *bit* better.' She was propping herself up in the pillows and patting her hands down on the sheet as if to settle it, as if to say that, just for now, she was looking after the sick-bed, and not the other way round.

'You won't give me the pox?'

'It's not chickenpox, it's measles.'

'Easy to lose track with you.'

'Daddy says you're not to call it the pox, anyway. He says it makes me sound like a Shakespearean prostitute.'

'Do you know what a prostitute is, Catherine?'

'A lady who sells herself.' This was the definition that

Catherine's mother had given when asked, and Catherine had the loose idea that it involved short-term slavery and cleaning work. 'We can't afford one,' she said.

'Really.'

'Anyway, it's all right,' she told him. 'I'm not contagious any more. Doctor King said so. I've got pens and paper.' She was leaning over the side of the daybed now, her hair tumbling down so that it swept the floor. She was scrabbling around with one hand while the other propped her arm against the parquet; a pale wader bird bending its leg at her elbow, rummaging in a mud of shadow. 'Bernie brought them for me,' she was saying, in a muffled voice.

Sitting upright again now, pens and paper in hand, face flushed, eyes tired already from that one small effort. 'She brought them in case I wanted to draw,' she frowned, 'but I haven't really been in the mood.'

Sam raised his head slightly, and his eyes grew warmer.

Catherine looked at him, and then she said, 'She keeps bringing me sick bowls. I wish she wouldn't. Sometimes,' she said, 'she's a bit annoying.'

And everything was changed. Sam was smiling at her now, but with his skin instead of his mouth. Such a smile: a warmth emanating from his pores that she could lie here and bask in. It filled the room, and all her joints were filled with it too, the happy laziness of his approval.

Bernie had gone to build a death slide with him, and left her behind.

'I'll go first,' she said, and drew the hangman's plinth, and the empty dashes where the letters would go.

Chapter Twelve

'Bulrush,' said Rosa, lying on the bottom of the drained pond with her blouse lifted up to her neck. No wind disturbed her hair as she lay with a pentagon of bare skin pointing down to the centre seam of her black broderie anglaise bra. Humberto lay propped lengthways beside her, with his hand hooked into her denim hip. His eyes followed her pointing finger to the tall reeds with their velvet brown spikes. 'Bull-rush,' he said, and turned his face towards her. '*Totora*,' he said.

'*Totora*,' she repeated, smiling up at him. Reaching sideways to unbutton his shirt, still smiling, her eyes still on his; and sliding her hand in to the fineness of his chest, its firmness, like the earth, she thought, that you could lie against, in which there was life. She could feel her hand pressing it. 'I like you,' she said.

'I like you too,' smiled Humberto, and she laughed and bit his arm that was there near her cheek; she only had to turn sideways and lean a little, to nip him like a cat might.

Humberto was laughing back at her, but quietly, seriously; and now he had stopped laughing and Rosa was silent; he was pushing the cloth of her bra aside, easing first one breast and then the other up out of it so that they spilled against the puckered ridge of cloth.

Rosa lay tense, gazing down her front at her ghostly sub-aquatic whiteness, and her papery nipples, extraordinary, brazen, there in the sunlight. She tried to smile but couldn't as Humberto bent his head and slowly kissed each one. She couldn't even look at him, not even the top of his dark head, but had to look over his head instead towards the thicket of bulrushes that grew around the pond's outskirts; the dragonflies that darted amongst them. 'Dragonfly,' she whispered.

Humberto raised his head, she felt the relief of it, of the prick of her desire drifting back to the constant ripple that she always felt when she was near him, soft and liquid again, the way that she was wanting him, instead of that fearsome solid urge that could not be smiled at.

He had laid his cheek on her chest so that he was facing the same way as she was; his ear against her breastbone. 'Dragon-fly,' he murmured. 'I never know your pond so full of beasts, Rosa. Bulls in the grass, dragons in the sky.' A proprietorial arm held her torso, but loosely, quite sure of itself; her navel cupped in the V of his elbow seemed to breathe in and out independently of the rest of her, as if it were his, quite happy to be there and to be so, sure enough.

Lazily his hand stroked the lonely hollow below her armpit. He seemed to like this the most: touching the parts of her that were strange almost to herself. He liked to stroke the backs of her knees, or run his finger up the secret skin behind her ears, slip his thumb between her toes. Parts of her she'd lost when she turned thirteen, all the bits that made you up when you were still a child, that gave way to the monarchy of breasts and furred pudendum which arose so suddenly from the old egalitarian way that you'd been used to. How easily you forgot it, until someone brought it back to you, made kings of your knees and queens of your toes.

*   *   *

And she liked lying here, with his head on her chest, as if she could give him something without his taking it away from her. It made her feel peculiar and strong, swollen and generous, happy.

He was speaking Spanish words. Again she tried to echo him, '*caballito*,' she said, and saw his head move lightly with her breathing as her lungs pushed the word out from her mouth. '*Del diablo*,' she finished, and watched his dark hair rise and fall again.

Clouds were coming in overhead from behind the mountain, still safely distant from the rushes and irises that grew around the pond.

The slope fell so swiftly to the river, and the ground beyond it was so flat, a haze of hazel tops, that from where Humberto and Rosa lay there was only near and far. There were the dragonflies that folded their wings and flashed, thinned glass blue and green in the sunlight, and there was the distant dun-coloured mountainside. The white rapids and the low shady woods in between these two things might not have existed at all, if it weren't for the sound of the water.

A dog barked somewhere on the lawn above them. 'Shit,' whispered Rosa, rolling sideways, staring at Humberto. 'Sam,' she said. Tugging her bra back into place and swiftly smoothing her blouse down. Running a hand through her hair. 'I'll go first,' she said. 'I'll meet you on the island. But wait, wait – ten minutes? Wait until I've gone.' She held up every finger on each hand. 'Ten minutes,' she said again. 'Go round the back of the house and come down from the drive.' Humberto nodded at her. He watched as she crawled towards the other side of the pond, climbing out but keeping her head down, keeping her body pressed close to the slope. He looked down as he fastened the buttons on his shirt, and when he looked up she had completely disappeared.

Humberto strained his neck outwards but then gave up

trying to see where she had got to. He leaned forwards instead, head turned sideways to better listen for Sam, to catch the sounds that carried on the air. He did not want to get Rosa into trouble; he did not want to be asked to leave: they had another ten days left yet.

All he could hear was the dog, stationary now, panting over something.

He couldn't hear any sound of Rosa's brother, not at all. But he waited all the same, like she'd said, for a minute or so, any mode.

And then he stood, and crept to the side of the pond, raised his head above the lawn's slope and gazed up the greensward. If Sam had been there on the flat turf above then Humberto knew he would have been able to see the top of his body, his shoulders and head at least. It was so narrow, that lenticular grassy terrace where the family picnicked, that even if Sam had been standing at the furthest part from here, pressed back against the poppy heads, he still would have been visible in part. But there was no sign of him; only the soft stationary panting of his dog, up there somewhere.

There had been no need, then, for Rosa to be scared and scurry from their suntrap. Humberto felt that he should have been bolder; should have come up here to look, and saved her the indignity of flight. He looked around to see again if he could spy where she had gone, but she seemed to have vanished. He felt a strange coldness. To go from a surfeit of human company – Rosa's, desired and held so close, he had had it right there beneath his fingers; Sam's, unwanted but in its menace just as near – to none at all, to lose the object of his desire and the object of his fear in only a minute or two, left him standing here with an uncomfortable emptiness in his stomach.

Humberto walked to the end of the pond and stepped up onto its low stone parapet. He had a wish to be belatedly brave. He would find something for Rosa, he would fetch her a prize, take it to the island and please her. He would go round the back of the house, as she had requested, but he would also perform some small act of bravery on the way.

He trod the slope to the azaleas, and on towards the high spread of the drying green and Mrs Farrants' cabbages that lay to the east side of the house, out past the kitchen rooms. He skirted the side of the earth beds, wondering if here he might find something, but there was only the tall beech hedge and the sound of cars that were startlingly close, just the other side of the leaves, on the road. You could see the colour of their paintwork through the gaps.

In the garden, you always thought of this house as inhabiting a quiet, idyllic spot, but in fact the quietness was an illusion sustained only by the overwhelming sound of the river, towards which the house turned its handsome sunlit face.

Humberto was close by the kitchen door now, which stood open. He could see no one inside. He stepped onto the herringbone bricks and passed into the shadow cast by the gable end, his sandals crunching as he found the dark gravel path that circled the northern, almost windowless walls in the narrow gap between house and hedge. Anaemic grass weeds grew among the pebbles here, under his feet, and he was glad of them, for their tufted roundels deadened the sound of his treading between the roaring of the cars that passed.

It was dull to be here, though, among the bins where there was no hope of finding a treasure for Rosa.

So he was pleased to reach the driveway at the other end, and walked to the gateway, relaxed now, and decided to look in the woods across the road. His spirits had lifted. He waited for a gap in the traffic and jogged across the tarmac, the glass pastilles in the nitre that winked in the dappled sunlight, cat's eyes, Rosa said; and he trusted her, he trusted the truth of all her animal words. Scaled the bank and reached a hand out for the fence post.

Chapter Thirteen

In the apoplectic gloom of her sick-room Catherine lay alone once again, now that Sam had left, but with the sheets of paper from their game in her bed beside her; the back of her nightie still sticking slightly where he had dabbed her spots with calamine ointment.

Really it was fine, because she had known that he would have to go. It was never as if he was going to sit and play hangman with her for ever.

She was drowsy after being lively for him for so long – it seemed long, though had only been ten minutes or so – and lay curled on her side, watching the sunlight on the red lipstick petals; listening to the flick-flack of the window cord. The exact same sound and rhythm as when he'd been here, with her. If she closed her eyes she could still pretend.

She closed them, and when she opened them again, a while later, she saw him, rounding the path that ran in front of the drawing room balustrade, like he were some kind of reward for her. For her earlier goodness in relinquishing him so gracefully. She could not have him, but here, she was allowed to look at him through the glass. Sam had stepped onto the flat grass now, the level terrace of lawn where Julab lay, panting behind the tufts of catmint. And now Sam was shouting, and running forwards. He was alarmed on Julab's behalf, Catherine saw, and she wondered what poisonous thing the dog had found. She edged herself up on her elbow, mouth agape, aware that she was witnessing a drama, would be able to regale the others with her share of it later. There was growling from the splash of nut-brown fur: was Julab afraid? Sam had picked something up: a thick terracotta pot, gifted by his mother. What was her resourceful cousin going to do with it, wondered Catherine. Up-end it over the poisonous snake? Trap it, yes, perhaps.

She watched as Sam strode over to the dog, bearing the pot. It was held up against his shoulder, like a champion or a knapsack, and then suddenly it was gone. At the same time, his arm had moved, pulled along and stretching out after it. Both his arms were down by his sides now, and his hands balled into fists. It was only as she watched him standing there that Catherine began to realise he had thrown the thing at Julab.

Still the understanding hadn't fully dawned as she watched him take a step towards the dog. The meaning of the scene continued to be kindly kaleidoscoped for a little while longer, fractured into its component appearances like sunlight on water hiding the things beneath even as inklings collect and the wind drops.

Julab's howl that only seemed to arrive at Catherine's ears once it had stopped: by the time she was listening to it, the sound had been and gone, and the real one in the world was now a pained whimper. The two noises bumping into each other, time jarred by the sudden swing from one world to another.

Sam stooping down over where the dog must lie now, wrenching something upwards, looking steadfastly at his hand rather than any of the things around it. A black plastic object in his fist like mangled liquorice.

Poppy petals wavering, one falling free and tumbling

67

upwards instead of down, floating past his waist. His pale blue T-shirt that was crumpled but dry. His trousers that were hardly wet at all now, losing the last of their dampness in the bright sunlight.

His face that was determined. Not glad nor angry, but most of all not surprised, and in the end this was how Catherine truly understood that he had done it. The way his face was all contained, part of the present moment and carrying forward. Like a complicated sum that knew what it was going to be, knew what it already was, all along.

Catherine was kneeling up entirely straight on the daybed. Time had jumped forward again, in the space it had taken for her to comprehend what Sam had done. He had been standing there behind the poppies and the catmint, and now he was almost gone. He was going back upriver, she realised, and she felt numb, and then crumpled back down in her muslin nightie.

She looked around her, at the wood panelled walls, the windows in the far corner, pale blank oblongs behind the pulled-down blinds, the long gleam of the parquet floor. The damp patch on the chair beside her bed where he had sat in wet trousers, before. She watched with a pointless diligence as the damp patch slowly cleared – twenty minutes, half an hour – and felt all the old things drain out of her as the water drained into the air, and felt it crucial that she should watch the seat pad dry.

Convinced herself quite completely that this was her task, and tried not to be upset by the sound of Julab's faint whimpers from the lawn outside, because that was part of the world beyond the glass, where things happened as other people planned and you had no idea what they might be so it was best, it was definitely best, to leave it all alone. Really, Catherine realised, it had nothing to do with you at all. It was stupid to even guess about it, because you could think that you had it and then you could find that you'd been wrong all along. It was like trying to imagine the ending of a story and then finding that everyone had died before it started.

It was very quiet. Now that Sam was gone, there was no one in the house. Perhaps she would have cried, if someone else might have heard her, but there was no point. Thank goodness for the window cord that went on, flick and flack against the wood, regardless of everything else.

The dog's whimpering grew softer and softer still, and Catherine lay and watched the dampness fade on the silk seat of the dining chair, until it had completely gone.

Chapter Fourteen

Sam climbed out the other side of the river from the rocks at the falls and set off down toward the hazel woods, the distant cycle path that ran by the mountain's foot. Everything that had happened, had happened. Everything that would happen, would happen. Everything he did merely moved things on: from the bucket in front, through the sieve that he held, into the bucket that rested behind him.

There was nothing from which he should hide. He would perform all manner of life-altering acts out there in the real world, but all of them would be right. Everything he did was necessarily part of that world, and history was his: even his knee-jerk vengeances belonged to it. He reached the cycle path, pushed aside the over-hanging branch, waded through the verge of tall grass, kicked a plastic bottle cap and turned along the way. Passing a stubby green litter bin, he dropped his chewed-up Raybans in.

When he thought of Julab's whimpers and felt pained, it seemed to him a weakness. In throwing the pot at his dog, he had done something that had happened now, was part of reality now, the wider world; and the world was not something from which a man should shrink. His actions were part of the green leaf, part of the hot pale sky, the world that existed for him through his eyes. To be angry with himself was no more allowable than to be angry with the sun for shining.

Chapter Fifteen

From a distance, Catherine was aware of Humberto's cry rising in the garden, but everything out there now seemed as far as the mountain. He could have been a bird rising from the heather, or a silent antler small on the horizon, there was something speckish and small about everything now: really, it was nothing to do with her. Everyone had already died, even as their bodies gathered vivaciously out there in the open air, Mummy and Aunt Ellie having chosen this moment to arrive. The sound of their wheels on the gravel of the drive; then the sound of Mummy's voice, how nice; Aunt Ellie shrieking on the lawn, dropping a carrier bag, look; Lori from next door standing behind her, saying nothing at all.

Everything now contained inside its proper bit of time, and would not escape again, would not run on ahead under the steam of her silly ideas, never again, never again would she find herself on a bridge that hadn't been built, did not exist. All Catherine was aware of was the contents of each second, in the second as it passed, sleeper by single sleeper. She wanted nothing to do with any of it. The purpose of watching it so closely was to make sure that your hair didn't get caught in things as they passed. You had to know where everything was, to keep yourself apart. She stood up straight upon the daybed and peered down over the catmint and the poppies.

Aunt Ellie's fingers were picking bits of raw-edged terracotta from the labrador's ripped-open flesh, quite precisely, as if she were picking coins from her purse. The side of Julab's nose looked like a soggy flower, big red petals folded back, and one falling down, under his messed-up eye. And Humberto, who had been standing waiting with a hand towel – it could have been for anything of course, you had to keep an open mind – now tied this around Julab's nose. Mrs Farrants – Catherine liked to think of her like this, now; *Mummy* gave too much of a clue to her own hiding place, but *Natasha* seemed mildly disrespectful – who had disappeared into the house on an unknown, not-to-be-guessed-at errand, returned to the scene and said: 'The vet says bring him in.'

Catherine got out of bed and opened the blind on the far window. Its sash had already been pulled up to let more air in. She walked back across the room, and watched some more the action on the lawn.

They were rolling Julab onto an old curtain, and Rosa was running up the garden. Appearing in the other window now, they were carrying the bulging curtain that almost certainly still contained Julab towards the driveway, and Rosa was peering inside it as she stumbled along beside them, her hair tumbling down and not hiding her eyes, that looked slapped by whatever they saw in there, not hiding the deep frown wrung in her brow. She was saying things, lots of things, but Catherine didn't really hear. She didn't pay any attention to words now, to the things people said, because it was the pictures that mattered. It was only the pictures, she saw that now. The words were there to describe the pictures, and that was all.

If you looked closely at the pictures, you really didn't need to know what the words inside them were. You could look at Rosa's face and know what she meant without listening, and probably you could know better by doing this than by listening to words that could always be wrong like ideas were. Whereas pictures could not, were not. A thing that you saw, how could it be wrong? As long as you didn't assume things, it always would tell you the truth.

Catherine watched as they loaded the curtain into the boot of the car, saw Julab's tail poking out sideways from beyond her mother's bottom bent forward stern and busy. Closed now, the boot, Mrs Farrants opening the driver's door. Lori standing separate with her hands at two loose ends. Inside the car, Rosa was kneeling up on the back seat, watching over the invisible dog. You could see the outline of her bent head. And then they were gone: Mrs Natasha Farrants, Mrs Eleanor Gill, and her daughter, Rosa.

They had put the dog in the boot of the car, and then they had all got into its seats and driven away, to the vet's, with Rosa peering into the back. But they might not get there, they weren't there yet, there was nothing to stop them breaking down in fifteen minutes, or being hit by a lorry in six, you couldn't tell that.

Lori was walking towards the porch: perhaps she would enter the house, or perhaps she would stand on its low steps under the arch and wait for something else. Last time Catherine had stood in the porch there had been fuschia bushes in tubs and croquet mallets, the smell of dry grey wood from the timber arch itself, beneath its hat of slates, and damp cobwebs scenting the corners of the cracked mosaic floor. Perhaps it was all still there. If she closed her eyes, it was all still there. It made her happy to think of this. Not the words: there was no need for her to list all

the things that the porch contained: but the things themselves, the picture of them, the feel of them – were right
there where the world had left them, rolled into a single
thing that was hers, in her memory. She had it safe.

Chapter Sixteen

'Oh, so you know,' said Lori behind her, in the room. For a moment, Catherine thought she meant: *you know*. But actually, all she meant was, you know as much as the rest of us know. 'We thought you were sleeping,' she said.

Catherine looked at her, next-door Lori, older girl and friend of Rosa when she visited, champion of weaklings at the primary school, head girl at the high school, left now, left school altogether, going away to Glasgow soon. Daughter of Nuala Farish, and Neil, from the other side of the green painted gate in the wall, the house to which Catherine was carried before she started primary school, the house where her mother drank coffee and talked. Catherine, sent to Lori's bedroom, had been allowed to play with the drawerful of horseriding rosettes, would lose herself for an hour arranging the satin whorls in rings of colour on the carpet, tangerine and lettuce green and scarlet. Her mother always left the door open, and so Catherine could hear the constant murmur of the two women's conversation as she sorted Lori's prizes. She didn't know what a lot of the words meant, but she could hear the space they left around them in a sentence. She could hear the way they echoed off the plainer words around them. She had always felt extremely happy, listening to the talking, and arranging the rosettes as if they were hers. She had felt happy listening to the calmness, the confidence, in her mother's voice, a way it never sounded anytime else. And like her own quietness was part of that happening; like by arranging Lori's rosettes she was somehow helping it, the thing of Mummy sounding happy and nothing being bad. She always put the rosettes back exactly right afterwards.

'You didn't see anything?' Lori was asking. That was the way she phrased it. When Catherine just stood there in the middle of the room, not responding, but staring back from under a gentle frown, this stood as agreement, acquiescence; but she might have looked like that whatever question Lori had asked. It was only as she was standing there, being misunderstood, that she decided to say, 'No,' and it was a decision that took its shape, as all of her decisions now would, from the shape of the present moment. 'I just woke up,' she said.

'Who's going to tell Sam?'

'I don't know. Maybe I could.'

Lori smiled. 'You wee darling,' she said. 'Don't be daft. You're ill. No, I meant – who's going to tell Sam?' Which made Catherine feel that she was somehow less than a Who, had failed to qualify, would only have hurt herself had she tried to ride among rosette-splashed lapels. Which was rubbish, because really she would have been the best person in the world to tell him a thing he already knew. She was the only one of all of them who could have looked him in the eye and meant: I know too. 'I imagine Mrs Gill will tell him,' she observed.

'Mrs Gill? Do you mean your aunt?'

Catherine nodded. 'Yes,' she said. Because it was, it was exactly what she meant. 'Why were you with her and Mrs Farrants?'

'Catherine, you sound like a policeman. You can't call your mum that.'

'Why not?'

'She'll be upset.'

'Why? It's her name, It's who she is.'

'Yes, but it's not what *you're* supposed to call her.' Lori moved toward the window. 'I can't believe someone's done this,' she said. Catherine looked sideways at Lori's face, at the shock and feeling shining there, and most of all, at the belief in her cheeks. She thought that Lori looked just as a real person ought to. She thought that Lori looked nice. 'Me neither,' she said, and copied Lori's expression as best she could: a mild scowl, but the eyes kept wide, staring at something, and the neck loose, as if ready to shake your head at any time. Then she turned to face the windows too. It didn't matter that Lori wasn't looking at her as she made this impression; it didn't matter that no one could see. Catherine wasn't like a name, that needed to be called, and cared who called it. She was part of the picture of things. She was here, between the daybed and the door. 'Should you be in bed?' asked Lori, turning round.

'I don't know.'

'Why are you looking at me like that?'

'Like what?'

'Like that. Like you're waiting for me to do something.'

'Were you in the car with Mrs Farrants and Mrs Gill? Or had you just come through the gate.'

'Mrs *Farrants* and Mrs *Gill* gave me a lift. I was walking back from Callander. Is that all right, funny monkey?'

'And then did you not know what to do? When you saw Julab.'

Lori looked at Catherine as hard as she could, trying to fathom her soft brown stare, her warm pillow-straggled hair, the thin summer nightdress, the way she stood, back straight, arms obediently hung by her sides like they were carrying two invisible and perfectly weighted pails of water, her head tipped up to look directly back like that. Meeting

Lori's own gaze that tried still to square the innocence of all this with the carefree callousness of what Catherine had said. Lori was plumbing the sweet openness in Catherine's eyes, wondering how deep it was and finding that really it went as far as she could see. Finding it impossible, then, to explain the coolness and the hardness of what Catherine was saying. Did she not feel anything? Surely she did.

And Catherine did not suffer from a lack of feeling: that was why Lori could see her sweetness, and be perplexed by it. It was just that, instead of feeling things in the normal way of crying or getting cross herself, Catherine was by now far more concerned with feeling the loves and upsets between the component parts of the world outside her. Her seeming coldness was also a lack of emotional selfishness that followed her always afterwards. By the time she was twenty she was empathetic to a point that verged on disability; could not help but view things from every conceivable perspective, which meant that she rarely knew who she was, which view her own.

She would stare at the vase on Rosa's mantelpiece in the summer of '92, after Parker's accident, a tall ceramic rectangle with a hole punched through the middle. She would picture how this vase would work with flowers in, how the stems would have to curve around the hole that from the inside would not be a hole at all but a vigorous bulging obstruction. She would look at the hole, and how you could see a circle of wallpaper behind this spot where the centre of the vase should be. Where was its centre now? Was it still there, by the rules of geometry, a heart in the one place where its being wasn't? She would be inside the vase then, thinking how dark it was at the bottom where no light shone in, blocked by the shape of the hole above. She would feel the intrusion of absence on behalf of stems that weren't there and this feeling would grow because she would not recognise it as her own until it was too late, rising sharply, unchecked, a spasm in her left breast. I don't like your vase, she would say. Crossing it out, looking away, to the roller blind pulled halfway down the darkening panes of the tall window, stretched from ceiling to floor on Annandale Street, first storey.

Pots of asters would be clustered on the wrought iron balcony outside, still vividly purple, but only through luck, Catherine would think, how lucky for them that their colours happen to coincide with the dusk.

But that is eleven years away, and it is another fifteen years on from that before Catherine will sit on the step one evening and wait, and fifty years again before she will lie face down on her empty bed with the metronome set ticking beside her.

Right now she was standing on the parquet floor in her bare feet, looking up at Lori's face. 'No,' said Lori. 'I didn't know what to do. I think you should get into bed, Catherine. You're not well yet.'

'Poor Julab,' said Catherine, because this seemed the appropriate thing to say, seemed the sort of thing that a girl *like her* should say. But she was by now one step removed, had trodden sideways from the world. Rather than living in a place where things had meanings, she had slipped back into a world where things meant nothing more nor less than what they were, the pictorial life of an animal, in fact. Her soul was making a backwards leap, invisibly, a retreat, into the world as it had been before speech transfigured it. And now, to move inside the other world, the human one which briefly she had inhabited and taken for one that worked, she picked her camouflage branches carefully, her words and tones. Her body would act in it very beautifully, but she would not live there again for decades.

All through the while that her body waxed into a woman's and then slowly exhaled towards its ageing, she would be someone like her: a mirage, created by her body. From now on, she could merely be whomever she chose to seem. Her true soul slept soundly somewhere else, carefully wrapped in crepe paper. Occasionally some outside weather might disturb the casing, some wind rustle the tissue, and then she would remember that she, Catherine, existed – but mainly it became a thing that was easy to forget.

Lori seemed content, the way she lifted the empty water glass from the bedside. 'I know,' she said, looking at Catherine with eyes that could share now. 'Poor thing. Did you see him? Do you know what happened?' Not asking now, but offering to tell.

'No.'

'They threw a stone flowerpot at him. It was still lying all around him, the pieces. They broke it across his nose. Who would do that kind of thing?' She looked at Catherine; Catherine looked back. 'Is he going to die?' asked Catherine.

'Julab's a strong lad, isn't he? I'm sure he'll be fine.' Lori looked down into the water glass for no reason that Catherine could see, and then Lori looked up again. 'He was still conscious,' she added, reassuringly.

'How do you mean?'

'Awake. He was still awake.'

'Is that safer? If he isn't sleeping.' Catherine was careful to keep her brow furrowed this time, careful not to allow her rude curiosity to show through the words. I'm just worried about Julab, she was trying to make the words say. Panning for facts inside the way she was meant to seem.

'Yes. It's a good thing.'

And Catherine was glad to hear this news. It would be all right if Julab died, because nothing had anything to do with her, but her personal preference, the way she'd like the story to end, even though she was only reading it, couldn't change it, would be Julab's surviving. It was a second-hand gladness, but a gladness all the same, and, as she spent her late-flowering professional career proving, second-hand feelings could be stronger than the real thing. Bundled up in a bomb-proof room, to be unwrapped with a robot arm from behind the guaranteed glass, that wouldn't break, all sorts of horrors and firework delights that you couldn't begin to hold in your naked hands. You could know every feeling a human being had ever known, and none of them need ever be yours. Always you could walk away unscathed.

The soles of Catherine's feet flashed white as she climbed back onto the daybed and pulled the thin sheet up over her body to cover herself.

Chapter Seventeen

In the kitchen Lori sat alone at the table, reading Ellie's copy of *Harper's Bazaar*. Sunlight fell from the high window in a broad flat ribbon that hung diagonally in the air, illuminating dust like sugar in egg-white, fell on the Formica and rolled horizontal like it had been pushed there by a pastry chef, a paper-thin leaf of it there on the cleanness of the surface that Ellie had wiped down after lunch. The rest of the room was very white and very dark, storm clouds in melamine and plaster, shading blue and grey in corners.

Certain items on the fashion pages had been marked with asterisks by Ellie's pen. It had never occurred to Lori that people might use swanky magazines like these as actual shopping guides. She was impressed, and felt comforted. It was nice to know that she knew people for whom the world functioned so perfectly. It took the edge off her waiting here alone and thinking about the poor dog, feeling upset by it, by a world that had malfunctioned quite badly this afternoon.

Lori turned the page and looked at a model in billowing, unbuttoned, navel-slit, turquoise silk boiler suit.

Chapter Eighteen

The sun was hurting Sam's eyes. His eyes seemed too far out from his brain, his lashes too short, there was too much light in the sky, too much bouncing back from the cycle track. White splashed on the green leaves. His brow was wrinkled, pulled down. He was narrowing the inlets to his head as best he could, and now he had to raise his hand, shade his face as he walked. He was approaching the flood meadows on the outskirts of the town.

In the throbbing red heat of his eyelids he could feel the old heat of his father's gaze. The pinkness of his father's cheeks was spreading over his own. The same consuming flush, far from joviality, the same enraged rosaceousness. Sam felt it gorging on his face, and he saw his father before him in the orange shadows, and the old dog Fergal standing to heel at his father's side, panting with every breath Sam took. They were waiting for him. *Come on*, rasped his father's voice from the dark orange bend beneath the trees, on the path up ahead, where the dry leaves scratched each other. The cross-hatched patch of shadow seemed to scrutinise his every step with an old familiar glare, one that knew it could afford to wait but reeked of impatience all the same. The shadow was measuring the centimetres by which Sam's own short shadow approached it. A breeze blew his father's breath across Sam's neck and made him twitch as his walking slowed. He didn't want to go there. He felt sick.

Stretching down to Sam's left, clouds of creamy scented meadowsweet puffed above the slow-worms in the reeds and long grass. On the river's lazy hip the mud glinted here and there with tips of wrappers, from cigarettes and chocolate bars, bleached down to white and dirty silver, handkerchief nibs. They were glinting in the sun. From here, they looked pretty enough – if you didn't know better, you might mistake them for scatterings of precious metal. But they weren't, were they, thought Sam, standing still as he looked at it all. They were just bits of crap. Just litter. Stuck there, in the mud.

On the opposite bank, the grass lay shaven down: women walked upon it with their children and brought them to the water's edge to throw bread to the ducks.

On this side was the mud, and the litter, stuck in it. Things that had been thrown out by the people over there, dropped, the things they didn't want. Not quite a part of this side either: not part of the world of reeds and peewits, serving no purpose among the fluid animal tangle that ran and sang around them. Pointless things which didn't belong but were stuck, stuck where they were, in the mud.

The sun was hurting Sam's eyes. He swallowed, and walked on into the burnt shadows where the cycle path slowly took its corner. The shade was one kind of relief: his stomach lurched once more, and he stepped into it.

Chapter Nineteen

Catherine had got out of bed again. She was standing at the dining-room table, which had been pushed against the wall. It was piled with her favourite story books, for the times when she was feeling well enough to read them. The books were in two piles, one either side of her. She took another from the left-hand pile, laid it flat in the space between, in the space directly in front of her, and opened it at the flyleaf. She was writing in it: *Everyone died before this story started.*

Closing the cover and placing the book on the right-hand pile; she took another from the left and now laid that one carefully in front of her, opened it at the flyleaf, raised her pen. Her face was calm, concentrating. She wanted to write the words as neatly as possible.

Chapter Twenty

When Bernie came back – everyone had forgotten about Bernie – she dropped into Catherine's sick-room first of all. She was feeling old and separate this late afternoon, responsible for things that hadn't happened yet; that was the difference. Always before she'd been made to feel responsible for things that had already happened, or were happening now, but this time she felt she had been setting up skittles instead of only knocking them down. The fact that Sam had stormed off instead of displaying admiration when she leapt into the pool, only made her powers seem grander. Her untried weapon had missed its target but crashing sideways had exploded all the same in a vision of might. Sam so far above, so wrapped up in his own world: she had made him leave. It wasn't what she had wanted, but it was an achievement. Although it might be a finicky business while she refined her actions, Bernadette was confident now that she could make Sam love Catherine. She looked at her little sister's upturned face, head rolled sideways on the pillow, and felt a surge of passion. 'Julab's been wounded in the garden,' said Catherine, gazing back.

'How come?' asked Bernie, not realising immediately that this was an important story, not being privy to the others' reactions, having only Catherine's calmness to go by.

'He was hit with a pot.'

'Somebody *hit* him? Who?'

Catherine shrugged as best she could while lying down. 'He's still conscious,' she said. 'Lori's in the kitchen.' As Bernie was walking to the door, Catherine asked, staring up at the wood-panelled walls, 'Did you go on the death slide?'

'Yes. I jumped off into the river.'

Catherine nodded and closed her eyes.

'It's funny that it's there now,' Bernie said. 'I don't think I like it, really, you know.'

'Why not?' murmured Catherine.

'It's our place, isn't it. And we wouldn't have put it there ourselves.'

'I'm ill, though, aren't I. It's your place now.' She sounded like a girl who was falling asleep. Bernie watched her for a moment or two and then she turned the door handle as quietly as she could; tiptoed down the hall until she thought she must be out of earshot, and flitted down the steps to the kitchen door, threw it wide.

'Hello!' Bernie called to Lori at the table. She was beside her already, opening a cupboard and pulling a glass beaker out; she was darting to the sink, turning the tap, coming back.

Lori was startled by the abrupt apparition, the slight person who moved and changed though her clothes and name stayed the same; it was strange after an hour spent with people who did not move, although their faces and their paper outfits changed. Bernadette appeared to her as a succession of fluttering magazine pages; it was at first the only explanation.

'I just had the funniest thought,' said Lori, now that Bernadette was sitting down on a tall-backed chair pulled in beside her. 'When the models are posing, they aren't really still at all,' she said. 'They're in between two things – they have to move into it, and then they have to move out of it again.'

Bernie nodded. She always liked the way that Lori talked to her, as if she were an older girl and not a child. 'I'll tell you something even funnier,' she answered. 'Their hearts are beating inside them. Look there, in the photo, even when they're still.' Bernie was only pointing, but then she took the magazine and closed it, held it vertically against her chest, tight closed in both hands. She was looking down at the fat band of thin, thin, page-tops: all those words and faces, worlds, vanished on end into tiny slivers that together made something else, a strip of muscle, here in her hands. 'Ba-boom,' she whispered. 'Ba-boom. They are in there.' She smiled at Lori. 'Where's Julab?'

Lori's face fell. 'Don't you know? Shit, of course. You were with Sam.'

Bernie shook her head. 'I do know,' she said. 'He got hit with the pot. Catherine said. But he's conscious, isn't he?'

Lori was nodding back. 'They've taken him to the vet. Sam's not with you?'

Bernie shrugged. 'He left a while ago. I don't know where he went. Humberto's looking for him. I wouldn't worry about Sam, if I were you,' she said. And Bernadette was so calm that Lori thought perhaps she'd been mistaken, carried away by the reactions of the others, Ellie's horror and Rosa's outrage. Perhaps these things just happened to dogs.

Chapter Twenty-one

Sam in Callander entered the outdoor clothing store and tried on sunglasses. The tags hung down in front of his nose. He would have rather had his old pair. He would have rather it were still this morning, when he was wearing his old pair.

So he didn't smile when he handed his money over to the man at the till.

But he wasn't going to get upset about it either. He pulled the tag off – the plastic dug a white line briefly into his forefinger – and he slipped the sunglasses on, and it was pleasing, in spite of everything, the way that their arms unfolded towards him, one after the other, functioning perfectly in his hands, waiting only to embrace his almost entirely certain face.

He set off down the pavement and the world was comfortable once more: just as bright, just as colourful, but it no longer hurt him to look at it. He passed the market square and the turning to the crags, the shops along the main street, the butcher and the baker that had always stood, and those begun by Italians after the war thirty years back or more: the ice-cream parlour, the boutique, Ferrinis, where mother sometimes went, the sweet shop and the chippie; the newer ones, for tourists, where kilts sewn in cheap Far

Eastern factories blew pleating in the breeze, hung from awnings.

Birdsong caught his ear nearby and stopped him, there on the corner before the Dreadnought Hotel. Not song in the normal nature of the thing, but a strange sound more leisured and spoken than song, lacking its danger, lacking the possibility of falling. This was the noise that the caged birds made inside the pet shop. Sam stepped up onto the threshold, and the flat Victorian emblematic swag across the tiles lay down beneath his feet, his rugged sandals, bare ankles, tanned, as he shifted and felt the darkness of the room, the purring of the fish tanks within.

He took a further step inside, and looked around, at the boxes of aeration and grazing, the sated gerbils dozing. It smelled of dried vegetables and intentional droppings; the warm, agreed-to odour of stramineous lives, where shit smells clean and mice are nice.

Bubbles rose and fish went gliding by, and by again, in spacious aquaria stocked with pondweed and glittering stones, looking out at Sam, looking in at them. He tapped the glass, and they darted away. This pleased him, because it was what he had expected. He stood up again and looked around, at everything in this spacious place where animals were ordered and small, arranged to fit inside the walls. The parakeets green and gold, exotically close and still; the chattering of fearlessly contented bills, the softness of it. He was already stepping outside when the proprietress walked in through coloured streamers across a doorway at the back and asked if she could help him. No, thank you, he said, and smiled, and stepped outside, into the sunshine again.

The main street ran in a straight line towards the mountain. The mountain loomed up tall beyond the vanishing tarmac, the shop-fronts, the sloping slates like lips or guttering for this channel that carried the cars east and west. Sam looked down it, and was disturbed, disturbed by the mountain that towered above, and glad that nobody seemed to have noticed it. All the buildings ignored it and talked among themselves, and the people criss-crossing from pavement to pavement seemed to lace the periscope of the street, its access to inhuman heights, more tightly shut. Nipping through sparse traffic to the Scotch Oven, to purchase loaves of white bread with pink icing, pulling wefts across the warps and weaving themselves in, weaving him too, weaving it all flat. He might have despised these people if it weren't for their casual scorning of the mountain, and the way that, today, this calmed him.

Chapter Twenty-two

The mountain was magnificent. It shrugged off the tree-line with its first easy shoulder, rose steep and green and dun with grass and heather lifted up against the sky. Grey striated rock like folded wings clasped the rounded fastness of its heights.

The forms of the Highlands all stand so singular and proud, and it is easy to imagine them as something forceful, self-created, statements in the sky that spoke themselves there. It is harder to imagine the truth, that they are accidental leftovers from a time of greater heights than ever their hilltops, an old plain above them gouged down by glaciers. That they were nothing but a part of some greater whole, part of the Earth, underground. Bore no names, were not Ben Ledi, nor Vorlich, nor Ben A'an, bore no identity at all but were just part of that undifferentiated nothing beneath your feet: the flat ground, the background, non-existent.

Like words, the mountains emerged only from the sounds that fell away all around them, could resonate only once this space of silence surrounded them. A language shaped by loss and not creation. A language in which it is the shape of loss, its speed and direction, urgent or loosely lackadaisical as it encounters points of resistance, that creates, carves the space in which singularities become apparent, take on the grammar of a landscape.

The narrative of a life is carved from memory's losses: must have spaces forgotten in its retinal riches before it can contain chained elements to make sense. The story that tells everything is not possible to tell. It stretches out above your head, in the past. It can only be imagined. Not in words but in the way that it felt, pressed in so perfectly against the contours that are left, until, if you are remembering and imagining well, they disappear again and you go with them.

The story that tells everything is also in the future, there beneath your feet. You can imagine the infinite arrangements of future landscapes beneath the surface that you walk on, there inside the flat ground, the background, the uncarved whole on top of which, for practical purposes, for want of an alternative, towns and cities must be built, and lives be lived.

Yet you cannot imagine it in words: futures imagined in words do not tell everything, but merely something, and are in that sense not so different from the present: which is, after all, a single outcome. Future imagined instead in the way that it would feel, to be part of the limitlessly, exponentially possible land into which the glacier cuts. To lose your skin and feel it, the great glacial force of accident and will, of history pushing time outwards with the weight of the past behind it. Then to peel away from that unbordered wholeness of untold time, to fall back into space and the all-pervading instant of the present, that glacier skin that washes up against things, and be done, or undone, one way or the other. These were the things that the mountain whispered.

The average interglacial period is six thousand years. The time between the past and the future is non-existent. But minds like to live as if it too were six thousand, as if time can lie stretched out and uniform, unchanging, like space. For Sam, the past was a sequence of still photographs that led him on to other still photographs in the future. If you flicked through them fast enough, they seemed to be moving, and each followed on from the other. The past was a row of stacked-up presents placed behind him. The future contained more presents, the only difference being that he couldn't see these yet. Although he could not see the future, he was quite sure that it would be made of the same stuff: of outcomes, slices of space, event and event and event, and would always make sense because he would always stand at the heart of it.

Sam treated time as if it were a space with him at its centre. Every letter in every sentence was turned sideways, and he was the thread that strung them together, these sentences that always, by their very structure, admitted to his existence; owed their own existence to his. He was the sense-making string that strung them, all in order, onwards, from left to right, through a world whose spaces readily translated into the letter of an instant and then, by juxta-position, a stream of coherent words that trailed behind him. He believed in himself instead of time.

Time for Sam, if he thought about it at all, was nothing more than a marker for arrangements and an order of events: the page numbers, and not the writing nor the reading of the book. It had no muscle of its own. He lived, like most people, in a world centred on himself and, seeing things always from his own point of view, therefore had to see them from the stance of the present moment, for this was where he was located. He was who he was, today, here and now; there was no going back. Nor any imagining different. He would not step back to a point in time where he could have understood things differently; he would not dream of leaping forward to a place that held the life he might have truly wanted. He was who he was, today, here and now. But of course the present moment is no time at all: the present moment is space.

The present moment now was happening to include the instance of Callander main street, in which Sam stood this afternoon. Here was history's slow-tampered template of domestic stone frontages with shop windows there enlarged; the painted signs, and cauliflowers in crates; a car door swung from the long row parked; the plumber's van. Trippers slim in city leggings and oversized shirts that draped their small breasts like hidden feasts or dead things, dotted shop and shop and shouted things, raw sound that time itself turned into part of sense. Into things that had been said, no matter who heard them. Men in tweed caps turned and girls with layered hair sprang from the pharmacy holding paper bags.

A picture doesn't need time in order to exist. Only words do. But even then they can manage to survive in this way: that words turn into part of the picture too, when you write them down. *Pharmacy*: a shape of green paint, pictured in the instant. Above it all, the mountain whispered.

Chapter Twenty-three

What a relief it had been, to walk into that pet shop, or rather, to have stood in it and now stepped out again. Once the pet shop had been accomplished – its regulated goodness – Sam felt a hell of a lot better. Everything in the pet shop contentedly making sense, animals happening inside thoughtfully catered boxes just as they were supposed to; and best of all he, he standing there amongst them. They had not blinked. The fishes did not dart away until the moment when he tapped the glass of their tank, which was done, in fact, not only to make them move, to prove the power of his touch, but to simply prove to himself that he was here. That the animals knew he was here. A splash that swallows a stone: they did know. That was what the darting fishes said: that clearly every creature in the pet shop was aware of his presence, and went on quite peaceably nonetheless. There is nothing wrong with Sam, rustled the straw in hutches, puttered the bubbles in the aquaria, ruffled the feathers on the perches. Sam is here and there is nothing wrong with him at all.

Once he had left the pet shop, it was a place where nothing went wrong. The pet shop was quite definitely a place in which he had not sinned, and it was joined up to the main street, which ran out towards the mountain, out to the river and the house, the garden and Julab. Julab was therefore in a world in which Sam did not sin.

With the comfort of its reminding behind him, and his sunglasses shielding his eyes, he pushed out of town along the main street that became main road, out along the avenue of trees that ran through the fields. After a while the fields gave way to woodland, the stately roadside beeches trimming the hem of a vast commercial Sitka forest, grown for props and pallets, which rose steeply on the right. He could hear the chainsaws within. The beech leaves down here were a beautiful, apple-fresh, cabbage-fresh, butterfly green. The road was twisting towards the pass where the house lay, and shadows fell thickly on the tarmac.

Somewhere soon ahead, his labrador waited. Sam was not sure how badly injured Julab might be.

He had hit him in order to get his Raybans back.

The Raybans were already chewed to fuck.

But he had had to get them back; they were his; that was the point. The point was that Julab was bad; Julab was wrong.

But it wasn't a punishment. He had to hit him, in order to get his Raybans back. Even though they were chewed to fuck. That was all.

Sam did not sin.

All of his actions were caused; the things he did were entirely the result of prior events, and therefore not his responsibility at all. He merely reacted with strength and clarity, in a logical way.

You couldn't say the same for Julab. Julab had no reason to chew Sam's Raybans.

Perhaps now he would have learned not to spoil things that didn't belong to him.

It was a shame. It was a shame that he had chewed Sam's Raybans, and made him hit him.

Sam would have preferred to have had his Raybans intact,

and not to have hurt his dog, which only proved how innocent he was. He hadn't enjoyed hitting Julab. He hadn't
derived any pleasure from it; it had merely been a logical
reaction. Whereas Julab had obviously been enjoying
chewing Sam's Raybans, had been wagging his tail, in fact,
when Sam found him.

It was clear, from this, which of them had been in the
wrong.

Sam stepped up onto the verge. The road had narrowed
and a slew of traffic heading north to the ferry terminal at
Oban dashed fast past him. He trod along the strip of sorrel
and plantains between black camber and stone dyke. Lorry
plastic flapped as it took the hill; *Warburton's*, said the next
one, silent letters and loud exhaust, and its white rear doors
were locked, over the rise it was gone in a fat floury thumb
pushed through the shadows, headed for the Western Isles;
and the cars that followed it had bicycles strapped to their
roofs, doing fifty although their spokes were still; and still
the shadows washed over them, and fell with a twig to the
tarmac in the silence afterwards. He stepped down onto
the road again and carried on.

Chapter Twenty-four

Among the uncoppiced hazels that grew lanky beyond the river, Humberto searched for Sam.

Bernie had said she'd seen him crossing the rocks below the falls. She hadn't asked why Humberto was looking for Sam, had just sat there high on her flat rock plaiting stalks together in her hands. She didn't even look up from this, but just said, He's gone across the river, and pointed, with a finger that didn't even bother uncurling itself fully from the rest, and soon went back to the peculiar handiwork in her lap.

And Humberto had been glad, not to have been asked why he searched for Sam, not to have been the one to explain this business with the dog to Bernadette, who didn't seem to like him any more. He had had the funny feeling, looking at her sitting there, that she would not have believed him even if he had told her. It was as if she had dismissed him entirely.

So he was glad to be away from her; he was glad to be going in pursuit of Sam, glad of the purpose with which he could leap from rock to rock, brush through the willows, tread the mossy tussocks that swept beneath the trees like the hats of so many Cossacks sunk into the soft ground, maybe that was partly why he trod so lightly, because it felt, standing on each one, that you were pressing down upon the tender head of something deeper. But it pleased him, too, to tread so lightly. Humberto liked the thought of being somewhere and leaving as if he'd never been. To be still, so still that the birds would land upon you and you could be one of them, or be a branch that could hold them, and feel their weight. To be trusted.

He had been travelling in this way for upwards of a year, at liberty abroad, whereas at home near Huesca he was known as what he had been and all his footprints held him. He liked being able to be the man of his own imagining, of Rosa's dreams; free to be himself as he might be.

Humberto searched for Sam among the hazel trees as if he were hunting for something he had lost: something stationary, and smaller. He checked behind trunks where a boy of Sam's stature could not possibly be hid, and even glanced upwards, into the slender branches above. He was enjoying the job of looking for Sam, but he had no real wish to find him. He was quite happy to be weaving thoroughly through the woods, happy to be mapping the land thus. Emerging onto the cycle track the other side, he glanced up the slope of the mountain. He saw no figure that could be Sam, yet this did not deter him. He would like to go looking for Sam upon the mountain. That was what he would like.

There was a stile further along the track, but Humberto decided to cross the fence just here. It would be easy enough for him to vault it, but he would not do that either. With strong and sinewy forearm, he pressed a palm against the fencepost, carefully picked his way over the wire, lowered himself gently on the other side. He liked to go where others didn't; he liked to leave no landing mark behind him.

He was making his way through the honey-scented whin. He was using the sheep paths that arced and bounded the hillside like the lines on your palm, that the sheep followed and wrote and forgot, those toughened ewes that stared as he passed or that trod sideways in salsa steps and carried on chewing. Disturbed enough to move but not to run.

He was slowly fading smaller, pausing at a higher fence before the heather, and almost indistinguishable from it now, from the dark ling furring like mink in swathes before the summit; he was faint on this coat that glowed with its deep pile even under cloud cover. The roughness of the heather caught and snagged what light there was, rubbed every nuance from a shadow, so that filtered grey dishwater light seemed pearly opalescent on the leaf tops against the trapped black grains thickly silting the scaly stems beneath.

Humberto was so distant from the bottom now that his movement to anyone below the mountain, looking up, would have appeared incredibly, terribly, slow. It was going to take him another hour to reach the peak. He was quite certain now that Sam would not be up there, but it had occurred to him that perhaps, from that vantage point, he would be able to see Rosa's brother somewhere upon the land laid out on all sides below. This now was his purpose and, in fact, it was not a bad one. Moving further from his object, he would have a better view of it. He would not be able to achieve his objective, but he would know a lot more about it, rather than casting around on lower levels, trying different paths, with one slim hope of success. From up here, he would be able to fully comprehend the distance between himself and Sam, and properly locate him.

Chapter Twenty-five

Rosa was close to tears. It was her anger, more than anything, that kept her from crying. Why, was the question she kept asking, silently, over and over again. She did not care who, she did not care when, or how the who got in to the where. She only wanted to know why. She kept running the question through her own mind, her own causal patterns of action and response, but found nothing matching. She could not be sure if it reassured or disturbed her, this unbridged difference. She could not imagine what wrong-headed reason there might possibly have been, and so she kept coming back to the thought that there was no reason at all, and this was what made her so angry. She was upset because Julab had been hurt; she was angry because she could see no reason why. It was an event that had sprung from nowhere: storyless, an ending. The people who did it must be held to account, and yet there was no accounting for it.

The town slid by Natasha's battered chocolate brown Mercedes estate car, speeding and slowed at zebra crossings along the main street. Rosa's elbow leaned against the window. Behind her the car boot was quiet and empty except for a soiled old curtain. The car seemed to rattle, Rosa thought; the door locks and flip-down hooks seemed looser in their joints. 'Are you all right, darling?' her mother asked. Rosa nodded, feeling funny to be asked that in the silent presence of Aunt Tash in the driver's seat, right there, just in front.

Ellie twisted in her seat to gaze back at her. 'You should be wearing your seat belt,' she said. And for once Rosa complied. Her mother smiled gently at her, and turned around again to face through the sun-smeared windscreen.

The doorway of the pet shop was dark and its windows were covered with a yellow plastic film to diffuse the sunlight. Rosa hardly saw it as they passed.

By the time Sam stepped out onto the street, his family were cresting the corner, passing the brief modern crescents at the town's edge in his aunt's old car, into the fields and woods that he would walk past. They were home in five minutes.

Rosa raged in the kitchen. She was shocked at the lassitude she found at the table there; Lori and Bernie actually laughing lazily at something or other when she came in. The way they looked up at her made her feel that in going to the vet's with poor Julab she had witnessed something that clearly they could neither imagine nor understand. This annoyed and thrilled her. She was, in fact, perversely pleased by the presence of the glossy magazine on the Formica, for it threw the raw authenticity of her own perspective into sharp relief. She was shrapnel falling on falsity. The deep-down crudeness of blood, torn flesh, sang more dramatically against the superficial shining of paid faces perfect in make-up; mortality grander when set against the magnification of an eyelash.

Reading is always an act of imaginative acquisition. To read a fashion magazine is to vicariously own this season's handbag; beauty; and this, in Rosa's world, was understanding nothing, but perhaps that was because she was already beautiful and no armful of handbags could have made her more so. Owning beauty was not a thing she needed to imagine.

The new thing that Rosa understood was ugliness. The discord of it, wreaked on Julab. The sheer physical mess. She had lived her entire life in an entirely beautiful world, grown up in a house with finely tuned lawns and box parterres, attended a boarding school with leafy avenues and carefully planted harmonious rustic vistas, known only the nicest of rooms and wardrobes. The only material ugliness she had ever encountered, until now, was her father in the hospital bed, his frail discoloured skin inside the ruthless pyjama top. But even this she had managed to understand as something saintly, because he had appeared so Christ-like, in his suffering, in the thinness of his wrists, the boniness of his head. And Christ was something beautiful, a thing that came in gold and painted wood, decked with precious stones, candle-lit. In her eyes, her father's death had been a noble and saintly exercise to which he had willingly submitted. Because if he had not submitted to it, then it could not possibly have happened, for he was a man of iron will. She never said, 'My father's dead,' but only, 'My father died,' which form of speech correctly represented her conviction that death was an action he had performed, or in which he had actively participated.

Dogs were different. Dogs often had things done to them to which they did not willingly submit: being put on leads, for instance, or having their tails docked. The thing that had been done to Julab had very clearly been done without his permission. Even Rosa could see no chink of nobility in this particular suffering. It was not like anything beautiful that she could think of, not at all. It was a physical, ugly mess. Rosa was brimming with its news, and struggling for a way to tell it, even as the space between it and the perfect arrangements of a periodical brought it into dazzling focus. Made the ugliness more aesthetically pleasing, in itself.

She strode over to the table, pulled the magazine up and threw it in the bin. 'How can anyone care about this,' she cried, as the swing lid closed. 'How can you be reading *magazines?*'

'We weren't reading it,' said Bernie. 'We were just looking at it.'

'But it's just pointless.' Rosa's brown curls were trembling at her collarbones. 'It's a stupid, pointless thing.'

Lori seemed to be remembering something. She was looking at Rosa, and realising that she, too, ought to be feeling something like this. She was aware that she had allowed herself to be distracted first by the magazine and then by Bernie's calmness. She got to her feet, put a hand on Rosa's shoulder. 'Are you okay?' she asked. The surface of her face was tender and crumpled like a muslin nightdress that might blow either way.

'No!' Rosa shouted. 'No, I'm not.' She was pulling away, she was standing with her back to them, arms forward, leaning with both hands against the worktop. Her head was slightly bowed. It was as if she was half-broken, overwhelmed, must hold onto something in case she fell but was too distraught to sit in a chair. Lori could not help but be impressed. She took a step once again towards her summertime friend.

'Did you see the vet do the operation?' asked Bernie.

There was a silence in which Rosa sniffed.

'Don't ask her things like that,' said Lori. 'She's upset.'

Rosa spun round unexpectedly, strong enough now to stand up by herself without a problem. 'Why?' she demanded. 'Why would anybody do that to Julab?'

Bernie looked at her cousin's hands, stabbing the air. 'I don't know,' she said.

Rosa put her hands to her head, raked her fingers into

her hair and left them planted there; her elbows like horns or wings hooked between scalp and shoulders. She stood still, not saying anything else.

'Maybe it was an accident,' Bernie suggested.

'It can't have been,' Rosa told her swiftly, taking her hands away and pulling out a chair.

'No,' agreed Lori. 'It can't have just fallen on him, because it was sitting on the ground.'

Rosa was nodding.

'Somebody must have picked it up and thrown it,' said Lori. Rosa nodded again. She was sitting at the table with them now, and Lori for one felt better now that they had found the correct tone. Of course she should not have been reading the magazine, and subsequently of course she'd been wrong to let Bernie's childish ignorance sway her own right feeling; no wonder Rosa had been angry with them. This was the right thing: to sit and ponder how it had happened. It was pleasing.

They imagined all kinds of scenarios: not reasons, for there could be none, but rather descriptions of the manner of the senselessness. A horror, being hollow, beyond comprehension, can only ever be conveyed in its details. This surface can be established, agreed upon, remembered, so that the episode acquires a sort of brilliant clarity compared to the events in the time around it. The girls were wrapping up the attack in the circumstances that surrounded it, and this basket of interwoven predicates – the hour, the visual scene – would be assiduously detailed until it was perfectly, perfectly real; a basket embroidered with blood-red flowers on the plain hazy lawn of another afternoon, picked out in the light of their attention. The more clearly it appeared, the more intricate its exterior construction, the less it distressed them to know that it was empty inside. If it could just be made to behave as if it were part of their world, then at least they would be able to talk about it. At least they would all be able to look and see something there.

'It was half past three when Mum got back,' said Rosa. 'The blood was dry.' She felt very brave; as if the blood were hers. She felt good to be talking about it so calmly. The calmness felt like a sort of sacrifice.

'Humberto had already found him,' said Lori. 'But only just, hadn't he?' She was glancing at Rosa, who nodded. 'I remember,' said Lori, 'his trousers were torn.'

'I was up the river,' said Bernie, wishing to add something. Rosa looked at Bernie gratefully, and nodded again. She was trying not to think about what Lori had just said. 'Mum bought the pot from Royce's,' she announced, after a pause. 'She got it as a present for Aunt Tash.'

Bernie was unsure how to respond to this. She thought maybe her mother was being implicated in the crime. She sat tight and looked at the tabletop. It was true, she supposed: if Mummy didn't exist, then Aunt Ellie could not have bought the terracotta pot as a present for her, and if it wasn't here then it could never have been used as the weapon with which Julab was attacked. 'Maybe they would have used something else,' she said, after a bit.

'Maybe they would,' said Rosa. 'But they didn't.'

The truth of this was hard to refute. The only thing that mattered was what had actually happened. Rosa's even-handed acknowledgement of other past possibilities only lent her dismissal of them further credence.

Owing to the fact that the act could only be understood in terms of its circumstances, those circumstances were now as inevitable as the act itself. The chain of normal cause and effect in human behaviour that the act of horror transgressed must now be borne by the normally contingent incidences around it. It was not like a wedding, that could happen in all manner of ways, subsume difference – weather conditions, style of dress, presence or absence of hatted guests – and still be the same thing. It was an aberration, and existed only in the precise manner of its happening. If it had happened differently, then it would have been something else. There was no internal logic to sustain it. It was raw violence, a black hole, and a hole can only be seen in terms of the edges around it, that are not it, but describe it nonetheless.

'I didn't see him,' said Bernie.

'He was lying by the flowerbed,' said Lori.

'By the poppies,' specified Rosa. 'There were bits of it embedded in his nose. It was ripped right open. Here,' she said, running a finger down the side of her own nose to show. 'And in his eye.' The worse it was, thought Rosa, the less likely it could be that Humberto's torn trousers had anything to do with it.

'His eye?' echoed Bernie, genuinely aghast, and Lori fiddled with her fingernails, ashamed that she had not told Bernie this; that she had merely sat there chatting, assuming Bernie knew, hadn't she said, hadn't Bernie said, 'I know'? Otherwise of course Lori would have told her. So maybe that was why she'd been so calm, Bernie had, and Lori should have been more upset after all, because she'd known, she'd seen it, after all. It was being on her own that had swayed her; sitting with the magazine; babysitting Catherine and waiting; the solitude and duty, the pleasant pictures to which to pay attention, had softly absorbed all the force of her emotion. She wished now that she could have gone with her friend to the vet's instead and been properly upset. Instead of sitting here feeling obscurely guilty.

'I didn't want to upset her,' she said.

'Bernie's old enough to know,' said Rosa. 'They cut his eye open,' she said, 'the boys who did it. They must have struck him from within a five-foot range or less. It was mashed right into his head.'

There was an awkwardness to her speech; its terminology, rather than delivery. Neither Bernie nor Lori could put their finger on it, but it was the technicality, the verb 'to strike', the detached consideration of proximity, which seemed quite alien coming from a girl like Rosa, from someone so comfortable and sensual. She was not the type to gauge such things, and then, as if she had discomfited herself, had tried to make amends by counterbalancing that scientific verb with crude emotive talk of *mashing*.

She was just not used to this sort of thing. But what language was there, to speak properly of ugliness? Perhaps it was not possible for her to talk of it and still be herself. Rosa had done many ugly things in her time, but always they had been dedicated to maintaining the superficial beauty of her life, and always they had stayed invisible beneath it. The knots of ugliness inside her had only strengthened the perfect fabric of her seeming self, and this had never been ruptured.

'The terracotta,' she said.

'Who were the boys?' asked Bernie.

'They must have come from the town,' said Rosa, looking at the table. 'They could have been on bikes.'

'They could have been staying at the campsite,' said Lori.

'What campsite?'

'You know. In the woods. It's not far, if you've got a bike.'

'Humberto was hitch-hiking,' said Rosa.

'I wasn't talking about Humberto. What's he got to do with it?'

'Nothing. Yes, if they were staying at the campsite, because the boys from round here wouldn't do it, do you think, Lori? You'd know.'

'Some of them might. Richie Small, Ian Bird, that lot. There've been some sheep going missing.'

'Sheep?'

'Oh, no,' said Lori, almost to herself. 'That's different, of course. They use the sheep for rituals,' she explained.

'Rituals?'

'Witchcraft. Have you seen the pentagram on the bridge above the cycle path? Richie sprayed it. He's a witch. Well, he says he is. I've never seen him do anything. And actually, I think they probably just used a sheep that was dead anyway. A lamb that the foxes had got, or the crows. Because its eyes *were* pecked out.'

'Its eyes! Like Julab – Julab's eyes.'

'Yes, but they would have taken Julab away if it was that, wouldn't they? Or there would have been something else. The lamb, the farmer found it in one of the caves and they'd had a fire lit around it, with pentagrams drawn in blood on the walls.'

'Oh my God.'

'They aren't real witches, Rosa.'

'Imagine what they might have done to Julab if Humberto hadn't come back in time.'

'But the blood was already dry. They must have left him ages before. At least half an hour, I would think.'

'How do you know how long it takes for blood to dry?'

'I don't. I'm just guessing.'

'But why would they have done that to Julab if they weren't planning on taking him away?'

'That's it. That's what I'm saying. I don't think it was them at all.'

'What's a pentagram?'

'It's a star, Bernie,' said Lori. 'I don't think they actually kill animals at all. I think they just say they do.'

'Well, Julab wasn't killed, was he?' said Rosa, flushed. 'So it still could have been them. And you said that lots of sheep have been disappearing. Not just one lamb.'

'Yes, but then it's easy, isn't it, when sheep disappear like they've always done, to say it was them because of that one.'

'You must have thought it was possible, Lori, or you wouldn't have mentioned it.'

'I was just thinking out loud. I was just thinking of possibilities.'

'It's such a shame Catherine didn't see them.'

'Maybe we should ask her again.'

'No, no. She's not well. We shouldn't upset her. I don't think we should tell her about the animal sacrifices either. She's too young. It might give her nightmares.'

'You can't sacrifice it if it's already dead,' said Bernie.

'Julab wasn't dead. He wasn't hurt at all before they attacked him.'

'But the lamb. If the lamb was already dead, then they didn't sacrifice it, did they?'

'That's what nobody knows, Bernie.' Since when, wondered Rosa, did children pay so much attention to detail? She kept going back, she kept remembering, a thing she might have seen or might not have done but kept seeing now, now that Lori had voiced it, a rip in that sturdy stone-coloured cloth, Humberto's torn leg. Did anyone else see but Lori? she worried silently, staring at the kettle.

'Did you touch the blood?' Bernie was asking her. 'To know if it was wet?'

And now it occurred to Rosa that in many ways it would be better if the blood had not been wet, if it *had* already dried by the time Humberto had found Julab – because that way it really couldn't have been him, could it? 'Actually,' she said, 'I think Lori's right. I think the blood was dry. Yes, you could see,' she said. 'You could see that it was dried.'

'Though Humberto did have to tie a bandage on him,' Lori frowned. 'I think he'd already bandaged him when you got there, Rosa.'

112

'Oh, but you could see. Around the edges, the dried blood, and there's a lot of blood in the head. Head wounds always bleed badly. Some of it was still bleeding, but most of it was dried. Most of it had stopped bleeding earlier.' Rosa was in charge of the facts. It didn't matter that she lacked Lori's status as an earlier eyewitness, her familiarity with the beginnings of the situation. After all, Rosa had gone with Julab in the car, which the others had not. Having accompanied him on his journey, having been closer to him then, when *he could have died*, she must surely have been closer to the truth. And of course the dog belonged to her family; having jurisdiction over him, surely she had jurisdiction over the story of what had happened to him? So the other two were silent, acquiescent.

'Maybe we can find their bike tracks,' Bernie suggested.

'That's a good idea,' said Rosa. 'Do you want to go and look?' Bernie, nodding, slipped out.

'Are you okay?' asked Lori again, now that they were alone. Rosa nodded. She was feeling a little happier now that Lori had asked her that; a little more able to think, and even to wonder how Julab was. She imagined him lying numb at the surgery. Her eyes moistened. She nodded again. She wanted to see Humberto, she wanted him to know. That she had forgiven him, if it was him, which of course it wasn't, was it; the more she thought about those boys, and the lamb in the cave.

Humberto would never do that, she thought, silently.

'Poor Julab,' she said. She was overwhelmed with feeling. She began to cry.

Chapter Twenty-six

Firm crunching footsteps sounded in the gravel. Something flickered in the far right of Ellie's field of vision, man-height. A dash of palest blue, which was not the colour of leaves nor cars, which were red and certain navy when they flashed past. That pale iced blue was the colour of the plastic sacks of animal feed on the estate Ellie knew as a child: this was what slipped somewhere through the back of her mind as she stood by the porch with Natasha, gazing down the garden to the river fence. A feeling of feeding the animals in winter, helping out, being useful and good. The happy slowness of this feeling, drifting towards her, even as she realised it was Sam. She was turning to face him gladly, and not sure why, because the news that she must give him was so bad. 'Sam,' she said, and Natasha turned as well now, breaking off mid-sentence, and moved aside and craned her neck so that she too might watch him approaching.

Sam raised a hand to greet them, half-ironical. 'Mother, aunt,' he said. He was right beside them now, he was walking past. Surely Ellie wouldn't let him walk past? thought Natasha, panicking. She mustn't!

'Sam!' Natasha cried – she just couldn't help it; but of course she should not have done this, because it struck a

114

dreadful note of melodrama, and just as Ellie was commanding his attention anyway, in her own way.

'Sam,' Ellie was saying, and he had turned round now, there by the corner window of the disused dining room. He was facing them, and it would be better if he weren't wearing those sunglasses, thought Natasha, she would have liked to see his eyes as he received the news. 'Something's happened to Julab,' Ellie was saying.

This was it, thought Natasha. It was happening.

'What sort of thing?' Sam was asking. If only he knew, thought Natasha, with a stab of sympathy; but of course he soon will. She watched him wide-eyed; Ruaridh's boy. She was here, she was looking after Ruaridh's boy. She was enormously pleased and relieved by how much sympathy this whole thing was making her feel for Ruaridh's boy. The more closely she could see his face as he received the news, the more she could sympathise with him.

'He's all right,' Ellie told him, reassuring him first. 'He's going to be fine, Sam. He's at the vet's overnight. He had to have an operation.'

'An operation? Why? What happened?'

He was such a brave lad, thought Natasha, because everyone knew how attached he was to that dog. He was frowning in consternation, but he was not losing his cool. He was gathering the facts in first. It was admirable.

'He must have been attacked,' said his mother. 'Somebody threw a plant pot at him.' Her face was very gentle and calm. 'Well, more a small urn, really.' A wisp of lank brown hair had come loose from her ponytail and slowly nodded as she spoke, backing up the news, seconding her every word.

'What!'

That was it. It had hit him now. He was shifting suddenly off the leg on which his weight had been leaning. He was planting his legs wide, and leaning on the opposite leg.

'What?' asked his mouth, and the word left his lips ajar. His palms were open by his sides. And now his arms were rising, it was like the ending of a dance, his hands were grasping his head, cupping the back of his skull, behind his ears. His head was tipping in his hands like it wanted to be cradled. 'Who did it?' he asked.

Sam did not ask why, because he knew the answer to that already. Who: because he wanted to know, he wanted to hear it, he wanted to know it wasn't him.

'We don't know,' came the reply, from his mother. 'We don't know who did it. I don't suppose there is much point guessing. He's had to have his eye out, Sam,' she said.

The pine trees were very thin and black against the sky. Julab's eye: blinking, still puppyish, when he licked your hand or leg or face, remembered Sam. Or keen beneath the table, down there by your knee, illegally, back when Sam had been used to slip him a strip of lamb fat from his dinner plate, giving none to Fergal – a long time ago, before Sam had banned himself from such childish acts. Julab's eye that always searched first for Sam. That had always started gladly at him with happy recognition, until this afternoon. Julab's eye, this afternoon, looking completely different. Things changed, didn't they, and you changed with them and found that you were just the same as anything you'd feared you might become, and maybe you'd only been afraid because you'd known it would happen all along. The full completing of it. Sam refused to remember any more, but stared instead, at the things that were outside him.

The pine trees were very thin and black against the sky. They were all Sam could see now: their organised branches, the bareness of them, spareness of them, whose needles knitted fine lines into a fur that only emboldened their bones. Not like the beeches, whose leaves erased their branches entirely, and then fell, and exposed them entirely.

Sam's eyes were clinging to the pines, to the needles. A million tiny actions not detracting from the ligneous thrust; and every cone nesting like a dark egg balanced magically against the wind. The clouds had blown under the sun and the scent of azalea blossom mixed with the pine sap, easy in the coolness. It looked cool over there. It would be nice to sit or stand among the pine trees, where the grey light was falling in, where nothing much grew upon the ground but just the branches above, the needles that never dropped a stitch without fixing it, all year round. It was the continuity and emptiness of the pine grove that he longed for. An escape from deciduous fall and rise. For the first time in his life, the only time, he wished he were not himself. He wished he were a pine tree, silent in space; one of them, over there. A low slab of orange nylon caught a bubble of wind, a bubble of watery sunlight, caught his eye to the left-hand side. He swallowed. 'Where's Humberto?' he asked.

'He went to look for you.'

Sam seemed irritated by this response. 'Julab,' he said, 'did he make it back to the house?'

'No. It happened in the garden. He was just lying where it happened. He was very brave.'

'How long.' He swallowed. 'How long was he lying there?'

'We don't know. Humberto found him.'

Sam snorted crossly.

'Don't blame yourself, Sam. You can't be with him constantly. I expect he came back here looking for food.'

'Yeah. No. He came back here with me. I was looking in on Catherine.'

'Oh.'

'And then I went over the river. I couldn't find him, so I just went on my own. You've no idea who did it?'

Ellie shook her head, and the loose strand of hair shook

too. 'Boys from the town, we assume,' she said to him. 'We've been to the police.'

'The police?'

She nodded. She didn't want to tell him that really there was no chance of finding the little buggers who had done this to his dog. She said, 'They're doing everything they can. It's a shame Catherine didn't see anything.'

'Catherine?'

'She was sleeping.'

Sam stared at her, then nodded. 'And the police,' he asked, 'they think they'll find the shits who did it?'

'Oh, I'm sure they will, Sam. There's forensic evidence now, isn't there? They can probably use that.'

Ellie was making this up. In fact, what the police officer had said was that without witnesses it would be impossible to know who to look for. If only dogs could speak, he'd said, with a rueful smile that had made Ellie rather like him, and wonder if maybe she couldn't go back and have another chat with him about it anyway. She'd noticed he didn't wear a wedding ring.

Sam was staring again at the trees. There was no chance really, there was no chance of not being him, no chance of being a pine tree over there. You did what you did and your actions decided you. He was not a man to waver: he would stand by his latest culmination, even as he felt the final good thing shrivel and fall away inside him. He would stand strong. This was who he was, after all, and hadn't he always known? He breathed in deeply through his nose. 'Well,' he said, 'they'll find all of our fingerprints, won't they, for a start.'

'Yes, I imagine they will.'

Oh dear, thought Ellie. Maybe she could persuade the officer to fingerprint the plant pot, in spite of what he'd said? If she asked him nicely; and it would help appease poor Sam. To feel that they were doing something.

'So it was Humberto who found him?' Sam was asking.

'Yes, that's right. Tash and I got here straight afterwards.'

'So Humberto was already there. Was he with anyone else? Before you got there.'

'No. Poor chap.'

'How long had he been there?'

'Oh, not long at all. He'd only just seen Julab when we arrived.'

'But there was nobody else there.'

'No.'

'And Catherine was sleeping.'

'Yes.'

'So nobody knows how long he'd been there.'

'Well, he *said* – I can't see why he'd lie, Sam.'

'Can't you. No. I hope you're right.' Sam was scuffing his foot in the gravel, and Ellie would have said something else to reassure him that of course, of course Humberto wasn't the type, but already Sam was asking about Julab's eye and wanting to know if they really couldn't save it.

'No,' Ellie told him, sadly, distracted. 'He's lucky to be alive.'

Sam's foot stopped in the gravel. 'Really,' he said, not even daring to make it a question.

'Yes. It was a very nasty attack. He'll be mighty glad to see you tomorrow, you know, Sam.' She reached out to tousle his hair, to draw him in to her shoulder, but he wouldn't be drawn, he tried to smile and pulled off an awkward grimace before loping off down the lawn towards the drained pond.

'Do you think he'll be all right?' asked Ellie, turning to her sister-in-law.

'He probably just wants to be on his own for a bit, doesn't he.' Natasha hitched her bra strap back up from where it had fallen down around her shoulder, inside her blouse. 'I'm amazed he's so calm,' she said. Although, in point of fact, she wasn't amazed at all. It was exactly like him: she just meant, it isn't normal. It isn't what you'd expect of someone else. 'Do you know,' she said, 'it didn't even occur to me to question Humberto.' But she said this very lightly, more in praise of Sam's thorough intelligence than out of any genuinely held suspicion of their visitor. It was a little curiosity, that was all, this thing that she said, a gentle specimen held in resin to look at. It wasn't going anywhere, was it, as she looped her arm through Ellie's and the pair of them walked towards the porch.

Catherine, standing by the window, stepped aside, to hide. She need not have worried: the women did not look up at all as they passed her. They were watching where their feet trod.

Chapter Twenty-seven

Huddled at the back of the old pond, Sam sat with his arms clasped around his knees. But his head was firm upon his shoulders: facing forward, his profile was resolute under the shiny dark flop of his hair. There were bulrushes to the side of where he sat, and black flag irises and gold, hilts brightly sheathed in sleeves. He knew the irises were there. He knew that they were beautiful but he did not look. He was staring ahead at the fence wire: the sheets of it, the chicken mesh rigged tight between tall posts whose bases could not be seen but were planted there nonetheless, down the slope. Each one sharpened to a point, driven down, into the earth, and that was the place it would stay.

Perhaps he would have felt happier if he'd lived long enough to understand that people and fences can be undone, shifted, built again. He had only seen the sort of undoing that did his father in, an unbuilding that was the end, and so it was all or nothing for Sam. He staked his heart in stone against the sky.

Through the wire swayed the distant tree tops, and he saw them only in the way that they appeared to him through that netting. Somewhere above and beyond them, the mountainside rose clear. If he were to have tilted his neck, raised his gaze over the fence wire towards it, then he could have seen the mountain.

Somewhere up there, Humberto had almost reached the plateau peak, on hands and knees now over the rock.

But Sam down here just looked at the fence wire: at the flatness of its picture, with the leaves of the hazel tops merely cast inside it, shifting inside that surface. He was looking straight ahead. He was seeing what was in front of him.

Julab's eye.

Sam did not cry.

Did not, in fact, feel anything at all.

He could have done, if he had chosen to turn aside, or look up; of course he could have done. But Sam was looking straight ahead, and did his bravery, his lack of remorse, make him any less human? For it wasn't that he hadn't the capacity for it. It was that he chose not to look that way, because life was all or nothing for Sam. His heart was staked in stone against the sky.

Beside him, there was his love for Julab, and Julab himself; things so good he could not look because he'd spoiled them. Above him loomed something bigger than he was, something to say how near or far he might be from the good: looking down, it could see him here; and he couldn't look back, because he didn't want to know it was there, because he knew what it would think if it was, if the mountain was there, if the mountain could think, which it couldn't, and it was not there, so long as he did not look back at it. He was looking at the fence wire and the picture of distant boughs in the mesh. The fence wire did not look back at him. That was why he liked it.

Looking at the fence wire, he didn't feel anything at all. There was a certain rigidity of thought, a kind of calmness, a flat and shallow trammel of visual facts.

He was not heartless. He merely thought he was immutable.

Onwards. He must always push onwards, because there was no way back.

The hazels acquiesced. They were just leaves, after all, shimmering in the wind. He could see them through the mesh. He could know they lay beyond it: there, but on the other side. He was glad of the fence wire.

The air was chill on his arms now that the sun had gone in. He would like a sweatshirt. It had been warm when he set out; it was cold now. And he was hungry, too.

Such reported dissatisfactions and desires re-inhabited his body, and comforted him. We're still here, purred his stomach and his skin. We are you. As blank as the fence wire, and always.

He turned himself over to them, thought: I'd like to go indoors for a bacon sandwich; pinpointing it. Looked around now. At the irises among the rushes, that were just pleasing shreds of sensual colour now, yolk-gold, or oil-black and purple sheened, cracked open and spilling in the leaves. One grand dragonfly, folding its razor wings. Nothing to do with goodness, now that his body was ruling him once more. And in the cooler air came smaller insects that showed up on the petals but vanished in flight, minutely crossed the air in degrees beneath his eyesight. Suddenly silhouetted their specks on something else, but you couldn't tell which one was which, couldn't track them.

Looking away, a square of turquoise silk caught his eye. A fancy Indian book covering: Rosa's notebook, hardback, embroidered. It was strange over there among the crumbs of sun-dried moss. He stared at it for a little while. It was strange that she had been here too this afternoon.

Again he remembered Julab's brown face looking up at him, contorted, growling, as if he hated Sam. Wanting to keep hold of the Raybans. Liking them better than him.

123

Eyes like a wild animal's. Not the cherished dog that Sam had thought he'd known. Like he hated Sam. Wanted the Raybans instead of Sam. A piece of plastic that belonged to Sam. Wanted that, and not Sam, not one bit.

Sam was cold.

He was hungry.

He wanted to go. He stood, and, on his way to the stone brim, he stooped, picked up the notebook. Rosa's innermost thoughts, cogitations, observations, wish lists, poetry. It could have been anything. He did not look inside to read it.

He carried it casually in his hand as he slowly climbed the lawn towards the house again. Green grass slid under his feet and his breathing echoed lightly in his ribs. Behind him, the river rumbled on, the mountain unseen. The book was closed in his fingers, not a part of where he was going, now, this instant. He was not tempted to look at all these things. He only paused once, and that was on the high lawn near Catherine's window. There were shards of terracotta by the flowerbed, right at his feet, but Sam did not look down at these. He only looked at the window. It stared back, the glass black, blankly. And already he was gone; carried on past the drawing room balustrade, tanned toes in sandals on herringbone bricks. Ketchup and margarine.

He tossed the notebook aside, into the grass. He saw where it landed, and sniffed, before taking the steps down to the kitchen door.

Catherine, who was lying on her side looking out, whose face had frozen when Sam looked in but failed to see her; now blinked.

Chapter Twenty-eight

Iain edged his nose around the door of George Farrants' office. 'Excuse me, hello.' Shuffled into the room, shuffling papers. A printed table showing pay and inflation: columns of numbers, screeds of them, far more than were necessary, and a hand-drawn chart tucked under it.

'You used our computer for this,' said George, slightly raising the top sheet of paper he'd been handed.

'Yes. I don't have one.'

'No. If you could afford one, there wouldn't be a problem, would there? Still,' he remarked, holding that paper with its green feint lines and perforated sides, 'I'm not convinced the office computer is content to be used for such ends.'

'It's a computer.'

'Yes! Yes, it is, Iain.' George said this as if Iain had just made some very perspicacious remark. He was fond of confusing people. 'But I do feel that you've *raped* me somehow,' he said, putting the printout down on his solid vast desk. 'I'm very proud of that computer, you know. It's like a *little* bit of me. And,' he announced, fixing Iain with his sternest eye, 'it's *new*.'

Iain nodded, looking back at George Farrants in his shirt-sleeves. It was always harder when you saw him in person; that was what he kept trying to explain to his wife. He never knew what to say. He was glad when George dropped his gaze. His heart skipped a beat when George picked up the sheet again, began to read it.

'Iain,' said George, without looking up. 'Why do these figures go back to 1746?'

'I thought it would be good to give some historical context. These are average figures from across the industry.' He shifted on his feet: that had sounded good, he thought; pleased.

'Where did you get them from? Have you had a private dick on Samuel Johnson's bank chits?'

'I was in London last month. We were staying with Ann's sister.'

George looked at him, waiting. He coughed politely. 'Ann's sister,' he enquired, 'she has a special interest in this? In the pay packets of dictionary compilers through the ages? Other than yourself, of course, as Ann's provider: some degree of sororial curiosity might be natural.'

'No, no! She doesn't have an interest. But I visited the British Library.' Iain said this as if it were self-evident, as if London were wholly synonymous with the British Library, all those sprawling suburbs and railway lines merely an extravagant life support system to keep the books breathing. As if to go to London actually meant: to go to the British Library.

And it was this, in the event, that made George smile and say: 'I'll see what I can do.'

And then sit wondering why he'd said that, once Iain had gone.

Still, he was happy as he drove home: not because he had had a particularly good day, but because he was a happy man. He liked sending Moira home early, he liked locking up as he left. He liked how well he knew his route: enjoyed slipping down the gears and up again in perfect time; coaxing the steering wheel, ready even before the corners came. He could have done it with his eyes closed, this road that carried him into the countryside, through the small towns, and finally wove under the overhanging beeches on the hill that swept him home.

He sat for a moment in his car, but he opened the door when he saw Natasha stepping out from the porch. She was standing on the gravel now, frowning at his hub caps and chewing her lip. Her eyes darted up to him as he walked towards her. 'Please come in, darling,' she said to him.

'Well, of course I'll come in,' said George. 'I live here.'

His wife didn't laugh. She cocked her head and looked down at his shoes.

What a relief, she was thinking, to see a solid pair of polished brogues. All day she had been looking at espadrilles and sandals. Humberto always wore hiking boots, but he was gone; he'd hardly been here at all. Just that awful moment when she and Ellie came home. She was so glad that George was here at last.

'Are you going to tell me what's wrong?' he asked, passing her as he stepped up into the porch.

Natasha was following him into the hall. She must clean out that porch; the floor was filthy in the corners with cobwebs. 'It's Sam's dog,' she said. 'He was attacked by some boys. He's had to have his eye out. I've left him at the vet's overnight.'

'Julab?'

'Yes.'

'Good God! How awful. Were the girls there?'

She shook her head.

'What happened?'

'We don't know. Humberto found him on the lawn this afternoon.'

'Here? Here in our garden?'

She nodded, water filling her eyes. 'Catherine was asleep, thank goodness. But right outside her window, George. Right outside her window.'

The door to the kitchen opened in the distance. The top of Bernie's brown head was bobbing up the steps, before she fully emerged at the far end of the hall. Gathered her elbows and started rushing towards them, George and Natasha with their faces turned towards her.

George stepped forward out of the wood-panelled darkness, protecting Natasha's tears. He stepped into the softer expanse of hall stretching out beneath the vast leaded skylight at the centre of the house, onto the sun-bleached rugs under great height and glass.

Bernie made her father's gin and tonic. She liked doing this. Alone in the drawing room at the drinks cabinet, with the French windows open onto the balustraded terrace outside. She was excited by the day's events and poured the gin into the crystal tumbler with aplomb. It seemed to her that she had set everything in motion when she leaped from the rope into the river: that was the moment when everything had changed. Julab had nearly been killed, everyone said, but now he was all right and they could all talk about him, including her.

Maybe it was better that Catherine was ill in bed. If she was up and about then Bernie would be with her, and be one of the girls, the little ones, the children still.

George took his drink from her quite sternly when she came back into the kitchen, and so she was bashful when she sat herself down, and stayed quiet while the others spoke. Please don't send me away, she was thinking.

'Maybe Sam would like a drink,' her father said. 'Nat? Ellie?'

'I'd like a drink,' said Rosa.

So Bernie was dispatched back to the drinks cabinet. But

not sent away entirely, and she smiled because she would still be allowed to go back to them: she'd have to, wouldn't she, to give them their drinks.

George stroked the head of his own dog: Kitch, with his liver-spotted pointer's nose, clean and right. Sniffing and nudged.

'Well,' he said, 'I imagine Julab will be a little subdued for a while. We shall have to look after him, but at least there'll be a lessening of the nocturnal latrations, eh.'

Nobody knew what this meant, but they liked it nonetheless, all of them, except Sam. They liked the low strength of George's voice, they liked being in a room with a man who knew words they didn't know, because maybe it meant he knew why this thing had happened when they didn't, maybe he knew how to catch the boys who did it when they didn't, or how to correctly forget about it when they didn't. And Sam did not dislike it either. He merely thought: it's Uncle George, and everything is normal. He even nodded and smiled, as if he understood what George had just said. And the others saw that George had made Sam smile, and relaxed a little more themselves, because they were taking their cues from him now. It would have been obscene for them to be more distressed than him when Julab belonged to him; when he loved Julab most.

Only Rosa seemed tense, holding her glass tight and smiling in a very determined way.

'Where's Humberto?' asked George.

'He's looking for Sam,' Rosa replied, too quickly, like her drinking. 'He went to find him.' She threw her head back as if she were bored. Looked at the dusty ceiling, the fine cracks up there: how clean it was, in a way, with nothing on it. How attractive she found it.

'But Sam's here,' Uncle George was saying, and so Rosa

had to come back down from the ceiling again and face them all.

'Before,' she said, putting her glass down.

And now she was uncomfortable speaking, now she would have liked to stop, now that they were all listening.

'I imagine he'll be back any moment,' said Ellie.

Rosa didn't look at her mother in case her gratitude swelled too fat and telling from her eyes, but nodded her head as sensibly as she could and concentrated on the project of pulling her thin blouse sleeve down over her bangles, and pushing the material in between each one.

George looked at Ellie, and thought, not for the first time, what an attractive woman she was, and felt pleased, not for the first time, that he harboured no lust for her; that her beauty in no way provoked him. It was one of the main reasons he liked her: perhaps the only reason. Before she had said or done anything, she made him feel virtuous.

But Humberto did not come back in any of the moments that followed. He did not come back as they moved through to the drawing room, George and Natasha, Ellie and Bernie, Rosa and Sam and Lori, settling on faded comfortable sofas whose springs had not quite broken. He did not come back as Sam almost straight away excused himself, and everyone excused him, to go walking on his own; I'll take Kitchener, he said, and everyone was moved by this; they watched him setting out across the lawn through the long open windows, with this other dog bounding at his heels, not his. He did not come back as Rosa slipped off up the narrow kitchen stairs to her bedroom in the old servants' quarters, now used for guests, and sat on the candlewick bedspread, thinking, and pushing the thin bangles up and down her wrist.

*   *   *

After a while she sighed, and wandered down the corridor, through the heavy door to the other landing, at the top of the grander stairs.

She pushed open the door to the billiard room, and it was very hot, very stuffy in here, close under the sloping ceiling with its small, high-hatted dormer windows fastened shut. She opened one, and then another. She walked over to the table, let her slender fingers drop and rolled a carnation-pink ball across the cue-scuffed baize. It hit the green, which knocked gently up against the blue. And now they were still again: slightly differently arranged, but no different. She was irritated by these billiard balls, and left.

'Catherine,' she whispered, letting go of a different door handle. 'Are you awake?'

The prone figure on the daybed shifted a little, moved its head. Rosa was moving towards her. She was crouching down on the floor. She was about to ask a question.

'How are you feeling?' she said, but that wasn't the one, and Catherine knew it, because it was too small for the long inhalation that had preceded it.

'I'm fine,' she answered flatly.

'Poor thing,' murmured Rosa.

A shallow silence fell, no deeper than the gaps between the pile on a candlewick bedspread.

'You didn't see anything?'

'I already said.'

'Were you sleeping?'

'Yes.' Catherine rolled over, away from Rosa. 'I've slept.'

'Do you want me to read you a story?'

'No.' Catherine didn't look round.

'Am I still pretty?'

'Yes.'

Rosa stood in the room a little longer. She walked over to the window in the distant corner. Someone had come

131

in and lifted these blinds too: usually they were closed. She looked out across the end of the gravel driveway, to the stand of pine trees, the ridge of Humberto's tent. He couldn't have fled. He wouldn't have gone, and left his tent.

She removed herself from Catherine's sick-room without saying anything else.

Still he had not returned as they sat down for supper in the kitchen.

'I'm not sure I like eating in here,' George said. 'It reminds me too much of being punished when I was little.' He made this seem very amusing. And then he looked enquiringly at his wife. 'Why don't we move the dining-room table through to the library?' he asked her.

'Yes,' she said, 'we could do that. I'll do it tomorrow. I'll get the young men to help me.'

'If the Spic ever comes back,' said Sam. He said it in such an affable tone that it was hard to think he was being rude. 'May I have the mustard, please, Bernie?'

In any case, only Ellie was in a position to reprove him, and she was gazing feyly up at the high windows. 'You know,' she said, 'I really don't think they *are* monkish, Natasha.'

'What? The windows?' asked George. 'No, more like a prison, I used to think.'

Ellie looked extremely relieved. 'Yes,' she sighed, 'that's it. It's like a nice cool dungeon.'

Because she could quite imagine being Mary Queen of Scots or some such, imprisoned in a room like this but perfectly comfortable, not unpleasantly secluded, that was what she'd meant about the room, earlier. A private prisoner could still have seat cushions and nice food, a wardrobe. It was vastly preferable to being a monk. Those poor souls, who wore the same clothes, day in, day out: when part of the joy of living, Ellie felt, was rising and looking from the window to see what the day was like, and gauging the mood in which one found oneself, and picking out an outfit accordingly: arranging oneself appropriately for the day, and then noticing, at various junctures, how well one had succeeded in this quest: this was one of the surest sources of her happiness. It was probably the only ability of hers in which she had complete confidence. She often tried on three or four combinations before breakfast, but it was not due to indecisiveness so much as a desire for perfection, which she knew very well she could achieve, and she would never come down until she was entirely satisfied with her choice. Likewise, when she changed in the afternoon, or again at eight, it wasn't because she felt she'd been incorrectly dressed before: you could be certain that it was because circumstances had changed, and the selection needed to be altered in order for harmony to continue to reign. The pastel dress had been swapped for twill trousers and a lawn cotton Liberty shirt on her return from the vet's, but not the cornflower one, because cornflowers grew with poppies, and that would remind everyone of the flowerbed and poor Julab. Also, something more sensible, more masculine, was required – hence the trousers – so she had picked out the William Morris art nouveau leaves, which was the sort of print Ruaridh might have worn on a tie, it swung both ways, she felt. When George's car had rolled into the drive, she had nipped into her room and changed again, of course: now that she and Natasha could relax – ought to, in fact – the trousers were laid over the chair back, her loafer-clad feet slipped swiftly one by one into a slub linen pencil skirt, the Liberty shirt switched for rust-coloured silk, and tucked in.

It was one of the reasons she spoke rather little: because she felt that, silently, she could do the right thing, if she just sat still.

*   *   *

Ellie was quite happy now, having finished her meal, leaning back and smoothing her palms over the perfectly fitting cream linen, letting them rest there, on her thighs.

Natasha was staring at her sister-in-law. She did not think her kitchen was like a dungeon, nor did she conceive of this as a possible compliment. She coveted that russet silk shirt. She knew the colour suited her. And she hadn't had time to make junket, what with the expedition to the vet's, everything that had happened.

'Ellie gave me an angora jumper,' she said, addressing the remark to her husband but gazing at Ellie's neck. The fine point of the shirt collar looked very delicate. It would quickly fray, she told herself.

'I'm sorry I'm not wearing it,' she added, looking up at Ellie's face now, and now away to her husband's plate. 'I haven't had time to get changed.'

'Oh, I don't mind! I expect it's more of an autumn thing, weather-wise. Or spring, maybe? The colour of it. It would be a lovely thing to wear at Easter, I think.'

'Where *is* Humberto?' asked George, frowning at the womanish turn of exchange. He could not tolerate any sort of conversation that touched on feminine pulchrification; even overly careful consideration of the seasonal shading of a sweater upset him.

He liked women to look nice; he didn't want to know how they did it. Not because of a lack of interest, nor because it would spoil it somehow, if you knew, how they did it, though perhaps that was true too, but because there was something deeply dangerous about allowing oneself to be implicated in such preoccupations. He always had the feeling that he might get his shirt tail caught in the machinery and end up naked.

It was one of the things he believed he liked best about his wife, that she had always got dressed in the bathroom, every morning they'd been married. He appreciated the completeness of her apparition through the heavy door that swept open across the carpet, in her seaweed-coloured things and skirts, her twisted hair in combs, her neatly darkened eyes. Some of her clothes had been getting a little stranger lately, but still. He was glad he did not have to look at her underthings.

George's chest swelled sternly as he gazed at the topmost button on his wife's blouse and considered the gladness, the definite gladness, with which he was always saved from her underthings. The suspenders on the washing line, the straps, the contraptions. With their hooks and tendrils, those sweet peas, creepers, whispering. It was the strapping – the splintering – the many things, harnessed to others – breasts to shoulders, legs to waist, cunt to hips – by scraps. It was the gaps between, and the dependency of one part on another, the interwebbing of all the parts speaking separately, satin and nylon subjunctive clauses talking all at once. The half-things, whispering, reaching. They horrified him.

Natasha's bra hooks were thorns in the heart of his desire. Sometimes he would feel them through the fabric that covered her back as he embraced her, and they pricked his skin like rose barbs. Made his hand recoil, and his blood seem to gush forth although of course they never really broke nor even bruised his skin. And if it was evening, and the girls were in bed, then Natasha, understanding his flinch, would save him, every time. She would go to their bathroom and George would follow her but he would stay on this side of the door. His fingers would curl in and out from his palms as, beyond the door, moving cloth made soft shifting sounds. And then he would hear her come towards him, the other side, and he would turn quickly and be sitting on the bed by the time that she emerged. He would smile up at her with sad, grateful eyes: at Natasha, bra-less and bare-legged, un-knickered in her dress. He would know he was relieved. He would also feel a faint despair, every time, even as he took her to him, safely.

He put a little butter on his salad potatoes. 'Has nobody seen him?' he asked.

The mood around the table was shifting, Rosa could feel it, but she was powerless to stop it. She could not hold it back. Suspicions were drifting in from the doorway, and thickened the longer it stayed empty, the longer that the shape of Humberto's shoulders failed to come and fill it and push them out.

Expectations around the table seemed to darken, and ripen, doubts that had been green and clung firm to the trees turning into soft beliefs that would drop into a palm easily enough if only someone came to loosen them from the branch. They didn't want to fall by themselves; it was a long way down.

'The French are careless rather than vindictive,' said Sam setting his fork neatly against his knife in the centre of his plate. 'Aren't they. Towards animals, I mean.'

'Oh, they're always neglecting their dogs!' Ellie seconded. 'Except in Paris,' she added, and nodded at her son. She quite agreed with him so far. 'Terrible pavements,' she said. 'The turds, I mean.' Took a sip of wine from her glass; George kept such a good cellar.

'But that's really civic neglect, letting your dog crap on the pavement,' said Natasha. 'It's not really unkind to the animals at all.'

'Oh yes, in Paris, the pooches rule the roost. That's what I meant. It's everywhere else. In St-Jean-de-Luz, for instance, we were very shocked by the number of stray dogs. There was an enormous thing that looked like it might have been part Alsatian, and it was actually quite frightening.'

'What did it do?'

'Well, it didn't do anything, Bernie, but it kept following me around. It looked like a *wolf.* And there were lots of them, all round the restaurant bins, scrawny awful things.' Ellie shuddered and popped a radish in her mouth, bit the main part off it, and laid the scalp and stalk down beside her untouched potatoes, munching. 'But no, no,' she added, when she had finished her mouthful, 'you're quite right, Sam, they aren't cruel. They don't torment them, they just let them starve.'

'And the Italians?' wondered Sam.

'Very indulgent people,' said George.

'I'd rather be a German pet,' said Natasha. 'They would take me for walks, and be fair and strict, and give me just the right amount of feed, and I wouldn't get fat on chocolate drops.' She said this in a voice that suggested she was addressing a child of Catherine's age, but of course Catherine was in the sick-room, tucked up in bed.

'Oh, you're not fat,' said Ellie.

'Of course she isn't,' said George. 'That wasn't what she meant.' He felt a twang of irritation towards Ellie, and suddenly disliked the fact that she was so pretty. He didn't find himself attracted to her but even so, right now he would have liked it much better if she were a little less of a blank-browed Modigliani. He would also like it better if his wife stopped speaking in that odd tone. 'The Spaniards are a very cruel race,' he said, putting his glass down. 'If you want to talk about vindictiveness, Sam. I believe there's an Iberian soft spot for tauromachy and taunting of bears.' Already he was feeling calmer. Just the feel of the words, rolling from mind to tongue as he needed them, just the right ones, in just the right order, all as it ought to be. With words he could pinpoint everything perfectly. With words, everything could be set in its perfect place. As he expounded on bloodthirst and bullfighting, his pulse slowed and the kitchen cooled. His harried thoughts flowed into a single line. 'Rome never left,' George said. 'If you want to see the spirit of Ancient Rome, go to Spain, not Italy. It's all there: the oligarchy, the perversions, the circuses of death as entertainment. The notion of *sacrifice*. The Italians can't bear to sacrifice anything, that's why they're always making such a fuss; the British are always making a show of sacrificing *themselves*; but only the Spanish have retained the rather splendid Roman notion of sacrificing other things, other creatures, other people, on one's own behalf. There is something simultaneously noble and bestial about it.'

'The Italians make more pornography,' said Rosa bravely. 'You can't say Spanish people are more voracious. Or perverted. Than Italians, you can't. Because Italy makes more porn.'

'Oh, that's not about sex. It's mere gynophilia. Real sex is sacrificial, and not in the stoic Morningside sense – no, in a Dionysian way, sacrificing somebody else for yourself and sublimating them in the process. Only – and here's the rub – knowing they're doing the same to you. The Spanish mentality grasps that mutual sacrifice quite perfectly, and is tormented by it. Whereas voyeurism avoids this, wouldn't you say, Rosa, must necessarily be intellectually as well as physically masturbatory; is not about intercourse at all.'

'I'm not sure this is an appropriate conversation for Bernadette,' said Natasha.

George turned and stared at his daughter. 'Do you understand what we're talking about?' he asked her. Bernie looked back at him and very carefully shook her head.

'The anguish, and the thieving,' George continued, 'the autophagous ambition of sex, the burglar burgled, immolating with one's own immolation. Feasting even as oneself is eaten. It's not for nothing that a marriage is *consumed*.'

Ellie was staring at him. The lower rims of her eyes

seemed to have been lifted by a tautening of muscles in the upper half of her face, even as her lips had fallen faintly ajar so that her lower lip showed a streak of the soft smooth pinkness normally tucked up inside her narrow sunbeaten pucker. Her hands had stopped moving on her thighs. She was fairly sure that this conversation – this monologue of his – should not be taking place, here, now, in this kitchen. She couldn't stop it, of course, but she could stop it happening to her. She pushed her chair back as gracefully as she could, whispered, 'Do excuse me, I think I have indigestion,' and walked to the kitchen door.

It was still light outside, though the temperature of the air had dropped. She would take the dark mossy steps up to the edge of the garden, the wasteland end, of cabbages and clothes pegs; she would stroll there and wait, for this feeling to subside, that she had described not entirely inaccurately: an inability to digest; a blockage of words, George's words, piling up on top of each other so that they had pressed up against her instead of simply flowing through her ears and being forgotten like words usually were. But had silted hotly, the weight of those arriving on top pulping the ones nearest her further, so they were fermented into something that she couldn't comprehend, whose splattered sense seemed to trickle against her unpleasantly. You could only take so much of George, that was what Ruaridh had always said. That's what she told herself, recovering now from the feeling that she had been wearing quite the wrong clothes.

Still not quite right, here stepping over blown mast beside the beech hedge that then gave way to evergreen lime-specked leaves, which gleamed like toad skins. Her silk and linen would be better on the terrace but those pleasant flagstones could only be gained through the drawing room doors and she had no wish to enter the house again. She stopped and sighed, looking around, away from the vegetable patch – how funny of Natasha to grow things, it was like that programme on the box, the one with Felicity Kendal, who had such a nice name, Ellie thought, like a happy-go-lucky mint cake, and that rakish half-drunk voice, and one of the things Ellie liked best about Ruaridh being dead was being able to think how attractive other women were without worrying that he thought so too, she could watch television and let her eyes wander across theatre foyers in quite a different way – and she saw the tangerine azalea blossom at the fringes of the lawn.

Stepping daintily towards it, she was being careful to avoid treading in something unsavoury, seeing as this was where the dogs went; she was paying great attention to the grass, and that was why she saw the turquoise notebook, that was why she picked it up.

'What do you think, Rosa?' asked Sam. 'What do you think about the Spanish attitude to sex?'

'Shut up.'

'Do you think sex is a sacrifice?'

'Leave her alone,' said Natasha, 'How would she know?' she asked, in a way that made it clear this wasn't a question he should answer. And then her tone of voice changed completely. 'The literal meaning of sacrifice is making sacred, isn't it, darling.'

George nodded. He was frequently glad that he had married a well-educated woman, and his wife seemed quite back to normal now.

'Well then,' she said. 'It's just coincidental that something has to die in the process.'

'But how else could you make it sacred?' George asked. He was frowning now, distracted as she'd hoped. 'Otherwise,' he said, 'it would just be a blessing. It would be a secular object bearing a blessing. A kiss!' The scathing way in which he voiced this word made Natasha blink.

'No,' her husband was saying, 'to make something sacred, it must cease being the thing that it was. That, my dear, is the difference between osculation and fornication mid the ferns of our fine conservatories.'

He seemed quite happy over there, finishing the last of the food on his dinner plate. It was a peculiar dinner service, thought Natasha, looking down at her own meat-crumbed porcelain, at the devouring eagle perched on the giant chrysanthemum bloom. Grandiose, doomed, his great beak and the flower that could never hold his weight, and really quite undomestic, she thought, and wondered not for the first time if these had strayed from an ambassadorial batch.

The gold leaf had almost entirely come adrift from his feathers. 'I don't have a conservatory,' she said, at length. 'And I think the cucumber frame would be a little cramped. Now—'

'I know who did it!' Ellie was standing in the doorway, looking dramatic. There were tiny dark blades of sweat on the silk beneath her armpits. 'It was Humberto,' she said. 'Humberto attacked Julab.' Her wide eyes were touring each of their faces with this angrily certain, clever proposition. 'He's Spanish,' she said. 'He's a stranger, and he hasn't come back.'

'Oh Ellie. I hardly think that proves anything,' said Natasha, but she was not smiling when she said this.

Rosa's chair fell over as she stood, made a clatter that she neither seemed to notice nor tried to end but ignored altogether. Her cheeks were pale, her eyes hard as she shouted, 'How dare you!' Her fists were clenched. 'Of course it wasn't,' said Rosa, but her voice was wavering now. 'Of course it wasn't him.'

It would have been better if she hadn't spoken. Her voice carried too much pleading, begged too much to be believed. So that everybody was embarrassed and looked away, except Bernie, who was staring at her cousin's face.

Nobody else said anything, not until Rosa had left.

'They *are* very hot-tempered,' Ellie insisted, as Sam was righting his sister's toppled chair. 'Look at Carmen,' she said.

'I thought Bizet was French,' said Natasha.

'But *Carmen* is Spanish,' said Ellie, as if she were explaining to a dullard.

'She isn't real, though.'

'Well, what about all the others in it, then? They're quite impassioned too, aren't they? It can't be a coincidence.'

Natasha was staring at her.

'Just like George said.' Ellie sounded very patient, waiting for Natasha to catch up.

'Did I mention operatic heroines or Humberto?' wondered George. He sat back in his chair, less contented than usual. He would be glad when it was just himself and his family again. He didn't mind Rosa's exhibition but Ellie was irritating him a great deal this evening. It offended his sensibilities for someone to have such a full and exact vocabulary whilst being so stupid. He flinched when he heard right words pressed into the service of wrong ideas, nonideas. 'Perhaps you have a diva of your own, Ellie,' he said.

'Oh, well,' flustered Ellie.

'Rosa isn't normally like that,' said Sam, quietly. 'She must be worried.'

His calmness, his fairness, impressed them, even as Ellie began to mutter darkly about the bad influences that were making Rosa behave this way.

Perhaps he was not so bad, this boy, thought George. His peculiar coolness felt welcome in juxtaposition with his mother's vapourised meanderings, her nonsensical logical bonds that didn't belong, forged in God knew what heated chemical fog of misplaced belief and emotion. 'You're handling this business very well, Sam,' George gruffly said. Sam looked down at his scratched eagle, at the absurdity, already noted by Natasha, of the artist's presumption that a garden flower could ever support the weight of a bird of prey. The wrongness of the tableau struck him greatly.

Everyone else at the table was stirred by Sam's modesty. Lori especially was charmed by his embarrassment. Silent throughout the meal, latterly occupied with wondering if she should go after Rosa to make sure she was okay, now she had entirely forgotten her friend and was gazing at Sam, at his downcast long-lashed eyes, the bothered sling of his jaw and the darkness of his cheek, the soft blackness of his hair that tumbled forward over his forehead in the gypsy's lick favoured by public school boys and pop stars. She had always thought there was something too lightweight about his vein of handsomeness – perhaps it was the literal slightness of his build, for Lori dated tall and thoroughly muscled boys who came from the farms – but now in his reluctance, his restraint in the face of praise, she saw a kind of sinewy contraction, a strength held back; and suddenly his face was fascinating to her, and would remain so for the duration of his stay.

Sam kept staring at the dinner plate, at the eagle perched on the spike-petalled globular bloom. Believe this, the eagle seemed to say. Believe this, because you can see it, can't you? Impossible things can work, in a picture that's been painted. You just have to decide to sit here with me, and stick with it. There now. Do you feel it? Do you feel the lightness of the petals underneath us? But we're here, aren't we. Look, we must be: everyone is looking at us and they see us here and we, we seem to be here.

Sam nodded.

Lori smiled a little, as if he had nodded for her. And the others also enjoyed this inclination of his head; it was good to be in the presence of nobility, however small a portion, here in this kitchen.

*   *   *

Talk turned to egg whites and pantomime dames. Often Bernadette tried to swing the conversation back to a discussion of Julab's injuries but no one else seemed willing to oblige her. They smiled at her, and yet pretended they had not heard. Eventually she gave up and listened, bored, fidgeting with her fingers in her lap, asked to get down and was allowed. Lori shifted in her seat, aware of being slightly pleased by something as Bernie left the room – now that it was just the adults, and her and Sam – but nervous too. For a moment or two, and then Natasha said how much nicer it would be to sit in the drawing room.

'I should go and look for Rosa,' said Lori.

Nobody tried to dissuade her, and so she found herself alone on the back stair, resting against the wall now that the door at the bottom was closed behind her, now that she could hear the voices of the others – the older ones, tones of her parents' age – muffled through its timber that was stained to resemble mahogany on the hall-side, but coated in durable white paint on the stair-side, this side. So that instantly she knew what side she was on: even if you took away the walls and the rooms, the stair itself, still you would know what side of the door you were on.

Chapter Twenty-nine

Humberto lumbered heavily down the mountainside, feeling the weight of his footfall spasm in the thin mattress of topsoil that overlay the rock, tremble out across its grassed skin. The clouds were pushing his body from behind. Each step shoved him harder ahead. His arms were worked as far back as they could go in his shoulder sockets, twin brakes on his balance and his head bent down to watch where his treacherous feet trod.

These mountains were not like the ones he knew. The roundness of their summits lent them a gentle air: from a distance they seemed much softer than the mountains of home. Here there were no craggy *cordilleras*, no daggered peaks to rip a storm on, no mica knife-edge heights glinting in the sun. Grand and mighty, these mountains were, but in the manner of stout pent bosoms, strained apron fronts on which little grew, swept clear with hands of cold mist.

Yet the sides were steep: the top was only round because its towering peak had been worn down in millennia of weathers, the likes of which seemed so bravely dashed by sharper heights that had in fact seen less. These mountains were old, that was all. They'd borne a brunt and still did, and their hidden strength was in the steepness of their sides that remained the same, that let the weather flow down them as if they were merely handy guttering, as if the summit, the roof, were the thing.

He thought that he could take any route down but too many of the animal tracks in the heather led only to cliffs. He had had to retrace his steps to the top and try another tack, twice, now. He was aware of the beat of his heart in his ribs, like an animal, something separate from him, almost some small enemy within.

Each time he had returned to that mild summit, laid out in a high hard blanket for a walker's pleasure, to stroll about or picnic on – that's what you might think, on reaching it: what a nice place for lunch – it had seemed a little more sinister, a little more dread, and its physical docility only worsened this. He was pinned in the sky by nothing, with nothing to beat. Nothing to fight against. Adrift without a wind on some absurd inflatable, the sort of thing that happened to children. At twenty, he was of an age, surely, to have earned a grander disaster than this. No rip current or rock fall, no snow-bound ridge. *He climbed the hill and couldn't get down.*

The weather was closing in. Screeds of mist rolled below him; watery breaths scalloped, overlapped and thickened. He went carefully as he could. Water settled on his skin from the air white and heavy with moisture around him, trickled cold down the insides of his arms. The cotton threads of his shirt were wet. The wet shirt suckered against his back, his sides, his abdomen. His many-pocketed shorts grew leaden. He was shivering.

The urge was to go faster, to break into a downward jog, but he would not: he knew there were sheer drops on this hillside, he had seen them from below, he had encountered them before. He kept treading steadily, blindly and cold, invisible. He was praying that the path would not end in a cliff, this time.

146

Chapter Thirty

Rosa ran up the bare stone steps in the tower, her left arm reaching always forward, pulling at the handrail fastened to the wall. She was breathing hard.

A great door met her at the top, there on the tiny landing by the high window cut like an archer's slit. She tried the blackened brass knob and found the door was locked. The handle turned, but the slab of dark-stained timber would not budge from its lintolled snug. She tried again, curling her peach-polished nails around that thuggish lump of iron-mongery that turned her knuckles white, but of course it did not open, because it was still locked. She pressed her body up against the wood, that was stained to resemble mahogany, like the smart doors far downstairs. People who mattered must have been used to climb up here. She laid her cheek against the door, liked its coolness, smoothness; liked its hardness, strangely, although it was the thing that stood in her way. Perhaps she had found a thing to cry against.

She stood there for a minute or two, and ran her hand up the wood, high above her head, and let it rest there. She was staring very hard sideways at the door frame. She was deciding not to cry, there, like a flamenco dancer standing still in silence.

She was alone, no one else here, at the top of the third and smallest stair. And yet Rosa's religious fervour meant that she was never alone, not really: God was in the window, and the doorpost, always she was being observed by the worthiest spy. It lent her behaviours a peculiarly romantic bent, and this was what so impressed Catherine, being the opposite of her own minute observing, her convalescent espionage, for she was turned the other way out.

'Catherine Wheel,' whispered Rosa, opening the sick-room door.

'Why does everyone keep coming in? I'm sleeping.'

'No you're not. You're standing up.'

'But I'm *meant* to be sleeping.' Catherine closed the book beneath her fingertips, perfunctory as a librarian at the table's edge.

Rosa was puzzled by this small cousin with whom she normally shared such fondness. 'Where's the key for the roof kept?' she asked.

'We're not allowed up the tower. Not without Mummy or Daddy.'

'I'm a grown-up. Grown-ups can go there on their own.'

Catherine stood resolute and silent, with her back to the piles of books now. She wasn't worried about Rosa asking what she was up to. She knew that Rosa wouldn't be interested, because Rosa just wasn't like that. Catherine was looking at the way Rosa's face was held together: too-tight, and sort of collapsing in the eyes, that were pulling the rest of it in. Like two umbrellas, she thought, with their spokes spread invisibly under her skin. Somebody has pressed the catches on the sides, that always pinch, but the hems are caught on her jaw, that's why her chin is buckling. Her eyes look funny, with that old water trapped in them. Wanting to have a good shake.

'Are you going to jump off?' asked Catherine.

'No,' said Rosa. She crouched down, and smiled, a small

spilled kind of smile that smudged. As if she were about to ask again, but then she stopped smiling, and her eyes became quite serious even though she was still looking at Catherine, like she was sad but didn't care who saw it any more. Like she was giving up.

She put her hand on the floor, about to push herself tall again. Breathing in.

'It's on top of the corner cupboard in the drawing room,' said Catherine. 'I can't reach it.'

Rosa didn't say thank you, but Catherine liked this. She was glad that Rosa's mouth simply broadened in front of her; glad that her eyes simply brightened, that she nodded, and left.

Catherine went back to her work with the books, inscribing her prologue notes slowly. From time to time she looked sideways through the far corner window, looked at the gravel beneath the foot of the tower where it rose beyond the porch.

She was keeping an eye with a cynicism quite differently inspired than Sam's. The two of them likewise were slaves to fate, but where Sam wielded its knife as if he were its automaton, Catherine stood immobile. If she could just touch nothing, cause nothing, nor prevent it either; give the key where her withholding of it would cause more different endings than handing it across; then she would be glad.

When she had finished with all of her books, and Rosa's falling body had still failed to materialise, then she went and stood close to the window once more, peering upwards. Rosa's hand was a tiny grey smudge like lichen growing high up, right up at the top of the tower, over the rim of the battlement. That was her brown hair tattered in the rain. Catherine stayed looking up at her for some time, at Rosa who stood looking south across the river and did not move, even though her hand must be getting cold out there on the stone.

Sam was hurrying in from the chill mist, Kitchener damply frolicking up the porch steps before him. Catherine had glimpsed him with the dog a few hours earlier, too. She wondered if Sam was going to hurt him and allowed herself to hope that he wouldn't. Sam was right there now, close to the other side of the window glass, but aiming only for the door. His arms were slim and softly muscled. He was stooping on the step to unfasten his Velcro sandal straps. She watched his hands intently. His hands, his arms, belonged to him.

They were the same hands that had done everything that he had done.

Maybe it was them, she thought, standing watching the deftness with which his fingers worked without him having to think. Maybe only his hands had done this thing, and not him. *You're getting carried away.* Maybe he had been carried away by his own hands, his own hands scooping him out of the way to get on with doing what they wanted. Look – he wasn't even watching as they pulled his sandals from his feet; he was looking sideways out across the gravel, towards the tent and the pine trees.

And then something drew his eyes towards Catherine's watching: he was looking at her. Now the weather was bad, now the sun had gone in, he could see her. She blinked and looked back, but she did not make a smile to answer his.

Once he had gone – or come, she supposed, from outside where she could see him to inside where she couldn't – she looked up again, seeking Rosa's hand and hair up there in the stone and the clouds. The hand had withdrawn but the hair still blew. Who knew if Rosa too had watched him coming in?

Catherine squeezed the hem of her nightdress, caught

150

up sideways in her fist. If it was his hands, and not him, that had almost killed Julab, then it was also his hands, and not him, that had lightly rubbed cream into the skin on her back while she'd lain by the window. She climbed back under her covers and drew them up to her chin.

She couldn't let go of the way he had touched her in the afternoon: it was the happiest she'd been in her life. It had to be him, and not just his hands, that did these things. She couldn't stand for him to be innocent of everything. She lay there, refusing it. Felt its way out closing, and a swelling in her ribs, a dread and a relief left here in the room.

She looked, and nothing was accidental, nothing could ever be accidental again. Not once it had been done. The window frame knew just what part of the garden it showed. The grooves of the panelling were as definite as if they'd drawn themselves there in stone. The green glass lightshade now had to hang from the ceiling on that certain length of chain, had to squat in that exact chunk of space. Maybe they'd been accidents when they were happening, but not now they weren't. The things that had happened just couldn't be otherwise, now. They were meant, now, all of them.

Turning her head sideways she felt, for the first time, the precise depth to which the pillow sank before pressing back to cup her cheek. It was not her pillow any more, but a pillow by itself that had travelled through time to meet her here. She thought of the feathers inside it, creaking and shifting, squashing each other down under the weight of her face. Suddenly she sat up and looked down at the dent she'd made in it. It wasn't an accident, not to a pillow it wasn't, it was not even an accident where you happened to lay your head. She lay back down and closed her eyes. He'd meant to touch her skin. Everything meant everything that it did.

Chapter Thirty-one

On the high slopes of scree, Humberto was sliding. His sturdy boots sank and clattered in the stones as he made his way backwards, holding his body close to the tilting field of rock, his cold raw hands gripping the lumps of spalled poor granite that slipped away, rolled under him to land on his ankles and bounce, rattle off to the distant bottom. All he could see was the blanket of stones, so close to his face, shifting but always the same, grey veined shapes that now seemed to be only rolling, the same water over a mill wheel, over and over again. He was sure he was getting no further down. The same rocks seemed always to come back around.

He could no longer be sure of the angle at which he clung to the world. Now and then he had a terrible conviction that the hillside had swung to the vertical, and then that it had tilted over so that he must sucker himself to its slippery underside or fall off into nothing: that in fact he was certain to fall, because at any moment the stones would tumble free and take him with them.

He lay down on the rocks, then, spread his arms and legs out as wide as he could, pressing against the slope, until the jabbing of the stones in his abdomen, his neck and thighs, steadied him and his head grew less giddy. He breathed in and out. The air was half water. It was no place for a man, this mountain with its ground that gave way like sand grains, its drenching of the lungs.

And yet it was tempting to stay, now that he'd found a place to be still. The terrible kaleidoscope sliding, the lack of all proper solidity, slapped at his muscles and skin only when he tried to move. It had ended, now that he lay still. He could lie here, quietly, and wait for the weather to pass. He could choose that: to close his eyes, and wait for the mist to clear.

He thought of it, but he was not the sort to give himself up to the mountain like this. Nor did he wish to begin to die by lying. With an effort, he pushed himself up with his elbows, dug his toecaps in and continued his descent. His strong tendons were trembling with every step, partly from the extreme cold, partly from the burlesque fluctuations underneath him. *Steady as a rock* – the stones mocked themselves as they slipped and rattled, that were meant to be more dependable than anything, and yet bled sideways over his hands, and went.

When he reached the end of the scree slope, Humberto stood still for several seconds on the stable turf. His kneecaps were shaking so he stooped and held them still. This also prevented him from being sick.

He was coming down a different side of the mountain, its west flank instead of the north by which he'd climbed it. He could hear running water somewhere below him: he would find it, he would follow it down.

The mountain burn joined a broader stream at the foot of the western slope. Humberto trod tiredly beside it, into the dark cleft where it became a bog tufted with cotton and kingcups. There was shelter from the wind here. There was a broad flat rock where you could easily lie down, a foot above the marsh. It would make a reasonable bed for the night.

Humberto walked towards it. He climbed up onto it, crouching, and then he stood, and held his hands up in an interlocking arch across his forehead to keep the rain from his eyes. He was trying to see if he was headed the right way.

There was nothing to see: the mist clung thoroughly across the mouth of this small gorge. But Humberto stepped down and headed onwards, the soft ground sucking at his boots, as if he'd seen a signpost brightly lit. He didn't turn, didn't glance at the rock as he staggered out into the open again, the howling wind.

Dusk was come, and his clothes worse than nothing, pressing the wetness to his skin. His shirtback like clayed muslin held the cold in folds that rippled over his shivering sweat, made places for drips. Water traced courses, needle-fine estuaries that laced his shoulder blades, made their way under a saturated sky of sodden cloth that with every other step weighed down against them and flooded the plain of his skin. Under the loose waistband of his shorts, pooling in the dent above his buttocks, the cold poured down his arse that was frozen numb, his fine gone legs; poured roughly like it were studded with heather stems that scratched as they went. He couldn't feel it: his arse was glass; but the scratching seemed to make a sound that his skin heard. His pores were deafened by it though his nerves lay deadened.

Still he could feel the air in his lungs, or rather, his lungs wringing air from the cloud he walked in, their wheezing burn. He could feel the gripping of the muscles in his calves. He could feel the rubbing of the wet serge fabric that chafed his thighs. The rhythmic pain was a kind of warmth, the way it flickered like a flame.

154

He was disappearing inwards, having lost his skin. The outside of his own body was something to be listened to distantly. The world beyond it had fallen. His own brain had slipped, and slept, as his lungs, his legs, still endeavoured to carry him home.

Blood trickled slowly from his crotch. It patched him with slow red leaf prints that washed away and grew again inside the sound of the scratching cold that was in fact the rain that lashed him. There were other leaves too, but Humberto scarcely saw them. There were hazels, and oaks, distantly in the grey; there were clumps of brambles closer by.

He no longer knew what the shapes outside him represented. His brain was too tired, too stiffened, to fetch answers from his memory. His past had seized up and left him. There was no time any more, nor meanings. There was only the shape of things, and rhythms of shallow pain breathing.

Yet something deeply in him stayed awake: something knew the things that he did not. That this ditch and that could lead him to the cycle track; that the treetop over there was one he'd never knowingly seen from the other side, and would carry him on to the riverbank.

He staggered over the hummocked Cossack hats of moss as if he were drunk or sleeping. He found the water's edge, and this was the last thing he remembered.

He had no recollection of how he might have crossed the river, how he must have stumbled upstream for another quarter mile before finding the falls, and how, here, he must have clung from rock to rock across the frothing chill.

In fact it took him half an hour to cross that which earlier, on his outward journey, he had traversed in five minutes. Several times he crouched on one rock, and stretched his arm out towards the next – his body knew that it could not make it on his legs, instinctively drew him onward by the fingertips, let his legs catch up through the rushing currents – but found it was too far. Sat back for a second or two before trying again, failing again, trying again. It could take him ten or twelve attempts to reach far enough, to touch the next rock, before the slow hauling forward of his weight. Twice he stopped altogether, for five minutes or ten. Waited in the shape of the middle of a journey, not its end, until his body bid forth again.

His limbs slipped on the black moss by the far bank. His ankles and his torso scattered suddenly across it, his face turning, that still contained him somewhere, locked in deep beneath the directings of his animal brain. He staggered down the gravel, boots splashing in the shallows as he gripped the long grass and plantains that grew along the bank. Like some old shoulder, and the grass for hair to grab at in his fist.

Scrambling up the gash of sand and tree roots where it led into the wild edge of the garden, his knees were useless now and he climbed instead only with his hands, that were like claws, paws, things that had never known how to use a pen or hold a spoon. His ankles digging in. A final heave of some small muscle behind his neck. The shape of the muscle was a crescent of steel that rocked against the wood that was petrifying everywhere inside him, crushing out the final juice of whatever blood still lay there. It wrenched him forwards, was enough.

He was crawling with infinitesimal slowness under the pine trees, towards his tent, and someone was watching him.

Chapter Thirty-two

'I think I saw a squirrel,' said Catherine, emerging from her spy hole where nothing could ever happen, finding her cousin in the hall.

'Good for you,' said Sam, carrying on towards the door to the servants' stair.

'It's injured,' she called. 'You should put it out of its misery, Sam.'

And that was when he'd turned, interested now. Thought about it, but only for a second or two before he went to fetch his gun.

It was all right, wasn't it, thought Catherine, to move people into a different bit of space where the things they did were still up to them. It was only wrong to believe that they would do particular things. It was all right to make the next thing happen, as long as you didn't try and make it into a particular shape.

Accidents happen, Mrs Farrants often said.

'*Accidere, accidentis*, of course they do,' Mr Farrants had once replied. 'Hard for them to do anything else,' he had said. 'An accident is that which happens, isn't it, Catherine,' as Mummy – Mrs Farrants – had dabbed the knee with TCP. '*Ad cadere*,' he had said. 'To fall to. So you needn't feel lonesome when you fall, for all the world's an accident and it's all falling with you.' Catherine had started crying all over again, at the thought of the whole world having an accident, but that was last year, when she had been someone quite different; had been a girl who thought that accidents were bad: wettings of the bed, car wrecks on the bend, broken legs and gashes on the head. Whereas now, she had decided, there was something very nice about accidents, about the things that just happened to happen. About the things that were happening *now*. Things that were happening *now* didn't mean a thing, not until they'd been done. You could just float in them and not look forwards or back. Not be wrong. Float in the big nothing right-now accident, holding the things that had already happened safe in your hands, tied up and done. But not ever mix the two up – not ever grab at that watery stuff all around you right now and try to hold any of *it* in your hand. You didn't try and steer the sea. It was not your business. And this was a nice thing, really, because it meant there was nothing to worry about at all. You just had to be part of the falling and never interfere. Just fall to. Fall into place.

Accident, as George once pointed out, means *to fall to,* and it is also the case that *intend* means *to stretch towards.*

'Intention can be part of the accident,' Catherine would one day tell her sister, but that would be twenty-six years later, on the terrace of the Botanical Gardens, over the newspaper report that Bernie had brought. 'You can fall and stretch towards the thing you are falling to at the same time, can't you.'

'Everything that happens, happens,' she would say, taking another drag on her cigarette. 'Everything that happens, will have happened. Today's accident is tomorrow inevitable.'

'Everything is an accident,' she would say, 'only not in the way that people usually mean that word. They mean accident to mean something that was random, or unintended, or aberrant. But really there is no such property in events: there is only that which was, and that which was not.'

These were some of the things she would say.

Catherine watched at the window once more, with a cardie pulled over her nightie, as rain spilled and dripped down the glass. Rosa had gone from the tower hours ago.

She watched Sam's long-loved figure striding onto the gravel, cocking the trigger with his head down, looking up to find his target. Halting when he saw the Spaniard lying distant beyond the pines.

And now Sam, in all his smallness, was standing over Humberto with the gun. What would he do, wondered Catherine. Knowing, this time, that he could do anything, and pleased by the safe feeling of knowing this. Detached as she observed Sam lay the gun down, crouch low on the ground, grip Humberto's shoulder. He was saying something: he must be, because she could see his lips moving in a way they only did when people spoke. He was pulling off his jacket, laying it round Humberto's shoulders. He was running back towards the house with such anguish that Catherine almost felt ashamed.

There was crashing of doors, there was shouting in the hall.

Rosa smashed first from the house, as if she had already known, had been ready and waiting for her brother to call her down from her candlewick bed. Flying to her lover with her limbs all terrified and strange. When she found him she could only think to cover him with herself. She dropped, and bound herself to him, pressed her warm chest, all her long body, onto the back of him where he lay; brought her arms around him, hugging his elbows in,

159

pressing her cheek against his glacial face that did not answer although she cried his name.

She was falling hair and moving lips, a trembling wish to save a man with her flesh.

Catherine stared, had the feeling, as she often did when watching Rosa, that she was witnessing something better than real. Her cousin was making a blanket of herself in a garden shrouded in mist.

She observed, with a degree of relief, the awkward movements with which Rosa was forced to rise when the ones with strong arms and real blankets came.

That was why, wasn't it. That was why you didn't.

Sam and George bore him between them. Natasha walked in front, and pointed at things that they might fall on: a tree root, the gravel (inexplicably), the step of the porch. Rosa behind seemed to be part of them, and there was a deep care in the way she walked, as if she were making sure that Humberto did not leave anything of himself behind: no shred of his life was to drip out upon the ground while she was watching, and if it did her hands were ready to snatch it up and hand it back to him.

Catherine opened the sick-room door a crack, a little more, slipped into the space she'd levered ajar and found herself the object of Aunt Ellie's scrutinising gaze. It was just the two of them, here in the waiting hall.

Ellie had not gone outside because she was not wearing a coat and it was raining. Her coat was at the other end of the house, in the scullery past the kitchen. She could not go out in the rain without a coat. 'Aren't your feet cold?' she asked. 'They're bringing Humberto in.'

'A glass of cold water, Bernadette,' George was saying to his eldest daughter in the porch, who ran now with

160

serious chin past Catherine and Aunt Ellie towards the kitchen.

'The drawing room,' said Natasha.

They were coming down the hall, Mr George Farrants and Sam, dragging the heavy ghost between them.

Catherine pressed herself against the door jamb. She saw his broken neck, his lolling head that rolled down over his own shoulder; she watched with frigid face in case it carried on rolling down his arm but it did not, it stopped, there above his breast, and suddenly, as it drew level with her, raised itself, opened blank eyes that stared askew to the skylight. He was rasping something, dripped it in spit. '*A-ladienna,*' he was saying. '*Ladienna de campo?*'

'What's he saying?' asked Natasha anxiously, and George also felt that he needed to know, but could not say. Even Ellie, with her eloquent cocktail French, was helpless. 'In the drawing room, Bernadette,' said Mrs Farrants, scarcely looking down as Humberto continued to garble at the rain upon the glass high up overhead. '*Ladiennamama, ahstoy enladienna,*' he murmured, and seemed to smile as his head tipped sideways again and all speech rolled far from his eyes.

'What's he saying?' asked Natasha again.

'I think it's nonsense,' said Ellie, and 'I don't know,' said George, 'he's delirious.'

'*La tienda,*' said Sam, with a heavy breath as he shifted Humberto a step nearer to the drawing room door.

'*La tienda de campo,*' said Rosa, opening it. 'He wants to be in the tent.'

'How strange,' said Ellie. 'It's freezing out there!'

'Of course,' said Natasha. 'He's staying in here with us.'

'We could tuck him in your bed, Mummy,' said Bernadette, and nobody spoke then, but all paused where they stood.

'No,' said Natasha. 'We'd only have to move him later.'

161

'But for now! There are blankets there already.'

Rosa was holding the drawing room door wider but she was looking at her aunt with eyes that seemed unusually clear while Natacha said again, 'No, Bernadette,' as Rosa, and everyone but Bernadette, had known that she would.

Rosa had the door as wide as it could go, now, and her bangles jangled strangely on her arm when she reached to touch Uncle George's passing shoulder, touching him because he was bearing half the weight of Humberto whom she loved. She followed the trio into the drawing room, and watched as Aunt Tash dashed in again, dashed around them all, to lay spare blankets on the sofa and with briskness appear to be giving much.

Rosa and the girls were banished then, because Humberto must be undressed. So it was not Rosa who unbuttoned his shirt and peeled it from his death-cold skin, and her fingers could only hang fidgeting in the hall as other hands, her brother's, eased his long shorts away from the bloody gouges in his skin left by their seams. It was Natasha, almost old enough to be his mother, who brought towels and bore his underpants away.

The men laid his frozen bones, still in the shape of him, down upon the blankets. Behind his empty head, the sofa arm, stood the ice-clean grate of the Gothic fireplace, its pristine summer hearth.

Rosa ran a bath.

She was not allowed to place him in it, but she could try the water with her hands, in the bathroom by herself. In this tub where he would soon be lowered in, she could gauge the temperature against her skin, of the water that in a moment would hold him. The electric heater on the wall lit orangely a tong of warmth, which curled the vapours from the bath. Steam clouded the window, and condensation kindly dripped upon her cheek. She shook her fingers now and stood, and with a sad demeanour but a firm straight back, opened the door.

They carried him past her, trailing blanket hems over the floor.

His body was so cold that the temperature of the bath water plummeted within a minute of his lying there, head held carefully up against the white enamel rim. They had to pull the plug, run more hot, time and time again. 'It's dropped again,' they said; and splashed the water that still was better than nothing, up around his neck and under his shivering chin, while the wastepipe sucked and the tap belched warmth, heat and heat again thrown stubbornly against the glacial bulwark of him.

Outside the bathroom, Rosa twisted her hands and tore her sleeve. She wanted to make more room in the world for him. There were so many things that didn't need to be here: if she could just get rid of a few. The ripping of thin Indian cotton that had begun absent-mindedly now absorbed her, and quickened.

Catherine, still watching from the doorway the other side of the hall, at once understood this activity that so appalled Rosa's mother. Even as Ellie cried out that Rosa must stop, Catherine was saying, in a calm and quiet voice, 'You can throw my books in the river if you like.' Rosa turned. 'Thank you,' she said.

'Or maybe I should,' said Catherine. 'You'll want to stay here with Humberto, I imagine.' She turned and, disappearing into the erstwhile dining room, said, almost to herself, 'Yes, I'll go.'

'*My* things!' Rosa called. 'Catherine, take *my* things.' Pulling a fevered hand through her long loose fringe, and walking across the hall in a stilted way, and then stopping, because every step took her further from the bathroom door.

Ellie would have prevented all this from happening, of course she would, if Bernadette hadn't suddenly started crying. Ellie hadn't even registered that she was there – you didn't, with Bernie, because you knew that she wouldn't cause trouble. Guiltily she pulled her little niece in, and gladly, because she knew perfectly well how to do this. She could easily comfort a small girl, easily smooth her cheek and say, No, of course not, Bernie. Of course he won't die.

So Catherine had been standing on the bridge for some minutes, and had cast several pendants, a highlighted copy of *Macbeth*, two prayer cards, a lilac lace bra, a Blondie tape and a cardigan into the roiling river before anyone ran to stop her, and the person who stopped her was not Aunt Ellie but her mother.

Chapter Thirty-three

Standing in Rosa's room, Catherine had felt the seriousness of her position. She was standing in Rosa's place. She was acting on Rosa's behalf. She must pick the things that Rosa would have picked, quickly, before someone came. Her eyes had swum over the dressing table and bed, weighing up their contents, the bric-a-brac objects, with a mind carefully coloured in by Rosa's way of thinking, seeing it all as if her cousin really were inside her skin.

Rifling through the jewellery, she had taken the pendants because Rosa would have thought it right to offer objects that were one thing hanging on another thing string. They were more dramatic, weren't they, than the ropes of shell and bead that were comfortably the same all the way along.

Rosa loved God, and *Macbeth* had ghosts in it, she knew, which were nearly the same as angels; the prayer cards, even better, wore pictures of saints. Gabriel was also an angel, and the book had Death in its title, so that went in too. The bra was a woman's thing, the opposite of Humberto, which would keep him from flowing down the river with the other things. The tape, which Rosa often played, had a song on it that went 'The Tide Is High But I'm Holding On', and he had looked as if he needed to hold on very desperately. Another tape box had a man on the front with death-white face and woeful legs; it also went in the bag, which was a pillowcase from Rosa's bed. There was an algebra book, full of things that seemed impossible; there was something to keep you warm, and it was soft. Catherine thought these were the kinds of things that Rosa would have chosen, had she been here herself, because Rosa was always one for making things stand for something else.

All this Catherine did in a matter of minutes, and was down the back stair, darting out across the corner of the hall to the kitchen and the back route out, so as to avoid the others who still stood under the skylight, Aunt Ellie and weeping Bernadette, Rosa who turned her head and silently watched her go.

She was gone. She was across the garden long before her mother emerged and wearily, in passing, asked for her whereabouts.

Catherine dropped each item over the bridge's handrail with deep care and reverence. She paused for a moment between each one. It was important to know what you were doing. It was important to watch what was happening as it slipped through your hands.

The Prayer of Saint Francis was falling gently from her fingers as Humberto trembled nearer life. A dove under laminated plastic kissed the water as his lungs fluttered and drew in their first slow breath, cleanly. The tiny pale blue card skated over the dark swirling surface of the river as Natasha squeezed out of the bathroom door and into the hall, to give this good report and then ask, 'Where's Catherine?'

'She's throwing Rosa's things in the river,' said Ellie, as if this were a plain and unstoppable fact. Rosa was standing motionless beside her, probably still in shock, thought Natasha as she strode towards the porch. 'For Christ's sake,'

166

she muttered as she went, but not before she had eyed her sister-in-law with incredulous disdain.

And now Rosa seemed to understand that Humberto was all right, and gasped in all the air she'd been refusing. She was bursting into the bathroom; no one could stop her. 'Rosa!' screamed her mother. 'He's naked!' But Bernadette still clung to her arm, and so she only dragged herself to the doorway in Rosa's wake and halted there.

Everyone saw Rosa bend over him where he lay, still in the bath, with a pained grimace in his eyes, the vacant smile of death vanished from his face. He seemed faintly surprised by something, but nothing in his nakedness surprised Rosa.

'Darling,' she was saying, and then her face swung up and away from him, like it were carried away on a crane. She was swooping back, though, from a tree whose branches were her arms on either side of the bath, and this made him want to laugh and stung his diaphragm and made him wince. Her ankles were in the water, her flesh against his, and all of her in them so that it could have been her breasts or wrists that pressed against him, holding her heart and stomach and lungs. He found it hard to comprehend how she could be there, and also speaking from somewhere else. Her face, up above, a constellation of features in the steam, seemed less truly her than the soul in her ankles that held fast by him there. Her face was too complicated, and too far from him, up there in the putty of the ceiling sky. He gripped her lower calf. He did not want to let her go, it was confusing, the way her face was speaking. 'You're all right,' Rosa was saying, and from the stars those arms stretched forward one by one, milky branches that might drown him, he was terrified, until he felt other flesh of her in fingers around the sides of his face and shuddered with

167

relief, held twice over now. 'You're all right,' her lips kept whispering, and kissing his cheek. He knew it would be better if her mouth did not speak but only pressed against him. The words seemed to halve her, and he couldn't understand fractions as he lay there, he could only grasp the whole of her. If she could just hold herself still against him, not split into eyes and mouth and hips doing different things. If she could just be everything. He was terrified that she'd splinter and fall into pieces in the bath water around him. If she would only stop speaking, stop looking at him, stop moving. He'd just feel her, and everything would be okay. No one would break, nothing. His grip tightened on her leg.

'Rosa, stop that!' shouted Ellie in the doorway. 'Get out of the bath at once!'

'Close the door,' said Rosa. 'It's making a draught.'

'Get out at once! You're embarrassing yourself!'

But Rosa was already getting out of the bath, she was treading on the bathmat and water was dripping from the sodden hem of her blouse and the wet patch across the arse of her tight long denim shorts where her bottom had accidentally dipped in. She was staring backwards at Humberto as if he were the only person who was alive in the room, and all the others just models of human beings that happened to breathe and speak, vocal accordions of no consequence. She seemed not to notice the way that Sam and Uncle George were staring at her, but resignedly took her mother's arm. Apparently submitting, and yet there was the pleased firmness with which she closed the door behind her, and thereby stopped the draught.

From the corner of her eye, Catherine could see her mother approaching. She did not hurry her work, but with the same slow measured pace waited and watched the tape box drifting on the current, taking its skyscrapers elsewhere.

Solemnly she reached and pulled out the cashmere cardigan. Her mother was shouting but nobly she ignored this, focusing her mind on what she felt was definitely the most important moment, the point where she held the thing between her fingers, out in the air above the far-down waters, just before the sacrifice. Meekly, splendidly, she released the cuff from her grip. Watched the cardigan's arm recoil away from her, in towards its heart, bundling itself and then folding out again as it turned and flapped into the water.

Her mother, snatching and scolding, could only frighten Catherine's face: inside, she knew that she was Rosa.

In the hall, Sam stood three feet from his sister, and slowly clapped his hands. His lip was curled unpleasantly, and his brown eyes regarded her with a particular coldness from a head held slightly to one side at exactly her height.

So George found himself alone with the patient in the bathroom, who was now running his tongue across dry lips, and looking back at him. Closing his eyes, thank God; and breathing.

George's eyes kept returning to the young man's hooded cock, trying to float on the water. And then at the space in the air above it where Rosa's bottom had hung a moment before with a wet patch the shape of an enormous heart. The real kind, the cows' hearts on butchers' slabs; not the sort drawn on Valentine's cards.

He turned frowning to the towel rail. He stared very intently at the chrome where it gleamed for an inch or two between overhanging blankets of thick looped cotton threads, dried stiff. The towels were white with a pattern of green bamboo leaves, but George saw only the colours of the threads as they curved around the shiny tubing like fur on skin around a clean wound, a slice of well-plumbed bone. Better, in fact, than fur, than hair, because each of the threads slid perfectly back in without an ending. How wonderful that would be, he felt.

Then George, touching the towel, finally gathered himself. He looked again at the visitor who may or may not have attacked his nephew's dog, and was struck by the strength of the stillness in the eyes that now held his gaze again. He felt deeply and unbearably the pleasance of being in a room with a weak and naked man who was yet strong. It seemed unbelievable that such a man could exist.

Half a sob wrung itself involuntarily from George's chest. Perhaps it was a cough. He shook the towel out, held it forward and coughed properly.

'I don't know if I'll be able to lift you,' he slowly, steadily, said, and his eyes were carefully averted.

'Yes,' Humberto answered, but he did not move.

So George sat down on the rush-seated chair beside the bath, with the towel on his lap and his shoulders hunched. It occurred to him that Humberto spoke a different language fluently. And George's upturned wrists rested loosely on his knees as if he were inviting arrest, and would just sit here until the time came and let the towel rail shine out at him from the other end of the bathroom.

George Farrants was forty-two and the years that crack facades had favoured him by informing his face with the lean intelligence that lay behind it. Humberto had turned his head and was looking incuriously at the older man's profile but he didn't notice any cleverness now, only the way that George was gazing across the room with such relief. It was the same face that Humberto's sister had worn after she'd given birth, a kind of elated exhaustion, and Humberto could not work out why this might be but he did not let it trouble him. He just lay there continuing to regard George sideways, and was comforted by the memory of Pili, and by the stillness of Mr Farrants.

A minute passed, and then George turned, because after all there was something to be done.

He had meant to stand, and somehow manage to lift Humberto from the bath, but now he found the young man staring up at him, it threw him slightly. Something in his gaze demanded a braver response. George reached out a hand and cupped the back of Humberto's head. With his thumb he smoothed his temple, as if he were touching a memory that had never existed.

And then he stood, after all, as he'd intended, and gestured for Humberto to sit up, to lean forward so that he might help him out of the great iron tub.

The Spaniard's hands grasped the white enamel rims either side of him. He was rising from the water, it was falling in loud pleats from him as he staggered upright, with George's left hand clasping his forearm; George's right arm bracing his shivering tricep, cupping its way firmly under his armpit to hold the front of his shoulder.

Natasha was here now, George had not noticed her coming in. She was holding out her arm for Humberto to lean on with his other hand as he heaved one leg and then the other from the bath.

George looked at his wife as she stood there, and the frail strong naked body of the man who might have died standing in between them, drenching the shell pink bathmat.

Chapter Thirty-four

Everyone argued over where Humberto should sleep. The best place would have been the blue bedroom that was occupied by Ellie, as it was on the ground floor at the end of the hall near the porch, in the base of the tower. It was a pretty, many-windowed room, but its real attraction was the fact that it lay so close to the entrance, was practically outdoors: it would be as if the foreigner were scarcely in the house at all. 'It would be best if he didn't have to manage stairs,' Natasha said.

But Ellie did not want to be moved, and eagerly Bernadette leapt in, said why didn't he sleep in Catherine's bed, seeing as she was sleeping in the dining room. Catherine's bed was sitting empty, just there in their room, which was downstairs too. So he still wouldn't have to manage the stairs. Please, could he? She could look after him. Clearly this was inappropriate.

So in the end, he did have to manage the stairs, up to an old servant spare in the roof, and it was only in the triumphal course of following the stretcher party up there that Ellie realised this meant he'd be sleeping in the room next door to Rosa's. At once she began offering to swap, but it was too late now, Natasha told her firmly.

Ellie looked at Ruaridh's sister in astonishment. She

wondered, with a shock something like cold water sluicing through her brain, whether it was possible that Natasha was really clever. Cleverer than her, cleverer than Ruaridh, maybe, in spite of being a woman, in spite of growing vegetables and being so busy, which everyone said was clever but secretly knew wasn't, because if you thought about Einstein, who was the cleverest man in history, well, he wasn't busy, was he, whereas poor people were often very busy indeed and they couldn't be clever at all, because if they were then they wouldn't be poor.

Yes – it was possible, from Natasha's tone of voice, that she had foreseen this whole dreadful situation. Ellie felt that she was somehow being punished as she watched her sister-in-law deftly turn down the sheets and draw the curtains. There seemed to be sadistic pleasure in her preparations.

Unhappily Ellie watched George unloading Humberto onto the bed. He was wearing George's dressing gown, and this unnerved her further.

'Sam and Rosa can swap,' she said.

'Why should they need to swap?' asked Natasha, even though she must have known, because Ellie had drawn her aside in the hall and told her, about the diary, and about how Rosa had now climbed into the bath on top of him. Ellie didn't know what to say in the face of Natasha's sour mischief. In fact, she felt as if she were being confronted by a new and disturbing version of Natasha for the second time in as many minutes, because she had never really thought of Natasha as being particularly mischievous, either. If she had thought about her sister-in-law at all, it had always been as somebody who *did* things, not somebody who *was* things; in the same way as children think about their mothers. Natasha bustled, had daughters, read books, grew cabbages, cleaned her own house (all of it), answered the phone to friends, mulched flowerbeds, cooked with strange cuts of meat. Somewhere in this house, once a year, her activities intersected with Ellie's own still life, and Ellie had always assumed that it was pleasant.

She left the room.

Chapter Thirty-five

In awkward silence, the women heard a round-up of the week's current affairs from the radio on the shelf. A sombre-nosed reporter reminded his microphone, told the women in the kitchen, how on Monday a sixth hunger-striker had died in the Maze, and that the dead man's name was Martin Hurson, and that his age was twenty-nine. Margaret Thatcher had once more decried the strike as the IRA's last card. Peter, what did you make of this? he asked.

Ellie, still drying up helpfully, said, 'Silly boy.' A sudden gush of Natasha's rinsing tap almost drowned her out. 'Don't you think? It's very selfish, killing themselves like that.'

'The men say it isn't suicide.'

'Well of course they'd say that. They're good Catholics, like you and Ruaridh, they wouldn't dare say that, would they? I mean, it's a sin.'

'I feel sorry for them.'

'Really? I think they're just showing off.'

'Like children. Yes, that's the thing, they're children.'

'Oh, I know. Their poor mothers.'

'I wouldn't say they're *good*. Good Catholics, to have killed people, or do whatever things they've done.'

'Rosa says he was innocent,' said Bernadette, slouched

alone at the table behind them. 'She says he was tortured into making his confession.'

'But I do feel sorry for them,' said Natasha, ignoring her.

'Sam says Rosa's a religious fanatic,' her daughter informed them.

'I'm sure he didn't. Stop telling tales.'

'I'm not!'

'Go and get into your nightie, Bernadette. I'll come and tuck you in. No,' she continued, once her daughter had noisily gone, 'I do feel sorry for them. It's sad, isn't it, that they should be so desperate, be grown men and feel like children.' Natasha carefully balanced an ashet in the rack. 'Ruaridh used to break his things, you know, when we were children. When he was upset.' She laughed. 'But then our father beat him, for breaking the things. So after that, he cut himself, did you know that? I imagine he told you. He hurt himself worse than our father could hurt him with beatings. It's one way of doing it.' She put her hands back into the sink. 'When you're children.'

Ellie was silent. She watched Natasha's back, the hula of her waist as she washed things. She wondered if Natasha were really telling the truth about this: whether Ruaridh, her husband, her great protector, could really once have committed such weak and vile self-martyrings. She thought that on balance she did not believe it, preferred to believe what he'd told her, that the scars were relics of schoolboy pacts of bonding. 'And you, Natasha?' she asked, flustered.

'Oh, I wrote a diary. Unlike Rosa's, with a lock. And then I burned it, once I'd grown up.' She was trying to find a place to put the dripping vinaigrette jug, which was difficult, because Ellie had stopped drying up and the rack was chock-a-block. She was frowning at it. 'What about you?' she absent-mindedly asked.

'Me?' Ellie exclaimed. 'But I never *was* upset.'

176

Why would you be? she wondered, still watching Natasha. Why in the world would you want to go round being upset? It was not a pleasant feeling. And how unfair of Natasha to bring Rosa into it. Ellie felt as if she might be about to start crying. It was not a pleasant feeling. She turned and ran out of the room.

At last, Natasha turned to look back at her, but by now there was only a flash of russet silk on the upward steps. A slim-fingered hand on the wall, and she was gone. Natasha stood staring at the closing door, and by herself heard a jollier reporter talk of the preparations for the imminent wedding of Diana and Charles, which Ellie would have enjoyed far more than she did, she thought; she found that sort of thing rather boring.

After a pause, she took the steps, opened the door to the hall and called. 'Ellie! They're talking about the wedding!'

But nobody answered, so she shrugged, and got on.

Chapter Thirty-six

Bernadette could not work out why her aunt had come into her room to talk to her about these things. 'I think it's appalling,' said Aunt Ellie, 'that your mother should allow him to remain here.'

'Please don't say nasty things about Mummy,' said Bernadette sternly from her bed. She was feeling treacherous for liking the smell of Aunt Ellie's perfume.

'She's a bit naive, that's all. But it's not your mummy we need to worry about, is it?'

Bernie didn't know what *nigh eve* meant. 'Who do we need to worry about?' she asked.

'Humberto,' Ellie told her.

'In case he dies?'

'He's not going to die. He's perfectly fine. They've put him to bed upstairs. In your father's dressing gown.'

Bernie thought about Humberto, about how much she had liked him, and how much he liked Rosa. She thought about Rosa getting into the bath with him. He must have been bare. She hadn't been able to properly see, but he must have been. 'I don't really know what's going on, Aunt Ellie,' she said.

'Poor little thing. Why should you understand? It's all

far too horrible for a sweet thing like you.' Ellie stooped and kissed her niece's head, brushed her cheek and let her hand rest there. 'Sometimes people aren't what they seem,' she said. 'Sometimes they can seem quite nice and really be quite violent. I think it would be better if you stayed away from him.'

'Humberto isn't violent.'

'He kills animals, Bernadette. He preys on things.'

'So does Sam.'

'That's different. Sam does it for sport, not to feed on. You have to be careful of men's appetites, Bernadette.'

'They do eat a lot. Daddy eats a lot.'

Ellie sniffed. 'Did you have a nice time on the rope slide?' she brightly asked, as if she were being very valiant.

'Yes.'

Ellie sat down on the edge of the bed, even though there wasn't really room for her, and patted the blankets that covered Bernie's chest. 'You should stay away from Humberto,' she said.

'Why?'

Ellie cocked her head. She was frowning at the painful news she must deliver to her angelic niece, who only this afternoon had been innocently playing with her much-loved cousin, Ellie's own boy, dear Sam, who was being so brave about everything. How tragic, she thought, that this summer idyll should have been shattered by the acts of the brutish foreigner who had insinuated himself into their lives. She wished she weren't the one who had to disillusion little Bernadette. 'We think Humberto was the one who attacked Julab,' she softly said, and patted Bernie's hand. Poor mite. She seemed shell-shocked by the news. Impulsively, Ellie drew Bernie's head in towards her breast and stroked her hair. It wasn't as nice as stroking

Rosa's hair. Rosa's hair was softer and also had more bounce. This deepened Ellie's sympathy for Bernadette, and she kissed her niece's forehead in commiseration before giving her a brave, encouraging sort of smile and leaving the room. She closed the door very tenderly behind her.

'Liar,' said Bernadette, tossing her head sideways on the pillow and gazing out at Catherine's empty bed.

Chapter Thirty-seven

The cries of fielding cricketers, the softly televised thwack of ball on bat, sounded intermittently in the drawing room. There was something strong and steady about it. The shared confidence of the silence before the batting sound, its stateliness. The recurring, like a slow pendulum, of that sound, coming from just the same place in all the wide green field.

Here in the room, there was also the solid calm of the raising and resettling of a glass filled with drink, the lazy leonine chests of concentrating men. Eleanor Gill pushed open the door and saw them. Spectating: she liked that. You could slip in beside it. George and Sam, on separate sofas, the strength of their fine male attention fixed on something else.

It was as if men's brains had bigger lungs, Ellie thought. They could pay attention to something and not be out of breath at all. It was as if their interest were always pitched at the same grand and singular level, and merely swung like the boom on a yacht towards one object or another. She relished this simplicity. It was reassuring in its purity and strength, its constancy. Whereas a woman's care was scattered, and could swell, or contract, around a dozen different points at once. With women, you could never be sure how much of their attention you were getting because the amount kept changing. With men, you knew that it was all or none, and Ellie was happy with either of those. It was not embarrassing to be unnoticed, but to be noticed and neglected – this was what mortified her. To be half-heard, half-answered, half-seen, made her feel a half-thing. Whereas so long as she was unseen, she could say to herself: it's all right, they simply haven't seen me, and this in no way detracted from her being there, and being a whole thing.

Watching men who hadn't seen you was just like looking in on sleeping children.

Or people on television.

And it was actually quite nice, in a way, to be so invisible that you could pat your hair, or even examine them: you could stare, you could do that, when the men hadn't seen you were there. Briefly she let her eyes rest on George. His was not the sort of face that appealed to her: she preferred men with broader brows, good strong blockish heads. Still, it belonged to George and, however much you disliked some of the peculiar things he said, the good thing about George was that he was a man of great confidence.

At times, of course, he had driven Ruaridh mad, with his outrageous and frankly treasonous statements. 'There is no such thing as Scottish nobility,' George had once said. Making harsh quips about the 'naive and foolish mess' over Darien that had led to the Union Settlement, and then something about Queen Anne sending spies up from London to bribe the big names further into signing, and she remembered George laughing about this, saying, 'They came home with half the money still in the caskets. Not because the Scots couldn't be bought – no – but because they managed to buy them so cheaply. Half price. That's Scottish nobility.' And then, ignoring Ruaridh's thunderous silence, he had gone on about the Clearances, as if this too were a suitable topic for discussion on a summer's evening.

182

No excuse for it, he'd said, not like in England where Norman conquerors came and screwed the natives, oh no, they screwed their own kin here – *screwed*, that was the actual term he had used. Nothing very noble about betting all your money on the wrong horse and then turning out your poor relations to put up the cash for the next one, he had said. Nothing very noble about deporting the people who'd trusted you to keep their land, in their name. 'Treachery,' he'd said. And then Ruaridh, who had been getting redder and redder, had said how that was bollocks, and George was just jealous, being from the peasantry, and that was when she'd stood up, realising it really wasn't right for her to be here. And then Ruaridh was saying how actually, he'd been too kind, George's family hadn't even been peasants, had they, they were bleeding little itinerant labourers, and then he kept repeating the word *itinerant* very slowly and carefully, as if he were very pleased with it, or pleased with being able to pronounce it despite all the wine. Anyway, she had slipped out of the room and left them to it. Natasha had looked as if she were going to intervene, but really Ellie thought it was better just to leave men to get on with these things, wasn't it. She could still hear Ruaridh as she closed the kitchen door behind her. *Sell a couple of curtains and—*

George shouldn't have provoked him, of course.

But anyway, the good thing about George, thought Ellie, looking at him still, was that whatever his faults, he had a great deal of *confidence*. His masculine sureness outweighed his strangeness, she felt. Vagaries of his that she saw as effeminate – his tendency to toy with words instead of taking them seriously, his silly ideas that really must also have been games because no one would actually think such things, would they, and it was wrong of him to provoke people with them – his skittish impetuousness – all these could be forgiven, in the end, because he always sounded so *sure*. His voice had a sonorous and only faintly brogued depth. So that the words, no matter how much they disturbed you, did always seem to be coming up from rock. From a solid confidence. And confidence, in Ellie's mind, was a grandly male preserve. If a woman was confident, it was because she was possessed of a great husband, father, brother, son: it was from them that her confidence came. Of course, lots of women lacked all of these and yet appeared sure of themselves. Jolly good actresses, Ellie felt.

She was so glad she had Sam.

Look at him there. Paying all his attention to the white-clad men on television. Looking at him, you would never have guessed what he was going through.

Julab was Sam's best friend. They'd got him when Sam was seven, in the spring of the year that he went away to school. Hardly planned, really, the dog had been sired on the sly by old Fergal, Ruaridh's dog. Who'd have thought he still had it in him? Got his leg over a gamekeeper's bitch, lucky, really, that she also happened to be pedigree lab. Otherwise they couldn't have taken one, could they. The gamekeeper should have had her spayed. It was his responsibility, really, to keep her kennelled when she was on heat. Ellie plucked at the loose ballooning silk of her sleeve. What was she thinking? Oh yes, that was it. Sam's face, when they'd taken him there and told him he could choose. So excited, but serious too, he hadn't rushed it.

Why did you pick that one? Ruaridh had asked him on the way home.

Because he liked me, Sam had said, and Ruaridh had seemed displeased by this answer. He kept trying to make Sam say that there had been some other reason, kept pointing out other possible advantages that the puppy had over the others, and waiting for Sam to agree, which he did, of course, but far too listlessly.

He likes me, Mummy, she remembered Sam saying,

holding him awkwardly in his small hands in the kitchen at home. Look, he's trying to kiss me.

You're going to spoil him, said Ruaridh, who had walked in without them noticing. Stop that.

They've got germs on their tongues, said Ellie, by way of softening the paternal decree. She often did this: agreed with her husband's discipline, of course, but at the same time made a gentler route for it that her children could choose to understand instead. It didn't matter, did it, as long as they did what Ruaridh meant. She was trying to help.

Let's take him to see his daddy, she had said. And Fergal hadn't recognised his progeny, but the puppy rolled onto its back, wagging its tail, and so they got along well all the same.

Sam adored the puppy. I sometimes think it was a mistake, said Ruaridh, getting that dog for Sam. He's obsessed with it.

Because Sam talked about Julab as if the dog were a person, and, when he was telling stories about him, would become so animated that he actually laughed, which was a thing Sam rarely did. Laughing as if he couldn't help it. One morning Ruaridh found him curled up in the dog bed, in his pyjamas, sleeping, with the labrador's nose driven deep into his armpit. He's just worried about going away to school, said Ellie afterwards, wanting to placate Ruaridh.

What's he got to be worried about? Has he told you he's worried?

No.

Needs to stop behaving like a bloody invert. Needs to start behaving like a man.

But it had all been fine after that, Ellie recalled, because Ruaridh had taken Sam out shooting that afternoon. His first time, with the children's rifle that Ruaridh had learned on. They'd come back with a rabbit that Sam had shot.

Ruaridh was bluffly satisfied and Sam had stood still and held the rabbit by its legs like Ruaridh told him, so that Ellie could take a photograph. Smile, she said. Say cheese.

And clever Margaret had skinned it, made a stew.

Dogs are for hunting with, said Ruaridh to his son at the table, and Sam had nodded. Well done, Ruaridh had said then. I think you'll be a fine shot.

It was fun, said Sam, in a level voice that sounded dreadfully bleak to Ellie's ears but was probably just the way that boys spoke when they were learning how to be men. I enjoyed it, he said. You couldn't keep them young for ever, she'd told herself, watching him. You had to let them go. You couldn't be selfish. So she'd smiled at him, and said, Jolly good, darling. I'm awfully proud of you. Shall we have some ice-cream?

And soon after that he had stopped building radios, and she was glad not to be finding bits of wire scattered all over the tack room any more, but in a funny way she missed it too.

Sitting on the sofa, Sam watched the tiny bowler's hooping arm, the progression of the even smaller ball, that red dot that was the whole point of it, passing from here to there and round again, dragging the camera lens after it like a girl's arse pulling at your eye.

He wasn't remembering anything. His brain was hushed and quiet. He was watching the cricket highlights, and that was all.

There were many things he chose not to recall. He did not, for instance, remember tying Fergal up to the ash tree by the dyke and carefully throwing stones at him, as if he were skimming them across a lake, the same calm concentration, only more important. He did not remember how pleased he'd been when he hit the dog's flank, and it had yelped, tugging panicky at the lead. And then it had realised

186

it was stuck there while Sam had aimed another. Something like pleasure: winning, at least. And more than that: knowing, once you'd hit your target, that this was what you were doing, because it was done. Not having to choose any more. A kind of relief, then. Being able to hit it harder next time.

Dogs were for hunting with.

They put up the birds and you shot them. Dead rabbits excited them. They liked to kill things, and you could be like them.

You could tie them up and stone them.

The more you did it, the more you felt like you were only one of them, but you could be the king of them. King of the dog that ruled your own one. The more you did it, the more you knew the things you'd known all along.

When he went back into the house, after the first time, he found that everything was much easier than before. He had a secret, curled inside him. Mother and Rosa were doing their special things, and he knew that neither of them loved him, like he'd always known, but now it didn't hurt. Finally it made sense: they were human and he was not.

When Mother came and tucked him into bed, and said, Darling—

when she softly brushed a strand of his dark hair sideways from his forehead and said,

You weren't too upset, were you? About the rabbit—

he wanted to laugh or cry or something, because he had a secret. If only you knew, he thought, you wouldn't be kind to me then. Then you would let all the hate out, and say all the things I know you're thinking.

Mother called everyone Darling. Mother was always nice, always polite.

She sighed.

Sam said No.

She smiled. I love you poppet, she said.

Sam looked back at her. She was lying. Wasn't she? It was horrid, not knowing sometimes, but then he remembered the secret again, that he had done, bought and paid for and given, non-returnable, and it was a relief, again, to know that he was right. Even if she thought she loved him, it was only because she didn't know what he had done. She didn't know what he was really like. It wasn't the real him she was loving. And he would never tell her, never take the secret back, give it up, because he liked so much the kindness in her eyes at times like this, he liked so much the quietness of her voice as if he were already sleeping, he liked the way she was looking only at him, and she was looking at him as if he were good. He liked the feel of it, even if it wasn't real, or especially because it wasn't real. He would keep the feel of it, by keeping the secret of his badness tucked inside him. He would just remember, of course, that what felt like love was not real.

He liked feeling something he knew wasn't really his. If you knew it wasn't yours to begin with, then you couldn't ever lose it.

When he drowned Fergal four years later, he didn't even enjoy it. It was almost an irrelevance, and yet necessary, there in the loch in July, up to his waist in water with the great dog held under his arm, pushed down. You mustn't forget, see, you mustn't forget you were bad. It had to keep on being done. Just enough to be always remembered.

It had been nice in a way, feeling Fergal go still. Go limp, and suddenly heavy, so that Sam had to heave his lungs to lift him. He felt like John the Baptist. All the water spilling like glass. The struggle of staggering under the weight, the sopping barrel body, the paws that trailed against him, as he carried Fergal safely to the shore.

I threw a stick for him, he told them. He was there, and then he wasn't.

Sam was neither ashamed nor proud of such lies. They didn't seem like lies at all. It was just that everyone had two lives, and nobody wanted to know your other one, not really. You told the truth about the way they wanted you to seem.

Father was sad, but said, Well, he's had a good innings. But also Father had taught Julab to raise grouse now and retrieve; he was going to be a good gun dog. Just like his pa, that was what Father said.

And Sam had a secret that was stronger than ever, would never break now. He loved the secret of his badness. It held him tightly, just as he held it. It explained everything and he knew that it would never lie to him. Never lie to him, and never leave him, nor send him away – the bad things that you'd done, they were there for ever, with you, weren't they.

It had been nice in a way, to hold the dog's head under as it fought against him. Not nice to kill him, because Sam had nothing against Fergal, but thrilling to hear that certainty inside his head that crowed: *This is me*. To know you were bad and not be afraid of it, that was the thing, as Fergal went still. And not be so weak that you would go crying it to everyone else, hoping to be rescued, and only upsetting them. To know you were bad and to keep it hidden, like a grown-up, that was the thing. The more his secret grew, the safer he knew he was from telling it. The worse he was, the more its certainties caressed him.

Yet the younger boys at school were not particularly afraid of Sam, for his cruelties towards his fellow pupils were casual and inconsistent. There was little danger at school of feeling loved, little need to protect yourself against the lie. In general he felt quite safe for so long as he remained within the school's walled confines. The coldness of the

189

pitches, the intermittent prefect beatings and the lumpen dumplings on his dinner plate, seemed just right. The way the boys lived, the way that they were ruled by masters yet still violently cared to rule each other, like dogs – Sam knew how to do that.

It was coming home that he could not stand. The only good thing about home was Julab—

Here boy! he shouted. Do you recognise me?

– and Julab did, he must, because he was sniffing Sam's leg and wagging his tail. He didn't do that to everyone, did he? – but the rest was sticky and unbearable. Mother and Rosa being nice to him. Seven's too young for girls, said mother when the time came, but he knew the real reason Rosa wasn't being sent away yet was that Mother loved her and wanted to keep her. He'd always known that.

At home, there was nice food and his bedroom that he slept in by himself. It felt strange, it felt of good things from long ago, coming to trouble and suffocate the new thing he'd become. When he lay here, warm and clean, he was feeling Mummy stooping over him even though he couldn't remember it, because it was from way back, before his recall. Her big eyes looming over him, and her hair. The smell of her, the sound of her, the exact ways of her voice when it still sounded like a song.

He couldn't remember it at all.

But he felt it sometimes, like now, and when he felt it, he wanted to scream. It was horrible. It made his legs go rigid with fright.

Sam on the sofa in nineteen eighty-one scratched his thigh through the fabric of his jeans. The cricket was finished.

'Hello, Mother,' he said, seeing her there in the armchair, watching him. He wondered how long she'd been there; it was strange the way that women had the patience for that sort of thing, for sitting.

190

It seemed to give her a jump when he spoke, even though she was watching his face, must have realised that he was looking back at her. 'Oh, hello!' she quivered brightly. She came and sat beside him, like she often did, she often sat too close to him. She was curling her body sideways on the cushions, she was folding her arm along the sofa back behind his head. He ducked his own neck forward, frowning.

'Are you all right?' she was asking.

'Of course I'm all right. I'm not a child, Mother.'

'We'll leave tomorrow morning.'

'Will you?' asked Uncle George.

'We can't,' said Sam. 'Julab's still at the vet's.'

Ellie chewed her bottom lip. 'Oh,' she said. 'I'd forgotten about that. No! I mean, of course I hadn't forgotten about Julab, that's why we must leave, isn't it, we can't stay here with that man in the house and Natasha won't ask him to leave. We can't stay here after what he's done to poor Julab. That's – that's what I mean.'

'That man? I presume you are talking about Humberto or myself,' said George. 'I wonder which it is.'

'Stop it!' said Ellie, agitated. 'Please, George, just once, stop pretending you don't understand!'

'But I would be a little more careful,' said George, 'about whom you accuse of attacking the dog. Thus far, your only evidence seems to be the fact that Humberto is Spanish. It is hardly a watertight case.'

'Humberto found the body. The person who finds the body is always the prime suspect, George. It's elementary.'

George was smiling. 'I think it's a great deal more likely that the culprits were boys from the town,' he said. 'Or drunken tourists. The campsite in the woods is strewn with cheap lager cans. It could have been any number of people.'

'Here? Here in your garden?'

George shrugged.

'That man,' said Ellie, and her lip was trembling now, 'has been preying on my daughter.'

George turned his head and contemplated the empty fireplace. 'Rosa is a grown woman,' he said.

'Just wait,' Ellie told him, shaking her head. 'When it's your daughters being seduced by a Dago vagrant with no education, I don't think you'll be so sanguine, George. One of these days you'll have to come down out of that ivory tower and grapple with the real world.'

'You're hardly in a position to advise, dear girl. Besides, let's be entirely clear: whatever amorous activities Humberto and Rosa are engaged in, it has absolutely no bearing on what happened to that dog.'

'I'm establishing his character.'

'I see. Are Sam and I the jury? Will we decide it between the three of us, here in the drawing room?'

'He is a moral degenerate.'

'I'd say he has excellent taste.'

'Don't be disgusting! She's your niece!' said Ellie.

George was laughing. 'Oh, come on,' he was saying, but he hadn't seen Sam, or rather, had seen him rise from the sofa but had not seen the look on his face as he drew his elbows back and launched himself forward.

Ellie screamed. George and Sam were fighting, there on the sofa, with their bare hands, she was quite sure that that was what was happening. Sam's back was bare around the waist, his shirt was rucked up. His jean-clad legs were pinning his uncle's, either side, and he was doing something terrible with his arms. She was screaming at the back of his dark head, but now his head was turning, the two of them seemed to be spinning, and rolling, onto the floor. Why weren't they screaming too? Why weren't they shouting? She stopped screaming, because she thought she must be wrong about them failing to shout, she thought maybe she just couldn't hear them. But there was nothing, now, and it was even worse than listening to the shrieking sound of her own voice. Just the sound of their huffing, and grunting, and the sound of knuckles on flesh. Ellie didn't know what to do. She ran out into the hall. 'Natasha!' she cried.

Chapter Thirty-eight

They were all stuck here now, thought Ellie miserably, undressing for bed. Stuck for the duration. They could hardly take themselves off, now that Sam had laid into George like that. Now that George had forgiven him, which was the really galling thing. Of course you won't want us here now, she'd hopefully said as Natasha swabbed her husband's lip, but when he asked them to stay and said, No, Sam's not to blame, it's been a strange day – well, it put her in a very difficult position. She could hardly insist against the wishes of the wronged party. Blast Sam, blast him, and blast Ruaridh too, for not being here when she needed him. Blast him for turning yellow and thin and disappearing.

She should go upstairs and check that Rosa was in her own room, she knew she should, but she didn't have the energy to deal with her daughter's bed either way. She couldn't face finding it empty and having to steel herself for what she might find next door. She couldn't face finding Rosa in it, there where she ought to be, righteous and cross at being checked up on, a scene. Either way, there would be a scene. Ellie sighed and unclasped her necklace, the amber beads that went so nicely with the russet silk shirt. She laid them on the little writing desk and sat on the edge of the bed, naked.

Her nightdress was folded under her pillow, where she'd placed it that morning. What a long time ago. She groped for it, and when she found it she tugged it out quite desperately, and buried her face in its white embroidered cotton, stitched in England.

She had been planning on crying into the nightdress. She was bemused to find that she couldn't. Her face was trembling, her ribcage was shaking, but no tears came.

She looked up, at the blue doves that flocked block-printed on the walls, and she clutched the nightdress tighter in her hands as if she were afraid of them, afraid of the birds.

Chapter Thirty-nine

Humberto lying upstairs in his blankets smiled like a ghost. He watched his lady as she tidied things away that weren't hers. She was picking up a pile of wire coat hangers from off the top of the chest of drawers and stuffing them underneath it, she was dusting the mirror with her sleeve. When he asked her what she was doing, she said that she was making it nice for him. 'You make it nice anyway,' he said. 'I rather have you than a tidy bedroom. And you so *un*tidy, *carina*.'

'Sh.'

He watched her as she continued. He stopped smiling. 'Why are you strange now, Rosa?'

She laughed. 'I'm not strange.' Walked over to the primrose yellow curtains drawn across the window, and reached up to pull down a cobweb that was hanging in tatters from the top of the hessian cloth. A spider must have spun its web across the closed-up folds of the curtains when they were drawn aside; they couldn't have been pulled over the window for a very long time. And now the web was broken, a dangling old breath here where you could see it, she was just sweeping it into her hand. 'You like things tidy,' she said. 'I know you do. I've seen your tent.' She shifted to the wastepaper basket. Humberto liked the way she walked;

it had a fine snappy roll to it, a proudness in the hips. Now she was standing still, though, frowning. 'Are you all right?' he asked her.

'Me? Yes.' The cobweb was sticking to Rosa's hand. She was glad of this. 'The cobweb's sticking to my hand,' she explained. She spent a great deal of time, poured a great deal of care, on the task of picking its tacky shreds from her skin, pinching them off her fingertips. She stooped, in the end, to wipe the threads off against the wastepaper basket's rim.

'It doesn't mind, you know,' said Humberto.

'*I* don't mind,' she absent-mindedly corrected him. '*I* don't mind, *it* doesn't matter. I know,' she said, standing up again and looking at him properly for the first time since she'd come into the room. 'I know you don't,' she said, looking at his greatly beloved face, and it hadn't changed, had it. His face still looked the same to her. She still loved him, then, didn't she. Yes. She breathed out with grave relief. 'Anyway,' she said. 'There you are. Spick and span.'

His gaze seemed to hold her rather coldly now. She wondered guiltily if he'd guessed what she'd been feeling, guessed that she had been so unsure as to whether she could still love him after what he'd done, guessed she'd come in here as a little test for herself, her eyes lined with litmus paper to measure her affections when the sight of him washed in. But it had come up all right, hadn't it. Like she'd known it would, hadn't she. Of course she loved him, even now he was no longer near death. Tentatively she tried to smile at him, but his brow was crumpled and his jaw was stern. 'Spic?' Humberto said.

'Oh,' she breathed, relieved again for the second time in half a minute, 'not like that,' she smiled, shaking her head. 'It's a phrase. Spick and span. It means neat and tidy. Shipshape. Neat and tidy, I mean.' She sat down on the edge of the bed and then she got up again, pulled the covers aside and wriggled down close to him, folded the blankets back over both of them.

'It's all right,' she carefully said. 'I don't know why you did it, Humberto, but it doesn't change the way I feel about you.' She kissed his shoulder. 'I still love you,' she whispered.

'Did what?'

'Hurt Julab. It was wrong of you, but it doesn't make me stop loving you. Nothing can make me stop loving you.' Ardently brushing away the doubts of a moment ago, briskly, chasing them with the sweeping of her fingertips over his skin. 'You know that, don't you?'

'You think I hurt Julab?'

'I know you did.' She pushed the fabric of his borrowed pyjama shirt aside and kissed his breast. 'You were the only one there, you were so late, I was waiting for you on the island, Humberto. I thought you'd changed your mind. I was waiting in the rhododendron bushes, I was starting to feel stupid. And then I thought, no, something must have happened, you wouldn't just leave me waiting there, Sam must have stopped you from coming to me somehow, found you.' She swallowed, frowning. 'But he hadn't. Sam was indoors with Catherine, and then he went off for a walk, he walked into Callander, Bernie saw him. He went past her at the falls. I don't think Sam saw you at all, did he?'

'No, Sam didn't see me.'

'I was waiting for you for such a long time.' She laid her head down sideways on his chest. 'Nobody saw you,' she said. 'Catherine was sleeping. You can tell me, if you like, why you did it. If you want to talk about it. If you don't, I'll understand. I know there must have been a reason. Maybe he attacked you. Your shorts were torn. It was self-defence, was it. Julab can get quite funny when he's got a bone or something, he can get quite possessive. Not with birds, of course, Daddy would have shot him for that, but with bones, sometimes he does. Did he have a bone? I'm sure he did. He probably thought you were going to try and take it from him, and went for you, and you threw the thing at him to stop him.'

'No.'

She lay very silently against him, and then she began to breathe again. 'Well, the thing is, it doesn't matter.' She was blinking. 'I don't mind why you did it, Humberto.'

'I didn't do it.'

'You don't need to lie to me. There's no need. You can tell me anything, Humberto. Nothing will stop me loving you. I don't know why you did it, but I don't need to. I know you're you and I know that I love you.'

'Why do you keep saying this?'

'Because I want you to understand!' Tearfully she raised her head and looked, over his dark throat, past his tightened jaw to where his eyes met hers. 'Don't look at me like that,' she told him. 'There's no need to be afraid.'

'I'm not afraid, Rosa. I am sad.'

'It's okay.'

'No. It's not okay, that you think I did this thing. It's not okay, Rosa.'

She sighed, perplexed, screwing up her face. 'Just. Oh. I wish you'd believe me. I know everything,' she said. 'I worked it out and it all makes sense. Why else would you have left me waiting on the island for such a long time?'

'I go to find a treasure for you. I go up into the woods and I tear my trousers on the fence. I find you a bird's egg and I bring it, for you, I bring it to the island but then first I see this dog, that is all.'

'Stop it! There isn't any bird's egg! And why else would you have run away afterwards? And nearly died.'

'I am searching for your brother.'

'No, I think you wanted to escape. Maybe part of you

199

even wanted to get lost and not come back. Because you felt bad, even if it wasn't your fault. You didn't want to hurt me. But I was so scared, Humberto I was so afraid I'd lost you That was when I knew, that anything's all right, and I can bear anything that you do, as long as I don't lose you. Thinking you'd gone, and then seeing you and thinking you might be gone for ever, leave me, die. It was worse than any silly small thing that you might have *done*. Because the things that you've done, they aren't *you*, are they? And I can forgive you anything that you do, as long as you always are. If you can just be you, and I can just be me.'

'I think you are very wrong.'

'Why won't you let me? Why won't you let me forgive you? Why won't you just admit it, and let me?'

'Because it is wrong, Rosa.'

'I love Julab! I do. I'm not saying that what you did is okay, you know, I'm not saying that at all, if you think I am heartless or – amoral – if that is what you're thinking.'

'No. You are not heartless. Too much heart, Rosa, too much brain, not enough guts.'

'Why are you doing this? You think I'm not brave? Do you think it doesn't take guts for me to come here, and forgive you?'

'I don't mean these guts, Rosa, I don't speak of *cojones*, I think you have those, no, I speak of *instinto*.'

She was shaking her head. 'I forgive you. I forgive you,' she was saying, over and over again, as if it were a shiver in her vocal cords, under the mended sheet, the weight of blankets.

Humberto swallowed. 'Three kinds of cleverness, we say: the heart, the head, the *instinto*. In the stomach, the guts. Like the shamans take from birds to make predictions of the future.'

'I forgive you. I forgive you.' She was repeating it like a

prayer or a spell, the ceaseless rustling of her lips against the Paisley that covered his skin.

'Your brain says I do this thing, because of informations. Your big heart says you forgive me. But no *instinto*, Rosa. This stomach of yours, it does not know me, does it? You are thinking and feeling, but you are not knowing, not at all.'

She stopped her whispering with a jerk. 'Everyone knows!' she pleaded. 'Mum told them. Everyone knows, or suspects, but we are still looking after you, nobody is throwing you out, Humberto, so you can stop, you know, you can just stop. Don't tell me the truth if you don't want to, but please, don't lie to me. Don't. It isn't fair.'

'Please go.'

'They can't prove anything. Nobody *saw*.'

'I don't want to hear you any more.'

'Do you think you have to be perfect for me to love you? That's what it is, isn't it? But you don't, I'm not, I'm not perfect at all.' Her hands became more frantic on his body the more his voice flattened itself, withdrew. She was determined not to lose him a second time. Especially she would not let him choose his own removal. She would not let him take his heart back, just when his body had been returned to her, was here, so frustratingly close to her. What good was it if he shut away his heart in the dark where it would rot? The possibility that she might only be permitted to see him as the whole world saw him, chilled her. To be next to him and as distant as a shop assistant, she thought would kill her.

She was gripping the other side of his ribcage now, his muscled torso, she had shoved her hand up under the pyjama shirt's hem – she needed to touch his raw flesh. She was trying to say, *It's us. It's you in your nakedness I want.* She needed to give him hers. She felt strangely ecstatic. *Show me your shame if I show you mine.* 'I bullied a girl at prep school,' she excitedly began. 'I poured sour milk in her coat pockets in the cloakroom, and I called her Pissbreath, and the worst thing was, she really did smell. I was horrible to her, Humberto.' She paused for breath. 'Jefferson,' she said. 'He was the tennis coach, I had a thing with him, last year. When they found out, I cried and said he had made me. Can you imagine? So I know, you see, I know about lying and saying it wasn't your fault. I know about trying to make everything fit. I know about trying to make it all be part of the way you want to be and not the way that you are.'

'Be quiet!' shouted Humberto, sitting upright, pushing her away from him, but she wouldn't let go.

'I refused to go to the police and the other teachers said I was too nice. They were angry with me, Humberto, for being too nice! I must have been very good, don't you think, for everyone to believe me? I wrote a fake diary. I used different pens and everything to make it look real, and then I let my roommate accidentally find it. She thought she was so clever to look inside it, but she wasn't at all, I planned her to. She said sorry to me, after, and it was really eating her up, Claudine, the guilt, how ironic. Your private stuff, she said. But you could tell she was pleased with herself too, so I don't really feel sorry for her. Everyone always does what I want, Humberto! I don't force them, but they do. I always get away with everything! I am so sick of it, you know.'

He was holding her back from him with his hand across her breastbone. She was stretching an arm towards him, trying to touch his shoulder, but he flinched sideways and kept his gaze fixed firmly on her own wide eyes. 'This man loses his job?' he asked.

'Yes. Yes. Now you see!' She laughed but coughed because of the pressure from his hand, which angled its fingers sideways toward her throat when she shifted. 'I've done bad

202

things too. We can be bad and good together, Humberto. Please, take your hand away.'

He loosed his grip gradually, let go. He'd thought she might lunge with an embrace, was ready to throw her off the bed, but she didn't.

Rosa was pleased that he'd done what she asked him in taking his hand away, thought his agreement meant she was doing the right thing, she thought it was working if she only gave a little more, and the useful thing she was discovering about her shame was that there was an awful lot of it to give. She smiled a little smile and leaned back on her haunches, resting her back against the wall before casting the next of her coverings off. Taking her time, positioning her words like fingernails for peeling off sunburnt skin. 'I kissed my brother,' she pronounced. 'With tongues. I got off with him, when we were younger. Nine or ten.' She was regarding Humberto's face devoutly, watching for any sign of disapproval, but he was only looking straight back at her without blinking. 'I was worried I'd make a fool of myself when I had to do it with a real boy, because I didn't know how to, so I wanted to practise, you see. And I was bigger than him, even though he was older than me. I said I'd give him money if he let me, and he said no, but then in the end he agreed. Everyone always agrees with me.' Rosa smiled uncertainly. 'He changed his mind again, we only kissed for five seconds, maybe ten, and then he changed his mind. But when he came back, he still wanted the money and I wouldn't give it to him. I let you kiss me, he was shouting, you said you'd give me five pounds, Rosie. And I just read my comic and said, I don't know what you're talking about. I never kissed you. Because I used to talk like that, like Mum does, all prim and proper. *I'm terribly sorry.* You know how she does? Anyway, she heard him, because he was shouting, and she sent him to his room, and told him he was a liar and a pervert, I heard her, and then she came to talk to me. So I knew I ought to agree with whatever she said, because otherwise, you see, *I* would have been a liar and a pervert. And I didn't want to be.' She moved her arm, he was watching her carefully, but she was only raising her hand in order to pinch her ear lobe between her finger and thumb. 'So then, really, I had to tell the other lie at school. Otherwise Mum might have found out what I was like, and then she might have guessed I was lying before, mightn't she. But why should I care? Why should it matter what Mum thinks? Why should that have mattered more to me than landing Sam in the shit? Or poor Jefferson. They didn't deserve it, did they?' She let her hand drop down again. It seemed to beseech him with the way that it fell. 'Aren't you going to say anything?' she asked him.

'What do you want?'

'I want you to forgive me. Like I forgive you.'

'Absolution.'

'So we can love each other absolutely.'

'I think I don't know you, Rosa.'

'You do. You do, now. I've shown you everything. Well, no, not everything. But I am trying to tell you the truth about what I'm like. So you know I won't judge you, my darling.'

'I am afraid.'

A broad and tranquil smile bloomed across Rosa's cheeks. 'Don't be.'

'No. I am afraid there is nothing for you to judge. I do not have anything to give you. I did not do this thing.'

She stared at him, and tears welled in her eyes. 'Why are you doing this?' she plaintively begged him.

'I think you should go to bed.'

'Please touch me.'

'Rosa.'

'Touch me!'

Humberto reached out a hand and touched the side of her face, and then he took his hand away again.

'You can't even touch me,' smiled Rosa woefully.

'Yes, I just touch you.'

'Not really.' She sniffed, and then her breathing began to gallop faster again. 'It was wrong of me to forgive you,' she said, scrambling off the bed, staggering to her feet. 'It wasn't up to me. And you – you sit there like a king, not admitting anything! I *know*, Humberto. I do. I know you did it.'

'I am sorry you are sad I leave you waiting on the island.'

'Do you think this is about my wounded pride?' Hands on hips in her baggy Blondie T-shirt. 'It's not! It's about *facts*.'

'I tell you *facts*, Rosa! Facts are, I don't know! Okay? This is the facts.' His face was turned towards her as if it had to look that way, had no choice, like a sunflower turned towards the sun. His eyes were parched, like he'd been looking at her too hard. 'Facts are, why do you create stories instead of not knowing the answer? It's so terrible, not knowing, that you have to make lies? It is so easy for you to believe bad things. But I make you the truth, and the truth is a good thing, and no, you don't believe this. Only the bad things. I think you want me to be bad, so that I am like you.'

'You think I'm bad.'

'You tell me all these things, Rosa. I don't ask to know.'

'You think *I'm* bad. At least I'm being honest.'

'No! No, you are not being honest. If you are honest, you love the truth. You have respect for it, okay, and you let it speak, this is what you do if you are honest. But you will not let the truth speak. You want it to say what you have decided. You decide I have done this thing. So, it is done. I think you can go to bed now and sleep.'

'It's not about my pride. I'm not proud. I wouldn't have

told you what I've just told you if I was proud, would I? Would I? I'm not making things up! Not this time! I know I'm not.'

'You say I lie.'

'But not because you are a liar, I just think you're too scared to tell me the truth, that's all. Because I know what it's like, I know it's frightening.'

'Maybe I am not like you, though, Rosa. You assume, but people are different, and maybe I am not afraid of the truth.' His head was tipped back against the wall, his face angled up towards her. 'Ah, but.' He half-laughed, half-sighed. 'This truth about you. Maybe it's better you never tell me this.' A hard knock at the bedroom door made Rosa flinch as if it were knocking on her body. 'Come in,' called Humberto.

It was Natasha's face that appeared above the turned handle. 'Rosa,' she said. 'Would you go and see if Sam's okay? He's just come to blows with George.'

'What?'

'He and George have had a fistfight in the drawing room.'

Rosa started laughing and, once she started, found that it was an intense relief. She was laughing very hard.

'It's not funny,' said her aunt.

'But you're not serious,' Rosa gasped.

'I'm perfectly serious.'

'Then.' Rosa swallowed. 'No. What happened?'

'I don't know. I wasn't there. But would you go and see if Sam's all right? He's locked himself in his room.'

'Yes,' said Rosa. 'Yes, of course.'

Rosa turned to face Humberto, once they were alone again. She couldn't be as bad as he thought, could she, if people asked her to help them. 'Poor Sam,' she said, quite unnecessarily, 'I must go at once.' His room was only two doors down the passage, but still she liked to linger here and enjoy the feeling of being called upon for help in front of Humberto. To show him how good she could be. 'I hope he's all right,' she said. Humberto's face was pale, but it had been pale ever since he'd been dragged in half-dead from the garden. 'Yes, go,' he told her crossly. 'Go to him. Get out!'

'You don't need to be jealous.'

'I'm not jealous. Get out.'

'I have to go anyway. I'm going anyway,' she said, as she wrestled with the door handle. Her T-shirt rode up as she pulled it, exposed the lower cups of her buttocks in black cotton knickers. Just for a second, but Humberto kept staring at where she'd been standing long after she'd gone. She was going to Sam's room, like that. '*Pon tus pantalones*,' he muttered, but no one was there to listen. He gazed around at the empty room, and wondered what he was doing in this place. He'd thought he'd found the world in Rosa's face, but now she seemed a foreign country, as strange as the rest of them.

Chapter Forty

Natasha adjusted the pillows behind her back. She sighed as her pencil slipped sideways into the bedclothes, pulled it back onto the notepad. She was making notes from a library book. 'Why did you do that?' she asked, without looking up, and George paused in the loosening of his tie.

'Do what?'

'Say that it was fine for them to stay. After Sam punched you. Look at your eye.'

'Don't fash. I caught him a nice one on the chin.'

'It's not a competition. Why did you say it was fine.' Her pencil made a soft scratching sound on the paper. 'For them to stay?'

'He's your nephew.'

'Yours too.'

'Well, even more reason, then.'

'I know you don't like him.'

'Nor do you.'

'Yes, I do! I'm very fond of Sam!' The pencil had stopped altogether.

'Then why do you mind them staying?' asked George.

'I don't,' his wife insisted. 'It just wasn't what I would have expected you to do.'

George sighed and took off his shirt. He always thought

it would be nice if Natasha undressed him. Every time he took off his shirt for bed, and looked down at his fingers on the buttons, he liked to imagine his fingers were hers. He was looking at his fingers now, but he was trying to just concentrate on the buttons. Tilting their slippery plastic moons sideways through the holes. He didn't like buttons, they were too precarious, had long gaps in between. He preferred zips, that closed themselves all the way. 'It's been a strange day,' he eventually said.

'Rosa,' said Natasha, but then thought better of saying anything further on that subject. 'I caught Catherine throwing Rosa's things in the river,' she said, by way of deflection.

George laid his shirt down on the chair. 'She said.'

Natasha had looked down at her notepad, but now her eyes flicked back to him. 'Who did?' she asked. George was half-naked by the chair.

'Catherine.'

'I really think we should get a new bed, George. You'll have to give me some money.'

'Not this quarter.'

'It's Rosa, isn't it,' said Natasha. 'You didn't want Rosa to leave.'

'Why do we need a new bed anyway?'

'Because there is something a little odd about making love with your husband in the bed in which his mother died.' She picked up her pencil, although she had no intention of writing anything. 'And the springs have gone.'

'No they haven't.'

'It's ancient.'

'Well, there isn't enough money in the business for me to take extra this quarter. Sales are slow, and lexicographers disgruntled with their pay.'

'Everyone says we're having a boom,' Natasha told him, like she hadn't quite made up her mind yet as to whether it was a party or a disease.

209

'I said I'd give Iain a rise.'

'Oh, for goodness sake, George.' Mice scratched and pattered somewhere in the wainscot.

'I'm sorry,' said George.

Natasha's anger dissipated almost instantly, but seemed to have been replaced by great anxiety. She did not like it when her husband apologised. It was a rare occurrence, and it always unnerved her. 'Don't be silly,' she quickly said. 'You've got nothing to be sorry for.' She set aside *Vegetable Parasites & Problem Fungi* on the bedside table, laid her notepad and pencil on top of its municipal plastic-coated cover. Smoothed her hands nervously over the top of the old satin eiderdown. 'I'm just being silly,' she said. 'The bed's fine.' She watched him walk towards the bath-room door; he had picked up her book. 'What are you doing?' she asked.

'I don't like having library books in the bedroom. Look!' said George, halting in the doorway to open the front of the book, to show her the flap of paper stamped with dates. 'It's like a dirty bib. And this,' he said, closing it again, indicating with distaste the protective cover. 'Plastic pants. Piss-proof sheets. What do they think you're going to do with it, Natasha? Smother it with strawberry jam and use it as a bath toy?' The bathroom door swayed closed behind him.

Natasha could hear the taps running, and closed her eyes.

'I've put it in the bath,' said George, when he came back. 'Seeing as they clearly think that's what you're going to do with it anyway.'

'You haven't.'

George blinked. 'No. Not really.' He sat down on the other side of the bed, with his bare back to her. 'You shouldn't be jealous of Rosa,' he said.

'I'm not. Don't be ridiculous.'

'Good,' said George. Because it wasn't Rosa, she wasn't the reason he'd wanted them to stay – or rather, she was, but not entirely, and not for him. He'd wanted her to stay for Humberto's sake. He had wanted to help the pair of them.

He was staring at his hands. Natasha was saying something else, but he didn't hear her. After a while, the mattress shifted violently beneath him, but he merely felt it as a force of nature, as if he were in a dinghy on the open sea, as if this were what mattresses did. He didn't hear the laboured sighs, or the switching of a bedside light. He might as well have been alone as he sat there thinking about Rosa, in the bath, Rosa and Humberto, and the shape of a bullock's heart. Humberto lying cold, and weak, but not afraid, and if you weren't afraid, perhaps there was no such thing as weakness.

If you weren't afraid to fall, not because you thought you would not fall, which was the bravery of fools, but because you weren't afraid of what lay at the bottom – then what might not be possible?

George had always been brave in his habits of thought; it was his heart and body that had stayed circumscribed, did not venture over the wall.

There had been no fear of any kind in Humberto's eyes, nor shame, when George had held his head. *I am*, his eyes had said. *You are.* And that was all. That was everything, that was all. As if hearts and bodies also could be brave: hearts and bodies also could know weakness and be strong.

He turned around to look at his wife, but she seemed to be sleeping, lying still, a quilted long barrow with its back to him. He got up and walked over to the great mahogany tallboy, and very quietly he pulled out its topmost drawer, the one in which she kept her most private things. Her underwear, her letters, little things the children had

211

given her, her jewellery. A conker. George lifted it from where it lay amid her knickers.

Steadily from the bed, head sideways, Natasha watched him, but she did not move, did not give herself away. Her eyelashes flickered silently, afraid. She had shored herself up against so many disappointments, but she had planted a palisade around her marriage, and its borders had always been the walls of this house. Here with George, in the bedroom they shared, here was the inmost penetralia in which she could brook no crumbling at all. She did not know what George was doing in her drawer. She did not know whether she ought to be jealous of Rosa. She thought of the old Mrs Farrants. She wished that she loved her children more. Many women, she knew, loved their sons and daughters more than the men to whom they'd borne them, and she had often thought, hearing them talk, that she felt sorry for them, but now she was wondering if maybe it wasn't more peaceful to have one's affections arranged that way. But she had decided to fall properly in love with George right at the beginning, and he had made it so easy, with that appealing nature of his. She hadn't really noticed how the other expanses of her heart had gradually been shrinking back towards this one reserve, staked out so blithely so long ago, like a garden in a lush forest that had turned to dust around it.

George stood with his back to the vast carved bed. The polyester satin of the quiet clean knickers ran slippery between his fingers, but their deep waistband of lace seemed to like his fingertips and rest there happily enough with its fine net of midnight blue threads.

He stood for a while, feeling it, the softness, the almost nothingness, and then he closed the drawer as quietly as he'd opened it.

212

Natasha was still watching as he turned with the scrap of fabric clasped in both his hands, as if it were a bird, and it was not until he had almost drawn level with her on his way to the bathroom that she realised what he was holding. She blinked, but she did not close her eyes, and George did not look down at her. He was content to hope that she was sleeping. He was almost content to hope that she was not. The only thing he dreaded was hearing her shout. But he took one step and then another towards the door, and still no loud cry came.

He was standing on the pale pink carpet of the bathroom floor. He was unbuckling his belt, and pulling off his corduroy trousers, his underpants, his socks – he put the knickers carefully on the basin edge so that he could undress – and now, with his clothes on the floor, he was picking up the knickers again, which had got a bit wet, despite his best efforts, because the rim of the basin was still flecked with water drops from Natasha's evening ablutions.

His nakedness in the mirror seemed like someone else. He was surprised when this reflection disappeared, went, rolled upwards over his head like an awning as he bent. His arms had reached down to the ground, and he could see the tufted wool of the carpet quite clearly around his pale long foot, and the dark, dark blue, satin spilling round his skin, letting his ankle in. He could feel the unsteady pricking of his breathing. If he'd ever thought about it, he would have liked to do this slowly, but he hadn't, not until now, not until five minutes ago, and he didn't. He drew the knickers up his legs as quickly as he could and looked in the mirror, feeling foolish in his erection and Natasha's underthings. Feeling both at the same time, deeply: aroused, and ridiculous.

So aroused, as he looked down, and slid his hand between his thighs, cupped his balls in their tight satin sheathing.

213

Then took his hand away, then brought it back, as if he could hardly decide. Ran his fingers across his hardness that was strapped in against him, half visible where it passed beneath the lace.

He lingered especially on the dark spots where the basin had left water marks on the satin. Touching these and frowning in the mirror, but happy in such a protective form of activity, because it was after all the business of ownership. Breathing as steadily as he could, when every muscle in his buttocks fluttered against the beautiful pants, the lace, especially, he could properly appreciate the lace now, its overall effect. A deep cuff of half-cloth, stretched down halfway to the crotch at the front, and arched all the way down the cleft at the back as well. George ran his finger inside the elasticated waistband. The yoke was cut in a V-shape, which gave the wearer the semblance of a shapelier waist. He lifted his hand away, lifted both hands, rested the backs of his upturned fingertips against the side of his ribs, and slowly he let his fingers trail down his sides to his hips. He was standing like that when Natasha came in.

Nothing happened for a long time. For a long time, George stood exactly where he was. In front of the long mirror, with the backs of his knuckles resting where they'd stopped against the satin as it firmly bit into his hips, either side. His hands were curled palm-upwards. Showing, in a way that asked Come instead of telling Go. There was room for all sorts of things inside the space that his hands cupped.

It made him seem less certain about what he was doing in the lacy undergarment, but then, at the same time, more feminine, in this uncertainty.

Natasha stood looking at him. Their eyes had met in the mirrored glass. Both of them were glad of this. It was easier than looking straight into each other's fleshly faces.

It was his reflection in the mirror that she was looking

at. George's body, its leanness, its length, in blue satin panties, in the glass. The way that his hands were rested.

'Come here,' Natasha said.

George turned round, and their real eyes met.

'I'm not gay,' George said.

Almost imperceptibly, Natasha nodded her head, and swallowed, and it was really only from seeing this movement in her throat that George could know for certain she had heard him.

'I'm not angry with you,' she suddenly said. And then, '*George*,' she said, but softly now, steadily and slow, as if she needed to hear his name, to use it on him still, so as to be sure that this was him. And then she turned, and walked back into the bedroom.

She sat down on the edge of the bed, where her sheets were pulled aside. In the new nightdress that Ellie had given her for Christmas she sat looking at her knees. She wished she were not wearing this nightie. The unstained smoothness, the scalloped edge. It didn't know her at all. She was very angry with the nightdress for how lonely it made her feel.

She rose from the bed, quickly crossed the carpet to the gleaming dark chest of drawers. Pulled open the topmost one, in which she kept her most intimate things. Soon found the old purple checked nightdress that she wanted, thin and three times mended: dropped button, ripped seam, broken spaghetti strap. All sewn back. Threw it on the bed, without glancing at the bathroom door, in much the same way that George had not wished to glance at her when earlier he'd made his way past her silent form. Bravery of this kind was a fear of feeling fear. She was pulling at the unfriendly nylon thing, pulling it off over her head.

She was standing like that when George came in. Mid-motion, with her back to him, but this time no mirror in which their eyes might meet. He stood in the doorway watching her nakedness increase. Notch by notch it scaled her spine, the paleness, and spread across her shoulder blades like wings. He watched as she turned and picked up the purple cotton thing he'd always liked her best in. He knew that she'd seen him now, from the way in which she studiously did not look at him but only at the nightdress, only at one particular square in all its broad pattern, so fixedly as she drew it towards her.

'I'm sorry,' he said.

She stood and looked at him then, and she was holding the old purple nightdress in front of her chest but her crotch was bare, her empty mat of pubic hair. 'Don't say that,' she said. 'Don't say that, don't. Please don't say that. There isn't any need.' She was dropping the nightdress on the floor, not intentionally but not by accident either: it was both. It was something that her fingers did. The nightdress was lying down there at her feet now. She was naked, but she had an obstacle, a rampart before her that saved her from wondering where to tread. She seemed relieved. Carefully, she smiled at him. She didn't want to do anything that wasn't real. She wasn't going to lie to him. That was why the smile was so careful, and only edged its way bit by tiny bit. 'Are they comfortable?' she asked him.

'Not really,' said George, and smiled also.

The strange thing was, thought Natasha, he didn't look unattractive. And now that something lay between them, she found that she didn't mind at all stepping over it, and her toe only lightly caught the thin checks as she walked towards him, now that she could choose this.

To stand so close to him, and George, dearest George, only standing there, breathing.

He did not reach out to her.

He was turning his head aside now, turning his face away from her gaze. He was looking down at the cast iron radiator in the ingo, and his cheeks were burning, she could

216

see their colour even in the dim-lamped half-light. His smile was so tentative now that it was hardly there at all. With his head dipped like that, and his face half-afraid or ashamed, he was striking an accidental pose of feminine seduction. Like he knew she was there, like his whole body burned with knowing she was there, but needed her to turn him towards her. The kind of modesty that made Natasha want to lift its chin, pull its lips towards her, slip right in. She found that she could stare at him quite valiantly.

It made her forget herself.

'Is this what it's like to be a man?' she asked, almost to herself, and now she was stretching out her fingers to touch his cheek.

'I don't know,' said George. 'Do you like it?'

She nodded. 'I don't mean that I want to be a man,' she added. 'But I never wanted to be a woman either.'

He breathed out, in a half-laugh.

'I'm not a lesbian,' she said. 'I'm sure I'm not.'

'Me neither. Not gay, I mean.'

'Sometimes I think I hate women.'

'They're better than men, aren't they, darling.'

'Men love you,' she said. 'But then, everyone loves you. Is it ever difficult?'

George looked her fully in the eyes with great bewilderment.

'Sh,' she said, although he wasn't speaking. Her eyes were running over his face as if he were a painting, nobody, nobody, had ever looked at George like that before. 'Do you want to put a bra on?' he thought he heard her ask him.

'Are you sure that you like this?' he said. 'I mean,' frowning crossly, 'don't feel like you can't – laugh at me, don't for goodness sake *spare my feelings.*'

'Sh,' she said, more firmly this time. 'For now,' she said, cocking her head.

'I think,' said George. 'I think I must look a bit foolish, like a clown.'

'Stop it, George.'

'You're beautiful,' he said, looking at the familiar planes of her face, half-familiar in the half-dark. The deep shadows beneath her eyes, and their upward tilt at the edges, the lick of her lashes like wing tips. The slowness with which she blinked.

'You. You are beautiful too.' She was nodding. 'Other men look handsome, but you have always been more than that. With you it's got nothing to do with the thing you're in, I think there's no splitting in it, yes, you're just beautiful in the way that things in the world are.' She wanted to give him some examples of beautiful things in the world of which he reminded her, but she couldn't think of any because it was such a long time since she had permitted the world to be beautiful outside the confines of this house. She frowned. 'Like the sun coming in through the curtains,' she said, at length.

'Maybe you just love me,' said George.

'No, no. It's that you just always look like you, in different ways. I should have realised. I've been so afraid, always, of losing you. When I needn't.' Because he seemed transcendent now, like an angel or something. Being neither male nor female, but being both instead, and still hers, and she could still be his. Being weak and strong, and permitting her also to be both, so that they could both forgive and be forgiven, given forth into each other's hands like this.

George stood very still, not moving at all, like he always did when he was afraid that something might come undone. It was like light: too much or too little would plunge you into darkness or dazzle, and both left you blind.

But Natasha just stood there too in her flick of brown hair, not moving either. He liked that she knew how to not frighten him at a time like this. He liked that she knew

218

not to frighten his fear by trying to kill it. Like she wasn't even waiting for him but was just standing there with him, not coming nearer and not leaving, just staying the same and breathing. He thought that this was tender insight on her part, but in fact it was only that she was disturbed by the things she had just said; was too afraid, herself. It was just their chance equivalency in this that did it.

When he looked her in the eye at last, and moved again, she felt the air in the room shift around her skin. He was like a bird, beating to the mahogany chest over there, the drawer that still hung open. 'You can take anything,' she said. 'You can take anything of mine.' And then stood chewing her lip, nervously.

But in fact, he did not take her up on this offer; did not rummage for suspender belts at all. She had said, Do you want to put a bra on, and that was enough for now. He was fetching out a brassiere. Not because he didn't want the rest – he was starting to feel that he did, badly – but because, when it came to hearts and bodies, George only ever did one thing at a time, in case it went wrong. Planning ahead required the confidence that everything was not on the edge of falling from under you. He had learned to fly precisely because he did not trust the ground enough to walk.

George was slipping his arms through the bra straps, stretching his hands awkwardly up against his back, trying to close the catch.

'Is that how you're doing it?' Natasha asked.

He stopped, stock still, staring at her. He nodded.

'There's an easy way,' she said. 'Do you want me to show you?'

He laughed, that short embarrassed breath of a laugh again. 'Yes. Please.' Stood half in the bra and half not. Suddenly roughly pulled it off when she was close and almost touching him, reaching out her hand; realising he should have done that already, shouldn't he? Shouldn't he have taken it off already, was that what she expected? He was holding it shakily in his hand.

Natasha took the bra, turned it upside down and inside out. Slipped an arm behind his back, reaching for the other end, pulled it round, like he was a hula girl. 'Here,' she said. 'Take the two ends in your hands.'

His nervous fingers touched hers, which were cold. 'Oh!' he said. 'Your hands are cold. Do you want to put on my dressing gown?' Offering her his, it was the least he could do, when she was giving him so much. He greatly wished to give her something. He only hoped his dressing gown might seem more attractive to her than her own. Why would it, though? he wondered. Hers was thicker, made of wool. His was silk: his grandfather's; it did feel nice, he told himself, against your skin; perhaps she would take it. But then, they had been married for twelve years and in all that time she had never borrowed his dressing gown once. Before – before they were married, when she had stayed with him in Cumberland Street – he remembered now, very suddenly, Natasha, twenty-one, turning a tap, seen from the back. The dark green silk wrapped round her hips. He could feel the winter daylight in the room, the heads of the nails in the floorboards beneath his feet like stars of grit in ice; he could see the exact drift of her tangled hair, the back of her head, every thread of her. The sash of his dressing gown bound in around her waist, her warmth inside it, shifting. He could hear the water glass held to her lips, her hungry small swallowing sips.

'Hasn't Humberto got it?' she was asking him, Natasha here and now in the room.

He stared at her, quiet and appalled. How terrible that would be. And he had lent it, she was right about that, and Humberto had been wearing it when they carried him up the stair. Oh, but then, he recalled with relief, Ellie, stupid Ellie, precious Ellie, had folded it very precisely on the sofa arm beside him, and primly said, I think you should take this back, George. He was shivering, and staring at Natasha, and telling her that Ellie had brought it back. Repatriated, was the word he used, as if now more than ever he needed the words to cover him.

And Natasha was saying oh to something, and stepping backwards, turning away from him when she neared the hook on the door. Reaching to fetch the dressing gown down.

Tall and straight, pale in the faint light, her edges disappearing into black, removing. He hadn't realised how dark it was over there. Her back turned. By the door. And he over here, the other side of the bed, why had he suggested it? Any second, the doorknob would turn. She would make her escape. He could not see her face.

But stood mute with the two sides of the catch separate in his separate hands in front of him. Dying on his feet. 'Natasha,' he finally breathed, in the half-gasp, half-laugh of his.

She knew what he meant by this, but didn't turn round because his fear assuaged her own. His insecurity seemed to lay itself like a glorious cool sponge on all the trepidation that she felt. She was holding it there all the while that she put the dressing gown on, slipped it over her shoulders with her back to him still.

Turning then, forest green silk hanging from her sides and down to her knees, her breasts less brave than they earlier seemed, harboured in its flanking, small and poor. Her nakedness spearing narrowly like a candle, tallow skin. She was stepping across the room, the slow rhythmic white flash of her knees seeming certain, towards George at the window and the shadowed velvet curtain, in the silk wings like a pterodactyl she was coming, like she might wrap wings of extinction around him.

'It's okay,' she said. 'It's me,' she said. 'Fasten the clasp.'

'It's the wrong way out.'

'It's meant to be. You'll see.'

George half-laughed again, relief at having her back and stupidity of not trusting her, a half apology.

'Now swivel it round so the clasp's at the back.'

The fear and pleasure of believing her instructions without understanding them. Trust. The bra facing forward now, with its triangles and straps hanging down like a climber's webbing harness. Blindly on a cliff face.

'And put your hands through the straps, so they slide up your arms. Onto your shoulders.'

Tenterhook high-wire calm. Hers were mouth-to-mouth instructions received over the telephone. His hands followed her, down through the loops like she said, pulling it up onto his body, perfectly.

'Can I kiss you?' she asked.

He nodded dumbly, half-laughed again.

Natasha took his face very gently in her hands, thumbs resting on his cheekbones, fingers splayed around his ears so as not to cover them, so as not to make him deaf, not to scare him. So he could still listen for alarms as she looked into his eyes that were spilled, all of him in them. And hers matching his, both of them wider than the other had ever seen them, like wide skims of water over sand, vast expanses brought there by the tides but now beyond their reach, at least for the time being. Until the tables turned. She kissed him very specifically and tenderly, leaned her cheek against his and rested.

When George shivered, she opened his dressing gown he'd lent her, wrapped it as far as she could around the two of them, drew her head back and kissed his lips. *Ah*, they both said, like they'd woken from sleep. Smiled and stepped apart, wondering how to be now, how they should be separately. Trying it out, trying out how to be themselves: George, a trapeze artist who had never held a spoon; Natasha, who had spent so long counting spoons and refusing to look up.

George ambled awkwardly to the dressing table against the far wall, fingered her lipstick that had fallen on its side, a twig of gold in the darkness. 'Can I put this on?'

'Yes. If you like.'

'You won't mind.'

'I never mind you.'

He swung round, sincere like a face on a postage stamp. As if he hoped he could really be enough to pay the weight. 'Really?'

She nodded, but not smiling now.

'I never mind you either,' he said, and then her face opened out in relief.

He was opening the lipstick, pressing it carefully to his lips. Were you more yourself like this, or less? In claiming all the rest.

Natasha gave him a skirt to put on, a coppery piece of evening wear that she'd bought in 1966. She didn't know how to throw things out, even things she never wore, and here, she'd been proved right, she'd finally found a use for it. There was still room in her practical brain for her to feel pleased by this.

Inspired by this – seeing the activity in a new light now – she was hunting through a chest, searching for the black chiffon blouse that had been her aunt's, that likewise was not her sort of thing at all; she was busy looking for it, it would be just the thing for George, and meanwhile George pulled the skirt on, and wondered if he was doing it properly, or whether there was a special way with these as well, it didn't matter, did it, if he was doing it wrong, Natasha had her back to him.

He was glad she had her back to him, and then he was not.

He was asking her to stop looking for the blouse.

'But you'd like it,' she was saying, still kneeling, with a pile of things pulled out on the carpet beside her.

'I want you,' George said.

'Here it is,' said Natasha.

She watched him dress.

She ran her hand over his chest, the fineness of the fabric slashed open at the neck. His bra blacker still underneath, and underwear inventing the things it was meant to hide, the triangles of fabric marking something to find. She pushed the chiffon wide and bent her head, kissed his breastbone that rose like the thorax of a ghost moth, planted there in his own thoracic breadth. She was pressing her lips against it, and you knew, now, that there was a life underneath it somewhere. George was really in his body, wasn't he, after all, when always she'd wondered about that and thought maybe he wasn't. Always she'd wondered, when they were making love, if it wasn't just a trick, because up until now, George had seemed only to be in his eyes. And he closed his eyes when they made love, that was the thing, so that when she'd looked at him, she had always wondered, who exactly it was that she was doing this with.

Bronze beads sparkled in grand circles on his thighs, like things seen in the sky: war-time aeroplane markings, things their fathers had flown in; or else orbicular stigmata, false eyes arranged in iridescent scales on lepidopterous wings. The metallic cloth reached as far as his fine knees drawn closed, resting. Her fingers brushed palely across it, catching his shortened breath when her hand ran near his groin, catching the glimmer and the roughness of the skirt, like fine gravel under her skin as she kissed him, coiling her other hand into a fist around a bra strap. How nice it was, she thought, to have so many things to push against. And he was in all of them, he was in all his skin.

Pulling back, she was slipping her hand between his

knees and slowly sliding them apart. 'This is it, you know,' she said. 'This is what it is to be a woman. More than the sex, it is having somebody push your knees apart.' There were so many things she had to tell him; there was so much he should know. She felt she could tell him anything when he was like this and know that he would not laugh at her.

'I like it,' said George. 'It feels like you want me.'

'I do.' She stared at him as she shifted the skirt up towards his hips and found the lace with her hands, the beating of him from inside it. The size of his sex perfectly wrapped in something so fine, twice as strong against it. It was like encountering a great cat behind the sofa, she thought. A tiger purring lightly among the bone china. She stroked his cock and bollocks, netted about with leaves and flowers.

When, later, she straddled him in the bed, she found that she was pulling on his cock at such an angle that it really did appear to be her own. She looked at George, looking back at her in a way she'd never seen him do. Looking at her, and she was there in his flowing silk dressing gown, stealing his cock, while he lay down before her in her lipstick and light night smock, skirt lost. Their faces were hard and red as she raised her buttocks, lowered herself again, onto him. She was rocking now, gazing wide-eyed at George's left ear and unable to comprehend it as such, because it was also her ear now, and her eye that saw it was his, and the pulsating bed was their shared heartbeat, but so was the shifting of the radiator as she moved, and the light on the wall above the lampshade was the heat of their shared palm pressed there, the shadows were their hair. 'I don't know who I am,' she breathed. With every awkward thrust of her hips she was swinging between gloriousness and revulsion, terror and love.

George was looking at her as if she had come to save him. She decided not to notice the look in his eyes. She decided only to notice the fact that he wanted to keep his eyes open, and keep his eyes on her, while she rocked back and forth. She would keep the look in his eyes for later; she could think about it then.

Natasha always had the feeling that she wasn't doing it right, she always did, and this was why she was feeling a little sad and ashamed, this was the explanation she could now forget for half of the way she felt as the linen-covered headboard with the dents of their two heads came faster and faster to meet her.

It was only after she came that she decided she had loved it.

Afterwards, she nuzzled him, slipped her finger up his anus. Heard him groan, knew he was closing his eyes with his quiet head turned, to the window. Felt the flesh inside him, his body letting her in and closing around her, pulsing and warm. Let her own head fall forwards against the skin of his back, his breathing and his spine that quivered with her wrist.

Her fingers disappearing, in and out of inside him. The way he was soft and hard at the same time, here where he was letting her come in. 'I love,' she whispered, 'being able to feel inside you.'

'I love it too,' murmured George, smiling under a pleasured frown. Natasha couldn't see his face, but heard it in his voice – the smile and the frown, the way that together these two things made something soft and hard, like the rest of him, of them, together, whichever way round – and she smiled too, loving him and breathing in the scent of his skin.

But she was also very drowsy, and in fact fell asleep with her finger still inside him, so that he had to carefully pull her hand away afterwards.

He lay watching her for a while, and then he went to fetch a piece of tissue from the dressing table, and gently wiped her finger. He knew Natasha hated germs. She didn't stir.

How strange, thought George. He wondered if he had just done what he always wanted. He wondered if Natasha had wanted it too. You never knew.

He felt that he was dreaming now as he looked around the room, at the fallen blooms of clothing. The bra constricted his ribcage in a way he hadn't noticed before, and this seemed to increase the dreamlike feeling, that of being in a place where normal bodily functions became difficult – breathing, speaking, running – while impossible things had become normal – flying like a bird, shape-shifting like a witch; these were things your body could do, in dreams. You could do things with your body, instead of just with words.

That was why you could travel through time, in dreams. Dreams didn't need words the way that your waking days did. In dreams, you could think in pictures, and be part of them: the body and not the word. Word, words, a picture tells a thousand words. Dreams were made of pictures, every second of which carried a thousand words, a string of thoughts that would have taken fifteen minutes to formulate sequentially, but here spooled out around you in an instant, a web, instantly understood. In dreams you could think a thousand times faster, you could soar on the currents of your mind, you could think in simultaneity, just as in the physical world your eyes could see a thousand things at the same time. This was why you could sleep for ten minutes and yet dream for hours within it. And this was why the pictures in your dreams changed so rapidly: four seconds in your dreams was an hour in normal time, an hour was the best part of a week. Sometimes the dreams flew even faster: sometimes you could sleep for a hundred years and yet wake up tomorrow morning.

Like music, each mental note of the picture could change at the same time as another. Not like words, not at all, that had to follow one after the other and wait their turn, or descend into nonsense. The language of music and dreams was of multiple things, of chords in concert that rose and fell and changed against each other. A dream was a million instruments conducting themselves in tunes that could frighten or delight you, yet the path of their conducting lay inside you: ruthless and truthful, not caring if you clapped because it could always come back, it didn't matter whether or not it was invited, always it had a home in that grand auditorium in your skull. Always it would show you what the possibilities within you could knit.

In dreams, you could think the way the world did.

George always found dreams alarming. Not their contents, but their nature. That physicality of thinking, its multiplicity, which was a kind of duplicity, wasn't it, but taken to the nth degree, in George's book. And the thing that George had always liked so much about thought, about words, was precisely the fact that it had nothing to do with bodies. Was better, he'd always felt: clearer, cleaner, in every way superior. One thing following logically from another, and each in its place, each in its time. Dreams were things he always bore diligently for the duration and promptly forgot; he did not laugh about them over breakfast the way that women did.

When he looked around and felt as if he were in a dream, this was not a comfortable thing. Too many different things were happening at once, and happening too fast.

He pulled his sleeping wife in against him, and found that he was crying into her hair. Gratitude within him like a hernia had grown too great to bear.

228

Chapter Forty-one

Natasha woke first. In the course of the night, she had drifted to her own side of the bed, and when she rolled over she was surprised to see that George's sleeping shoulder was bound by a narrow black lingerie strap. She was still in the first moments of waking, when you could be anyone, living in anyone's life, rather than specifically the life that left off in your bed last night. Everything was different in the morning. In the morning, you had to decide. Whether to carry it forward or tuck it under your hat.

Natasha lay watching George for a while, and then she reached out a hand and gently stroked his hair, and smiled. She was feeling happy, generally, as she moved around the room, tidying up. She paused at one point, watching George sleep, feeling sad, in a way, as she folded her nightdress, that he wasn't awake, that she should be alone. But mostly she was glad, and the sadness itself was not unpleasant, being a longing and not a regret. She did feel very much that she would have liked it if he could have been awake and watching her move about the room this morning; if they could still be sharing everything. Her strong desire in this unnerved her slightly. She hung his dressing gown back on its hook. She pulled her own bathrobe on.

That was better, she thought, looking around.

She went into the bathroom in order to run her bath.

The black rubber plug on its chain was not wound and hooked around the tap. It was fixed plumply in the plughole, and the bath was filled with two inches of water, and there was a book in it.

Natasha stared, for a second, before swooping her hands down into the cold, cold water, so fast that she hurt her back. She was lifting out her library book, and then she didn't know what to do with it.

It must have been there all night. George had put it there. All the time.

She was wrapping the book in her bath towel, but clumsily, because too many other things were stumbling through her head. Too much was changing, treading backwards. The morning had stepped backwards and trodden on her bare foot. She dried it as best she could. Patting its sodden pages with the cotton-looped cloth. Her eyes fixed upon each page: here, a cutworm, its caterpillar body buckled by the wet. Next to it, she read,

Cutworms are usually brown and live in the soil, though they may feed above soil level at night. They gnaw the base of the plant stem. The plant gradually wilts and dies.

Her eyes flitted down the page to a paragraph which began with reassuringly bold type.

CONTROL *by treating affected plant with a soil insecticide as soon as damage is apparent.*

She turned the page, but this time she didn't look at the picture, or the description of the pest. She had decided that it was the final paragraphs that mattered. They were the things she needed to check were all right.

CONTROL is difficult or impossible once the grubs are in the roots. Where carrot flies are known to be a problem, use a soil insecticide when planting or sowing.

She turned the page again.

CONTROL is difficult, and soil insecticides have only a limited degree of success against the weevil.

Page.

CONTROL is best achieved by a systemic fungicidal application.

Page.

CONTROL is impossible. Remove and destroy affected plants promptly.

Page.

CONTROL with chemical treatments is not practical for root rots. Avoid recurrence by raising plants in sterilised compost; destroy affected plants as soon as damage is apparent.

The next two pages were stuck together. Natasha was trying to prise them apart, it seemed very important. She was picking and peeling at the soggy corners with her fingertips as she knelt on the pink bathroom carpet, but they wouldn't let her in. Her hands were shaking.

All the time. The book had been in the bathwater, all the time. She had thought, at the time, that perhaps he'd done some such thing, she'd been ready to forgive him, because with George, there was something endearing in such mischiefs. She always felt them as a kind of intimacy. But he had said, *No, not really*, and she had chosen to believe him. She had believed him, and he had known, all the time, that really the book was lying here. Had known all along that she was believing his lie. It had been laughing at her all along, this book in the bath. He had made her weaker than him, all along. His own weakening of himself for her had been a pretending.

She couldn't get the pages apart.

Chapter Forty-two

Lori perched herself on Mrs Farrants' kitchen worktop. It was good to be unusual. It was good to sit in unusual places.

It wasn't even a proper worktop, which was weird, wasn't it, in a posh house like this. It wasn't fitted units. Just really big cupboards, with thick tops, pushed in rows against the walls. The Formica was sticky underneath her thighs so she adjusted her position from time to time, and this was no bad thing either. It was pleasant to move her knees while talking to Sam.

He was changing the dressing on Julab's eye, and she was telling him about the technical terms for various parts of arches. 'You have your keystone, the coign in the middle,' she said, 'and then the *voussoirs* either side. I think it's clever, the way they stay up. Not that I'll be having any in my buildings, though, you can't, it's too expensive. They only did them like that because they had to. They didn't have steel construction.' Her voice when she said *steel construction* was warm and pronounced.

Sam thought she had said *coin*. Now Lori was talking about architects he'd never heard of. Lee Corbussier, she said, he did a chapel, but it was more like a cathedral, it was huge, it was in France, it was like a huge concrete mushroom, but in a good way. She would like to go there in the snow. He was French.

'Why?'

'What do you mean, why? He can't help it.'

'Why do you want to go there in the snow?'

'Oh. Because it's grey, it's concrete, I think it would look nicer surrounded by white. Than green. Like everything does, doesn't it. I mean.'

Sam looked at her then, and nodded. 'But it isn't,' he said.

'Well,' she smiled, 'in the snow it is. Or in art galleries.'

He nodded again and sniffed. 'It's not a very French name, *Lee*,' he said.

Lori started laughing. She enjoyed laughing while sitting on Mrs Farrants' worktop. '*Lee*,' she said, 'not *Lee*. *Lee*. French for *the*.'

'Your pronunciation is wrong,' said Sam, but he sounded preoccupied, he was taping down the sides of the dressing. Anyway, he felt happy, happier than he had done in a long time. 'I don't know much about buildings,' he said, releasing Julab's nose from his grip, stroking his nut brown fur, flinching as the dog shook its head.

'Well, I'm teaching you,' she said.

'Don't.'

Tenderly he carried on stroking the dog.

'Well,' said Lori. 'You tell me about something, then.'

He was walking to the bin, he was pushing the lid aside and dropping the old dressing in. He was standing with his hands on his hips, thinking, and now he was telling her about the technical terms for various pieces of armour. 'A vambrace,' he said, 'is the piece that protects your forearm.'

Julab was whimpering.

Sam crossed the room quickly, crouched back down where he'd been sitting earlier. 'Ssh,' he said. 'Ssh boy, it's okay.'

Lori craned her neck to watch him.

It was as if she wasn't there. Sam seemed to have forgotten about everything except the labrador and the pain it was in. He was caressing it, talking to it gently. Lori, watching him, seeing his kindness not done to impress but pure and heartfelt, real, fell entirely in love.

Chapter Forty-three

The bed was empty when George woke up. At first he thought he must have got the sheets tied round his chest. He fingered the tightness of the bra, lazily for a second or two, as if to be sure of it, and then he tried to take it off. He couldn't imagine the tricks Natasha might have showed him last night, naturally could not then work out their reversal; had to fight with the thing as he pulled it off over his head.

That was better. That was all right. He threw the bedclothes aside, swung his legs around and sat, holding the bra in his fist. Everything was all right.

There was lipstick on the pillow.

George got up, looked at his face in the mirror. His mouth was still smudged with colour. He still liked it. Where was Natasha? He loved her. He loved her so much.

Chapter Forty-four

'Hello, Mrs Farrants,' said Catherine, putting her book to one side as she lay on the daybed.

'Don't you *Mrs Farrants* me. What are you doing still in bed?'

'I'm ill.'

'No you're not,' said her mother, and then she laid a palm against her daughter's forehead. 'You feel fine today,' she said. 'People who are well enough to throw books in rivers are perfectly well enough to get out of bed and get dressed.'

'I am dressed.'

'Your nightie doesn't count, Catherine.'

'Why not? It's a dress. I think I might wear it as a dress.'

'Get up!' said Natasha, and when Catherine just stared at her, she pulled her sharply by the shoulder, yanked her upright onto the floor. Catherine's bedclothes erupted behind her, and the book slid into a loud bang on the parquet. 'Do as you're told, will you?' Natasha shouted.

'Don't cry, Mummy.'

'I'm not crying.' Natasha turned, and bent down, to pick up the book. 'What have you written in your book? Why have you written this?'

Catherine shrugged. 'No reason.'

'*Everybody died before this story started.*'

Catherine just looked at her.

'You shouldn't write in books.' Natasha was walking towards the table, she was laying the book down on its gleaming wooden surface. 'It spoils them,' she said.

'You look upset.'

'I'm sorry. I didn't mean to shout.'

Natasha went outside, to where she had propped open *Vegetable Parasites & Problem Fungi* to dry in the sunshine. She stooped to touch its pages, to check its progress, tending to it as if it were a vegetable of hers. She wondered what it would recommend for its own curative treatment.

Chapter Forty-five

Rosa wasn't there. Lori hesitated in the doorway; thought about retreating, thought of the way the door would feel if she did that, her finger softly nudging its latch back, closed.

A chink of sunlight twinkled through the skylight, into the room, there where she was looking. She took this as an invitation: and it did look like one, a small gold card dropped carelessly on the carpeted floor, the rust woollen peneplain. Her fingers trailed down the paint of the door that was closing, now, behind her. Dust in the air made the shaft of light seem almost solid ahead. She could look at it and pretend that she was not standing next to Rosa's empty bed.

The sunbeam faded as clouds recovered overhead and Lori affected an air of disappointment at this, tilted her head and frowned at the skylight. Sighed and glanced sideways, almost surprised, it seemed, to find herself here among Rosa's things, alone. She sat herself down on the half-made bed, the candlewick bedspread tugged halfway up, a raffish spill of white cotton sheet from this low-cut neck. Rosa was so messy, thought Lori fondly, looking around. All her mascara tubes and knickers, her crumpled clothes, her *NME* with the cover gone, her perfume bottles and books – *The Poems of Federico Garcia Lorca*; Sidney Sheldon – three different bottles of perfume she had, Lori realised, swinging her gaze back. Imagine that.

Lori was not an envious soul. She was only gently fascinated that other girls her age might live like this, like grown women, with bottles of proper scent to pick from when they dress, and wear some every day, not just at discos. Imagine having three different perfumes with you, even on holiday. She got up off the bed and stooped over the small chest of drawers in the corner where the bottles and books stood and sat among hairclips, pebbles. She reached out and her fingers touched the phials: they had to, to turn them, so she could read their names. *LouLou, Joy*, said the first two, but the third bottle was the most beautiful. It was a frosted glass apple whose stem and perfect crystal leaves formed the handle of a stopper. The liquid inside the apple glowed the colour of a Golden Delicious: still three-quarters full, it looked as if it were three-quarters a live apple and one-quarter a glass one. Lori turned it around and around, but could see no name nor label on the bottle. She picked it up and carefully lifted out the stopper. She was expecting it to smell of apples but it did not, it smelled deep and warm and musky and strangely exciting, strangely unnerving, when you had been expecting apples, she thought. As she breathed the scent right in, she felt it wrap around her heart and tighten it. She was afraid she was going to steal a little bit of Rosa's perfume; she was afraid she was going to dab a small drop on her wrists to find out how it would smell upon her skin; so she put the stopper back in and, with both hands, firmly replaced the bottle on the top of the chest of drawers. The sound of the door startled her. She pulled her hand away quickly, too hastily, knocked the apple on its side. Her body was slow and wanted to go back, wanted to set the bottle straight, but her neck kept pulling it round because it must, it must see who was at the door – it must be Rosa, and Lori must be ready to explain. The stopper was in the bottle. She could stand it upright later, in a moment.

She was starting to explain, with her lips and tongue that were delivering words – the truth, because Lori never lied – but her eyes were seeing Sam. His face, his body, there in the doorway of Rosa's bedroom.

'I was looking at the perfume bottles,' Lori was saying. 'The apple, I was looking at the apple.' She laughed nervously.

'*Fille d'Eve*,' said Sam, but Lori neither understood what the words meant, nor the fact that this was the name of the perfume. She did not even understand that he was speaking French. 'How appropriate,' he said, in a kindly tone of voice, and she smiled uncomprehendingly. 'I think you knocked it over,' he said, and his fingers uncurled around the door knob, letting the catch click out.

'Yes. Yes, I did.' She was looking at him. And tucking in her chin, she turned back, stood with her back to him. Leant over again, the way that she had been standing when he first saw her in here, a few moments earlier. She picked up the toppled bottle, more slowly than she needed to. Maybe she was just being careful. She breathed out in a queer little sigh as she set it back in its place. She took the trouble of turning it round so that its crystal leaves were in the exact position in which she had found them. Because she knew she would not want Rosa to know she had been in here. She was sure of that now.

Lori turned around and also knew, from the way that Sam had not moved by an eighth of an inch, knew that she was not wrong to walk towards him. From the way he still remained the same, now that they were standing right up close, she knew she was not wrong to lean her face in to his. And yet at the last second she weakened – perhaps it was his hand still on the door, as if half-ready to leave

– and slid her eye past his, and stopped there, cheek to cheek with him.

His eye had still been staring forward, she had noticed that, as her face went sailing slowly past it. Why was that, she wondered. What did it mean? She had the feeling that he was still staring forward, even now; she was certain he was not glancing sideways at her hair, the back of her head. She would know, she thought, she would feel it if he were, and anyway, it would not be like him.

This feeling of knowing him thrilled her: to know what would be like him, and what not. And it was good, to be close to him; it was good to stand here, like this, with him.

The skins of their faces were touching. His was weirdly cool, she found. She could feel a prickling heat flooding through her own capillaries, scratching like fast roots through sand, casting out blooms on the surface.

Lori's breathing was very bothered but she turned very slowly, and gently kissed that cool cheek of his. She glanced toward his eyes: he was staring straight ahead. She blinked.

The clouded daylight caught their young heads softly, as if it were pressed through one of Rosa's thin silk scarves and not just the scum on the skylight glass. It caught his frozen stillness that was by no means peace or rest. It caught her cajoling nervousness. Thin fibres drifted up from the carpet as she moved her feet, her Converse baseball boots, four shifts at the Byre Inn.

The room had long seen similar things, and did not flinch but let them carry on, here between its walls papered by the old Mrs Farrants in 1953, turquoise bleached to aqua, patterned with a scatter of white diamonds, curling away from its glue along vertical fault lines.

Lori was resting her head sideways in the hollow of his neck. Blue Perspex baubles gleamed like brand new buoys on the elastic band that fastened her ponytail, and floated, reflected, in a corner of the mirror, there on the low commode in the corner.

Sam was looking, not at the hair bobble, but at Lori's mirror face turned sideways there on his sister's chest of drawers. Her cheek above the perfume bottles and books, the tubes of squeezed-out sun cream; her nose beneath Rosa's necklaces of coral and lumpen shell that swagged the corner of the mirror's wooden frame.

His own face reflected there too.

When he turned and began to kiss her hard on the lips, it was a small leap from intolerable cliffs, in which the ground far below threatened to refuse him. Gravity seemed weakened. He was fighting to fall, he was pushing for it with all his might.

He kissed her because he did not want to see her face.

He didn't want to see his.

Lori's warm tongue. He didn't like it when she tried to pull away. He pushed closer, carried on. And she was still kissing him back, if a little less certainly.

When she turned around and stepped towards the bed, it was not in submission but in order to escape a little, to exercise her will. To sit there on Rosa's rucked-up bedspread, where she often sat in summers like these and was happy. When she was sitting here, on this bed, often she was smiling; often she laughed. She was sitting here now, though, feeling quite different. She laughed a little, trying for the feeling that was missing. Her laugh was tiny, more a reedy cough.

Sam's eyes were darker than usual as he moved towards her, their black whorls larger, pushing the colour out. His hazel irises, which were normally so soft and reminded her of her friend, were smelted down to thin encircling rims for those broad deep pupils. Lori was sure she'd read in a science book that perfect circles didn't exist. *There are no perfect circles in nature*, the sentence had said. But she was looking at them, wasn't she? Those circles in his eyes that were still small, really, weren't they? Smaller than half-pence pieces but the centre of everything, now, bearing down on her. She was going to be ready for this.

She leaned an arm out behind her on the mattress, so that her shoulder was pulled back, her chest pushed up and out. She smiled seriously up at him.

It was the normalness of Lori that Sam found so inviting. Her average mouth, her little button nose adrift in her moon face, her soft chin, broad hips. Her big breasts inside that Western-style denim shirt. And she was so open with him: open eyes, open face, open shirt at her neck. She was not Rosa, here on Rosa's bed.

When he tried to undo the topmost pearlised button on her shirt, he found that it was not a button at all. A mere popper fastening that came easily apart in an unexpected way in his hands. It shocked him a bit, when he'd been expecting something averagely difficult. In the wake of the fright, in the relief, a rush of blood drained to his cock, and he was ripping the rest open now, one by ripping one, with slight sharp breaths, slices of air that hardly graced his lungs but only ripped over their surface, in time with the glorious sound of the press stud cascade, down to her hem.

He had never been this hard in his life. He loved these buttons. He'd have been happy to close them all up now and do it again. But they were done, they were all done now, and he would long for American women for the rest of his youth, and then be almost content with them and not know why, because of this, because of this Trossachs girl with her baseball boots and her cowboy shirt. Her cleavage plump and firm as a birthday cake in white synthetic satin bra. He did not bother to unhook it, but left her in there, because he liked the effect it made. He was intent on unfastening her waistband, and kissing her again, but pulling away from time to time, teasing her, because he knew he'd got her now.

'I don't think we should be doing this on Rosa's bed,' she said. He didn't even answer. 'I'm not sure we should be in her room like this,' she tried again.

'She won't know,' murmured Sam, gruffly for a boy.

Because he was just a boy, Lori thought, looking at him as he pulled back to tug her shorts down. She'd always thought he was just a boy, even though he was older, but now, being with him like this, he seemed to know just what he was doing with her; seemed exactly like a man. He seemed to know her body better than she did as he slid his fingers inside her. He hadn't even bothered to take off her bra. It was this, in the end, that cemented her infatuation with him.

Yet when he rummaged in Rosa's drawer for a condom, she demurred: 'We can't use hers.'

'Why not.' It wasn't even a question, the way he said it. He was looking at her, he was waiting. And when she didn't reply, he carried on looking at her and his gaze shook a little as he tore the foil corner; his nostrils flared as he slipped it out. 'Have you done this before?' he asked, just before he entered her.

'Yes,' she said, thinking how different it was with Ahab. Something worked up to over many months, a thing he'd won from her with steady love. A thing she had refused all the others, but was giving to Sam because he assumed it was his. And because she loved him. And because this is it, she thought, this is it. She had never been this afraid, this excited, in her life. She had never done *this*.

Her eyes screwed closed as she felt him pushing in, stretching her, filling her. She tried to ignore the feel of the candlewick bedspread under her naked skin.

Sam breathed out, surrounded. Lori's hot narrow core pressed against him, all around him, holding him as he went over and back, over again. In and out and in: that most decisive indecision. It felt like choosing between two different kinds of death, in which one meant never dying, but you never knew which.

Lori on the bed, it would be better, he thought, if her hair were spread out behind her head. He paused for a second, leaned his elbow down. She thought that he was cradling her for a kiss. He felt for the hair bobble and slid it out, bright blue, the colour of a shooting cartridge. He raked her hair out a little and smiled at her when he noticed she'd opened her eyes, was staring up at him. 'I want to see your hair,' he said, by way of explanation. Thrust deep into her again.

'I'm getting a little dry,' she shyly said. 'I'm stressing in case Rosa comes in.'

He had to stop, then, and took some baby oil from the dressing table, and this time Lori didn't bat an eyelid at the distastefulness of using Rosa's things. He lifted up the chair on whose back Rosa's clothes were draped and wedged it against the door – in truth it would have been useless in stopping anyone who wanted to come in, because the latch was high and the chair weighed little, but it made Lori feel happier – and then he ministered to her cunt, which was reddened, with the oil. 'Poor thing,' he said. In his other hand he kept his cock moving. He mustn't let it go soft. He was watching those fat furred folds of hers, the nuder lips within, the hood of her swollen clitoris. They were shining now, and the hair greased into flat dark curls; his fingers slipping over and in. He glanced sideways at the carpet, the rust-coloured threadbare carpet that covered the floor of both these rooms, Rosa's and his, his and this, the room that Rosa always slept in; and simultaneously suddenly he thought he was about to come. 'Okay,' he asked her, but it wasn't a question, and he was already inside her again as she nodded and said, 'Yes.'

He was looking sideways at a used water glass beside the bed, at the musty imprints of his sister's lips on its rim, when he came and it almost surprised him, not to see it there, curling whitely down through the inch of water that remained.

Looking back, at Lori, her face half-surprised looking back at him. 'I'm sorry,' he said. Withdrawing, slipping off the condom, and bringing her off in his hands, slowly and with what she thought was a great deal of expertise.

Chapter Forty-six

Natasha was with Ellie all morning. It was impossible for George to get her alone. He watched her talking, and sometimes he stood near her, still watching, waiting for her to look at him. At length he would speak, ask her some mundane question, the location of a wanted object, the nature of the coming meal, but each time he did this she met his gaze so frankly, so blankly, and answered him so coolly and politely, that by mid-afternoon he had desisted.

He was sitting in the library now, trying to concentrate on Dante's *Inferno* but kept finding himself distracted by Beatrice, beatitudes in the darkness, alabaster skin, his wife's, that unsunned portion bearing down on him, heat, the heat.

He heard her laughing in the kitchen, underneath, and it was too much for him.

'Who on earth is that?' asked Ellie, as a din shaped something like Shostakovich blasted from the hall.

'George.'

'I didn't know George could play the piano.'

'He can't. He hates music. I don't know why he's playing it. His mother made him learn. He never touches that thing.'

'Well,' said Ellie. 'It's good to have an instrument. Ruaridh insisted that the children did. I think they're glad of it when they grow up, aren't they. Music's a thing that can give one so much pleasure. When they're young, they've got all their friends, and they think that's how it's going to always be.'

Natasha looked at Ellie sharply, interested in her in a new way. 'What do you mean?' she asked, and at the same time, the piano playing abruptly halted.

'Well,' Ellie began, but that was as far as she got, because George was flinging open the door.

He was standing there on the steps, above them. Natasha, looking at him, felt furious that Eleanor should have been interrupted at this juncture when for once she might have been on the verge of saying something worth listening to.

She also couldn't help noticing that, pale and elevated over there, preparing to make an annunciation, he looked something like an angel. She was reminded of the way he'd seemed to her last night, in the darkness, the way things had seemed like they might have been. This made her angry with herself, as well as with him.

'Rosa and Humberto are holding a passionate convocation in the porch,' said George, and Ellie, believing him at once, bolted from her seat, ran past him, was gone, while he still stood staring at his wife. His eyes had not shifted. 'Nat,' he said.

'Don't call me that.' She was turning her head aside as he took quick steps towards her.

'I love you,' said George.

'It makes me sound like an insect.' Should she go and stand somewhere else? Or would that make too much of it. She fixed her eyes on the tap. Why wasn't he speaking? Why wasn't he saying anything else? It must be a trick, to make her look back at him; she wouldn't fall for that. 'Nothing happened,' she said, and even she was surprised by the evenness of her voice. She wished that Ellie would come back. For the first time in her life, she did not want to be alone in a room with George. And yet, when Ellie did come back, and George left, once the door was closed, once he had very definitely gone, she wanted to run after him and weep. How dare he.

Chapter Forty-seven

Lori came over more often than she had done when she was Rosa's friend. She liked watching Sam take care of that poor dog of his. He was so gentle with it, seemed to get so much pleasure from watching its slow healing. She liked swinging her legs from the worktop while they told each other things. Neither of them had really mastered the art of asking questions yet, so this was how their conversations went: taking it in turn to tell things.

They played billiards upstairs in the evenings, and sometimes they made love, but sometimes Sam didn't even try, and this raised him further in Lori's estimation. He wasn't like other boys. He took her or left her, and either way, he loved her. She knew this, because when she had asked him, Do you love me? he had said, Yes. And kissed her.

Catherine, who was not entirely better, but was at least vertical and dressed in day clothes, sat frowning on the daybed. Her mother could not understand why she wanted to stay in the same room. 'Aren't you sick of it?' she wanted to know. 'Aren't you bored,' she asked, more kindly in the stout silence that followed, 'of looking out of the same window? Come outside, darling.'

But Catherine liked sitting here. Her skin was cooler

now, and she could enjoy the view. She liked the gentle flick-flack of the window cord against the wooden panelling. This was the only place from which it felt safe to watch them, Sam and Lori, out there in the garden. If she were to sit out there too then they would behave differently in front of her, wouldn't they, and she wanted to know, she wanted to see. She was not afraid. As long as you knew the truth, nothing could scare you.

So she watched them over the coming days, and noted the degrees of closeness quickening between them. It began with Lori straightening her skirt when she stepped out from the path that came out by the pines from the far rhododendrons, glimpsed in the distance through the right-hand window. As she passed the left-hand window five minutes later, Catherine was near enough to see the heightened colour in her cheeks, which she presumed was produced by shame, although you never knew. It could have been sunburn. She examined Lori's face at tea-time, and the colour had gone, which made her think it was probably not sunburn. It probably was the shame of sexual intercourse after all.

Still, it was happening in the bushes, wasn't it, Sam was keeping it in the bushes, which pleased her. It was good that Sam's liking of Lori knew its place, and that Lori was obedient to this. It was good that he was ashamed of her.

Catherine noted with displeasure the way that they then smiled at each other after tea.

By Wednesday, Lori was touching his arm quite brazenly, in the course of normal speaking. There, in front of Mrs Eleanor Gill, who was laughing with Sergeant Jonathan Hope and not paying attention to them like she should have been. Why wasn't he in his uniform? That was interesting. Catherine noted it and tucked it in the box inside her head where she kept all the things that didn't quite make sense. All the things you didn't know the answers to yet. They were like odd socks: you mustn't throw them out, or forget them; you kept them, there in the box in your head, and one day you would find the missing partner, the answer. You mustn't throw them away or forget them, and especially you must not wear them with a wrong partner that lies easily to hand and *looks* okay but isn't. No, you waited.

And watched.

Lori touching Sam's arm as she spoke.

Mrs Eleanor Gill going out by herself one night. In a peach satin dress.

Sam rubbing sun cream into Lori's shoulders, but only because she'd asked him to, maybe he was just being polite.

Catherine hadn't had to ask him to rub cream into her back, had she. He had offered.

Rosa and Humberto standing by the wire fence at the bottom of the garden, the top of the river cliffs. Talking to each other. Catherine was irked by the fact she couldn't hear them. When people stood on the terrace or the flat oval lawn up here at the top, she could hear every word, but there was a point on the slope of the garden where the sound of the river rose and covered everything beneath it. It sounded like water and it acted like water, the way it submerged things. Even though she could see their lips moving. Rosa was standing with her back to the fence, shading her eyes with her hand. Humberto was standing sideways on.

Catherine wished she could hear them. Rosa had now stopped shading her eyes and was running her hand back and forth over the wire. She wasn't looking at her hand, though, she was looking at Humberto. Catherine could see Rosa's mouth moving. Her bottom lip was dropping down, so that her mouth hung open for a moment, then almost closed itself up but not quite, before falling down again, like it had to scoop up more, and then sealed itself shut, and blew something out, the last word, almost like a kiss. It looked like she might be saying *I love you*. Those were the shapes of words that her mouth was making. It was hard to be sure, though, from here. Then Rosa swivelled her body loosely, like she could hardly be bothered with it, and touched Humberto's arm, seemed to be playing with him. It was annoying that Catherine couldn't hear them, but she could see the picture they made. Humberto being stiller and stiller, Rosa moving more and more. And now Rosa was turning right around, for no reason, so that she had her back to the house, even though this meant that she must now have her face pressed uncomfortably against the fence. Maybe she was looking through it at the river. Maybe her eyes were closed.

Humberto going away, with his tent packed onto his back, and thanking everyone for allowing him to stay, he had enjoyed meeting them he said. It was good to be able to know a proper Scottish family, he said. They offered to take him to the station, but he said he would just hitch, he said he liked it, the fortune, he said.

Rosa not speaking to anyone, after he'd left, and refusing to eat. Ellie saying, 'At least he had the decency.'

Lori appearing in the late dusk from among the rhododendrons again, and this time with Sam beside her instead of a polite ten minutes behind her.

Catherine knew you could have sexual intercourse and

not be in love. Like in *Diamonds are Forever*, or *Moonraker*: you knew that James Bond wasn't in love with the women from the way that he smiled. Like they were ice cream. You liked ice-cream, you liked it very much, but you didn't *love* it. People said they did, but they didn't mean it. They just meant they liked it, that was all. Maybe Sam was like James Bond. James Bond killed people, and he was still good. James Bond wouldn't think twice about hurting a dog.

Lori stroking Sam's hair on Friday morning as he lay with his head in her lap, outside. Where was her mother? wondered Catherine. Where was Mrs Farish? Talking with Natasha Farrants in the kitchen, that was where, gassing over Rich Tea biscuits the way that they always did.

Lori talking in a babyish voice to Julab, who was Sam's dog, not hers. They had put him under a parasol to shade him.

Sam watching Lori as she talked like this to his dog.

Sam leaning and reaching out for Lori without being asked, turning her face towards him. Holding her face in both his hands, looking at her eyes very steadily, as if he were asking something, or telling, and not just wanting. Sam beginning to kiss Lori's mouth very seriously.

Catherine stared. Fat tears were rolling down her cheeks. Because nobody, nobody, ever looked at an ice-cream like that. After everything she'd done for him. She wept. Tore herself from the daybed, and hurried slipping and sliding across the floor. She was gulping great drags of air as she half-ran, half-staggered down the hall.

'It was Sam,' wailed Catherine, almost falling down the stairs into the kitchen. 'It was Sam who threw the pot at Julab, I saw him, I saw him do it, Mummy, it was Sam.' She hurled herself against her mother's elbow and her lungs retched with tears. It was done. She had done it. I have betrayed him, she thought, and he deserves it. She didn't know which part felt worse. When she thought of him looking at Lori like that, it took up so much soreness that she couldn't feel anything else at all. She screwed her eyes as far closed as she could, until it felt like her eyelashes were jagging the other way round, into her skull. Her cheek was hot against her mother's bare wet skin.

Natasha was trying to lift her daughter up onto her lap, she was pushing her chair back, hoisting Catherine up by the armpits. But Catherine was screaming, she was shouting, 'No, no, don't lift me,' and clinging onto her mother's arm, with her face still buried behind its elbow.

As it turned out, nobody believed her anyway.

Natasha had a fair understanding of the way that these things worked. 'She's upset about Sam and Lori,' explained Natasha afterwards, to Ellie and Nuala in the deep cool kitchen. 'She's always had a crush on Sam,' Natasha said. Which was true; and when Ellie thought about it, once she'd recovered from the shock of it – because Catherine was a *child*, after all – then the truth of it became so self-evident that she felt she'd always known it.

'That's why she's saying this,' said Natasha, and this also made perfect sense. 'Don't be cross with her. She's just a child,' she said. 'I'll talk to her, Ellie.'

'Yes. Perhaps she isn't really better yet.' In fact, everyone felt that it was quite pleasant to sit here and discuss the mishap. And no one had lost an eye. It was only a sweetly hysterical child.

Chapter Forty-eight

Rosa's fingers were gripping the handrail of the bridge very tightly, but still they trembled a little, as if there were insect wings in the knuckles trying to uncurl the fingers so that the palms would rise, and then the arms too as the wings would carry the fingertips higher, into the air, and carry the whole of Rosa away with them. She was gripping the handrail as if it were the only thing stopping her from being carried away by her own hands. White water roiled beneath the bridge, but Rosa was staring out into the middle distance where the water was far enough away to seem not like water but just the river, the river taking the course it always took between the steep grey rocks. She wanted to look on a thing that held its course. She did not want to think about the water in there, about the chancing of its particular atoms ending up here. She only wanted to see it doing what it always did once it arrived. Flowing onwards, downwards, along the riverbeds that had been carved out for it by all the water going before. Not water at all, but a river now, with a name. People called it the Leny and wrote its name on maps. It couldn't help where it went. It couldn't help what it was, could it.

*   *   *

George had stepped onto the bridge from the garden side. He was taking strides across its planks and Rosa could feel the whole construction shake beneath her feet. It was making her feel sick. She turned her head and eyed him with pleading horror. 'Afternoon, Rosa,' called George, and touched his forehead as if he were saluting her, and all the time he was coming closer and the reverberations were getting worse. He was squeezing past her shoulders, pressed against the opposite rail and he was making off towards the island with a book in his hand. The unsettling tremor of the bridge settled back, safer and safer the further he went. Stopped altogether once he had gone. She looked out at the river again, where it bent between the rocks. She tore from the handrail and ran after George.

'Uncle George!' she shouted, as she landed on the grass, and the planks, bound in chicken mesh, shivered back to stillness behind her. 'Uncle George!' The air was so loud, out here on the island, surrounded on all sides by the river rapids, but she knew where he was, she'd seen his funny sun hat through the willow branches.

She was out of breath when she caught up with him, and he was already settling down on the carved wooden seat in his tennis clothes, his unfashionably small seventies shorts and white Aertex T-shirt.

George did not possess any summer clothes other than those worn for sporting activities, as if it were somehow in bad taste to expose one's skin unless for practical purposes of athletic cooling. Baring oneself to the sunlit breeze in idleness might be too dubiously pleasurable, too suspiciously German, but everyone knew that intentionally exercised sweat deserved its outlet. The necessity of it countered all possible accusations of immodesty. In hot weather, he therefore appeared to be perpetually en route to a tennis court, despite the fact that the house did not have one.

He was settling down nicely now, enjoying the feel of

the weekend air that, cooled and oxygenated by the tumbling river, rushed up the hair on his legs, licked his thighs briskly, washed the ghostly white skin inside his elbows. He was opening *Witch Wood* in the pine grove. The sun soaked the double-spread page, and this added to his pleasure, because that was how his skin felt too, like thick paper in which every pore was pricked out like a brightly separate letter, and now he was one with the book, could lose himself entirely as the light dappled over the tree roots and the sound of the river closed out the rest of the world.

'Uncle George!'

The cloth on Rosa's body was the first thing he saw, it being such an unnatural shade of emerald green, a sheened peel of clinging jersey dress blowing into the clearing, flecked with those startling white polka dots. She was step-ping from the shadows of the footpath into the shifting sunlight under the pine trees. 'Can I talk to you?' she was asking, and he was saying, 'Of course,' and lowering his book completely. Rosa was looking around for somewhere to sit. She was considering the tree stump, discounting it. She was coming towards him and now she was perching herself on the broad arm of his sycamore seat. George liked watching her face as she did all this. He always liked watching people choose things.

Rosa shifted her buttocks on the solid arm rest, and scuffed her sandals against the ground. She was frowning. She was silent. George picked up his book again, but found it difficult to concentrate with her sitting there, next to him. 'What is it?' he asked her, lowering the book to his lap again.

'Do you think the truth is important?'

'Which truth?'

'Do you think there is more than one?'

'Depends which kind you mean.'

'You must do. If there are two kinds, then there's already more than one.'

'No. There's one of one kind. There are infinite numbers of the other.'

'What kinds?'

'The whole, and all its parts.'

'That's just one thing, then.'

George leaned back and smiled. 'Ah, dear niece, come to mop my fevered brow with cool epistemology? How glad I am that you came to talk with me. Yes,' he said, closing his book and slipping the bookmark in, 'let us moil ourselves with the loveliness of logic. So,' he said, laying the book down on the seat beside him. 'No. They behave differently, you see.' He paused for a moment, staring at the scoop of skin above the neckline of her T-shirt dress. 'Look at you,' he said, but it was an instruction rather than exclamatory praise, and now his eyes were on her face again. 'You're sitting still, but inside you, a million things are moving. All in different ways and different directions – your blood, your breathing apparatus, electric messages in your brain. And yet you, who are all of them, can be sitting still. That's what it's like. They're part of you, but they behave differently from you. The different truths are part of the whole truth, but they behave differently from it, and differently from each other too.'

'But what about truth and lying?'

'Oh, lying. You didn't mention lying.' He frowned. 'Lying has moral overtones, wouldn't you say?'

'Yes. That's the thing.'

'There is nothing very moral about your blood cells. But you, you are a moral person, aren't you, Rosa?'

'No. That's the problem.'

'Yes, you are,' George insisted. 'Perhaps your morals are pristine, perhaps they are filthier than a fish-gutter's finger-nails. But undoubtedly you have some. The parts of you

260

do not – your hair, your kidneys – but the whole of you does, because it chooses. You choose what to do with your body as a whole. You do not choose what to do with your platelets, your tendons, your heartbeat.' He laughed. 'So in fact, it is the opposite. With you, the parts of you do not have morals but the whole of you does. With truth, the parts of it have morals but the whole of it does not. Morality arises out of freedom and then choice, but the whole truth is entirely free without ever having to choose, precisely because it is the whole truth, and contains everything.'

'Well, if it's free, though, it's half-moral, isn't it.'

'Oh, it is the freest thing in the world, because there is nothing above it. And it is always good, but no, not in the moral way we understand goodness. If it contains everything, which it must, because it is the whole truth, then it holds all that is good and also all that is bad – all the moral elements, if you like. Above that, it is good, but in a different way, in its own way. In the way that it is something that exists beyond matter in a universe of absence, of unhappened nothingness. It is something. Something containing everything. In the way that God subsumes everything, too, and really they are the same. Everything is part of the same stuff. Lucifer was an angel, wasn't he. The light-bearer, for goodness' sake! Badness is not so much the opposite of good as its perversion. It is the exact same stuff, only twisted the other way round. In a way everything is good, because it shares the same base material of truth, of being, of goodness, or whatever you like to call it. Not good for us, but good in itself. No matter what we do with it, we can't beat truth. We can be blind to it, if we choose, but we only make our blindness part of it. Lying is an irrelevance to the truth, it bends around and gobbles up your lies, because, you see, it is *true that you lie*.' He looked down at his hands. 'Nature abhors a vacuum, and morality abhors vacuity. More than anything else, I think, that is the worst thing we can do: to pretend we are not free. To refuse to choose. That is the insult, isn't it?'

'Yes.' Rosa was looking at her uncle intently, and then seemed to relax. 'Maybe it was because he carried the light,' she said. 'Maybe that was why Lucifer fell.'

George's eyes brightened gladly. 'He was jealous of it?'

'No. I don't know.' She sighed. 'Light holds all the colours, but you can only see them when they land. White light is like your truth, isn't it? It comes streaming in, holding every possible colour under the sun, but none of the colours are visible until they land on things in the world. Every thing reflects it differently, or refracts it. Every thing tells a speck of colour, and thinks it made it.'

'Oh yes.' George was nodding. 'Go on.'

'Perhaps it made him cross. To be carrying all the colours, and no one could see.'

'He probably started out contentedly enough.'

'And then it was harder. Doing a good thing invisibly. Because he wasn't the sun, after all. He didn't make it. He wasn't God. He was just the one who carried it, and nobody saw, nobody knew he was there.'

George was eyeing the footpath where it entered the clearing. 'Imagine,' he said. 'Being asked to prostrate yourself before a creature that looked straight through you. Yes, perhaps he didn't fall that far to begin with. Perhaps we pushed him further with our own blind ignorance, or arrogance, call it what you will.'

'Maybe a rainbow is a reminder and not a promise,' said Rosa.

'Maybe it's both. It says, "Look, the colours aren't yours." It says it wherever it chooses, and you can't touch it.'

'But how is that a promise?'

He looked back at her. 'It's an assurance that we are less and more, after all, than we think we are. A reminder that

262

we're less, like you mean, Rose, because the colours don't belong to us, but a promise that we're more, because in being able to reflect those colours that come from somewhere else, we become part of something greater than us that can't be touched. Something that can't be touched, touches us.'

'Light and colour.' She stirred the moss on the side of the seat with her finger. 'And words, George, where do you think words fit in?' She had never called him George before. Maybe it was the way he'd called her Rose.

'In the beginning. They're all hooked up together, aren't they. The word, the truth, and the light.'

'God. You are talking about God,' said Rosa, and wasn't sure how she felt about this, about God being equated again with truth and abstract concepts, because she had always seen God as head boy of the angels, captain of the First XV. Religion to her had always been a panoply of winged beings, a hierarchy of saints and a book of stories; the crucifix a reminder of the romance of self-sacrifice and a kind of wishing tree.

'Yes,' said George. 'And you do have to have a word to call it. But the mistake is in thinking that God needs words, that he needs to be called God. He doesn't need it at all: he is it. I don't think, when he spoke to prophets and told them what to call him, that he was doing it because he wanted to be called Yahweh or Allah or Jehovah. I think he was doing it because it was the truth, because he and those words are the same. God is the truth behind words. A kind of impossible point where the word and the thing it denotes are finally the same. I mean, actually, *the same.*'

Rosa was quiet for a moment. 'That's really not possible, is it?' she said.

'Not in our heads, anyway,' he agreed. 'No more than we can hold the world in our hands; no, we cannot hold God in our heads.'

263

'Then what's the point of words? If we can only understand them as lies.'

'Symbols.'

'Same thing. If they aren't the truth.'

'Lies can tell the truth.'

'The truth can tell lies, if it isn't the whole of it.' She gazed gravely at George's bare white knee. His legs were very slender, she noticed, not like Daddy's; not like Michelangelo's David, nor Humberto, not at all. She'd always thought that all men's bodies were broad and densely muscled, that slender men like George and Sam were mere anomalies, but maybe she'd been wrong about everything. She'd always thought it was the whole truth that liked to expose itself to her – that only people, not the world, lied. She was chewing her lip. George's knee, the fine sculpting of its scapula, seemed to be at the crux of everything. It was as if she had been falling all day, ever since Catherine's outburst that had come too late, and now she could finally see the bottom. 'I think there's no such thing as the whole truth,' she said. 'And it's dangerous to believe in it. Otherwise you can think that you know it, but you can't, can you? Because it doesn't exist. There are just lots of different things that can be true, all at the same time. They don't match. Some of them do, but they don't have to. No. There isn't a whole truth. There's just all the bits.'

'They're part of something greater.'

'Well, it's nice to think so, but that doesn't make it real. You can't know there's a whole truth, can you, when you can't ever see it. Maybe there's just all of us thinking differently, and thinking we're right. Maybe there's just everyone being right for themselves, but wrong.'

George was quiet for a while. He was looking at the pine trees, the high branches above the water that he'd climbed as a boy. 'We are all working in the mines,' he said, 'but we are coming up to the air with different rocks, every time. Nobody says the Earth is not whole because it contains both diamonds and sandstone. But none of us can go down there and come back up with the whole Earth itself in our hands.'

'Of course not. We live on it.'

'Like we live inside the truth. That's why we can't hold it: we'd have to turn ourselves inside out and cease to exist as parts of it. I believe it's called death.'

'But you're cheating. Everyone knows the Earth exists.'

'And everyone knows that truth exists. It's a question of whether we say it exists as a single whole, or only as the different and mutually conflicting particularities that constitute it. Truth or truths. Unlike the Earth, we can't go into space and photograph it.'

'It's dangerous,' she said again.

'It's dangerous if you think you can grasp the whole of it. It's dangerous if you start mistaking your pebble for a planet and fancying you've got the universe in your pocket.'

'And if you don't? Then what? If you know that all you've got is a lump of rock, then still, what's the good of that. If you can't ever know if it's right. I know, you said, everything's true, but that's not much *use*, is it? You might as well say everything's false.'

'I suppose that's why I like books,' said George, but Rosa was only partly paying attention to him. She was concentrating mainly on the thoughts inside her head, which were pulsing through the pattern of the pine bark as she stared at it. 'There's nothing to stop you, is there,' she suddenly said, 'from going back? You could go down and dig in a different place, you could dig up another rock, couldn't you?' Her voice was gathering pace. 'You could keep going, in different places. And some rocks *are* better than others. Some rocks have diamonds and rubies in them.' Her eyes were darting over his face, and then she was tilting her neck back, gazing up at the brilliant blue sky.

George had been looking back at Rosa's face, but it seemed intrusive now that she was no longer looking at him, so he looked down at her arms instead, tawny soft-looking limbs that were hard and strong, like the velvet on a stag's antler, that was how her skin would feel. 'Jewels aren't shiny when you find them,' she said. 'I know you have to cut them. But then the light shines through them,' she said. Sometimes it was hard to believe she was Ruaridh and Eleanor's daughter.

'You're very brave,' he said. 'In your head.'

Rosa swivelled her eyes towards him, met his gaze very directly and said, 'I'm trying to be. It's my new resolution, George.'

'Bravo. Still, don't dismiss what you've already got too easily. It's worth hanging onto. The bit you've got is the bit no one else has. The outside of your body is the inside of the rest of the universe, that's what the philosophers say.'

'I don't like my bit.' Half-sulking, picking at the moss again. Half-expecting Uncle George to remonstrate with her and point out how lucky she was to be her.

'But it's connected to all the rest,' he merely said. 'The outside shape of your life is a membrane that connects with everything else. If you map the bit you've got, properly, then you can know the rest of the world from the indentations and vibrations printed on you, I think, if you listen. If you follow these things outwards from the point where they touch your skin, by imagining. Just as the moon can show you where the sun is, even in the dead of night, when the sun is nowhere to be seen. You can imagine where it must be shining from to hit the moon at such an angle.'

'I am a very imaginative person.'

'There you go then.' How young she was, George thought, and felt relieved to be reminded of it. As soon as he heard a person describe themselves, he knew they would not trouble his heart too greatly, that he could merely enjoy them or not as he chose.

'Why are you smiling? Don't patronise me, Uncle George, you'll spoil it.'

'No. It's just that,' he raised his eyebrows, 'if you say,' seemed to be trying to excuse himself for what he was himself about to say, 'I am an imaginative person, then how will you imagine what it is like to be an unimaginative person? Maybe you don't want to. That's fair enough.'

'I'm just telling the truth.'

'It won't be very useful to you, though, that sort of truth, if it's usefulness you say you're interested in. It's fixing things. It's fixing yourself at a particular point in time, isn't it, and then sticking with it always. Which in a way is false. To pretend you stay the same while everything around you changes. Maybe it's more useful to say, I like imagining things. I have often imagined things. Rather than fixing it permanently to your pronoun, and saying, I am an imaginative person.'

'I don't think it makes any difference how you phrase it.'

'But of course it does! Grammar is the structure in which you think, or the structure in which your thoughts make themselves tangible to you in words, which might as well be the same. It matters very much. The best advice I can give you, Rosa, is to rid your person of adjectives and make love to verbs. Be a person who feels pride, but do not be a proud person.'

'How would you describe yourself, then?'

'I wouldn't want to. Not any more. I wouldn't want anyone else to describe me either. It means writing down, you know, *de scribere*. Which has a certain permanence, not like spoken words that vanish as if they've never been there. You have to be careful about the way you write yourself down.'

'But you love books.'

He nodded, and looked sad, she thought. 'Yes,' he said. 'And I always thought I knew who I was. But I can't have done, because I never did like describing myself; I always did get angry when other people tried. When people said, George is so impatient, or George is clever. I hated it either way. I went along with it, Rosa, but I must have always known, that in fact I didn't know who I was at all and didn't want to. I think I have always wanted to be no one, or everyone, which is the same thing. I needed someone like Natasha but then, you see, I didn't know what to do with her once I'd found her.'

Rosa was staring at her uncle, who continued to sit there, having so suddenly made these confessions to her. What had, up until a moment ago, felt like a brave conversation, now seemed vaguely sickening. Her face prickled, it wanted to be covered up so much. Rosa did not, she discovered, want to know everything after all. At least, not right now she didn't. Maybe later, when she was on her own, in her room or somewhere else; then she would think about the things he was telling her now.

'And now I've buggered everything up,' said George.

'You shouldn't tell me this, it isn't right,' said Rosa in a rush. 'Maybe I won't mind knowing it later, once you've gone, but I really don't like it right now, Uncle George. It is making me feel uncomfortable.'

She meant, I am discomfited, and discomfiture is being unprepared. I am discomforted, and discomfort is being un-strengthed. I am unready. *All over the place.* Here and now, in space. Whereas later, it would be fine, because she would not be in it. Later it would be a thing to remember, a story. A chain of events which she could not change or choose in, and this would be nice.

Rosa was an occasional reader of novels; mainly she liked teasing out stories from the lives of herself and her friends, and this sort of history-telling held much the same pleasure as that found bound between covers. Things that had happened were done and dusted down, complete.

George loved books. Not necessarily because the stories in them were better than the stories all around you in real life, but because, in a book, there was nothing to be afraid of.

Normally when someone is telling you what they think, you are listening and thinking, well, that's not what I think. You are gauging the difference between their thoughts and yours, the space between. But most of all, you are thinking, What should I do next? What shall I say? How to bridge the gap in a way that they expect, or do not expect (depending which you value more), and that is also intrinsically pleasing to yourself; that shores up whatever opinion you have of yourself today, or the view you want them to take on you. Because when a real person tells you their thoughts, they are changing part of the real world that you live in, and you cannot help but respond to that. You know that it affects you directly. Mental kneecaps twang over your ego. No matter how much you enjoy hearing other people's thoughts on things, you can never experience them as thoughts in your own head, unless the speaker is a person with whom you are deeply in love and therefore of whom your whole raw being is deeply unafraid. Otherwise, instead, they will always be thoughts that you are thinking about, meta-thoughts, which is not the same thing at all.

But when you are reading, other people's thoughts can easily be yours, because you can be in a world in which you have ceased to personally exist. Losing yourself in a book was not just a platitude for George, or once upon a time Natasha. Beneath his eiderdown in Cumberland Street they had both lain quite lost in books. It had been like being in love twice over. To lie in bed with the one you

269

loved, lazily sated, and read a book as she read hers: there could be no greater pleasure, George thought.

But then, reading is itself a little like being in love. Its pleasure is the pleasure of being in someone else's world, a pleasure which love and books both make possible. With love you had to have earned your lover's trust. With love, you also gave your own world back, handed over your keys and let your loved one walk in you the way you walked in them. With books, you merely had to open the first page, and it was always there. It waited with eternal patience to be found, demanded nothing from you but belief.

Still, once things had happened, they might as well have been in a book. Once they had happened, you knew the order they had happened in. You could run through it in your head, but it was happening somewhere else. You were imagining it. It was safe: you did not need to be afraid because it wasn't asking you to choose, and therefore you could do no right nor wrong.

This was what Rosa meant.

'I don't think one needs to be so reliant on one's imagination,' she crossly and contrarily said. 'I don't think truth should be imagined, not at all. It doesn't seem right. And anyway, there must be another way. To get at the world, from your little piece of rock.'

'I am sure there are many.'

'Atoms,' said Rosa. 'You could learn the atomic structure of your rock, for a fact, and then you could – you could –'

'Extrapolate?'

'Extrapolate from it.'

'Extrapolation is a nicer word for imagining, isn't it. But yes, yes, you could learn a lot about the universe that way. If you are brave enough to hack into yourself, yes, I think you could learn a lot. Why shouldn't there be an emotional physics to the universe?'

'And people can tell you what their part is like, can't they.'

'Yes, of course.'

'It's wrong to assume they're built the same as you, isn't it. You should watch them, and listen.' She was swallowing hard. 'I think I've been an idiot,' she said.

'You think Catherine is telling the truth.'

'I don't know. But I think Humberto was not lying.'

'Humberto was a very good man.'

Rosa nodded. 'He still is,' she said, and looked at George, and saw that he agreed with her from the way that he was being silent and not speaking in long words. Yes, it was all right to be intimate like this with him, it was fine now that she could choose it.

When things were happening, it was unpleasant to feel that you were being dragged into them without your permission. It could feel as if you were a character in a book that someone else was writing, and nobody likes that. It was unpleasant to feel that you existed but were powerless.

Nicer to stand invisibly behind the sofa, unseen and not-existing but only looking in on past or future things, or distant told or televised things, where your powerlessness made sense and was in fact rather relaxing; the kind found in reading.

Or, seen and existing, to see and to choose, to exercise that freedom which is, after all, the essence of being.

But nasty to feel that one existed yet had no choosing. Rosa was happier now that she had chosen. In fact, it felt as if she had truly chosen something for the first time in her life, even though all she had done to exercise her choice was remain seated on the arm of a sycamore seat and not walk away.

*　　*　　*

Rosa, wondering whether it was right for her to feel so much less anxious now than she had done on the bridge, and deciding it was fine, glanced over at the skinny tree trunks, the rough bark, its black kohled markings like snakeskin that were really not markings at all but just the shadows of all its edges.

'I love you,' she said.

'Yes, that's the thing, isn't it,' said George, because he was thinking about Natasha, and because Rosa seemed to be reading his thoughts very correctly. Naturally: she felt the same way about Humberto, didn't she. It seemed to him that she was voicing the way that each of them felt about others. It did not occur to him that she was expressing her own feelings for him. She meant she loved him in the way she wanted to begin loving everyone.

'Hello!' called Natasha's voice across the clearing, and both their faces turned instantly towards her. 'What are you two doing?'

'We're talking,' said Rosa.

'What about?'

'Lucifer.'

'Conifer,' said George, now apparently fixated by the nearest pine tree. Rising to his feet and walking towards it.

'Jennifer,' said Rosa, playfully swinging her legs.

'What does a Jennifer carry?' asked Natasha.

'Gin.' Rosa started laughing. 'Oh,' she said, turning to her uncle once more. 'Thank you. Thank you, George.'

George only shifted his gaze from the tree to the river, and nodded, without looking back at her. 'No, no. Thank *you*,' he said. He knew Natasha was staring at him. He could not hear a sound as light as Rosa's sandals on the fallen cones, not above the roar of the water whose constant churned-up freshness washed over him still in air light with ozone, but he knew that she was leaving. He knew that soon he would be alone with his wife, who had been avoiding him assiduously and every night pretending to be already asleep. Why had she come to him now, all of a sudden? Pricked by silly jealousy? He felt mildly angry.

'I'm going to have to pay for a replacement book,' Natasha was saying, now that her niece had vanished into the trees. 'My library book,' she added, when George made no response.

'I've got plenty of books at the office.'

'The one you put in the bath.'

'I'll do them a swap.'

'They don't want a swap. They want back the same book they lent me and frankly I don't blame them. It is the usual arrangement, isn't it, George.'

He turned around. 'This is precisely the problem with public services,' he said. 'Nobody has any initiative, nobody has the authority to make any kind of decision at all and this flaccid imbecility is a direct result of the triumph of training over education. We are becoming a society of espaliered minions incapable of standing up by ourselves.'

'It's a public library. They have to have a system.'

'They have obtunded you.'

'Please, speak English, George.'

'I am speaking English!'

'In words that only you can understand.'

'Oh, come on. It's not as if you're Ellie.'

'Ellie isn't stupid. Well, maybe she is, but she can speak perfectly properly. She understands words as well as I do. We both comprehend English very well.'

'Then whence this nematocystic outburst? Honestly!'

Natasha was staring at him. 'You hide behind your bloody sentence constructions as if you think no one can see you there,' she said. 'But I can see you, George. I can see you. Remember that.'

He laughed, but the laugh was a short dry bark.

'You throw up your words like nets,' she said, 'and you

run sideways behind them. You may like being so elusive, but you know what, George, maybe I am tired of being eluded. You are like a child, hiding your eyes behind your hands, thinking you're invisible. You're not. I'm just sick of your refusing to look at me. You just lie, and lie, and lie. Do you think I can't see you there?'

'I've got a very good anthology of Lallans verse. It only came back from the printers last week.'

'Shut up! The library doesn't want your poetry, George, it wants its book on gardening back!'

'I never knew you hated me so much.'

'Don't even try that.'

'I resent your saying that words are a thing I use to hide behind. I don't think you are being very fair, Natasha.'

'Is it fair when you ruin my book and laugh at me?'

'A gardening book! A book on grubs and weevils! With fact boxes! And *tips*!'

'You looked inside it, then. '

'Yes.'

'Why?'

George seemed flustered and didn't answer her. 'You used to read novels,' he said, and then he cleared his throat. 'I did tell you the truth, in the kitchen,' he said, 'and that night.'

'I don't want to talk about that,' said Natasha.

'I am sorry I put your book in the bath. But I wasn't laughing at you.'

'Yes you were, George. You were laughing at my book. You still are.'

'Perhaps a bit.'

'How would you like it?'

'Oh, come on. I think you have seen me at the height of my ridiculousness.'

'I didn't laugh. And all the time, George, all the time, you were laughing at me. You were laughing at me not laughing at you while you knew. You think I am a fool, just because I am not so clever as you.' He made no reply. 'Or was that the point of it?' she asked him. 'Was it some kind of ghastly insurance, George? Perhaps you played this prank on me because you are so afraid of your own stupidity, was that it, George? You're so afraid that your body might be stupid when your wonderful, brilliant mind is not, that's why you never let it do anything, isn't it, in case it lets the bloody side down. Was that it? Were you nursing your body through it at my expense? It is very babyish.' She stopped, swallowed, looked around the pine grove as if she had only just noticed the trees. Flapped her arms out from her sides, but was flightless. 'I feel so stupid. You made me feel so stupid.' She breathed deeply. 'I thought you were being brave, and you were not. But I was, George. I was.'

'I didn't know. I didn't know what was going to happen, when I put your – gardening book – in the bath.'

'But you did when you sat on the bed and lied about it. You had made up your mind by then, hadn't you.'

And George didn't answer, because he didn't know if she was right or wrong. He thought she was wrong, but he couldn't be sure of it. How could you not be sure of a thing that had happened inside your own head? He remembered very clearly deciding to get up and go to the chest of drawers. He remembered it seeming difficult but important. He remembered feeling brave. He remembered deciding to open Natasha's drawer instead of his, and that when he did this, the feelings increased. But it wasn't until he'd had his hands in there, it wasn't until he was holding her underwear in his hands, that he had decided to go into the bathroom and take her knickers with him. And even then, it wasn't until he was in the bathroom, was it, that he had decided to put his foot through the leg-hole.

He remembered how white his foot was against the midnight blue satin; he remembered with perfect clarity the pink tufting of the carpet beneath and around it. He remembered the exact mounding and shaping of his foot; he could see every hair, and its exact placement could have marked each one with a pin. He remembered the vertical stripe of white keratin that stretched the full length of the nail on his biggest toe. He remembered it disappearing briefly as the dark blue satin rode over it. He remembered the ghostly white, sharply defined ridge of the tendon that ran from the root of this toe to his ankle flesh, and this too, disappearing bit by bit beneath the cloth and then returning.

That was a kind of choosing, wasn't it. Seeing everything perfectly clearly in the moment that you did it. Being perfectly and consciously aware of what you did.

Things that you remembered were things that you had chosen, or chosen to accept.

But this was the thing: he could only remember his constant succession of actions and, though each was in total clarity, he could not remember a point at the beginning in which he had chosen, in advance, to carry out all of them. Did you really just make things up as you went along? And if you did, then why had he had that great feeling of bravery and purpose? He must have known, mustn't he? Must have had an inkling, when he stood, when he rose from the bed, he must have known. Natasha seemed to think so. But how could she know what he meant when he did not?

'You can't know what is in my head,' he said.

'You left too long a pause,' she said. 'When I said, you haven't, and then you said, no, you left too long a pause. You were deciding to do something. You were deciding to lie and then do something else.'

'Then you didn't believe me! Then you knew from the beginning that I was bathing your blasted book. So I didn't fool you at all, clever Natasha, and I don't know why we are involving ourselves in needless controverse.'

'But I did believe you! I chose to believe you, George.'

'Wherefore? If you knew that I was lying?'

'I didn't. I just told you. I.' Natasha reddened and looked away. 'I could tell you were lying, but I chose not to think it. I chose to believe you.'

'That's not possible! You can't know one thing and choose to believe the opposite! You are making no sense.'

And yet this was not what George believed at all. When he was sitting in his library, or writing in his journals – when he could think calmly and clearly, with no feelings, the way he liked to think – when he was not momentarily distracted by his passion for Natasha, by her accusatory blush that flustered him, or by the freshness of Rosa's youth and skin – then he knew very well that you could know all sorts of different and entirely conflicting things. The truth of your mind was the same as the truth of the universe, could hold everything within it, but this just happened to be of no use whatsoever to you. That was what he hadn't wanted to admit to his niece, because he'd wished so much to please her. He'd wanted to talk to her about all the things you could do, not the things that you couldn't.

The terrible thing was that your mind truly did hold the universe within it, only it was invisible to you, all of it except the single thread, the one lump of rock that he'd described to Rosa. The rest of it was in there all right, but you could never hear nor touch it, never grasp it, it always slipped sideways and was already on the other side of the room even as the part of it you'd grabbed stayed here in your hand. You could not read it because it made no sense, did not follow word upon word, but played all at once. Language was like mermaid's feet: without it, you never could walk to meet other people, and tell them about the one thread currently inside you, and hear news of what lay inside them. But with it, you were cut off from the reality inside yourself. You could love language, you could love it very much, its beautiful linear logical strings like links in a silversmith's chain, and yet you could still long for the garden of meaningless phenomena which you'd traded in for it. That whole, unbroken place in which you did not exist, and everything was you. You could stumble towards it, and think you'd found it in bed with your wife.

'You made me feel so stupid, George.'

Natasha stood looking at her husband for a moment longer, and then she turned to leave, and he let her.

'You make me feel so lonely,' he said, after she'd gone.

Chapter Forty-nine

It is memory that allows you to see the whole truth. Only because of memory can you go back and choose to make another voice from all the roomful that could have spoken; choose to string a different kind of sense than the one you at that time had made. Memory is multiplicity, many minds, many lives, in the single mind, single life, that is yours. From the light of the future, you can transport yourself back to the present you inhabited and reread it, quite differently. Memory stores all the ingredients, every colour and word and note, they are ready and waiting for you.

Back then, Bernadette stood at the dining table in Catherine's sick-room, gluing flowers into her scrapbook. 'You ought to press them first, Bernie,' said Catherine. 'They'll just go mouldy like that.'

'No they won't,' said Bernadette. Then she began to get cross about the way they wouldn't stay stuck down – the paste wasn't working on their fresh, watery flesh. She kept insisting that she just needed more glue, and was layering it on thickly, but Catherine, watching her, was doubtful. She left Bernadette and went to look for their mother, who told her they should try using Sellotape, just a little bit. The roll was running low and Sellotape wasn't cheap: Catherine knew this, but she still could not work out why her mother looked as if she were about to burst into tears. 'It's all right,' said Catherine. 'We'll leave it.' She went back to the sick-room, to tell Bernadette, but Bernadette had disappeared.

Chapter Fifty

The poppy heads shook. Catherine watched them from the daybed indoors, and watched the slice of Rosa's forearm in the leaves, the industrious stoop of her neck. She didn't like Rosa's dress today. She thought it was a bit tarty. The part of her that thought this was quite separate from the part that looked out and watched.

Rosa was standing back now, straightening, and staring down among the thick leaves with her hands on her hips. She didn't know how to look for things at all, thought Catherine, and wondered what it was that her cousin was searching for. She was startled when Rosa turned and looked straight at her. Because nobody had done that before. Not the whole time she'd sat here they hadn't. She did not move.

'Come and help me,' said Rosa, and she didn't even bother raising her voice. Of course, Catherine could hear her perfectly clearly, because of the window being open, but that wasn't the point. The point was, that usually when you couldn't see someone, you spoke more loudly, didn't you. It unnerved her that Rosa should simply speak to her as if she were quite visible, when she knew, she was sure, that she was not. Otherwise others would have noticed her before. 'Help me, Catherine,' Rosa said.

Catherine stayed kneeling on the daybed, holding her

281

breath, looking at Rosa who was looking at her but not, Catherine now noticed, looking at her entirely correctly. Her gaze was focusing somewhere ahead of Catherine's face. She was looking in the correct location, but at a different depth. She was looking at the area in the pane of glass behind which she knew Catherine ought to be.

Catherine could pretend, couldn't she, she could easily pretend not to be here after all. She thought about it, looking at Rosa's face, turned towards her, outside in the garden. She thought about it, looking at the way Rosa was looking at her but not seeing her, not seeing her at all, nor even trying to, but rather trusting to. She looked at the way Rosa carried on looking and then tucked a long curl of hair behind her ear, still looking at the window, with a faint squint in the sunlight, before bending her head once more towards the flowerbed.

Catherine breathed out. After a while she climbed down from the daybed and walked towards the door. Her bare feet made a soft padding sound upon the floor, like bakers' palms on kneading boards.

The room was empty now, as Catherine made her nervous steady way towards the porch.

Or rather, the room was still. The glass lightshade hung upon its chain, the cushions and the dragged-in quilt lay crumpled in the sunshine on the chaise longue. A couple of books were stacked on the dining table, over there in the corner, and gilded glued-together crockery, too fragile for use, waited thick with dust, undiscarded but forgotten, in a glass-fronted cabinet on the wall. There were chairs, and there was the door handle, but all of it lay still: no breath nor touch disturbed it any more. The unattended things, gone from thought.

*   *   *

282

Beneath the droop of a whiskered poppy leaf lay a pale blue eggshell, flecked with brown. It was right at the front of the flowerbed, close up to the hem of the lawn. Catherine found it at once, because she knew how to look for things. Always you began with what was nearest to you. The things that could be hidden there.

'This might be it,' she said. Staring inside the shell, at the blood-stained putamen from which its bird had hatched and flown.

'Maybe we should check,' she said, as Rosa, beaming, had taken it and turned to go. 'Maybe this one was here anyway. Maybe we should check for others, just in case.'

Rosa looked aggrieved. 'No,' she said, but then she breathed in and out a couple of times and suddenly changed her mind, and so they carried on searching through the foliage.

At length Rosa stood, chewing her lip. 'I don't think there *is* anything else here,' she tentatively said. 'Do you?'

Catherine shook her head. 'No,' she said.

So Rosa bent then and tenderly scooped the eggshell from where she'd laid it on the lawn, and carried it indoors. She carried it up to her bedroom, and cleared a space for it on top of the chest of drawers.

Around the egg, Rosa built a different story. Trawling through the past week, over the same ground with different, finer nets, she plucked out every glimpse and glued these into a kind of nest around it. Each of her conversations with him polished up and laid within. Every frown and every nuance of his lips, every wild smile, the way he built his sentences and the tremor of his skin.

It was a labour of love, her remembering of him, but also an admission of defeat. Such memory is the scrapbook of the exile, exiled from the past, and one who is not exiled from her happiness has no need of it. The shrines of the mind are built upon small deaths.

Chapter Fifty-one

'Why did you take so many pictures of Sam?' asked Bernadette, sitting on Rosa's bed with the packet open beside her and the photographs pulled out, onto her lap. The inside of the packet on the bedspread showed a smiling woman with ecstatic hair and glazed pink lips, who appeared to come in many different sizes. 'He isn't doing anything,' she said, looking perplexed from one photograph to the next. 'He isn't even smiling.'

'I wanted to finish the film.'

'He could have smiled then, couldn't he. To make them pictures. They aren't really pictures, are they? He isn't smiling, and he isn't doing anything interesting at all.'

Bernie pilfered one all the same, seeing as Rosa didn't really want them, these photographs of Sam. She took one and carried it excitedly inside her thin indigo jumper, secretly down the stairs to Catherine.

'I stole it,' she said.

'I don't want it,' said Catherine, looking at the photograph of Sam being bored in an armchair in the drawing room, that once she would have found passionately exciting. She would have thought he looked thrillingly grown-up, if she had been a girl like Catherine used to be. She would have revelled in the brave cowboy sling of his careless, adult knee. Even his boredom would have seemed to speak of wisdom, if she had been the girl she used to be. How could she ever have thought so grandly of him? He was just a horrid boy sitting in a comfy seat.

'But you love him,' said Bernadette.

'No I don't. I've stopped.' Catherine had put the photograph down again, and was staring out of the window at the laburnum, which Mummy said was poisonous. 'I wouldn't be surprised if somebody kills him.'

'Why would anyone want to kill Sam?'

Catherine turned accusingly towards her sister. 'You don't believe me either, do you?'

'You mustn't try and murder him.'

'Who said anything about murdering?'

'You did. You said, I wouldn't be surprised if somebody kills him.'

'Accidents happen.'

'Don't, Catherine. You'll go to hell. And be sorry.'

'Do you believe me? Do you believe me about what he did?'

'Why do I have to?' cried Bernie, getting to her feet crossly. 'Why should I have to believe anyone? Why do you always want to make me think things?'

'I don't!'

'You do! You do, Catherine. And I love you, Catherine, and it isn't fair. Don't ask me to believe you, okay?' She grabbed the photograph from the table. 'I stole this for you!' she said, and thrust it into Catherine's hands.

Catherine stood there, holding the lacquered paper, the imprint of the room next door exactly as it had been yesterday evening, containing Sam in one corner. She knew that Bernie was glaring at her very upset and angry and she also knew that she had done this, she had made her sister feel this way, and she would have liked to make amends somehow but could not imagine what to say. She didn't know what to do at all. And now her big sister was leaving her, was walking away across the floor with her head bowed. As she went, Bernadette ran her hand through her hair in just the way their mother did when she was most upset; she had been learning this.

'Thank you,' Catherine said. Bernadette turned round then, in the open doorway, and nodded her head. And then she carried on.

Catherine ran after her, into the hall. 'I don't care!' she called, to her sister who was under the skylight now, close to the hulking hip of the grand piano. 'I don't mind if you don't believe me!' she called. 'It's fine!' Half because she meant it and half because she wanted to shout something. Bernadette turned for a second time and nodded, and smiled at her quite weakly, and then she carried on walking.

But it would be nice, thought Catherine, going back into the dining room. It would be nice if you told the truth and people believed you.

Chapter Fifty-two

'Hello Rosa,' said Catherine. She had knocked, of course: she always did. And Rosa had said, Come in, but still Catherine felt funny about being here. It didn't feel as if she had Rosa's real permission. She felt like rain coming through an open window. Rosa was writing in a notepad with a fancy pen that you couldn't refill.

'Shall I leave you on your own?' asked Catherine.

'No, you're fine,' murmured Rosa, but she didn't say anything else. Just carried on sitting there with her back to the pale bluey-green wall, thinking and scribbling.

'I like your pen,' said Catherine.

'Thank you.'

'What are you doing?'

'I'm writing a letter.'

'To Humberto?'

'Yes.'

'What will you do if he doesn't write back?'

'I'll go and see him.'

'In Spain?'

'Yes.'

'Do you love him?'

'Yes.'

'Why?'

287

'Why? Because he is him. Because he is him and I am me. Because we are us.'

'You'll be all right, then,' said Catherine. 'It won't matter if he writes back or not, will it,' she said. 'Because you'll always be you, and he'll always be him. Even if you never see him again.'

'I *will* see him. I will go and I will see him,' said Rosa, as if she were reminding the notepad on her knee.

'But even if you didn't,' Catherine insisted. And then, 'Do you believe me, Rosa?' she asked. 'About Julab.'

Rosa didn't answer her straight away, but looked up, looked straight at her, and her eyes were like the counters on an abacus, Catherine thought. 'Yes,' she said. 'Probably.'

'Probably?'

'I can't understand why you wouldn't have said sooner.'

'Well. I'm not lying.'

'No. I said. I probably do believe you. I think maybe what you're saying is the truth, even if I don't necessarily trust you. Not a hundred per cent, anyway, Catherine Wheel.'

'So you know it wasn't Humberto. Otherwise you wouldn't be writing to him.'

'No, I know it wasn't Humberto,' said Rosa. 'And I should have known before. But I would still write to him. It wouldn't matter what he did.' Rosa stared at the paper and for a second or two looked as if she might be about to cry. Her and Mrs Farrants, thought Catherine, thinking about love and Sellotape. She regarded her cousin with a puzzled frown. 'I only love people if they're nice,' she said. Rosa looked up at her then, and didn't seem to be about to cry any more. She sniffed, and then she was busy writing in the notepad again. It looked very messy, from what Catherine could see. There were lots of crossings-out, and bits of small diagonal writing crumpled in the margin.

'Will you write it out again neatly?' she asked. 'Before you post it.'

'Yes.' Rosa wrote some more, and turned the page. She carried on writing, and Catherine carried on standing there, listening to the sound of her fancy pen. 'There are so many things you forget to say,' said Rosa. 'And you don't even know, at the time. Because you aren't remembering. Why would you be?'

'Where's the eggshell?' asked Catherine.

'It's over there. It's with my other things of him.'

Catherine twisted her fingers, and walked towards the little pile of items on top of Rosa's chest of drawers: a pale blue speckled eggshell, a leather bracelet, photographs, in a space cleared amid her own personal detritus. 'Would you like me to put these things next door?' she asked. 'On his bed? Then it will be like a bit of him's still in the right place, won't it.'

'No,' said Rosa quite violently. 'I want them here. With me.'

'Okay.'

'Anyway, that wasn't his place. He belonged in the garden.'

'Do you think Sam loves Lori?'

'Oh, probably,' said Rosa carelessly, failing to observe the distraught rigour of her small cousin's carefully held face. 'Why wouldn't he,' she said.

'But Rosa!' cried Catherine, her self-control finally collapsing. 'Why should Sam be happy? Why should Sam be happy when we are not? We are good and he is not, so why should he be happy, and kissing Lori, and stroking her face? It isn't right! It isn't fair, Rosa!' But Rosa only looked at her and laughed.

Chapter Fifty-three

'What is it?' asked Lori. 'What is it?' she said again, under the pine trees on the island on the blanket they had spread. Sam, intent upon her shoulder, pursed his lips and did not answer. Flicked the insect from her skin, from the nook of her collarbone where a film of sweat and sun cream had gathered into a small shimmering pool. The insect stuck to his finger. He flicked it from his own skin with his thumbnail.

'Nothing,' he said. 'It's gone.'

And Lori subsided gently in her swimsuit.

Sam sat staring at her, the whole feminine mass of her, from the great shadow in the low scoop of her sparkling spandex bust to the easy sigh of her shifting thighs, the quivering of her soft expanses settling to stillness now, settling into the slow and peaceable rhythm of breathing in and out, lying down, with her eyes closed.

He didn't know how to touch her. It was okay when he was taking her, or kissing her, or doing useful things like rubbing in sun cream or flicking insects from her skin. But he wasn't sure how he might be able to touch her now that they were just lying here, calmly, like this. He had never touched a woman fondly at rest. Another woman once used to touch him like that, but that was before he was him, he could scarcely even remember it.

He looked at her lying next to him, and he glanced at Julab stretched out on the grass the other side of their discarded shoes. They had brought the dog's blanket, or rather Lori had. Sam had said, It'll be too hot, he won't want it, but she had insisted that he would want it. It's familiar, she said.

Sam had felt very tender and brave at the way he had allowed Lori to bring it, with good grace, at the way he had allowed it to be the case that she might be right and he could be proved wrong. He was braving the possibility that she might have to then try and carry on loving a man who was wrong, and that she might quite understandably fail. Yet as he followed her across the bridge – Lori taking Julab on the lead, she had insisted on this once more, and Sam following behind them with the blanket – he had found himself hoping that Julab might want the blanket after all, for her sake. It was the trusting gladness with which her baseball boots trod. A trust that made you want to trust it in return.

Julab had not wanted the blanket. Lori had set the dog down, and taken the blanket from Sam, and arranged it in artistic folds, but Julab had turned up his nose, trotted off, sniffed about and promptly lain down on his side, panting in the shade. Lori had picked up the blanket and laid it out right next to Julab – obviously she had picked the wrong spot, she had said, laughing. Sam recalled it as he lay staring at the mole on her thigh, which was next to him now: she had been she was laughing and saying, Obviously I picked the wrong spot. I should have let him choose where to sit. Knows his own mind, doesn't he. She had been smoothing her hands over the blanket once again, close by Julab's hind quarters, making it as enticing as she could. Here boy, she was saying. Here, Julab, look! Look! It's your blanket!

She was trying and trying and Julab wasn't shifting an

inch. She was trying very hard and then she was starting to laugh again, and Sam was laughing too, because it was funny.

He couldn't remember the last time he had laughed because something was funny. He had grown very used to laughing for other reasons. He was laughing as if he were surprised and relieved and also hugely amused, and Lori was trying to suppress her own laughter and saying, Shut up! Shut up! as if she loved him. And their laughing kept getting louder and louder, especially Sam's, but it was all right because the water in the rapids was making so much noise that nobody could hear them, nobody would come and say Shut up and mean it.

Wearily Julab had closed his one remaining eye.

Sam, remembering the laughter, felt a laughing tremor in his breast, quelled it. Shadows of branches and cones cast a fine net over Lori's basking stretch next to him. He glanced guiltily at Julab but Julab was happy. Julab was sleeping. Sam looked back at Lori, and he was smiling, and then he was not smiling at all. He was gazing at her dormant form very seriously. She had the numbers 8 and 0 printed in blockish numerals across her front, as they might be expected to appear on a digital watch.

Last year's costume, which made him love her even more, because he knew that Rosa would have been wearing this year's model, and knew also that she would have chosen a bikini, had many from which to pick. Didn't she always? Couldn't his sister always choose whatever she liked? (Whereas Lori knew what it was to not have everything, and was not bothered by it.)

He was looking at the numbers on Lori's swimsuit, and listening to the comforting smothering roar of the water in the gorge, and knowing that Julab was asleep.

* * *

292

Sam heaved himself up onto his elbow. He was lying sideways on to her. He slid his hand, his wrist, his arm, onwards under her skin, gently but surely under her neck, and began the process of drawing her head in towards his chest. His chest was tight, his breathing shallow.

She finished the movement for him: shifted her hips sideways into the hollow of his groin, let her hair catch in his elbow and spill in a grand luxurious mess over his forearm. Laid her head with the smallest of sighs right there, closer than he'd planned it, right there where his arm met the trunk of his body, his torso. Her head, there against the chest that he soaped in the shower. With an undulating heave, Lori breathed out again. He felt it.

Sam closed his eyes.

He didn't seem to exist.

It was the weirdest feeling.

It was like he had all of his being in her, being him, being her, being him.

Chapter Fifty-four

'It's too hot like this,' said Catherine, standing in the bedroom she shared with Bernadette. The room in which she had always slept before she was ill, the room to which her mother had now briskly returned her. She was plucking at the frilled cuffs of her quilted nylon dressing gown, which she was wearing back to front, the way they used to do when they were dressing up. It looked like a robe, this way round, with the frilling collar turned to make a high regal ruff that pushed her small chin out and upwards. Blue and yellow flowers splashed down her front. 'I'm too hot,' she said, and sighed.

'You're better, Mummy said so. She said you should get up and dressed.' Bernadette sat sideways on the bed, twisting tinfoil around a broad plastic hair band. It made a busy crinkling sound, like something hatching, Catherine thought. She frowned again.

Sometimes she looked older than Bernadette. She was looking older now, looking down her high-robed self in a way that made it very clear she was aware that she was wearing a dressing gown backwards and not a fairytale ball-dress. She couldn't wear it, she kept thinking. Sam would take her for a baby, wouldn't he. She examined the nylon closely and imagined him laughing, but then, which was worse, she imagined him not laughing at all, and not being surprised, because what if he actually *expected* her to dress up like a child? She deeply wished to be recognised as a worthy adversary. She was someone to be reckoned with, wasn't she? Why did everyone think she wasn't, just because she was smaller? 'I'm too hot,' she repeated, desperately, and the redness of her cheeks seemed to lend this credence.

The crinkling sound stopped.

Her sister was looking back at her across the carpet strewn with bits of sewing and record sleeves, *My Fair Lady*, *Sergeant Pepper's Lonely Hearts Club*, a half-embroidered laundry bag spelling *Bernad* in looping chain-stitch letters. 'Okay,' she said, but then she dipped her head and the crinkling tinfoil sound started up again. So Catherine just stood there for a moment or two, and then gingerly she peeled the dressing gown sleeves forward from her shoulders, hunching forward, tugged the sleeves off over her hands, inside out.

Bernie was still being busy.

'I don't mind,' Bernie was saying. 'It was only to cheer you up.'

Catherine holding the inverted nightwear didn't answer, but looked at her sister's bent head. A second later, she was concentrating on pulling her dressing gown the right way out and hanging it up on the back of the door, on the hook that was hers, beneath Bernie's because she was smaller, even though she could reach Bernie's hook perfectly well. It wasn't even a stretch, not slightly. It annoyed her that her hook was lower down even though she could perfectly well reach the top one.

'Let's put some music on,' she said. 'It made my head spin when I was ill. I haven't had music for ages.'

'It made your head spin?'

'Yes.'

'You sound like Mummy, saying that.'

'Lots of people say their heads spin.' Are we fighting again? wondered Catherine. We don't usually.

She watched the record turn, and the stylus in her hand, pinched between her fingers like a sugar cube in the Ancaster Tearoom when Nuala and Lori once took her. Slowly she let it drop. *I'm singing. In the rain.*

'This is your favourite song,' said Bernie.

'It isn't.'

'Yes it is, you always say so.'

'I don't have one any more. And anyway, always is a stupid word. It's meant to mean for ever but it doesn't. If you say somebody always does something, you only mean they used to, up till now.' Catherine looked around and saw again how messy their room had become in her absence. In her thin cotton she crouched on the carpet, gathering things up and treading solemnly to bookcase and chest.

'What are you doing?' asked Bernadette without looking up.

'I'm tidying.'

'I wish I were as tidy as you.'

'Then why don't you be?'

Catherine dropped a fistful of beads into a jar on the desk. They rattled like hail on Fred Astaire's umbrella.

This was in fact the last year that she would be tidy in her habits: she would grow up to be a teenager whose free-ranging lingerie and belongings outdid her cousin Rosa, and then she would live with dishes jammed into the sink, right up to the faucet. All through her twenties and thirties, still she would live in a mess to such an extent that when her mother says, You were a very tidy child, Catherine will think that she must be mistaken and say, No, not me, you must mean Bernie. Bernie's the tidy one.

She will like not deciding where to put things. She will

prefer to not move them, to let them lie where they fall until next time.

The beads settled down in the jar. Lumps of jewel-coloured glass, porcelain pellets, black resin roses and dull wooden balls. There was wire, there were clasps, somewhere. The beads came from jewellery-making kits – except for the roses, which had peppered the cuffs of granny's worn-through gloves – which had been given to them by Aunt Ellie, but Bernadette and Catherine had agreed not to make the expected necklaces. If we make the necklaces, we won't have the beads, Bernie had said, and Catherine had agreed, that it would be better to keep them as they were. Loosely in a jar, you could rattle the beads in your hand, or look at each one all the way round, or spread them on the floor like treasure, a sultan's mosaic, a trail. You could use them to bet with at cards.

'Lady Di wrote to me,' said Bernadette. Catherine flicked her head round. 'Really? What was she asking you?'

'Don't be silly. She doesn't ask things, does she. She's a bloody princess.'

'Not yet.'

'Almost. And then she's going to be the Queen.' Bernie was setting the hair band aside, she was opening her bedside drawer and pulling out a stiff sheet of paper. '*Dear Bernadette, thank you for your letter,*' she read aloud. '*I'm afraid I have never ridden a motorbike, but it looks like it might be fun to try. Yours sincerely, Lady Diana Spencer.*'

'I wonder if she can type fast, like Mummy,' said Catherine, walking over and squinting at the sheet.

'Let's practise forging her signature.'

'Okay.'

'You know,' said Catherine, as the two of them sat at the desk with their pencils and paper, 'I don't think anyone will really think we're her.'

297

'We could send letters. They wouldn't know if we just sent letters.'

'We don't have enough money for stamps.' But Catherine continued to copy the loops nonetheless, content with the fact that it was all to no purpose, even as her older sister stopped, frowned and pressed the end of her pencil against the outside of her nostril, eyeing the laburnum sternly.

Chapter Fifty-five

Lori was laughing at something Sam had said. Her prettiness, plainer than Rosa's, lay in its youth and kindness rather than any particularly melodious selection of features. Prettiness is, perhaps, the speed with which a face can be grasped. Features that make clear exemplars, unclouded by age that fades the edges and roughs up the background, lying in perfect symmetry for being known in half the time, folded out like a butterfly, fly home. In your hand in no time. Other faces take longer to land: are distortion, complication, failure to match.

Lori's looks were averagely imperfect and asymmetric, but the calm underlying her skin and the readiness to meet you in her eyes, made her face as clear as a face could be, and set it travelling faster to your heart. The prettiness belonged to her, rather than her nose or lips. Because it was a subtle sort of allure, people felt clever for noticing it, and this made her seem even more attractive to them. She had always had strings of boyfriends, and yet if you were to have seen her in a photograph you might have wondered why.

Lori was laughing, and Sam was lifting his head to look at her – he'd been poring over the map spread out on the kitchen table, planning their bike ride. He knew she wasn't beautiful, but more and more he found he loved the sight of her face. It seemed to well up with prettiness as he looked at it. Sam was feeling happy and wise to love a girl like Lori, as he looked into her laughing eyes. He smiled at her, and his hand slipped on the map, shifted it. A pen rolled off the table edge.

He bent to pick it up, from where it had rolled, next to Julab's nose.

Lori screamed.

She was running round the end of the table – it seemed to be moving, blocking her, getting in her way – her hands were batting at its edge.

Sam was screaming too, but not in horror, his voice was not quivering outwards the way that hers was. He was screaming with shock, in dry inward drags of air. Her screams were emptying her lungs of every scrap of air they held. He was screaming inwards, she was screaming out. Neither of them were speaking a word.

Sam had his free hand on Julab's head, pushing the dog backwards, trying to get it off. Julab's one remaining eye glared up at him through the agony. It was a huge eye, and it was hard with aggression and terror, and most of all it was wild. It was the eye of a wild animal and not a dog at all. It was a look in his eye that Sam had seen there once before.

Sam, retching, slid his hand to cover it. There was the relief of that, of not having to see the look in Julab's eye, but at the same time the hardening of Julab's head around his screaming right hand, the tightening of the jaws. The shaking in his free fingers that pressed hard against the labrador's head. The softness and the agony in his other hand, the one he couldn't see.

*   *   *

Lori's hands. Two of them. Either side of Julab's ribcage, digging themselves in. She was pulling Julab's body backwards, and she was pulling his jaws with it, and now there was bleeding, and snarling, and Lori crying and screaming while she kept on holding the dog, and her arms were shaking. There was blood, everywhere.

Lori was straddling the dog in order to hold it, and its head was twisting backwards towards her. 'Help me,' she was screaming.

Chapter Fifty-six

The dog would have to be put down. Ellie was impervious to Rosa's pleas.

Rosa, in fact, seemed to be becoming quite unhinged. She had come into her mother's bedroom, which was not a thing she often did, and said perfectly seriously that this attack supported Catherine's version of events. Perhaps it was Sam who had attacked Julab in the first place, she said. And that was why he went for him. She was wearing that ugly black baggy T-shirt. Which had somehow reassured Ellie that of course she was talking nonsense. She was just saying the sort of things that people who liked to wear those sorts of clothes always said. Ugly, disloyal things. It wasn't Rosa's fault. It was just the behaviour of the sort of person she thought she had become.

Still, Ellie didn't like to argue with her children. 'It doesn't matter why it happened,' she had said. 'Dogs can't go round attacking people, and that's all there is to it. We will all be sad to lose Julab.'

'Lose him? We're not losing him. We're killing him.'

'Rosa, he has to be put down. Imagine if it were a small child next time.'

'What next time? If he only did it because he was provoked, there won't be a next time.'

302

'Sam was only picking up a pen. Lori was there. Lori saw what happened.'

'If Sam was the one who took his eye out.'

Ellie ignored her.

'Stop ignoring me.'

'Animals get a taste for blood,' said Ellie. 'There is always a next time.'

Rosa had stood for a while, looking at her mother, and then looking around the room. And then she had said, 'Well, good night then,' in a pleasant enough voice, and gone to bed.

Chapter Fifty-seven

Everyone sat together to watch the royal wedding. Catherine was wearing a back-to-front dressing gown and a tinfoil tiara. She seemed quite better now, ever since Sam's mauling in the kitchen. She was entirely back to her old self, and had stopped lingering under the laburnum in that interested way that had been causing Bernadette so much concern.

The cheering from the crowds as the girl stepped out of her carriage was so loud, it was like the racket of the river in the gorge, foaming out from the television set there in the corner. 'Look at the length of that train!' said Ellie, and Bernadette told her the exact length, seven point six two metres, she said, and Ellie said, Gosh, although it made no sense to her because she only understood feet and inches. Still, you could see it, you could see the length on the television. The woman from Emmanuel, the dress designer, was dashing in from the side to straighten its end. Lady Diana was walking down the aisle – well, not really walking, because you couldn't see her legs, it was more as if she were simply moving – and the white fabric was flowing slowly after her, inch by inch. It seemed to take for ever. There were close-ups of Diana's face in the veil. She looked as if she were glad of the netting, or maybe just glad. 'Charming,' said Ellie.

Sam sat with his arm in a sling, over there in the armchair, and Lori was curled by his feet, resting her head against his knee. Sam was staring at the screen with a peculiar expression, as if he were extremely angry about the wedding, or else angry about Lori resting her head against his knee, though neither of those things seemed likely to Ellie. Of course it had been hard for him, she thought, to have Julab go for him like that, after all his care and attention. Of course he must have been upset by that, mustn't he, and, Sam being Sam, was quite likely noble enough to also be feeling upset that Julab must now be put down. But his voice was quite level when you asked him a question, and he had taken a second glass of Pimms, and was drinking it fine left-handedly, and not too quickly, so really everything was all right, wasn't it.

'Isn't it funny,' said Bernadette, 'to think she wrote a Get Well card to Sam, and there she is on television.'

'Yes,' said George. 'And hand-delivered. I imagine an equerry was passing.'

Rosa had been standing in the doorway, leaning against the jamb, in that liminal way she always had. She had been standing looking at Sam's face instead of at the television. Ellie had glanced around and seen her, and then decided not to look in that direction any more, had turned back and said, 'Look at the length of that train!' So nobody noticed when Rosa slipped away.

Chapter Fifty-eight

Across the country millions of people watched their televisions as Rosa put Julab on his lead and set out along the road to Callander. The tarmac was utterly silent. No motorists were abroad, no lorries bearing loads, but it didn't occur to Rosa that this was because of the nuptials in London. As she walked along the empty road, sticking at first to its edge and then walking down the middle, seeing as she had it to herself, she felt the world was emptying for her and the dog. It was right that there was only the sound of birdsong to accompany her footsteps and Julab's tap-tapping paws, his gentle pant. There were the two of them in one world, and everyone else in another.

The boy Roderick at the dodgems had said the fair would stay till Thursday. He would take him, he had to.

The plan to save Julab was typical of Rosa in its exoticism, its unlikelihood of success.

She was startled when, just as she reached the signposts on the edge of the town, traffic began materialising in front of and behind her.

'Roderick,' she said, over and again to each person who worked the stalls and rides, but she said it each time just as if she were saying it for the first. There was no note of desperation or tiredness in her voice, because she always had complete faith in her enterprises. She smiled warmly at everyone who told her that they did not know, and brightly at last to the man who said that Roderick was in the blue caravan over there. Knocked and found him peeling the backing strip from a plaster, looking up at her. 'Hello,' he said.

'Hi. It's Rosa. I met you on the dodgems last week.'

'Aye, I do remember you.' He smiled. 'I do mind your lips,' he said, and Rosa smiled too.

'I've got a dog,' she said. 'Come out and meet him.'

They leaned against the warm metal side of the caravan while Rosa told him what had happened. 'Some boys attacked him,' she said. 'You can see, he's lost an eye.' And she watched while Roderick squatted down, held Julab's face in his hands, and she hoped that Julab wouldn't bite him, but it was all right, he didn't, and Roderick was making soothing sounds to the animal, and saying sympathetic things to Rosa. 'Ech, some boys are spoilt,' he said, 'that's what it is. Folk say we treat our dogs badly, but you'd never see us hurt one. They eat what they find and they come with us, and that's fair enough en't it?' He was stroking Julab's neck now, and Julab seemed to like it.

'Yes, I think so,' said Rosa.

'Folk that get their kicks from hurting beasts on purpose, ech. And he's such a handsome fellow,' he said. 'They must be spoilt, that must be it. But he'll be all right with his one eye, won't he?' And he stood, smiling again at Rosa, leaning in against the caravan again, closer to her than before.

Rosa was looking back at him, and he could see, to his surprise, that she was trying to hold back tears. She was swallowing, and then she was shaking her head, 'No,' she was saying, 'that's the thing. It's awful.'

'What is? What's awful?' Roderick was putting his hand

307

on her waist, but she just kept shaking her head, and trying not to cry. 'What is it?' he asked again. 'Please, tell me.'

'My father can't bear to have an ugly dog. He says Julab will have to be put down. He's taking him to the vet's tomorrow.' Rosa pictured her father's face as she spoke. She felt slightly bad for using him in this way, but the thing was, this situation called for desperate measures. Only a father would do for this part of her story, and it wasn't her fault, was it, that she only had one, and that he had gone.

'No!'

Rosa nodded.

'What a bastard.'

'I know.'

'He's a fine dog. He's fine with just the one eye. Ech, that's terrible.'

'That's just what my father's like. Everything's about appearances! He doesn't want his friends to laugh at him for having a dog that isn't all handsome and conventional and normal. He doesn't care about Julab at all.' Rosa was picturing her father when he was cross, and in her head she swiftly made that all of him, just for a moment. 'I hate him,' she said with feeling.

Roderick looked at her. 'I'll take him,' he said.

'What?'

'If you want. I'll take him. I don't care what people think.'

Rosa said yes and kissed the side of his neck very passionately against the hot tin side of the caravan.

'Here's his dressings,' she said, and Roderick chose not to understand that this meant the girl must have planned everything. Chose to believe that he himself had chosen to save the dog, and why not, it was what he would have done anyway.

Chapter Fifty-nine

'Where were you?' cried Ellie, when Rosa came back. 'I've been so worried.' She wished she didn't have a small bowl of peanuts in her lap, as it made her look less worried than she would have liked. She set it on the side table, so as to have an emptier expanse of lap in which to twist her hands.

'I'm sorry,' said Rosa. 'I just couldn't face sitting and watching a wedding.' She raised a hand to her throat, let her fingers trail down to her breastbone and looked away. She had been studying the pictures in that big tome by E.R. Gombrich in the oriel-windowed library at school. History of art had always appealed to her not for its academic analyses but for all the useful things a woman could learn from the women in the paintings, the infinitely various ways in which they stood. If your body was a language the world insisted on reading, you might as well learn how to speak it. 'Humberto,' she said. 'You know.'

'Yes,' said Ellie, who could afford to be generous now that Humberto was safely out of the way. 'Yes, poor you. I hadn't thought. Not that you would have married him, of course.'

'I took Julab for a walk.'

Ellie hoped her daughter wasn't about to embark on another plea for the dog's life. She feared the worst when

Rosa suddenly burst into tears. 'He escaped,' Rosa said, and then she started laughing at the same time as she was crying, she seemed really quite hysterical, Ellie thought. Bernadette had thrown herself into her cousin's arms and was consoling her. 'It's all right, Rosa!' she was saying.

Ellie stood looking at her daughter.

'He'll come back!' said Bernadette.

'It's better if he doesn't,' said Catherine, whose cheeks were flushed from sitting in the nylon dressing gown on such a warm day in July. She was looking at Sam.

'Yes!' cried Bernadette, suddenly seeing the sense of this. 'Now he won't have to be put down, Rosa! Maybe it's all for the best? He can bite things in the wild, can't he, he can catch things for tea. Don't cry, Rosa. Please.'

'Oh, thank you, darling,' said Rosa, wiping her eyes but still crying slightly, as she drew Bernadette to her more tightly. 'Yes,' she said, wiping the back of her hand under her nose. 'Maybe you're right.'

Lori stood apart from the others, watching Rosa in a new and baleful way. Draughts of cool summer air washed over her where she stood, there by the open French windows, and she was aware that the breeze felt pleasant but yet she was not pleased by it, how could she be, pleased by anything, when Sam was sitting by himself on the end of the sofa. I need a bit more room, he'd said, getting up from the armchair where she had been happily, tentatively leaning her head against him. You have the chair, Lori, he'd said.

It wasn't his hand, was it. You didn't need more room in a chair just because you'd injured your hand.

And yet, it was ever since Julab had bitten him that he'd been behaving like this. Angry with her, and she didn't know what it was she might have done to so offend him. Silent with her, and most of all, not wishing to be touched by her.

You might have thought it was because of the pain, but

310

it couldn't be, because he was totally normal with everyone else. Seemed often to be reaching out his good hand to tousle Catherine's hair, or play-fighting one-armed in the garden with Bernadette. *En garde.*

Oh, don't hurt him, Ellie had cried, worried under a big hat. While Lori stood, by herself, under the wisteria, watching and feeling awkward. Always now she was standing by herself, and watching, and feeling awkward. It was a feeling that was alien to her. She did not know what she had done to deserve it.

Lori stood here now in the drawing room, watching Rosa being comforted by Bernadette. She watched Rosa smile and be bright. She looked over at Sam, who sat upon the sofa-end by himself.

You thought you knew someone, and then you found you didn't. She'd thought Sam really loved her. There was a hungry sickness in her belly as she hooked her thumbs down through the empty belt loops of her denim shorts. She'd never felt so alone as she did now, here in this nice room full of pleasant people. In a room with the man she longed to touch but could not, because, for reasons that she did not understand, it was no longer permitted. What could she have possibly done?

Sam must have felt Lori watching him. He turned his head away from the scene in the doorway and blankly met her gaze. The look in his eyes seemed to ask her what she was doing here. They stared at each other for a long minute as the women's voices rose and fell beyond them. Lori's searching plea, her wounded eyes, could find no comfort in his face even as Bernadette cried over and again to someone else, 'It'll be all right!'

Lori turned and was disappointed by the airy openness of the French windows through which she could walk so

311

easily. There was nothing to stop her from stepping out onto the terrace, and she would have been so glad if there were.

There was the balustrade, over which she would have to climb, but that was a thing between her and the garden, a private business observed only by the sun and the laburnum tree. There was no person to watch her, least of all the man whose gaze she most desired, as she tearfully placed one hand upon the lichened stone. No one to stop her as she clumsily straddled its sill. She scratched the skin on her inner thigh as she heaved her leg over it and staggered onto the path, veered out across the lawn. The gate waited hidden in the far wall.

Sam stood, after she'd gone, and watched the empty doorway to the terrace. After a minute or two, he walked towards it, stood in its sunlit breeze by the dragging curtains. He stepped outside, where she had gone, and looked down at the brilliant brass espagnolette as if it confused him. Its finished indoor glossiness flung outside into the garden seemed impossible. He laid his functional hand upon it, but Lori hadn't, had she, she hadn't needed to touch the door handle at all. That was how easy it had been for her to leave him. And right: right that she should leave him, as he watched her there, distant now and glimpsed above a flowering bush, her brown hair disappearing. He had thought that he might be someone different, that he could be another man – she had made him imagine such a possibility. He had forgotten who he was, after everything. But Julab had reminded him. Sam felt slightly guilty for selling her tickets to a country that didn't exist; mainly, though, he disliked Lori for her stupidity in falling for it, in falling for a version of him that wasn't real. And blamed her, too, for her part in creating the whole illusion, and then colluding in it. She had tricked him into tricking her. If she hadn't believed that the other him existed, then it never would have happened, this stupid mirage of the last few days. She shouldn't have made it happen. Now it was worse than before, being him, the real him. He knew that things would be back to normal soon, knew that soon everything inside him would be entirely calm once more, but right now, the day seemed to flay him. Everything that he saw pierced him, with its beauty, or pride, or humility, or loneliness: every plant in the garden, every expanse in the landscape. At the far edge of the garden, Lori was opening the gate. Sam glanced up at the mountain.

His hands were too hot. There was one that felt the burning brass of the door handle; there was one that sweltered in a bandaged useless weight. His hands were too hot. That was why he turned and stepped back into the room, out of the heat of the sun. That was why he did not watch Lori's final vanishing, but instead stood by the still-chattering television set, head bent.

The others were drifting from the room. First Natasha, who glanced at her husband and then turned quickly away when she found he was not looking at her at all, swallowed and slipped out. Then Ellie announced she was going to sit in the sun, out by the rhododendrons, and asked Bernie if she would like to join her, and Bernie said Yes, if Catherine comes too. And finally George, who had been standing staring at the clock amid the porcelain clutter on the mantelpiece, blinked and jerked his neck, seemed to realise where he was, and also strode out into the hall.

Only Rosa was left as Sam walked over to the mantelpiece. He picked up a china figurine with his one good hand, a Dresden belle, and then he carefully put it down again. Turned, and now was regarding his sister very levelly. Swallowed, and cocked his head to one side, and tried to smile. Rosa looked back at him as if she had seen everything now. She looked very old, and worn, but not unhappy.

Looked as if she were tempted to laugh at him, but he did not mind this in the end, would only have minded if she'd pitied him. 'Thank you,' he said at length. 'Thank you for rescuing Julab. For letting him go.'

Rosa just carried on looking at him in exactly the same way, and then she walked towards him and kissed his cheek. He felt the catching of her dry lip that stuck to his skin for a splintering second. 'That's all right,' she said, and then she left the room, and Sam sat down in the armchair again where earlier Lori in all her dreadful heavenly ignorance had laid her head against his knee. The television was still on, and he was looking at the screen, but he wasn't really paying attention to it.

Catherine and Bernadette filled watering cans at the sink in the kitchen, ready for the sunbathing trip. 'Come with us, Mummy,' pleaded Bernadette. Natasha was glancing up at the doorway to the hall, but it stayed resolutely empty and so she agreed. 'Has anyone seen my magazine?' Ellie was asking in the corner, as Catherine chased Bernie outside and water drops gleamed on the black and white chequerboard floor.

Chapter Sixty

'Thank goodness for that,' said Natasha, after they'd all left and she was standing on the gravel by herself. It was in fact the last year that Ellie and her children would come to stay for any length of time; they never again came back like that. Natasha thought she was glad to see them go, but it was strange then that the sound of the engine as the car turned into the road, the smell of the exhaust, made her feel sad. 'Thank goodness everything's back to normal,' she said, but she glanced over at the space among the pine trees, and frowned, as she walked into the house.

The afternoon was very quiet. It wasn't unpleasant, she insisted to herself. The quietness was not loneliness. It was peaceful, wasn't it, she thought, mopping the kitchen floor with more vigour than usual and being crosser than usual with her children. She kept going back into the kitchen, and then couldn't work out why she'd gone in there. She kept finding herself looking at the little clock on the Trinity cooker, despite the fact she had nothing cooking and was expecting no one.

Natasha was upstairs when George came home many hours later. She was stripping the sheets from the beds in which Sam and Rosa had slept. Stripping beds always made her feel melancholy. George was not coming to find her and say hello, in the way that he usually did. She was waiting for him, but he didn't. Maybe he had only carried on doing it because Ellie had been here, she thought to herself, this last week. Maybe he only hadn't wished to embarrass her in front of Ellie, by not coming to say hello to her all the other evenings, up to and including yesterday – maybe that was the only reason he had still been coming to find her and say hello during this last week. She had needed him to keep coming to find her; she had needed to keep being short with him. Partly because he deserved it; partly because she could know she could stop. She shook the sheet out. She folded it, because it was easier to carry the sheets if they were folded, even if they were all going to get crumpled in the machine. She stood there waiting, but George did not come up the stairs to find her, and now she did not want to go down. Stripping the beds always made her feel melancholy, she told herself. She was trying not to cry.

In the lean-to shed by the kitchen door, George was unbuttoning his shirt. Scant daylight smudged a single small and grubby glass pane that looked into the shadows, so his clothes were in darkness where they mounted in a heap at his feet. He sat down on top of the enormous sack of dog food in the corner, naked.

George was not doing it in the shed out of shame. He was doing it in the shed because he wanted it to be complete before Natasha found him. He wanted to do it properly for her. He lit a match, and lit the candle. Put the matches on the windowsill and held the plate over the candle so that the flame licked the underside of the porcelain. After a while it was ready, and he began. Took the flame away, ran his finger round and round in small circles, over the bottom of the plate, and began to write it. Wrote the first one on his chest, in large letters, and the second on his left bicep. And then he thought: maybe I should let her be able to find me halfway through. Maybe that has to be part of it. So he took the candle and the matches and the plate, which by now had a good disc of soot on its underside, marked round and round where his blackened fingertip had swept it, and he opened the door. Beech mast cracked under his bare feet as he strode across the grass, over the fallen blown things. He was standing naked, six feet out from the hedge. He looked down and saw his bare feet, every line and vein and hair on them there in the grass. A shining leaf curled and gleamed down there to the left of his left foot, and the leaf was mottled like toadskin. His cock was hanging down and it was pleasant in the breeze, and startling. George swallowed, and lit another match, and lit the candle.

Slowly in the wavering shadows of the beech trees the words grew over his skin. *I love you*, he daubed on elbow and arse-cheek, calf and shoulder, twisting and stooping, as far round as he could reach. It was written in black soot on his pale skin, which the late sun and shadows turned a kind of bronze underneath the beech trees. It was written different ways up and in different sizes. It was written in places you liked and places of which you were ashamed. It was written on skin that was public and private. Hand and thigh, forehead and loin. Finally it was written on his right foot.

George put down the china plate when he was done. The gilded giant eagle on the side of the plate which he had not needed lay clutching its chrysanthemum in the grass as he walked away towards the vegetable garden.

It was not a large plot of earth. George only needed to put his foot down once, and then take one more giant step to reach its centre. He took care not to step upon her vegetables. Then all that remained was for him to wait.

*　　　*　　　*

Why didn't he come to her? wondered Natasha. Why didn't he still come to her, so that she could still be short with him? She would be extra-short with him at supper. She would. She felt a terrible nausea in her guts about him not coming to find her this evening. Carefully she folded the sheets into eighths and then decided she had not got them straight enough. It didn't matter that they were going to be thrown in the machine. It just mattered that she got them very straight right now, or here, which was the same thing.

After half an hour, the sheets were very straight. They could not have been straighter. So Natasha had to go downstairs, and by now she was glad, by now the sheets had become a kind of enemy. As if they were keeping her from George all by themselves; as if it was not she who had invested them with this power in the first place. She was feeling a little excited as she finally left the safety of the servants' corridor and made her way softly down the narrow stair. She pushed open the door and stepped out into the hall.

She had expected something to happen. She looked up the few steps that led to the door of the library, where she knew George must be hiding. He was being absolutely silent. Perhaps he was being quiet because he had heard her. She would be quiet until he thought she had gone. She put down the laundry and stood very still. She stood like that for almost twenty minutes, waiting.

Still no sound from him. Natasha eventually walked towards the shallow library stair, its dark-stained balustrade, and three steps up, halfway, she called out, *George*.

He did not answer her. She stared at the library door. She would not go in to him, she would not. She turned, and went to fetch the laundry from the floor, and down in the kitchen she stuffed it into the twin tub washing machine with violent elbows and a slam of the lid. She went to check on the children, who were sitting in their room cutting things out from Rosa's discarded pop magazines and seemed perfectly happy without her also. She went back to the kitchen, and stood surrounded by the noise of the washing machine, and ran her hand through her hair.

George, standing in the vegetable garden, watched Natasha laying the drawing room rugs out over the balustrade.

She had come back into the kitchen to get a broom for beating the rugs, which she had draped over the balustrade, and then she realised that it was time to get supper on. She took the mackerel and yesterday's beetroot out of the fridge. The tinfoil shone in a bright brave way as she wrapped it round the mackerel, and the red light on the cooker as she turned on the oven also grimly pleased her. There were still some things which obeyed her, still some things did what she wished. But it also distressed her: the distance between these things and the one thing, the one thing she truly wanted. The one thing she had always allowed herself to go on wanting, and now found herself wanting more than ever. Her husband, her only weakness. She had been wrong to trust him with it, she told herself, staring at the obedient light on the fascia. She looked around her at all the other things in her kitchen that never tricked her, and she breathed deeply. She took a knife from the drawer, with which to cut a fresh lettuce from the vegetable garden.

Natasha did not notice George until she was halfway across the grass. She was wrapped up in her own thoughts and feelings, and concentrating on the knife and her breathing. It gave her such a jump, when she looked and saw him. She stopped still. It wasn't a ghost, or a lunatic, was it. It was George. Naked, but with something on him. She was carrying on walking towards him, and she could see quite plainly now what was written, where it was written largest, across his chest. *I love you*, it said. She carried on walking towards him. *I love you*. When she had just managed to lock it all in. Her sandals were at the edge of the bed now. He was not far away from her at all. They were both standing still now, and she was seeing what he'd written, over every different bit of him. *I love you* said all the parts, at the same time, together. *I love you* said his throat and his arms, his groin and thigh and shins, his face and hanging cock.

Natasha didn't know what to do. She wished she knew what to do. She kneeled down at the edge of the flowerbed and with her knife she cut a lettuce, because that was what she had planned. But she knelt there for quite a long time, even after she had cut the Webb's Wonder and had it in her hand. She thought she might think of the right thing to do, but she couldn't. She could just feel the cool lettuce leaves against her skin, and the closeness of George, and all the different parts of him on which he had written. George was being completely silent. Natasha loved him back, just like that, the way that he said. She loved him so much. She wished she knew what to do. She got up and went back across the grass. She looked back over her shoulder when she got to the kitchen door, and George was still standing there. He hadn't moved. He was standing there all the time, just waiting. He was looking at her and he didn't move. 'Come in,' she called. 'Come in and eat.' And she blushed, and went in.

Natasha sent the girls out quickly, after they had eaten, it had nearly been more than she could bear, to wait. With George sitting opposite her, at the other end of the table, faint dark smears on his freshly bathed skin. With George looking back at her. She thought that he would never look the same to her again.

When the girls had gone, she pushed her chair back and walked, almost ran, around the table to where he sat. She was standing beside him, and then she didn't know what to do, again, all she'd known was to get here and be next to him. She pulled his head in sideways to her body and ran her hand through his hair and to the side of his neck. He pushed his chair out and she staggered slightly when he did that, because it pulled her with him. But now there was space for her to sit down sideways in his lap and be kissing him.

Chapter Sixty-one

Two weeks later, Lori slipped into the pharmacy on the main street, the one with a green painted sign, and came back out with a package in a paper bag. *One Test*, said the letters printed on the end of the small cardboard box inside it, and then Lori looked down and blushed, and folded the top of the paper bag over it so that the words were quite invisible.

'It might have been the baby oil,' said the doctor on Tuesday. 'You can't use baby oil and condoms. Did no one ever tell you?'

Lori left the surgery and stared at the brazen cherry tree shrugging off the last of its pale pink petals in the cold grey breeze, there by the side of the road. She was staring at the late-flowering blossom, at the way that it fell and drifted across things, hiding the things behind it in its slow and lazy shower of paper hole punchings. Suddenly she looked up the road, to where the iron footbridge took off across the disused railway. Frowning, she looked the other way, at the sign board of the guesthouse down there on the main street, and then up at its chimney-tops. Her eyes kept flitting, now to the high stone wall directly opposite, which bordered some private garden, and now beyond that to the tip of the church steeple, and back again as if they were looking for something else.

Pulling her baseball jacket more tightly around her, Lori walked along the main street and let her gaze flicker sideways into each shop window: the jewellery and the postcards, the hammers and the books, the fishing tackle and the candy jars. But still she glanced up, and around – at the eaves of the Bank of Scotland, at the telephone wires – and still her face fell back, troubled and dissatisfied.

She almost walked into Alison Petrie on the corner, and had to stop and say hello. 'How are the horses?' asked Lori, fixing a broader smile than usual to her face, making sure not to look Mrs Petrie in the eye because nobody who worked with animals could look in her own eyes now, she thought, and fail to know. 'How's Rudy?' she said.

'Very good, very good,' nodded Alison. 'Missing you. You haven't been out for a while. Come for a hack before you're off to Glasgow, won't you?'

'Yes. Isn't it windy?' said Lori, glad of the way the wind was blowing her hair across her face and hiding one half of it. 'I think I'm going to blow away,' she said, and touched the arm of Mrs Petrie as they said goodbye.

Her throat was tightening as she walked on. She thought she might be about to cry. It took her a while to realise that she was staring at the mountain. It was so far-off and quiet that you always forgot it was there. You could look at it without noticing, in the same way that you might see glass or sky. But now that she had realised she was looking at the mountain, Lori found herself fixated by it. Something in its high horizons gripped her. The way that it lifted the earth upwards like that and pressed it against the clouds.

She remembered Rudy's hot flank in the spring as they had jumped the ditches, that sweet saddle sweat that rose in the dark woods where the only light was the pale green moss that coated all the tree trunks, luminescent in the shadows. The perfect rhythm of her lungs, his hooves, in the silence. She was feeling brave, looking at the mountain, remembering the way that she had ridden. She thought of Sam, and the way that he had so gently pulled her in towards him as she lay half-sleeping on the island. She thought of his coldness later, and it almost made her lose her nerve for remembering, because of how much she had hated it. Not hating him, but hating the coldness – this was her enemy, which had crept in and bitten him, frost-bite in the dog's bite, and then spreading over him, numbing him, it seemed, to her presence, no matter what she said, no matter what she did. She hated that terrible coldness which had stolen him. And he'd gone, hadn't he, she reminded herself, staring out at the mountain. And here was a new thing. Here it was, she thought, with the wind in her face. She was letting it be, she was letting it be real.

'Lori just ignored me,' said Bernadette, breathless from running back down the vennel from the main street to the car park and the soft bedraggled riverbank, the wandering ducks. 'Mummy says no, by the way. Lori ignored me, I said hello to her twice.'

'Why not?'

'She says you'll catch your death of cold.' Bernie sat down on the green painted bench next to Catherine. 'Do you think Lori is lovesick?' she asked, but Catherine just shrugged. 'Are you still jealous of her?' asked Bernadette, scrutinising Catherine's face. 'I thought you didn't love Sam anymore.'

'I don't. But how would I know if she's lovesick?' Catherine pulled a strand of hair away from her mouth. It had blown there in the wind while she was speaking. 'Where is she?'

'Standing outside the Dreadnought Hotel. Staring into space.'

'I mean our mother.'

'Oh. She's in the greengrocer's. She's just heading up to the butcher's.'

Catherine bent forward, pulling off her plimsolls.

'What are you doing?'

'She'll be at least quarter of an hour.'

'She said not to.'

Catherine waded in anyway, lifting her brown skirt up above her knees. Coldness lapped her legs but the mud felt warm, the way it squelched between her toes like something melted. Only, now that she was in the water, and the startled ducks in flight, now that she was standing in the river with grimy feathers washing up against her knees, she wasn't really sure what to do next. It didn't seem that there had been a *point* to it. Bernie was just standing there looking at her. And she was just standing here in some dirty duck water. 'Well,' Bernie was saying drily from the bank, 'I'm going to go and look for something to give the ducks. Over *there*.' Bernie jerked her head towards the far end of the riverbank, where some of the birds had taken refuge and were now settling fussily on the grass.

Catherine stood in the water, watching her go. Then she turned and looked around, away from the ducks, upriver. The overhanging branches of the weeping willow seemed like a point, she thought, wading now towards them. She was striding but the weight of the water made her movements very heavy and slow. Once or twice the shock of its restraint almost toppled her. She was holding her skirt higher and higher, and glancing round anxiously all the time now, to check that Bernie couldn't see her. She wished she could go faster through the water, as she watched her sister closing bit by bit on the litter bin at the end of the grass, her yellow back receding. If she could get to the tree before Bernie turned round, if she could hide in time and watch from behind its hanging leaves as her sister tried to find her – that would be a game, wouldn't it. That would be a point. Catherine's heart was beating hard, and she found herself holding back a laugh. She hadn't been this happy for weeks as she grabbed hold of a wisping branch and pulled herself through the curtain.

It was very dark in here. For a moment, Catherine felt scared, but only because it was so different from the world outside. Here, the wind didn't touch you. The air was still, inside this strange room roofed with branches and walled with trailing limey tails – maybe that was the strangeness, too: a house built from the roof down instead of from the ground up. She looked around. There was just the quiet murk, secretness, and the slow rhythmic slapping of water against the riverbank. Over there, something was caught against the mud and roots of the bank, half in and half out, nesting in a pile of washed-up sticks. It looked like dirty waterlogged white bread. Wading further into the darkness, she poked it with a twig, and found that it was solid. Bernie had already started calling for her when Catherine, stooping so close over it that her hair fell into the muddy water, saw it was a book and picked it up.

She brushed an old and rotting leaf from Macbeth's haggard cheek. All the plastic coating that once covered him had been peeled back by his long soak in the water. The remnants of it still hung in little squeamish tatters from the spine, like the edges of sunburn, a frill of old skin. His troubled brow was mud-smeared now and his eyes were strangely bleached. He was just paper now, like all the rest – the cover the same stuff as every page beneath it. For some reason, she liked him better like this. Not that he hadn't looked noble before, when she had sent him from the bridge to his almost certain death. It was just that now he seemed to understand. Yes, she preferred him like this. She pressed him to her green woollen chest and used the

326

end of her jumper sleeve to dry him. In the process, she let go of her held-up skirt and its hem fell into the water.

'Catherine!' Bernadette was calling, somewhere beyond the curtain of hanging leaves. 'I've found half a sandwich! Catherine, where *are* you?'

Chapter Sixty-two

By Saturday, the weather had warmed again. Bernie and Catherine lay on their backs, together on the flat river rock, not speaking. Bernadette had asked Catherine if she wanted to go on the death slide, but Catherine had said no. I have no desire to end up splattered in the oak tree, she had said, waving an arm over her head, in the direction of the tethering tree on the other side. She had sounded like their father when she had said this, even though she hadn't used his clever words, and Bernadette had the definite feeling that this was cheating. Well, Bernie had said, after a pause, I have *no desire* to lie around being bored. And then neither of them had said anything else.

The afternoon was heavy with the sweetness of sifting pollen sinking into the skin of slow water. The air hung so still that the striping shadows of the ash leaves overhead did not move at all on their bodies but seemed instead to have been painted there. There was not really enough room for them both to lie down on the rock anymore – they had both grown a lot since last summer – but neither of them mentioned the fact, and both of them pretended to be comfortable although Bernadette's feet were poking off the end, into the plantains, and Catherine was cramped up against one edge.

Bernadette began to slide herself along the rock, so that her feet were now resting on it and her head pushed off the other end, tilted backwards into the water. 'Ah!' she said. 'Oh, it's cold. It's nice. Come and try it, Catherine. Come and dangle your head off the end.' And Catherine did it, and they both pretended that this meant it was a good and a fun thing, the fact that they could no longer fit on the rock comfortably together, even though it occurred quite plainly to each that they still could have chosen to play this head-dangling game back when the rock was big enough for both of them. They lay with their heads cupped in the cool river, their hair tangling outwards and around their faces in its indecisive drift. Bernie rolled her head sideways a bit, and at the same time so did Catherine. They were looking at each other over the dark surface of the water glinting with plant dust and tiny insects. Bernie smiled at Catherine, and Catherine smiled back, and they both understood that they were deciding to be friends. They both understood that this had become a thing that had to be decided. Catherine blinked, and a pale ash key washed up against her cheek. Suddenly she scrambled upright, crouched on the edge of the rock and, without looking at Bernie, ducked her head and tumbled off. She was rolling in the darkness, in the water, with her arms still wrapped around her bent-up knees, holding them tight. Her eyes were wide open all the time. She was blinking at the dark underwater thighs of the rocks as they slid upwards, past her. When she rolled onto her back and craned her neck, gazing up through the water, she could see her sister's splintered figure leaning out from the side to watch where she had gone.

Their hair was still wet when they got back home, and their father had made a mess of their bedroom. 'Daddy, what are you doing?' asked Bernadette, standing in the doorway.

329

'Mr Farrants,' said Catherine, peering up from behind her sister's shoulder to where their father stood on a broad plank slotted through the tops of two stepladders, painting something high up on their bedroom wall. She squeezed past her sister and found that he had moved their beds and chests of drawers and the toy box into the middle of the room. 'Is this so it's easier to get your ladders round?' she asked him.

'Exactly so,' George replied, without turning round.

'What are you doing?' asked Bernadette again.

'I'm making you a nursery frieze.' He dipped the brush back into the pot of white paint, which was showing up like skeleton leaf on the green walls.

'But it's all words,' said Bernadette.

'Well, don't you have enough pictures? Isn't the whole world made of them? Look around you, girl! Haven't you got eyes?' Bernadette stood chastened for a while. The writing began halfway across the previous wall, the one that formed a partition with the hall, a few feet above the doorway by which the girls had come into the room and found him. It performed a complete loop of the room, and then formed a second row of words underneath the first. It was this row that George was working on, slowly moving from left to right.

The first row said: '*Once there was a garden whose name meant delight or pleasure: Eden, in the Hebrew. Once there was a time when humans still were animals upon a grandly sifting evolutionary line. Men and women who didn't know that they'd been born, would one day die; did not understand the world as separate from themselves, a thing still persisting when they closed their eyes. But lived their lives in a whole and undivided universe devoid of self-awareness: blameless creatures who could do no right nor wrong because they did not know that they existed. Gifted beasts, driven by instinct to shelter and to mate, to rear and hunt. Once there was a time,*

330

when you were a child, a baby in your mother's arms, when
you were like them too. All the world and all the creatures in
it an extension of your breathing and your feeding and your
dreams: no boundary, no dividing line of I. You did not exist.
Or, everything was you. But slowly those ancient hominids,
and you, the babe in arms, began to understand that you had
being. A clear white tooth pierced the skin of a perfect, rounded
fruit. And that was the beginning of everything, that first inci-
sion, the first dividing line. That was the point from which a
story became possible to tell, because now there could be separ-
ate parts: a beginning, a middle and an end;

And then the words fell into a second row, so that underneath the opening words, there read: *the clock of the universe*
set ticking. Was, and is, and shall be, can only exist around
the centre of an I: a point of view around which the vista
shifts. The wheel can only turn around an axle that is separ-
ate from it. And at the same time came the words. Symbols
attached to things, the very ideas of things, purring up from
this newly divided world. The word

– which was as far as George had got. He was just
finishing off the downstroke of the last letter of 'word'.

'It's quite difficult to read, daddy,' said Bernadette.

'Is it really for us, Mr Farrants?' asked Catherine.

'Of course it is. I told you, it's a nursery frieze.'

'But we aren't babies,' said Catherine.

'Make up your minds. Are you adults or illiterates? It
can't be too difficult *and* too infantile, can it?'

Bernadette left the room.

for a tree can not exist until

'Has your stunkard sister renounced us?' George
enquired, still not turning round.

'You're nearly at the end of the plank,' Catherine
observed.

'Ah. Catherine. It's you. Yes, yes I am nearly at the end
of the plank.'

'Would you like me to help you move the ladders?'

'Yes.' He looked round at her with the paint pot in his hand and a broad smile. His dark eyes were shining. He climbed down and she helped him move the apparatus. Their ladders clattered over the floor, and she kept looking up to see if the plank was going to fall, but it didn't. 'It's an experiment,' said George. 'No. It's an example.'

'Of what?'

'Well of course that's why the Jews and Egyptians had scrolls, isn't it.' He was climbing back up the stepladder, over its top with the tin of paint hanging from one hand.

'You might drop the paint,' said Catherine, as he stepped onto the bending plank carefully. He didn't answer. He was dipping his brush and painting again, right where he'd left off.

the

'Because, theoretically, it is possible to unroll a scroll and see all the text at the same time, isn't it. Not just two pages, but the book in its entirety, beginning to end. It can exist outside of time! It has no need for time in which to turn a page. Perhaps they were written for the End of Days.'

'I'm not sure you could read a whole scroll at once,' said Catherine. 'I think some of them could be quite long.' She too had done the Romans at school.

'Theoretically,' said George. 'It would all be visible. Even if you were to stand several hundred yards away – a mile, even! – in order to see it all at once, it could be done.'

'I think you might be too far away to see the writing,' said Catherine. 'And actually, even if it was only a little scroll, you still couldn't read the whole thing at once, could you? Well, I couldn't. And I am quite a fast reader.'

idea of a tree

'It would be part of the picture of things, don't you see?' said George, and he actually interrupted his work now to turn and glance at her over his shoulder, as if he really wanted her to understand. So Catherine nodded to please him, but she didn't really understand at all. He went back to his brushwork. 'Your eye doesn't take time to read a picture, does it?' he said, with his back to her again. 'You open your eyes, and there it is, all of it, at once. It doesn't have blank white spaces in it, does it?'

Catherine shook her head. Her father couldn't see her, because he was busy with the painting, but in any case he didn't say anything else. There was just the soft scratching scoosh of the brush, high up, as it drew the words.

exists, and the idea of a tree

Catherine stayed in the room. She helped her father move the ladders each time he had sideways-walked to the end of the plank. She watched him painting for a bit, when she wasn't moving the ladders, and then she stopped watching because she didn't really know what the words meant. Or, she knew what most of them meant, on their own, but she didn't understand what the sentences meant. Which was strange, she felt. You ought to understand a sentence if it was made of words you understood, oughtn't you. And it wasn't as if the sentences were complete nonsense, just that she couldn't quite *get* most of them. She sighed and sat down on her bed. It was like being in a boat, having the beds out here in the middle of the room with everything piled around them. She felt like Robinson Crusoe on his raft. There was a picture of that in one of her books, of Robinson Crusoe and the crates and the goats, and he was paddling them over the water towards the beach. In the background of the picture was the ship going down. She frowned and lay back, closing her eyes. She was thinking about what her father had said about how pictures didn't have blank white spaces in them, and she was thinking about how that didn't necessarily mean you understood them all at once. The scenes in the real world that you saw with your eyes. She was thinking about how sometimes you could be looking at one thing, and be thinking you were looking at another, because you didn't *want* to understand it, or because you had *assumed*. The time it could take to realise. She could feel her throat tightening. You could see it and still not know what it *meant*.

And in a book, she thought, when you were reading – it wasn't that the bit you hadn't got to yet looked blank. It wasn't white. It was just that it didn't make *sense*. Was that what her father was saying? That everything should be like the words you could see but hadn't read? Patterns and pictures, and nothing meaning anything else? Just the way that they sat, was that it? Like she had decided back on that sickly afternoon that already seemed ages back. 'Does this mean that nothing is to mean anything else?' she asked, in a small voice, her eyes still closed as she lay upon the bed. Pello had disappeared: he had probably fallen under the beds and she knew she ought to rescue him but she just wasn't in the mood, and she lay holding pillow pig across her chest instead. Her own callousness impressed her but also added to the funny tightness she was feeling in her breathing. 'Good Lord!' said her father, and she could hear that he had turned round, from the way the second word rang out very clearly across the ceiling. He laughed. She thought he was probably looking down at her, but she did not open her eyes. 'Such a world-weary tone for one so young,' he said. 'And you are so correct. But the crucial thing is, that everything means itself. You mustn't forget that, Catherine, or you will descend into anomie and silliness.'

'Okay,' she said, as if she knew what he meant.

can not exist until it can be separated from you. No longer just a leafy extension of your world with tree-like attributes, in the same way that your hand was an extension of your world with hand-like attributes, but something quite apart. Out of the breach flowed language, trickling down the side of that bitten-into fruit, through time. Innocence and ignorance punctured, once and for ever, because, once you know, there can be no unknowing of it. It was awareness of ourselves that forced us apart from the garden; awareness of ourselves that created time, and through time, death. Awareness of ourselves as being separate from the rest, that clothed us in a grammar with present, past, and future tense, on which successive words might then be threaded, and each mean something else. We are all clothed in language that was bought at the price of exile from

George had almost worked his way back, for a second time, to the starting point above the door. 'If Bernie comes back in that door, you'll be knocked off and fall,' observed Catherine, opening her eyes.

eternity

'Or maybe you won't,' she said. 'Maybe the door just won't open properly and she'll be stuck in the hall.'

'All things are possible,' said George.

'I know,' said Catherine, in an affronted tone of voice. 'I'm not a baby.'

and

'Damn it,' said George. 'I thought I was going to be able to finish this line.' He was standing at the far end of the plank, and his right arm was stretched out as far as it could go. He put the brush back into the pot and began to climb back over the top of the stepladder. He was moving quite gingerly. 'Will you help me move the ladders again, Catherine?' he asked as he descended. And once the ladders had been moved, and George had mounted onto the plank once more without falling, then Catherine stood to the side, looking up and watching him as he lifted the brush again. She was watching him now because it looked like he was nearly finished, and usually it was interesting or fun or exciting to watch the end of something.

innocence.

She watched as he put the full stop in.

'Well,' she said. 'I think it looks nice. It's very clever of you to get it to end in just the right place.' He had also written the words very neatly. She admired these skills, even if she wasn't sure what was the point of the whole thing.

But her father was writing another word now, and shifting sideways along the plank, writing another.

Once there was a garden,

Catherine watched him with a frown. He was repeating the top line, wasn't he. Was it all going to go round again?

whose name meant delight,

It was, wasn't it.

or pleasure: Eden, in the Hebrew.

She went and sat back down on her bed, and found pillow pig and held him close, leaning back and closing her eyes again. Didn't words *have* to mean something else? Otherwise they stopped being words, didn't they? And just turned into shapes. If that was it, if that was what he was doing, then what was the point of it? You might as well paint gobbledegook words, you might as well paint *pygaliffy smork h neld,* or pictures of rabbits and fairy-cakes. What was the point of making the picture be sentences that could mean things, if they were only to be shapes of paint?

Once there was a world in which you

Opening one eye and squinting up, Catherine saw that the third line was in fact not a copy of the first one, two rows above. She was glad about this, though she didn't know why, but she still felt cross that he had started it in exactly the same way.

From time to time she helped him move the ladders,

did not exist,

and the white letters unwound across the green walls like bits of thistle seed,

or were everything:

or like when the sheep wool got caught along the fence

wires. She just looked at that, at the way that it was looking. And then she closed her eyes once more.

wholeness, and ignorance, and bliss.

The brush carried on with its nice soft sound on the wall.

Language is the fruit of partition, and the pay-off of loss. Perhaps, one day, language will lead us back to wholeness. A different wholeness, at the end of our exile: not innocence, which can not be regained, but in its place goodness – a thing not inherited, but fought for, and built; not ignorance, which can not be regained, but in its place wisdom – a thing not inherited, but fought for, and built. Words can be swords and shields, scal

The latest line of words had almost reached the third corner of the room when Natasha opened the door, with Bernadette beside her. George turned round. Natasha was gazing around the walls, looking at what he'd written. 'I gather you are making the girls a nursery frieze,' she said, in a tone of voice that suggested she did not believe this. Yet she did not sound troubled, the way that she usually did, faintly, when George became absorbed in some new lexical adventure. There was none of that nervousness in her voice. Why should there be? The words weren't taking him away from her, were they? He had dedicated the writing of words to her, hadn't he, back in the vegetable garden. Natasha would never again be jealous of them.

'It's just words,' explained Bernie to her mother, brow furrowed in complaint.

George was beaming. 'Catherine likes it,' he said, as if this dismissed Bernadette's objections, and Catherine, lying on the bed with her eyes closed, blushed, and kept her eyes tightly shut. She hadn't meant *that*. 'It's an example,' she said.

'Do you really like it, Catherine?' asked Bernadette. But Catherine was saved from having to make up her mind

337

and answer, because their father was talking in a hurry to their mother now, in that excited way he sometimes had. 'You know that programme we watched last night, about Heisenberg? Atoms consisting of a nucleus surrounded by circling electrons that can only be conceived as mathematical matrices? Not in material terms?'

'Yes,' said Natasha.

'*Mummy*,' said Bernadette.

'Mathematics is a language, isn't it,' said George. 'I mean, of course, our own language is very debased, in every sense of the word – adulterated, and cut loose from a real base – but if you take an original written language like ancient Hebrew, where each word contains its own meaning, where the meaning is composed of the inherent meanings of the letters, and through their ordered juxtaposition – it's the same thing, isn't it! In an original written language, where each letter has a constant meaning – or set of meanings – which interact with the meanings of the letters around them to create the meaning of the word – in that case, don't you see, language can behave mathematically. Words can mean themselves the way that numbers can. Of course, I can only write in English, so, ha, it isn't a very *good* example, is it, but I just wanted to try, you see, and I haven't thought it all through yet, but – in spirals, look, it's Bohr's electron jump, one more letter and you have to start a new layer, don't you. And – and of course, *of course* it behaves differently depending how you look at it. Is it the shapes of the letters, or is it the meanings? *Does* it mean anything? It doesn't have to, does it? If you look at it without time, if you snapshot it, then it's a picture. If you look at it within time, over time, through time, then it becomes its meaning.'

'I think you might be approaching nuclear physics from a slightly biased perspective,' said Natasha. 'Shush, Bernie. Are you saying that the universe is composed of words at a sub-atomic level?'

338

'Well,' said George, 'it might be.' He laughed. 'Maybe I am biased, ha, but that doesn't mean it's wrong. It would explain so much, wouldn't it? The paradox with matrix mechanics, in describing electrons, is that the equations are dependent on the ordering of the numbers in a way that makes no sense, mathematically. In maths, three times four ought to equal the same as four times three – they both ought to be twelve. But in the atomic matrices, that doesn't happen. In the atomic matrices, it matters which order the numbers go in. There, three times four does *not* equal the same as four times three. With numbers, that makes no sense – but with words, with an arrangement of letters, it makes sense perfectly. AB is not the same as BA, in ancient Hebrew. They are related, but they are not the same: they are opposite sides, opposite results of the central set of possibilities. The multiplication sign in maths can also be verbally expressed as *of*. AB – the strength of the home – is not the same as the home of strength. It is its mirror image – identical but opposite. Synonym and antonym. Each letter has its own meaning, but that meaning is affected by the surrounding letters and by its placement within the word. Good God, do you see how exciting this is?'

Natasha was nodding, as if he had just made a present for her which she had opened and, to her surprise, found she liked. 'Yes,' she said. 'Yes, it's beautiful. A lexical atomic theory. You must write it down.'

'I've started. I will. Oh, if it were words. If it could be. It would explain the extra dimension that physics can't. A complex numerical equation – a formula – can exist pictorially – the shape of the figures. And it can exist as the expression of a *relationship* – the instance of mathematical or physical law that it is presenting. Yes, and in just the same way, a sentence – presuming you're using an original written language like ancient Hebrew – can exist both as a pictorial shape, and as an expression of a relationship, both of the relations between each letter in a word, and then between the words also – the grammar of the sentence – which latter part we actually also have, even in our own language. But those words would do something more, wouldn't they. That sentence would have a third dimension – more than just the sum of its parts, more than just an expression of a relationship between its parts – it *is* something new! It speaks. And then, sentence upon sentence – do you see? They truly do create a parallel universe. And liaise, don't they, between one universe and the other.'

'In the beginning was the Word,' said Natasha.

'Mummy,' Bernadette was saying. 'Mummy, can you put some flowers in it?'

'It's very interesting, George,' said Natasha. 'I like it a lot. I think you've got something,' she said. 'Don't forget to write it down properly.'

'I won't.'

'Maybe you could publish it. In a pamphlet.' And then Bernadette was tugging at her hand, and the two of them left the room. Natasha was murmuring something to her daughter.

pels and telescopes and microscopes and bricks. Words can be needles, that pull our understanding through from one world to another. Perhaps language can bring us home to a place where no words are needed. Perhaps language will one day sacrifice itself. Might it not be possible to stitch closed, with words, the hole that has been ripped? The very gap from which they originally flowed. To make whole, knowingly. And lie down, once all is done, in silence, and in music, and never need to speak a word again.

Catherine had sat up, once the others had gone, still hugging pillow pig as she watched the words progress. They trailed out from behind her father's left shoulder as he kept shifting to the right.

Nor indeed be able to, for we would at last be ended, all our separate selves brought back to one, and

She helped him move the ladders again.

time sealed closed behind us.'

He marked the full stop on the wall, there, beneath the first starting-off place above the door, and beneath the place where she'd thought it had ended last time, when it hadn't. Then he added the closing speech marks. That was how Catherine knew that this time it really was the ending. Because the words had finished speaking.

George was dismantling his painting apparatus. He asked Catherine if she wanted to help him, and she said Yes, and it was true, she didn't mind helping him at all, but when she was standing with one end of the plank held high up above her head on her fully upstretched arms as they pulled it off the ladder, she suddenly felt like crying. She didn't know why. And she couldn't cry, she told herself, because then she would drop the plank. She wished Mummy would come back. Mr Farrants left the room, with the plank of wood over his shoulder, and she had thought that *maybe* he might come back for the ladders, but he didn't. Still, it wasn't as if she had been so silly as to actually expect it. She pulled back her blankets and climbed into bed, pulled the bedclothes right up over her head so that she was entirely hidden. It was nice in here, like this. She liked it.

Eventually her mother and Bernie came in. Catherine knew it was them, because she could hear them talking before they opened the door. She had heard their voices outside in the hall. She breathed very seriously into the darkness, the bedclothes.

They didn't seem to have noticed she was here. She could hear them talking, she could hear Bernie saying, 'Oh no. Daddy's taken the plank away.' She could hear her mother saying, 'Oh, we don't need it. I can use a ladder on its own. I'll just go up here and there and do patches of them. Will that be all right?'

'Yes. Like in nature,' Bernie was telling her. Catherine breathed out and in, Had they really not noticed her? They couldn't have done, how strange. She lay beneath the bedclothes. But then all of a sudden she felt as if she were going to die. If she stayed underneath any longer, she felt, she was really going to die. She pushed the blankets from her and lurched upright, panic-stricken.

They were turning round and staring at her. 'Oh good God!' said her mother. 'I didn't know you were there!'

'We've made a stencil,' said Bernadette. She was holding a cardboard rectangle. She was waving it around. On one side it was grey cardboard, and on the other side it was a man in a kilt and a vest getting ready to throw a very heavy ball like he always did on the Scotts Porridge Oats packet. He had bits cut out of him. Catherine wished that Bernie would stop waving him around like that. She wished she had some way of telling them how dire everything was, but she couldn't explain it.

Bernadette said they had been looking for old paint in the shed. They had a small and rusty tin of something that looked like it had blood around its edge, dripped and crusted. 'It's red,' Natasha said. 'Is that all right, Catherine?'

Catherine nodded. She was definitely not dead. She pushed the blankets as far back as she could and unhooked her legs from the bed.

Mrs Farrants was climbing the stepladder and standing on its topmost step. A small cloud of stencilled crimson roses bloomed around her head.

'Which one did you do first?' asked Catherine, when her mother had come back down. Some of the flowers were above the words and some were beneath. 'Where did you start?'

'Gosh, I don't know,' said Natasha. 'There, somewhere.' She was pointing at the lower flowers.

'But which *one*? Which one was the first?'

'It doesn't matter, Catherine,' said Bernadette.

'I don't know,' said their mother. 'Now, where shall we do the next lot?'

Catherine stared, first at her mother and then at Bernadette. It didn't matter, did it, she supposed, with just a picture. Where it had started, but still. It was a bit unnerving that you couldn't *tell*. 'I'll help you move the ladder,' she eventually said.

'Over here,' said Bernie, pointing. She looked so sure about everything, thought Catherine, taking in her big sister's blithe movements, the easy swing of her yellow shirt sleeve, the daisy clip that held back her hair from her face. Catherine glanced at the window beyond. The window, which *meant* itself, because it had happened that way. The window, which was the way that the window was with every other thing. The way the window was with things that stayed the same – the wall and the floor and the ceiling – and the way the window was with things that regularly changed – the going up and down of the roller blinds, the flowering and bareness of the laburnum outside. The way the window was with things that might change but mainly didn't – the table normally pushed up against it, that had been taken away and put in the middle of the room, maybe that was why Catherine was staring at the window now with such a pang, because suddenly it looked so different, suddenly it *was* so different. And then the way the window was with things that always changed when they felt like it – the sky, and the weather, and Catherine, and Bernadette, and anyone else who cared to come in and be with the window. Catherine was staring at it now, at all the things that shaped the window, from the outside in, everything, everything else. The way that everything washed up against

343

it. That was what it meant, wasn't it. The way it pushed back against each one.

And that was why she was feeling upset as she looked back at her sister's hair slide. Because suddenly she was sure that for Bernadette the yellow shirt was just a thing she wore which sometimes itched her wrists, and that the daisy clip was just a thing that held her hair back and which she liked because daisies were her favourite flowers. The bed was just a thing she slept in which was comfortable for her, and the window was just a thing she looked through, which handed the sunshine in for her eyes. And that was all. You could tell by the carelessness with which she moved, as if it didn't *matter* where she threw her hands or ordered their mother to paint things. And Bernadette turned round just then, and smiled, as if she wanted to check that Catherine was also having fun, and Catherine felt horribly lonely, and smiled uncertainly in reply. Of course the world pressed differently against her and Bernadette, she thought – you'd expect it to – but she had not expected to find that they pressed back against it in such completely different ways. They were not the same thing any more, not Catherine-and-Bernie, and more than that, they were not even the same *kind* of thing. They were quite different, and here they were, and they had decided to be friends.

Chapter Sixty-three

Strange things happened in the Farrants' garden. Once, the following summer, in the middle of the night, the children saw two women kissing on the bridge to the island, half-clearly in the half-moonlight. Sometimes the flowerbeds would be crushed, as if an animal had been rolling among the poppies to make a bed for itself, and when this happened, Bernadette always said, 'It's Julab! Julab's come down from the woods. He's been back.' And Catherine said 'Yes,' although she knew that it wasn't.

Catherine had embarked on a correspondence with Rosa. It had begun a few days after she found her cousin's copy of *Macbeth* washed up under the tree by the ducks. She had written to let Rosa know that Macbeth was safe and well – he is a bit weathered now, she wrote, but definitely all whole – because she knew how much Rosa liked it when things were saved. She was trying to give her cousin something back in return for her saving of Julab. And then Catherine had signed the letter as Lady Diana Spencer, so as to make a half-secret of herself and at the same time a joke.

Rosa had replied a few weeks later, expressing surprise at Diana's progressive and feminist retention of her maiden name, and wondering how long she intended to stay at her current holiday address, and all this had made Catherine laugh as she read it by herself, and afterwards hide the letter from her mother and Bernadette.

The letters grew longer, and increasingly confidential. On paper, Rosa and Catherine built a closeness that had never existed between them as breathing people, being so different in the way they lived. In their letters it did not matter that they had such different personalities, such divergent opinions and outlooks – the only thing that mattered was that they both wanted to pick their worlds apart and present them to the other, turn and turn about. Each of them wrote as if she were writing to herself, so that each became the other's keeper. When Rosa invited Catherine to visit her the following summer, she seemed surprised that the repository of her innermost thoughts still only came up to her armpit. They had been awkward for a moment, after Rosa's initial claspings, and then they had somehow agreed from now on just to speak as they wrote whenever the two of them were alone together.

Catherine had sat and listened to Rosa's latest tales of how she had tried to win back Humberto. When she was listening, she always tried as hard as she could to impersonate a sheet of paper that Rosa was writing on. Flat, with expanses of blankness on which to write, but also showing what had already been done. She would sit holding up to Rosa, in her face, the things she'd just been told – reminding Rosa where she had got to. But not saying much, scarcely speaking at all. Listening, to Rosa writing letter after letter and getting no reply (Catherine already knew this but she listened anyway). Listening, to Rosa spending half the contents of her building society account on an aeroplane ticket to Zaragoza. Listening, to the sharp Pyrenees below her. Zaragoza looming from the soft farmed plain between those mountains and the grey dusty folds of the Sierra de

Moncayo, feathered with dry riverbeds. Listening to the F-16s taking off from the American military airstrip alongside the airport, as Rosa's window juddered and slowed along the runway. Listening to the heat, and the wind that blew her hair everywhere as she climbed down the steps. The men in dark blue uniforms who looked right at her and smiled. The sound of their smooth black shoes on the glassy floor, and the sound of the foreign language curling everywhere around Rosa's head, the sound of Humberto's language flowing from women and men around the luggage carousel. Listening to the paper uncrumpling from Rosa's hand, as she handed it to the taxi driver, the blue ink address. The slam of the boot, and then the lilting pop duets on the radio for miles, hours, north towards the mountains she'd crossed in the sky. The window wound down, the broad hot growl of the road to Huesca. Listening to Rosa's stomach rumbling as she sat there, as the time went by, she hadn't expected it to take so long to get there, she said. Excited, she said, and nervous, in case he wasn't there. If he was there then everything would be all right, she wasn't nervous about seeing him, no, she wasn't – only nervous in case he wasn't there.

In the small house on the edge of Loporzano, Humberto's mother had told Rosa to take her shoes off – smiling, with shoe-removing gestures, to explain – and Rosa had assumed that this was so she would be comfortable, and Catherine did not say that she supposed it might really have been in order to keep the floor clean, but just listened to the version in which Senora Morales wanted Rosa to be comfortable. And Rosa had sat like that, with the bare soles of her feet on the beautifully cool tiled floor, and had drunk the coffee and smiled a bit. 'Humberto, no,' his mother had said, and Rosa was still taking this in as she sat and smiled at the two of them, at Humberto's mother who must have given him his eyes, and at the young man who was also there and who wore a yellow belt and was handsome although not as handsome as Humberto and did not really look anything like him. 'Pili's husband?' Rosa had asked, and Humberto's brother-in-law had understood this, and nodded, and said, "Tomas', and smiled. But there wasn't much more that any of them could say, because Rosa's hosts spoke no English and she had no Spanish. 'Humberto, Argentina,' said his mother. 'Argentina,' said Tomas. Rosa was nodding, and saying, 'Argentina. Okay.' It was clear she understood the concept of Argentina but, there being so little other information they could give her, Tomas went to fetch an atlas anyway, gave her the same information twice over. Laid it out on the sofa next to Rosa at the double page where Argentina hung whitely dislocated from all the land and sea around it, a single tongue rolling down across the page fold. He pointed loosely at the tiny yellow square that represented Buenos Aires. 'Thank you,' said Rosa, '*gracias*.' Tomas had smiled at her and nodded, bashfully, half apologetic. They had all smiled at each other some more. Rosa perused the atlas as she drank her coffee, and did this for as long as she could, and then eventually had to lay the map down again on the sofa beside her.

Catherine imagined the silence, and to her it felt quite sweaty and thick, the way it was in your dreams, when you tried to speak but couldn't. Rosa had known she would have to go soon, she said. Because there was nothing she knew how to say. Rosa had smiled again at Senora Morales, at Tomas, and she had looked around. At all the things that were here, at all the things that were in some way Humberto because he had been around them. And then she suddenly thought of something. '*El caballito del diablo!*' she cried. And made a fluttering motion in the air with her fingertips. She was very pleased – Catherine could picture it exactly, and she thought Rosa must have looked very pretty, because she always looked pretty when she was

348

pleased by something, but also a little bit unnerving, because it was always like she was asking you to come with her too – demanding it. '*Si*,' Humberto's mother had agreed, and Catherine imagined her uncertain tone. '*El caballito del diablo.*' And after this, Rosa was quite content about leaving, she surprised herself by it, she said. Senora Morales was asking Rosa if she would like to stay the night – at least, she was making a sideways pillow sign with her hands, and raising her eyebrows – but Rosa was saying, 'No, *gracias*, hotel, *gracias.*' There was nodding and kissing of cheeks.

Rosa had been happy after that just to wander around the alleyways with her holdall over her shoulder, to follow the end of the lane out to the field of olive trees. The grass beneath each tree was thickly starred with white daisies, so it seemed as if they were casting light instead of shadow. Dark blue mountains rose beyond, into a heavy bird-belly sky that pressed down against the rocky heights and rolled squawking streaks of cloud from their peaks and ridges: this was how Catherine saw it as she listened to Rosa talk.

And Rosa saw with her own eyes the places that Humberto had mentioned – the bell tower, the cattle gate. She saw the difference between how she had imagined them from his descriptions, and how they really were. She worked out the ways in which she had misunderstood – her tendency to imagine things as bigger or more beautiful than they were. Realised that she was thinking of what they *were*, and that what Humberto had been describing was not in fact the bell tower nor the cattle gate – a crumbling block of stone, a rusting piece of metal – but places where things happened. Do you know what I mean? she asked, and Catherine nodded vigorously and said Yes. The place where the bells rang, the place that announced itself. The place where slow good beasts passed from village into pasture.

In Huesca too, with her holdall left on the bed in an

evening-shaded hotel room, Rosa walked the cobbled streets and plazas where Humberto had been. She seemed peaceful, but it wasn't what Bernadette would later have termed *closure*. Instead, Rosa made of it an opening. Gave herself over to what she thought would have been Humberto's way of seeing things. This could be hers and no one could take it from her. She had found a way to be with him always, now. She could always be her being him.

Years went by, but Rosa only found herself nearer and nearer to Humberto the deeper his silence and his absence grew, because she was freer and freer to imagine him. Catherine watched as year on year her cousin grew more deeply wedded to the idea of him, found him beside her in the strangest, smallest things. The way that fresh catkins would swing from a bare branch, giving their all in a cold March, pollen before leaf, spring before sun. Anything brave, anything true, took on the being of Humberto. No wonder no one could compete with him, this lover who was the world, and lit up hers, this lover who did not exist. Hugos and Reubens came and went, undressed and passed through her kitchen, but none of them could touch him. Never more than half-interested in anyone else, all this time, quite content to spend the last of her beauty among cut blooms in her Broughton Street flower shop, slowly Rosa's skin had turned from a likeness of petals to something more papery in which you might wrap such, and she seemed almost glad of this. Relieved to be a little more free of the pretenders who had always pursued her.

Chapter Sixty-four

Catherine pressed the ridge of her sunglasses back up against the bridge of her nose. Her hands were cold, and yet she didn't want to put them back in her jacket pockets. She tapped out a cigarette, and dipped her head as she did so, and the sunglasses slid minutely back down her nose. Morning sun tripped on her pinned-up hair under a haze of shattered catkins that were brittle now and coloured rust. A million fine tails hanging from the green-bloomed paper birch, whose roots only slightly disturbed the paving on the terrace of the botanical gardens. 'That's mother's,' she said, thumbing her dry lighter for a spark, two times and four before it lit. The words were squashed by the shape of the cigarette between her lips. 'What, this?' asked Bernadette, pinching the front of her angora sweater. 'Yes, she said I could have it. The colour doesn't suit her.' Catherine was pushing her sunglasses back up against the bridge of her nose. 'I brought the newspaper,' said Bernadette, rummaging in her oversized lilac leather handbag. Catherine was staring at its ornamental buckles, the way they shook as her sister moved her hand inside it. She winced and looked away.

Bernadette's neat fingertips were smoothing the pages flat upon the café creosote, she was holding the news down in the wind.

'I've already seen it,' said Catherine. 'You don't need to show me, Bernadette. Fuck, it's cold. Why's it so cold? It's June.'

'It's the haar.'

'I know it's the haar. But it's still weird, to be so cold in June.'

'Well, it's clearing now. The sun was out a moment ago.'

'I know it was.'

'It's terrible, isn't it,' said Bernadette. 'All those poor people. And just so random.'

'Nothing is random,' said Catherine. 'Randomness implies the opposite of intention. And things don't happen intentionally, therefore they can't happen randomly either. A thing can't exist if its opposite doesn't. Things just happen. They happen, happen, happen, and that is all. Everything is an accident,' she said, 'only not in the way that people usually mean that word. They mean accident to mean something that was random, or unintended, or aberrant. But really there is no such property in events: there is only that which was, and that which was not. Intention can be part of an accident, but it can't be *instead* of it. There is no such thing as a fully intentional thing. But intention can be part of the accident, that's the thing, isn't it. You can fall and stretch towards the thing you are falling to at the same time, can't you. In a nice way, I mean. You might as well. At least that way you might steer the falling and land properly, in a good place. But it's fucking idiocy to think you can *fly*.'

'I'll bear that in mind.'

'Everything that happens, happens,' said Catherine, taking another drag on her cigarette. 'Everything that happens, will have happened. Today's accident is tomorrow inevitable. Bear *that* in mind.' She was trying not to look at the newspaper.

'Stop being so bloody bleak,' said Bernadette, but there

was fondness in her voice, which Catherine heard as a patronising tone. She flicked the ash from the tip of her cigarette, tilted her neck to watch it fall on the paving stones. '*Thirty-five killed in Maddaouira blast,*' read Bernadette out loud. '*The Al Warda restaurant was filled with holiday makers enjoying a balmy evening on its opulent terraces overlooking the sea.*'

'What was the food like?' asked Catherine, sarcastic.

'It doesn't say.' Bernadette tucked her honey-streaked hair behind her ear. 'Gosh. A terrace,' she said. 'Like here.' She looked around the place where they sat, regarded the cotoneaster and the crows, gravely, the pensioners and pigeons, and then began to read again. '*Nobody noticed the modest young woman who slipped between the tables with her head covered,*' she said. 'I can't believe it was a woman,' she added, and for a moment Catherine thought this too was part of the newspaper report.

'How do they know nobody noticed her?' Catherine asked.

'They must have asked the survivors.'

'Still, the dead people might have noticed her. Don't you think it's rude, not to take them into account? They weren't dead *then*. And anyway, if none of the survivors saw her, how do they know her head was covered?'

'They must have found her headscarf.'

'She blew herself up.'

'Maybe people saw her on her way there. It isn't really relevant, Catherine.'

'Do you think the journalist is trying to make a more interesting story?'

'Interesting?'

'More pathetic. Do you think he is trying to heighten our emotional response to this undoubtedly hideous incident.'

'*Maddouira is an elegant town on Morocco's Atlantic coast. Richard Burton and Elizabeth Taylor retreated here during*

*the 1960s. Subsequent decades have seen it become a Mecca
for surfers as well as sophisticated visitors drawn by its artistic
bohemian vibe. Our travel writer Maryanne Phillips dined
in the Al Warda restaurant in Maddouira last week. "My
Narrow Escape" page six.'*

'God. Bugger that. Stupid fucking egotistical cow.'
Catherine was climbing out from the bench. 'Her, I mean,
not you. Do you want another coffee?' Hoping Bernie
didn't, because really she didn't have enough money for
two. The price of drinks in the Botanical Gardens was
extortionate.

'No. And don't go.'

'Oh shite. My cigarette.' Catherine was looking at the
half-smoked Silk Cut in her hand, thinking maybe she
could stub it out and then relight it when she came back.
But it always tasted horrible when you did that; also she
didn't want to be seen scrimping in front of her sister. At
the same time she couldn't afford to bin it.

Bernadette had laid the newspaper aside, was pulling a
copy of *Paris Match* from her freshly assaulted handbag.
'This is the bit,' she said, finding the page with its corner
turned down, opening it out. 'Sit down, Catherine,' she
said, and Catherine did, because this course of action
coincided with that towards which her own practical
considerations were leading her. '*Humberto Morales, forty-
two.* God, can you believe he's forty-two? Was. God. I
will always think of him being twenty. Won't you?'
Catherine shrugged. 'I'll translate,' said Bernadette. 'I've
already been through it. *Married with two children, aged
five and six.*'

'Don't, Bernadette.'

'*His wife Maria was waiting outside with their son and
daughter. Señor Morales had gone back inside to collect his
wife's coat, which she had forgotten.*'

'For fuck's sake. Why do they have to include that?'

'It's what happened.'

'No. No, they're doing it for you. They're telling you a story, Bernie. So as you can yearn at its tender avoidability.'

'But it *was* avoidable. It *is* tragic, isn't it, that Humberto died because he went inside to fetch his wife's coat.'

'He didn't die because he went to fetch her coat. He died because a woman standing next to him blew herself up. And the sadness isn't for you or for me, it shouldn't be.'

'What's wrong with sympathising, for Christ's sake?'

'They're trying to make you sympathise with its opposite. They're making you imagine it not happening. The subtext is, ah, what would have happened if he hadn't gone back for her coat? Or if she hadn't forgotten it but had taken it with her when they left. And all these other stories, with the details, of why the dead were there. Inviting you to think, what would have happened if they had decided to holiday somewhere else? Or eat in a different restaurant that night? All of it, all of it, is designed to make you sympathise with a world in which things could have happened differently. You are not sympathising with what happened. You are sympathising with its unreality, with its not-happening. It is all to make you feel that this is random, when really there is no such thing as fucking *random*.'

'Things *could* have happened differently, Catherine. Even if she'd still done it, twenty-one people might have died instead of thirty-five.'

'It doesn't matter! It didn't happen that way, did it. It happened like this. There was a time when it could have happened differently, but it's gone. Time isn't an arrow that you can pull out of your skin. Time is not a linear thing. It's three-dimensional – no, more than that, it has more dimensions than you can imagine – tentacles – exploding outwards from the point where it began. It's shrapnel, and you can't take shrapnel back, Bernie. Or it's a glacier, cutting through a landscape, and you can't put the hills back.

Because it's still there, it's still growing, outwards, and because there's too much of it, in too many countlessly different directions.'

'Your shrapnel analogy is kind of infelicitous, in the circumstances.' Bernadette pulled a stick of salve from her bag, slicked her lips. 'Anyway, I'm not saying anything about taking it back. I'm just saying, it could have happened differently.'

'And I'm saying, that doesn't matter. The only thing that matters is the shape of what has happened, morally, not materially. We're at the membrane of time, pushing outwards –'

'Membrane? I thought it was a glacier.'

'Okay then, the membrane is the outer edge of the glacier, its skin. That's time, always pushing outwards, expanding. But the *shape* of it – that's up to us! It's our actions that press it one way or another from the done things into the undone things. Into all the moral possibilities of the universe. Oh,' said Catherine, stopping suddenly. 'I wonder what will be the shape of what is left behind? What is it that we're carving?' she asked, frowning sideways at the birch trunk. 'Anyway. It's the moral shape of the thing, that's what matters. That's it.' And this was the worst shape, she thought, this thing that had happened. The stone that blows empty rings out through everything. A bomb that pricks a hole in a restaurant, blows out nine or forty-nine lives, that sideways prick their own holes in homely kitchens, office canteens, empty beds: the ripped edges of other hearts and lives draw the spaces of the dead. Wives and fathers, friends, carry holes in their own selves, soldiering through the frying of an egg. And forward too go all the undone things: forward sprawls the lack, the other shape of death, its unborn depth: the hole itself. The walks not taken, thoughts not grown and words not said, things unmoved by fingers, people never met. This life that hangs all silent

356

in the dark, and can't be seen nor touched nor had, this unworn dress, this is the stretch of death. Forward it goes, into the future of the world, from every hole that killing rips. Here it is, she wanted to say, looking at the photograph on the page of the magazine, the building blasted open, the torn bits of things that used to have a use, the stains of blackened red. Here is the kaleidoscope flowering of death: here is the shape of ruptured ends: be it acts of terrorism, or more soldierly bombs dropped, or schoolboy shootings in a classroom in baking Tennessee. Here's the instant spatter of it, here's its shape, its breadth, and there, where we can't see it, snakes its depth. Who knows what might have swum.

Catherine was sorry for the lives, that had lost the people to lead them. She was sorry for the world, that had lost these particular shapes from inside it; their only ways of moving, ways of seeing, the singular turn of their heads. Lungs like stingray wings to beat them forward through time, had stopped. She couldn't be sorry for what floated now, there on the top. Silent corpses had no life with which to share in feeling. But everything inside her ached for the fullness of life that had been torn out: her heart bled not for the dead, nor even for the worlds in which their death could be avoided: not for other pasts nor presents but for the future. For all the undone things, the things they would have shaped.

'I think the number is not the point, for us,' Catherine was saying. She pulled out the newspaper from beneath the *Paris Match* and jabbed at the page from which Bernadette had first been reading. 'The time of day, *Greenwich Mean Time*, is not our *business*. The layout of the restaurant is not our *business*. This informative spew. Should it make us feel better? To know the details? The edges of a hole might describe it, but they are not it! They are not the hole itself. There is a difference. Look! Look at the picture! What else do you need to know? All the rest, all this, it is just distraction. They always write the wrong things.'

'What would you have?' wondered Bernadette, upset. 'Full-colour centre spreads, no difficult text? *Art*? Do you think this is art, Catherine? Like that idiot said about the Towers? Please don't say you think that this is art.'

'No! There should be writing, but – not like this. It is like they are talking about a painting, and all they can do is go into raptures about the gilding on the frame. They think it's a normal thing. They keep trying to describe what it is, and that's why they get stuck, I suppose, because they're looking at the wrong thing. You can't describe what a hole is, can you. You always just end up talking about edges.' Catherine's voice was puzzled and calm again. 'And if they can't describe what it is – not really – then maybe they should be talking about what it is *like*. Because it doesn't mean anything otherwise, does it? But no, it is certainly not art. Art is beautiful and good.'

'How very old-fashioned of you.'

'Art makes ugly things beautiful, it makes bad things good. It transfigures them. If it doesn't, then it isn't art. Violence is the opposite. And maybe that's a useful thing. Because if this bombing is the opposite of art, then it's a lot like it. Opposites are never as different as people think.'

'Black and white,' said Bernadette, emphatic, seeming to slap it down on the table, but sideways, in her distaste; like she was leaving an envelope of money there for a black-mailer whom she did not want to touch.

'Are both colours, yet both not,' said Catherine, opening this up, unappeased. 'Are absorption or reflection: opposites that are both a reaction, taken to an extreme: they are both totality. And yet are passive states. Do not exist with the lights off. You can only say, they *will* be such when the lights go on.' She looked up at her sister. 'Really,' she explained, 'they are very much alike. And quite fragile, really, because with a grain of absorption, white disintegrates into something else; and a grain of reflection will be the end of black. Other colours aren't like that, are they? Blue can bear a thousand different shades, but you can't have pale black. You can't have dark white. They are what they are, or they're nothing. They break.' She smiled at Bernie. 'Opposites are never as different as people think. And they need each other. They create each other. As soon as black exists, then white exists too. It becomes conceivable. Ask Rosa.'

'I don't think Rosa will be much concerned with ontological musings right now, Catherine.'

'So she knows?'

'She will once you've told her.'

Catherine was silent. She frowned and pushed her empty coffee cup aside. When she spoke, it was as if she hadn't heard. 'Rosa says that God created by creating opposites,' she announced. 'He divided night from day, and that is what created them. Divided land from sea, and that is what created them. All creation is in fact division.'

Bernadette sat looking at her, saying nothing.

'If this bombing is the opposite of art,' continued Catherine, 'then that is a useful thing, because opposites are never as different as people think. It means, look at it in the same way and you might actually find something. You don't look at a painting and say, oh, it consists of a patch of French ultramarine two centimetres by three, and here, at square D13, a dash of green! You say what the painting is *like*, don't you? What it resembles. Not what it *is*. So then. What the bombing is doesn't make sense, any more than a painting does by itself. Maybe we should stop describing it and say what it's *like*.' Still Bernie wasn't saying anything. Catherine shrugged. 'It's like the Trojan horse, it's like a bullet hole, it's like throwing stones in a pond.

359

It's like the hand of fate, an act of God, but not. An act of men and women who presume to know the mind of God. Who *dare* to try and second-guess the universe.' She was trying to light another cigarette. 'Arrogant fools,' she said. 'It's people culling other people's lives, not for their individual parts but for the whole they represent, the whole that's present in their part of it – you see. It's a murdering that's utterly rooted in metaphor. And that is its stupidity. Do you see? It is unreal.'

'People have *died*,' whispered Bernadette at last, and there were tears in her eyes. 'Can't you understand that? Thirty-five people have *died*. I think it is real all right, Catherine.'

'Yes! But that is the hideousness, do you see? The murdering is done as if it is something unreal – because the victims are stand-ins, aren't they, symbols? But look – here in the real world – really, they are gone. Those exact, precise ones. It's like some terrible mistake, where the guns in a movie are real and the actors are dead and the crew and then the coffee boy comes and look, look, it's just a terrible mess. Because it was done to make sense in a pretend world, only it turns out to be real, and in the real world it makes no sense at all.' She was gesticulating wildly with her cigarette. 'And as for them, as for the dead, the real dead – can you mourn them, really, as anything other than symbols? Aren't you making the same mistake as their killers? Or do you presume to miss them like their mothers, husbands, children, sisters will? Is it you who will go through their clothes, and fold their underwear in the bin? Is it you who will try, and fail, to believe that they are gone? And hear them laughing sideways in the park? Or know exactly what they would have thought of such and such a thing, but now can not? And dread forgetting? Is it you who will wonder how your heart still works, and know the guilt of it? Is it? Don't be so sentimental. You haven't their permission.'

'I know you're still affected by Parker,' said Bernadette, as if she were insisting on it. 'I know it was hard for you to lose her,' she said, but she was refusing to look her sister in the eye. 'I know that's why you're saying this. But really, sometimes, you sound as if you have no feeling.' To her own surprise, Bernadette let out a shrill and nervous laugh.

Catherine eyed her calmly. 'And what good do you think wringing our hands can do?'

'At least it means we're human.'

'But our job is not to cry, that's for the ones who loved them. For Rosa, maybe. Us? We knew Humberto for three weeks in the summer once when we were children. Nor is it our job to collect evidence, that's for the police, surely. It's wrong for us to cast ourselves as a victim's lover, an investigating officer, a central figure in the drama. Maybe we should cast ourselves as someone in the background, a member of the audience. That's what you and I are in this particular incident.'

'We just sit tight in our seats, then, do we Catherine? We just buy ice-cream and watch the show? Wow, this is fun! No? Well then, you can see the problem.' Bernadette laughed again, and looked away.

'I'm just trying to see things as they are.' Catherine stood up. 'It's important to remember who we are, that's all. Be moved by the others, by all means, and let them enter into us,' she said, 'but don't forget. Don't forget we are not them.'

Her sister was silent. And then, 'I don't agree with you, Catherine,' she said. Yet Bernadette did not seem angered anymore and had shifted her hands so that she was no longer gripping the magazine in quite the same way. She had turned her shoulders sideways, bent her head. Slowly she let the article drop entirely, began to pick at the surface of the café table. 'You think it is wrong to enter into other people's lives,' she was saying. 'You think we should always be remembering our own place, Catherine. But then, you see, incidents like this become nothing more than wallpaper, everything a backdrop. It's selfish to only ever see the action from our own perspective.' She looked up once again. 'Why should the world revolve around you or me?' she asked.

Catherine's head was shaking vehemently. 'That's not what I said. That's not it at all.' But suddenly she was very tired, and when, after a moment, Bernadette said maybe she did want another coffee, but she would get them, she needed the loo anyway, Catherine only smiled wanly and watched her leave. Sat back down again and glanced around her.

She had been unable to explain. It was the prurience, but most of all it was the sentimentality, that was the thing she hated. The fakeness of it, the egotism. Of people who co-opted other people's dramas for their own drab lives. People who presumed to place themselves within the drama in some cheap sham way. Most of the people who imaginatively entered into victims' lives, did so, she suspected, not from any selfless desire to understand, but rather so that they could enjoy the sensation of the world revolving round them. And when they stepped back into their own worlds, she wondered, wouldn't they be sitting in the exact same spot, however much they'd been titillated by the trip? For they would have been absent from themselves for the duration. And in the meantime, how could they do anything to compensate for what was going on, when they weren't really there? It was a self-indulgent wallowing: a catharsis that meant sacrificing others for oneself, only never returning the favour. Using other people's pain as a moral cleansing lotion. And then putting it back on the shelf.

To have compassion with respect – that was the thing, she told herself. If you were to put yourself in someone else's shoes, you could step out of them any time you liked. The thing was to let them step into yours. She looked down, at her blue leather flats, their scuffed poulaines. Anyone could step into them, any time they liked. Anyone did. Always they left things.

Listen, whispered a voice in her head, listen to all the things they would tell you, and so many questions they'd ask.

She pulled the newspaper towards her and re-read it, after all. Was sitting like that when her sister returned, carefully with a balanced tray that lapped at her attention, reflected the purity of her concentration back upon her chin, like a buttercup, thought Catherine. She liked watching her sister with the tray. She was smiling gently as Bernadette slid back in, and Bernadette smiling also, now that she had satisfactorily settled the tray and seen Catherine's face.

A pigeon flying low flew so close to their heads that their hair fluttered out after it. They both turned, but the bird had landed on the lawn, was oblivious to them as it pecked up crumbs from the grass.

To give your hands to the people who had none, thought Catherine, to let them use yours in the balancing of what had been done. Doing its opposite, here, in this real world of yours – did mean doing something, didn't it, after all. All her life, Catherine had lived as a non-combatant. Had thought it could be enough to *feel*. That to fully understand the pains of the world was an end in itself, but now – now she wished to dare on their behalf. This was what had become clear to her as she talked to Bernadette. That, understanding the things that had been done, she must now feel the shape and pressure of all the things that pressed against her, and then exert just the right degree of life and of control, an exact direction, in the way that she was pressing back. You couldn't undo things, but you could balance them out, couldn't you. It happened all the time, in the alternating of the night and day. Sometimes one seemed to be winning, and sometimes the other, depending on the season. They didn't undo each other, but they balanced each other out. And now she felt she must do what she could to balance out ruptures, the arrogance of violence; you could do that, couldn't you, by mending harmony in the corner of life against which you daily pressed yourself – by protecting the small and quiet notes, acting with respect for the integrity of every element. In this way, she was suddenly sure, you could fight the brash tunelessness of average greed, of cruelty and violence. By nurturing harmony in this part of the song. It was not enough, she decided, it was not, to simply understand the song – you had to protect it, too, didn't you. You had to lift up the weak and quiet flutes, so that they might make themselves heard. You had to contain the megalomaniac urges of the drums. Within yourself, yes, but also all around you. 'Do you think justice can be a musical concept?' she asked her sister. 'Harmony. Nurturing harmony,' she said.

'We like to think it is,' Bernadette assured her. 'I think the law treats everyone fairly equally.'

'But the quiet ones, the small flutes – maybe they should be given *more* attention than the drums. Otherwise the drums run away with the tune. Don't they. And at the moment it is easier for the drums than for anyone else, and that doesn't make sense, does it? Giving the best lawyers to the richest people is like holding up a microphone to the loudest instrument in the room.'

'Justice isn't for sale, Catherine, whatever you think.'

'But lawyers are.'

'Well of course we are. We have to make a living.'

Catherine was looking at her sister sideways on: half-seeing the expression in Bernie's eyes, half-seeing the Weigela, its perfect flowers that printed themselves so carefully upon the summer morning air. The purple shapes of the flowers, practically identical, that were really two things, she knew: the front-on daisy shape, and the sideways-on

364

trumpet that had got it there. She was looking at their fronts, at those long-planned prettily symmetrical faces which each held out, saying *Look at me this way*, and the stamens nothing more than dots in the centre, but if you were to see the flowers from the side, or if you were to cut one open, then you knew that the stamens went all the way back. Only, on this bush, today, the blooms were massed together so closely that you couldn't see a single one from the side. They were like a Roman battalion in tortoise formation. *Look at me this way*, each flower said, and the closeness of the ones next to it meant you didn't have a choice. In front of them, strands of Bernie's honeyed hair caught the light. Catherine's attention settled once more around her sister's cheek and head. Bernie's gold stud earring with the amethyst inset was moving very slightly, almost imperceptibly, up and down as she breathed, in and out. It juddered suddenly as she coughed. Catherine knew she did not really want to start arguing with her sister, properly, on personal ground. 'Do you remember that thing Father painted on our bedroom wall?' she asked.

'At Falls? Yes, it was fun.'

'Was it?'

'Yes,' said Bernadette firmly.

'You know he still thinks that. He still thinks we're made of words. Sitting on chairs made of words. In a universe made of words.'

'I thought it was just a theory of his.'

'It couldn't be true, could it?'

'No, of course not. You'd need someone to invent the language in the first place, wouldn't you. You shouldn't take Dad so seriously.'

'He thinks it pre-exists in the same way as mathematical relationships. He thinks it comes to life when we uncover it. Like a book when you read it, he says.'

Bernadette was quiet. After a bit, she roused herself and

said, 'I like it, that Dad has these ideas. I like it, that he pursues them all. But our father is not a practical person. He doesn't live in the real world.'

'None of us do, according to him,' Catherine replied. Observing the slight tightness in her sister's jaw. She knew that Bernadette subsidised their parents, even now, in the smaller house. She also knew that in taking his daughter's money, however generously and unbegrudgingly given, their father had forfeited all respect. To Bernadette, he could now only ever seem some sort of pet. 'It's the world that we live in that matters,' Bernie said. 'Call it what you like.' When Catherine did not respond, she went on, with a shallow laugh, 'Don't you think there's enough in this world to be getting on with?' Scraped her spoon around the inside of her empty cup, catching the leftover foam from the cappuccino. 'Why concern ourselves with questions beyond it?' Sucked the teaspoon and put it back inside the cup.

'But you like it that Father does?'

'It's the way he is.' Bernie frowned. 'I don't know. Sometimes it is entertaining I suppose.' She looked up very sternly from beneath her lowered brow. 'But it is not to be taken seriously,' she said, and blinked. 'It is of no relevance in day-to-day living.' Still Catherine remained silent. 'Much as I'm fond of him,' said Bernadette, finally, removing the spoon from the cup and laying it down on the wood.

The rust-coloured catkins hung above Catherine's head and behind her shoulders, their antique bait flaming in the grey morning. Bernadette was watching Catherine's face closely. 'I'd go and talk to Rosa if I thought that would be best,' Bernie said. 'But it will be better coming from you. You know that, don't you.'

'Yes, yes,' said Catherine. 'It's fine. You're right.' They both sat in silence for a while. Catherine didn't notice the way that her lit cigarette was grazing against the down-fallen edge of the newspaper page. Neither of them noticed for a second that Catherine had set fire to it. To begin with, it was just a tiny blackened hole with fiery orange edges, on a page that also held pictures, so it could have been that, it could have been part of the page. It was only when the flame leapt up, and they smelled its burning, that they realised what had happened. Bernadette, horrified, blew on the paper, waved it in the air, slapped it on the table. 'Did you do that on purpose?' she cried.

'No! No, of course not,' protested Catherine. 'It just happened,' she said. And then she felt like laughing, but did not. Looked up into the branches of the paper birch instead, and felt like crying.

'No, of course,' said Bernie. 'I'm sorry. Of course you wouldn't have.' And now Bernadette was saying something about how she didn't know if she'd be able to get another copy, it was from yesterday; maybe her assistant would have one – Simon always bought the *Times*. If he hadn't thrown it out. Actually she could phone him. Don't worry, she was saying, after she had thought of this remedy, this almost-certain source of very exact replacement; it wasn't your fault, Catherine.

On the fine morning skyline rose the grey spires, the castle rock. Around them sat women and children, a slew of white plastic trays on slatted wooden tabletops. 'You aren't meant to smoke here,' said a blunt au pair at the next-door table. 'It says so on the sign.' Catherine looked at this young woman with the beautiful jaw and the hard eyes, and smiled, and stubbed out her cigarette. 'So it does,' she said. And then she went back to watching Bernadette, the pained care with which she was folding the damaged page. The respect in which she held it.

It's nothing, Catherine wanted to say. It's only words as printed by a stranger on a page. Do you not know how easily those words can be laid and twisted? The human ones, the ones that do not speak themselves. It's the pictures, she wanted to say: it's the words inside the pictures that count, not the words that people make on top. She meant, trust your eyes, trust the world as it's read by your body. Trust your body the way you trust your mind. Because your mind is part of your body, isn't it, and our human words can be part of the picture too, if you use them right: that is their point, surely, their true treasure: to gather the unreal in, to make it part of the picture. To make the unreal real, fleshed out by pen or lips. To make you realise. Beside her, the tree roots slightly disturbed the paving stones.

It was the words on the newspaper page that Bernadette was interested in. It's all right, she was saying. It hasn't actually damaged the article. You can still read it. It's just the picture, she was saying. It's fine.

Catherine was looking at her sister. Not just Bernie's face, but the whole of her, or all that was visible above the cutting line of the picnic table: the precision with which her pale throat plunged into her collarbone, met the encircling rim of the pale green angora sweater. She felt a sudden desire to save her sister's life, although she knew quite well that Bernadette's life was in no immediate danger, especially not here in the betulated shade on the terrace of Edinburgh's finely, stoutly, secluded botanical gardens; among its precisely labelled specimens. She often felt this kind of urge, despite the fact that Bernadette was older than her, and probably, in most people's conceptions of the matter, safer, securer, healthier, happier. She wanted very much for someone to appear – some physicalised threat which her sister might recognise – and in response to this, she wished that she might throw herself across her sister's lap, holding the lilac calfskin handbag up in front of the pair of them, and thereby save her sister's life. She wanted Bernadette to know something which she herself still only half-knew, could not entirely put her finger on. A feeling that words were meant to illuminate the pictures, to explain them, but not to be worshipped and obeyed in themselves in a way that was so easy to misuse. They were only meant to take you through the picture and into the real words inside it. Catherine did not share her father's delight in language for its own sake. She held human language in deep mistrust. She could not bear its slipperiness. She was faintly appalled by its sensuousness, its tricks, but perhaps this was because she knew she was always on the verge of being seduced by it. Because it would be so nice, wouldn't it, to believe it? To listen to its whisperings in which humans seemed so much higher, so far above, the mere picture of things. It was always so tempting to cut the ropes free, to let its hot air carry your basket skywards. Her father thought you could use language, be its master, but Catherine was more cautious about that. Perhaps she had less faith in her power to control it, or perhaps she better understood the reasons why it whispered, why it wished to lead you upwards and away. Because if it submitted to your hand, if it let you drive it down, through the surface of the earth, pulling you through the hole after it – if it went home to the place from where it came, to the words inside things – then it would no longer exist. And Catherine very well understood that you could simultaneously want to give yourself up like that, and yet be terrified of showing yourself, do everything in your power to hide yourself and stay away. You could splinter yourself into a thousand tongues just so that you might never be one.

Bernadette was pushing her sleeves up. It couldn't be because she was too hot. The air was chill. The haar was clearing but the sun had not yet decided properly to shine, although it looked like it might do, soon, was on the brink. Perhaps she merely wished to exercise some degree of control over her coverings, which was an urge that Catherine recognised. Watching Bernie push her sleeves up, Catherine felt a fresh rush of affection, of companionship in part. And yet also she was deeply aware of how different she and

Bernadette were. How strange it was, she thought, that this was the person she loved most in all the world. That this person could be so very different, so entirely alien, from herself. Like words, sibling love towed the unfeelable in to your own world. You could imagine it quite perfectly.

Catherine was looking at it now, across the table from her: at Bernie's world, and Bernie within it, the soft brown hair on her forearms that shivered in the faint breeze. She was imagining it. She was feeling the trusting simplicity of it, of being in a world where you believed what people said and where everything was no more nor less than what it seemed. Where your main concern could quite validly be your happiness, and the happiness of those you loved. Where happiness was being with people you loved, eating good food, with nice shoes upon your feet. It was a nice world, thought Catherine, with much to recommend it. It had a peaceful, pleasing internal logic. Like a beach ball inflated to perfection. She only did not like the way it blithely rocked against other worlds, rolled over them. The way such a world could blow sideways in the wind, fall into other people's picnics, and yet remain so unrepentantly, beautifully, round; its colours so unblinkingly bright.

Bernadette was pulling her cuffs down again. Their milky mint-green softness brushed her wrists, the perfect loops of their hems. Catherine, looking at the wool, remarked, 'She must have hardly worn it.'

'What?'

'Mother. She must have hardly worn it. It looks like new.'

'Oh. No, I don't think she did wear it much. I don't ever remember her in it, do you?' The last drifting layers of the morning's sea mist were disintegrating, puffing into softly glowing vapour among the Chinese bushes and Himalayan shrubs. 'Oh good,' said Bernadette. 'Looks like it's going to be beautiful again.'

Chapter Sixty-five

Catherine rubbed her knees to keep warm, and tried to call Rosa again. It was gone nine. I'll be home by eight, Rosa had said, when Catherine had come by earlier and got no answer at the door. I'm in Tranent, she'd said, when Catherine had then called her at her florist's shop and been redirected to her mobile. And Catherine had not said anything else, other than, I'll see you at eight, then. Catherine had sounded like a woman making plans to see her cousin. Rosa had sounded busy and said that this would be nice. They saw each other at least once a week; there was nothing unusual in it.

Rosa wasn't answering her phone now, it was going straight to voicemail. Knowing Rosa, the battery was probably flat, but that was all right. Catherine could wait. Catherine was happy to.

The main door of the neighbouring building banged closed behind footsteps. 'You're still here,' remarked the man who had gone in there before. He was lighting a cigarette. Catherine lifted her head. 'I didn't know you'd seen me,' she said.

'I'm Larry,' said the man.

'I know,' she told him. 'I heard you at the intercom, before.'

'You were listening,' said Larry. She looked back at him and smiled. 'I like the way you're sitting,' he said.

'I liked the way you were standing,' she replied. 'At the door. When you were waiting.'

'I didn't know you were looking.'

'It would have been different if you had.'

He hesitated, cocked his head. 'Would it?' he asked, and she nodded. Larry took a drag on his cigarette. 'Perhaps I'll follow you,' he said. 'Perhaps I'll watch you one day walking down Queen Street, when you don't know I'm looking.'

'But I'd like that,' said Catherine.

He smiled. 'Do you mind waiting for people?' he asked, gesturing at the location of her waiting, there where she sat.

'Not really. I'm thinking.'

'What about?'

Catherine thought about it, about Rosa and Humberto. She thought about telling a stranger that she once knew a man who had been killed in yesterday's newspaper story; that her cousin, whom she loved, had loved him; that now she had to tell her that he had been among the dead. That he had been unlisted in the British press because he was not British, and that this struck her as a peculiar kind of idiocy, as if killing could be more or less grave depending on where and upon whom it was committed. As if one life meant more or less than another. She glanced up again at the window of the second-floor apartment, and thought about that whole strange summer, back in eighty-one. She thought about all the things you could see when someone didn't know that you were looking. She felt sorry for God and for spies. The things they had to look at.

She chose to tell Larry the story, in brief, of how the cousins had come to stay in her big old house one summer like they always did. How she'd seen Sam throw a pot –

'A terracotta one, ornamental, sort of,' she clarified. 'At his dog, and almost killed it, it lost its eye.' She told him how she said she hadn't seen anything, because she had a crush on him—

'On your cousin?'

'Yes,' said Catherine, tucking her hair behind her ear primly. 'And everyone blamed the Spanish man who was camping in the garden.' Catherine did not name Humberto; perhaps she was afraid to in case her voice gave the edges of another story away. 'The man who Rosa was in love with,' she said. 'So he left.'

'Who's Rosa?' asked Larry.

'Oh, sorry. My other cousin,' she said, choosing not to tell him that Rosa lived here, that it was Rosa she was waiting for, here on this doorstep.

'Sam's sister?' asked the listening man.

'Yes. And then Sam started seeing Lori, who lived next door. I was a bit upset,' – Catherine smiled at this – 'and being a vengeful brat, I told everyone that it was Sam who had attacked the dog.'

'But that was the truth, wasn't it?'

'Yes. I suppose so. Anyway, no one believed me. A few days later, after the dog had started getting better, Sam dropped something next to it in the kitchen. He went to pick it up, and the dog went for him. Bit him. Nearly took his hand off.'

Larry laughed. 'A kind of justice. If he'd attacked it.'

'I know. But nobody had believed me. They said it would have to be put down. Only it escaped, the day before.'

'Lucky dog.'

'Oh, I think Rosa had something to do with it. And, I don't know, I was just thinking about all that. I was lying indoors, you see, that's why I saw Sam do it. Because I was sick, I'd just had measles. I was lying in bed in the dining room, I'd been put there to recuperate because it had a nice view, floor-to-ceiling windows over the garden. And you know, in the summer, when it's bright outside, you can see out through the glass one way, but nobody out there can see in. That's how I saw him do it without him realising.' Catherine gestured towards the window on the second floor, which was the other way round, the opposite, from the story she was telling. It was indoors brightly lit against the outdoor dusk. The same thing, the other way round.

Larry's gaze followed her pointing hand. He stood watching the people who thought they were invisible. He made no comment but merely continued watching them as Catherine turned her head away and picked at the hem of her blue and white skirt. 'It didn't matter though, did it,' said Larry, still staring up at the man and the woman, there in the apartment. He watched them calmly, seemingly unsurprised and unmoved by their ignorant exposure. 'It didn't matter that you saw him. Everything would have turned out just the same if you hadn't seen anything at all.'

'Yes,' she said. 'Well, I think that's how I like things.'

'Is it?' he asked, looking down at her now, and she shrugged.

Yes, thought Catherine, it was, until today. The only thing I have always wondered is, perhaps it would have been better if he had known that I had seen him, at the time. I could have still not said anything to the others until it was too late to be believed. Everything could have still turned out how it wished to, effectively, I needn't have forced any change in it. But I have always wondered if maybe it wouldn't have been better for Sam to have known I was there. If he could have seen me through the glass afterwards. Perhaps he would have righted things himself, and Humberto might have stayed, at least a little while longer. He and Rosa might have turned out differently, or the same but painlessly, blamelessly. Always I have wondered if I should have knocked on the glass. She chewed her lip.

And then Larry asked her what happened to everybody else. Afterwards, he said. How did it all end.

Catherine thought about it. About how everyone said that Rosa had made a fool of herself chasing after Humberto like that, all the letters she had written, and then what Ellie had referred to as the 'silly journey' that left her standing on a doorstep in a small town outside Zaragoza where she learned that Humberto had gone to Argentina, and by way of consolation drank black coffee with his mother and his brother-in-law on a leather corner sofa with a Messianic antimacassar.

Catherine thought about Rosa's abdication. She thought about Humberto – whom, as she'd pointed out to Bernadette, she had hardly known, though Rosa talked about him so often, you almost felt you must have done. Thought of the way he'd moulded all of Rosa's years, after he'd gone. Thought of him there in the folded magazine. Married with two children, one of each, everything you needed, and a noble career. She thought about Bernie, who had made lots of money and married a rich man too, just to be sure. Their parents pretending that Bernie didn't give them money. Living in a smaller house. She thought about Aunt Ellie, who had married a hispid therapist and drank and was too jolly whenever you saw her, and always said *Carpe Diem* and avoided looking in mirrors and regarded pretty waitresses with nervous suspicion. She thought about Sam, who worked in Washington now. How the last time she saw him was five years ago. How he and his wife had found they couldn't have children, and went round to Lori's house with presents for David.

But most of all, she thought of her parents, and the way they'd been when she had visited them at the cottage last. How it had seemed, all afternoon, despite their politeness, as if she were interrupting them. Why invite someone, she wondered, if you didn't want to see them? She thought about her father asking what she was working on, she thought about the way that she'd been telling him – answering his question – and how he had paid no attention, none, because he had been staring over her head at her mother, who had walked back into the room. And then both her parents had made a great and sudden show of loving her, had fussed and pulled out special words to use on her, but really, she knew, they were doing it for each other. There were silences between their sentences, and in the silences they looked at the floor or at Catherine as if they were trying not to look at each other. They were like children, Catherine thought. She remembered, once, having been a child herself. In a different world. She felt the dust of the day clinging uncomfortably to her skin. It seemed to have got down into every pore and be sitting there, clogging every inch. 'There was a fire,' she said, scratching her arm. 'At the end of the summer. Everyone died except me and Bernadette.' She sounded like a person who was telling the truth.

Larry looked at Catherine. He was almost certain that she was lying, and lying in just the same way that he himself did. He was not so certain of it that he could say so, though. It would be terrible to accuse somebody of lying about a thing like that if they weren't. 'Do you still see your sister?' he asked at length.

She looked back at him eagerly. 'Yes,' she said. 'I saw her this morning.'

Larry, smiling at the relief with which Catherine told the real truth, ground out his cigarette butt beneath his shoe. 'Would you like to have dinner with me some time?' he asked, and Catherine's eyes dulled with dismay. She was hesitating. She knew she would have to say no, because she would never be able to admit to the lie she had just told. It wasn't even funny, a lie like that, he would think that it was loathsome, and he would find it out very soon if he ever got to know her. And yet, it would have been nice, wouldn't it, to sit in his company some more. She had liked the way he was standing at the door, by the intercom, before. She liked the low roll of his voice. She liked the way that he spoke, as if he knew as well as she did that words could be a joke but that nonetheless he was not laughing at them, because also they were all you had with which to do this, these funny fragile flints. She liked the way he was looking at her now with those pale blue eyes. Behind their playful invitation she thought she saw a strange kind of pained unflinching strength, something which might be enough to see you and let you see inside it too. Something with which you might at last go home. She wished she had not pretended to be someone else. She wondered if she could still afford to risk it. Cross with herself for having spoiled it before it might begin, she blinked.

'You can lie to me as much as you like,' said Larry.

Catherine swallowed, and smiled. 'Oh well,' she said. 'In that case.' She was smiling as she gave him her number, and she still felt like smiling after he had gone back inside. How strange, she thought, sitting there alone again but differently so, tapping her fingers against her knees as if she might find a tune in them.

Beyond the floor-to-ceiling windows on the second floor of the new apartment block over the road, a man and a woman were doing nothing at all. They were doing nothing bad nor good, on an expensive Italian chrome-legged sofa high above the street. Sometimes one of them moved their lips, but mainly they were just looking at something the other end of the room, and their bodies on the sofa were slack with ease. They seemed to float so high, there above the kerb-grown weeds, the fallen wrappers, the accidental passers-by; there in the land of the invited. They were doing nothing at all, in a place where nothing might happen to them, and they thought that nobody could see.

Catherine looked up, and all expression faded from her face as she watched them there. After a while she frowned and looked away. She hugged her knees and, for the first time this evening, felt impatient.

She did not wish to be sitting here anymore.

She was almost glad when Rosa came.

'Hi,' she said, standing up awkwardly on legs that were stiff, brushing flakes of sandstone from her thighs. 'Hello,' said Rosa, slipping her car keys into her left-hand jeans pocket, kissing Catherine's cheek in the usual way. She pulled back and smiled at Catherine, stepping past her to open the glossy black front door. 'God, I'm so late,' she was saying, glancing at her wristwatch as she pulled a different set of keys from the other pocket, on the right-hand side of her hips. 'You haven't been waiting here all this time, have you?' Her peach cotton drumskin back vibrated a little as she fitted the key into the lock.